RARE BIRDS

RARE BIRDS

BOOK ONE
of
HANGFIRE

L.B. Hazelthorn

ALLEGORIE PRESS

ALLEGORIE PRESS

First published in Australia in 2024

Copyright © L.B. Hazelthorn 2024

The moral rights of the author
have been asserted.

ISBN: 978-0-6486473-0-0 (TPB)
ISBN: 978-0-6486473-3-1 (eBook)

A catalogue record for this book is available from the National Library of Australia.

I give you the end of a golden string
Only wind it into a ball
It will lead you in at Heaven's Gate
Built in Jerusalem's wall.

WILLIAM BLAKE

1

April 1923

Rom blotted a word and belligerently crossed it out. Quarter of an hour to go: open the archival box, check its card, and transcribe into the ledger—*portion of coffin text* or *funerary figure in green Egyptian faience*—deciphering the geriatric script of some worthy conservator.

Probably Mr Bignall, currently eating a cheese sandwich in the corner.

Rom shook out her cramping hand. Her writing wasn't even the tidiest, dipping reckless over the page, but the workroom ran on patterns she was starting to identify: thou shalt give the females all the paperwork. Bignall never had to handle paperwork; he was happily buffing the grime from an ivory chess piece with a tiny sponge and a wad of spit.

Their basement in the British Museum was almost empty this afternoon, just Dr Carr and a few other second-year students, and Rom scribbled amid the lamps and open boxes. She kept her left hand gloved to readjust the artifacts or lift out a shabti figure, a palmful of serene blue glaze.

Movement in the doorway; nobody had entered. Rom nestled the shabti back in the box and itched her neck. But the steel chair wasn't exactly restful and she now had a clammy discomfort between the shoulder blades as if she were being stared at. The shelves behind were only ranked boxes, bone shards at the most; they wouldn't be watching.

Not a comforting notion. She turned in her seat.

The white dog stood behind her, blinking wintry eyes.

'Go on,' Rom said, low as she could, 'get out,' but Dr Carr was already calling across the tables.

'No animals in the archives, Miss Godden, I do believe we were clear, unless they're mummified, petrified, or rendered otherwise inert.'

One of the students snorted and Rom grabbed the dog's trailing leash. 'Mummify your damn face,' she said under her breath. She marched Pixie back to the staff room and tied her again to the tea table. She'd leave the dog at home if only the beast wasn't such a yelper —her whole first year at the College Rom had returned each day to the landlady's bristling complaints. Hard to believe; Pixie never so much as whined in Rom's presence. But Mrs Martin, if left unappeased, would never again turn a blind eye to a young man entering rather late at night.

'Hold on,' Rom said, 'we'll be out of here soon.'

She rubbed her tightened wrist as she dropped back into her chair. Probably the dog didn't plan to be obnoxious. Some creatures only have one master; maybe Pixie couldn't belong to anyone these days.

And the workroom wasn't Rom's idea of delirious joy either—just a shabby imitation of field work.

'Must you?' somebody said across the table. One of the boys had been whistling. Now he sang the words and even Rom could hear.

'His tomb instead of tears, was full of souvenirs—'

'God, shut up.'

'Old King Tut Tut Tut Tut—'

'That's enough, please,' Dr Carr said, but Rom knew resistance was doomed. Half the country was singing it. And every nightclub was called The Pyramid or something—Egypt was everywhere as if it spilled from her mind and flooded London.

'Andromeda?' Meg Crawford leaned over Rom's table, right in the way of the lamp. 'I've just been talking to Dr Carr. You see, I'm going to the Mediterranean this winter and he thought you might suggest a place to visit.'

Meg went off somewhere different every year and always wanted an audience. 'I wouldn't know,' Rom said.

'Didn't you go? I thought you went.'

Rom thought of saying something crushing but she'd been practising forbearance and absolute mastery of her temper. 'I haven't visited recently,' she said instead. Meg walked away, and still seemed irritated—so really Rom thought she might as well have been rude.

Meg planned to be a missionary; her essay on museum management had involved a proposal to stick little bits of paper over all the hieroglyphic penises. The other students doing Ancient History were going into teaching; only Rom had archaeological leanings, apart from Hobson, who was whistling again, and all he liked was Anglo-Saxons.

Local digs meant bones and Romans. Graduation felt distant.

Rom turned a fresh page in the ledger. Three more years; then Mother would finally stop sending postcards about the gorgeous Cairo sunlight, and Rom would be lifting these glistening bits of blue from the sands of Saqqara instead of packing them back into boxes. Or maybe she'd be deciphering inscriptions in the Greek isles.

Or grubbing around the Sumer in her lipstick and knickerbockers, with the silence, and the bones, and the stones, and the clay tablets like lovely old biscuits.

The issue with dreams is they're never convenient. Driving you all sorts of places, submerging your thoughts while you forget to look at the clock. Rom groaned and shoved her chair back. 'I'll miss the half-past five.'

'You can catch a cab,' Dr Carr began, but she was already in the staff room grabbing her coat and hat and lumpish great pest of a dog. She and Pixie pelted through the narrow corridors, grim linoleum, heading for the exit.

They emerged into a tang of rain and mundane suddenness of natural light and didn't slow, dashing the length of the Museum's putty-coloured backside. Then street after street of Bloomsbury terraced houses until they dived at last into bus-jammed Oxford Street just as evening turned the shops transparent.

Rom halted on the corner and scanned the crowds for a familiar hat. The glitter-windows of department stores glistened with beaded gowns, reflecting every passer-by in marching profile like the temple walls of Dendera.

'What a face.' Ditto's warm hand slid under her elbow. 'Plotting something?'

'Escaping class.' Rom couldn't find a spot on Ditto's cheek that wasn't powder so she picked her neck instead to kiss and get swatted. 'We still have to stop at the grocer's—we're going to miss our Tube.'

'Not if we gallop.' Ditto bent to caress Pixie and her dark hair swept forward, bobbed sharp as a helmet. Her blush-coloured dress flapped like busy petals around her legs and Rom wondered again—today, as every day—what luck had led her last year to the tea-house noticeboard, *room-mate wanted*. The vilest apartment you ever saw, but Ditto made up for it.

She caught Rom looking. 'Am I horribly crushed?' She straightened and hopped and let Rom check the back of her dress, her slip caught on a brassiere strap. 'I've been in my knickers all day. Costume fitting, I hope it's going to be feathers.'

So did Rom, rather. But Ditto looked nice in anything—sleek hats like this silver one, clean pinks and a flash of green beads. Her father was Japanese, and she stood only as high as Rom's chin, and that seemed to be one reason for her brave bright clothing: *nobody takes me seriously*, she said, *I'll dress to please myself.*

Rom, neither neat nor small, who suffered wearing girdles and got stares when she didn't, knew something about being seen, and how you make a choice one day to either vanish like a sofa or stand up, wear sequins, be the chandelier.

Ditto's clicking heels fell into step beside her. 'Are we getting chops?' she asked, wistful, and Rom was counting through their pocket change when they intersected a noisy stoppage on the corner and found a troupe of Ditto's friends.

'Jolly dog,' said a boy in a candy-striped shirt, and Pixie raised her head for pettings in a way she never permitted Rom.

'Glad somebody thinks so.'

'Pretty collar, too. Is it gold?' The boy hooked Rom's other arm. His name was Ollie, she recalled from last weekend, but it was hard to keep track when Ditto's crowd comprised half of Soho. 'We're on our way to Gordey's, can't you come?'

Ditto shook her head. 'Rom will be the last one dancing. I'd have to drag her home.'

'And we'll miss our train,' Rom said.

Ollie howled. 'Taxi!'

'Can't afford it.' But music drifted from a basement window and she hesitated. Each coin in her pocket was accounted for; she and Ditto had agreed already there'd be no Gordey's this week—nor the picture theatre, nor the music hall, just work and discipline. But the streets were admirably fresh, hissing with restaurant steam. Lustrous motorcars hummed under the waking neon lights like an unexpected festival.

Ditto was laughing. 'Haven't you got a lecture tomorrow?' Red-lipped, open-mouthed, beautiful Ditto, and Rom decided.

'Gordey's,' she said, and arm-in-arm behind Ollie they all swung between the brick backs of theatres into the cooling wedge of night, a crowd for the passers-by to step around. 'But we're going to be sensible tonight.'

'Yes, Mother.'

'I'm serious, dear, three laps and then home.' Rom pulled up short as somebody caught her wrist.

'I am looking for the way-station.' The little woman's voice was oddly deep. She had one hand cupped against her shabby fur collar and something fluttered there, a sparrow confined by her fingers. 'Is it north?'

Rom tugged her hand away. 'Don't know,' she said, 'the Tube's just past the taxis.'

The woman frowned from under a strange hat. The wrong sort of hat, like a film cowboy's. 'Where are the crow's people?'

'Perhaps at the train station if you ask—do come along, Pixie.' But Pixie sat watching the woman and her small birds and wouldn't budge.

The woman hitched her narrow shoulders. 'Ben darkmans, mistress.' She tipped her strange hat as a man might. 'I thought you were somebody else. Ben darkmans, dog.'

Rom stared after her. 'What was that?'

Ditto strode onwards. 'Hashish, I should think.'

The other thing about these streets—they belong to all the oddities, frantic and glorious, crammed between stairs up to bookshops and down to cafes. Painted boys and a girl in trousers shared cigarettes outside the pawn shop where Rom and Ditto dived left and pulled Pixie up the tatty stairs.

Here the band was already tuning up behind the cigarette smoke. Gordey's churned with people getting off work or gearing up for late shifts; Rom's dark skirt and tie didn't look so out of place.

Ditto put her lips to Rom's ear. 'Will you hold my purse? I want to dance.'

Rom went for drinks—just her rotten luck, it wasn't the usual barman, and she had to send Ollie instead.

He came back with a tray of vodka. 'Dicks are good for something,' he said.

'You might as well present it at the bar for stamping. Mother Pierce would have let us buy.' But Mother Pierce was a dear old cat; she didn't mind if girls bought their own drinks or boys wore rouge, and she never let any coppers lurk in the toilets—touch wood—which made Gordey's rather popular.

At least in Edinburgh Alec would buy for them. Rom wished he was here tonight; it might be bad form to dance with your brother but he'd be better company than Pixie, who'd folded beneath a table and gone to sleep.

By the time the band stepped up to foxtrots, four drinks in, everything glowed with a filmic blur. Ditto was on the dance floor, apparently doing Isadora Duncan, making great slow bounds with outstretched arms and a smile of saccharine vacancy. Ditto could mimic anybody and she sashayed back to Rom, swishing with one hand poised high. Another impression. Not *quite* a society lady—a translated translation, because the Piccadilly pansies were playing girls, magnified to mockery, schoolgirl French and crossed legs and *which mascara, darling?*

Rom weaved through the dancers trying to avoid a girl in a pink dress who was grabbing everyone's arms and scrawling rude words. 'One more drink,' she said, shaking her purse. Ditto's friends had found people they wanted to kiss in peace and they all settled in a booth near the coat-room. Rom refused to sit on anyone's lap and went hunting for a chair, but the only spare was under the elbow of a hatefully intoxicated boy.

'That one's mine,' he said. 'I can get you thrown out of here.'

She wanted to pin him against the table. 'Piss off.'

'Don't mind him,' said a young man in a red jumper, corduroy trousers like he'd just stepped out of somebody's stables; he pushed the chair into her hands.

'Well,' Rom said, 'his manners are dreadful.'

The young man winked. 'Agreed.' He looked jolly enough to dance with. She'd have asked him if he'd hung around.

The air sang as Ditto swept her through the next samba and Rom was aching for an intermission when Ditto waved a cigarette case under her nose. She followed gratefully down the back stairs to the alley, to lean a shoulder on the cool brick and listen to the tumble of upstairs voices.

Rom snuffled. 'These are strong.'

'They're Ollie's, who knows where he nicked them.'

'Fine night for it, butterflies.' The man in the alley stepped closer. A blondish shortish type, hands hanging almost to his knees. Rom thought he planned to moralise about vicious young women who drink, but he held out his felt hat. 'Any coin for an old gunner?'

His shoes were new; he had a gold watch chain. Rom felt Ditto's hand on her back. 'We're out of cash ourselves,' she said, 'heading home.'

'Not even a jingle in your pockets?' He reached the light from the doorway.

There was something wrong with the shadows. With his tunnelling shadow, the alley's mouth, and Rom sobered. She stood unsteadily.

'Turn 'em out,' the man said.

'Don't be stupid, we don't have anything.'

The door bumped wide and Pixie pushed past Rom's knees, trailing her lead. She stopped in the puddle of light and dropped to her haunches.

'That's a pretty necklace for a pup.' The stranger's teeth glistened in the dark. 'Hand it over and we'll call it even.'

Pixie barked, quick and rough like a crack of thunder clearing its throat. It echoed down the alleyway. The shadows repeated themselves in shudders.

Blue violence behind Rom's eyes, and she winced at the burning stench. 'You alright?'

Ditto didn't answer. She was looking at the other animal.

Yellow fur hung matted from its hackled neck. The size of a lion and it swayed cat-like, shoulders bunched and muscular. Rom stiffened. It must have escaped from somewhere. But its tail dragged thick and wet, long as its body. It lowered its ugly head and the pricked yellow ears fanned out like ragged bat-wings.

Pixie's growl rumbled from behind her jaws.

Rom didn't need the warning. Her dizzy stomach turned over. 'Ditto. Get the others.'

As soon as Ditto's pelting footsteps died away on the iron stairway Rom regretted it. She had no plan, just her and Pixie in the dark. She blinked wildly. In a dream you're able to shift things, change it, but this bore down on her too real—the alley smell, a slap of cold wind and the animal, not a dog, approaching on weighty paws.

But nearly a dog. Four legs, same thing, and Rom's hands tingled. This wasn't a nightmare. It existed, it must have a weakness. If she could just find something, big enough, loud enough—

Rubbish bin lid. She threw it. The crash woke echoes and the creature recoiled, opening its jaws onto a silence that fizzled her teeth.

Rom screamed.

The dark air split and wavered as Pixie leapt. She closed her jaws on the creature's shoulder and it turned on her, rolling heavy. Tossing her. Pixie yelped as she struck the brick wall.

The doorway was abruptly full and somebody shouted from the steps. 'Is it a fight?'

'Quick, where's a broom—'

And Ditto's friends were there, and Nell in the pink dress, and Ollie, and the young man in the red jumper, and they all spilled into the alleyway and the world felt human again. Rom's ears hissed, just voices and distant traffic as Pixie scrabbled to her feet.

'Where is it?' Ditto said.

Rom spun, scanning the rain-slick alleyway. 'Gone,' she said. 'Completely.' It hadn't passed her and she hadn't seen it retreat. 'Pixie scared it off.' Or it vanished, she thought, as sudden as it came.

'Oh, good old dog. A man tried to rob us,' Ditto was explaining, 'and then we saw some kind of bollocks-mad animal. *Not* a rat, this was enormous.'

The man in the red jumper kicked the rubbish lid. 'Shall we call the dog-knobbler?'

Rom wondered if he was a policeman, nosing around the nightclub in his heavy boots. She didn't want to talk to anyone tonight. 'Pixie.' She found her voice, starting towards the dog. 'Come on, old girl.' Pixie made soft rough sounds, whining along the gutter as though she was searching, and Rom bent. 'Oh, bloody Christ. Her ear—'

Ditto peered around her shoulder. 'We need to get her home.'

Ollie made everyone shake out their pockets and throw together coin for a taxi, and Rom held the dog's head against her knees as she and Ditto rattled back through the midnight streets.

They hauled her up to their tiny apartment, hushed and bumping on the stairs, and woke Miss Gwen, Ditto's little spaniel, when they turned on all the lights.

Rom boiled water on their chipped gas stove, which hid behind a folding screen of scarlet Victorian decoupage and pretended to be a kitchen. The yellow lamps made everything feel small and normal; their mismatched sofas, ancient paisley carpet, the music sheets tacked above the sideboard—impossible that anything existed past these walls, hideously striped and blessedly familiar.

But Pixie. Rom downed two glasses of water and attempted to feel undrunk. 'Is she bleeding?'

'It's not blood, just wet. But she's hurt.'

They got Pixie onto a chair beside the sink and Rom patted the warm cloth over the dog's ear. The fur was matted around the torn skin, a slip of raw pink flesh. 'Did it bite her?'

'*It.*' The emphasis was dangerous. 'We should never have gone to Gordey's, Soho's a mess at night.'

'Poor doggo.' Rom pressed the towel down, drying gently, but Pixie shook herself free and stalked to the sofa. 'Maybe we imagined it. I hope so, we were rather pizzled.'

'Still are,' Ditto said, 'your hat's on backwards. You know you've got *whore* written on your arm?'

'Shut up, yours says tits.' Rom plunged her hands back into the sink and scrubbed the scrawl on her skin. The ink wasn't permanent, at least, and streamed off in rivulets.

The black line ran fine as thread across her right hand. 'Ditto.' Her voice rose.

'What have you bloody done to it?'

'Nothing.' Rom scrubbed anxiously. 'I've never seen it before.' Under water the mark showed clear and delicate around her little finger as it crossed the back of her hand, twining to loop her wrist in a flourish.

'Invisible ink,' Ditto said, 'like spies have. Did Nell get you?'

'That's the other hand. Nobody's touched it.' The marking faded as Rom rubbed it on her dress. Once her hand was dry you could imagine you'd never seen anything. 'But did they? I can't think.'

'The place was horribly crowded.'

'If somebody had drawn it I'd remember.'

Ditto stood on tiptoe to pat her head. 'Now it's a tomorrow problem.'

'It's already tomorrow, that *is* the problem.' And they couldn't even console themselves with mutton chops for breakfast; they'd forgotten the shopping. 'God,' Rom said, 'I've got a lecture at ten.'

She ate two oat biscuits, whose main charm was their nutritional value, and stretched herself on the shabby velvet sofa, whose main charm was its almost-adequate length, and rubbed the back of her hand, listening to Ditto humming from her bedroom. But long after the lights were off she lay restless, staring through the street-lit dim at the wicker chair where Pixie slept.

'The dog's cursed,' Ditto said at breakfast. 'Look at her name. She's a faery hound, isn't she?'

'I think she's a sort of bull terrier,' Rom said uneasily, and took a bite of toast. She flexed her fingers. No mark had appeared this morning as she washed. Pixie's ear was healing already. And Ollie dipped his cigarettes in hash oil, apparently, so none of their theories came to much at all.

Daylight was telescoping last night into something pitifully small but logic didn't satisfy.

'Whatever that animal was,' she said, 'Pixie broke her leash to stop it. Did my grandfather train her?'

'Real question,' Ditto said, 'why would he need to?'

'That was luck,' Rom said, 'coincidence. If it hadn't tried to rob us—' She laved another chunk of toast with raspberry jam. That sentence wouldn't end well. She'd equated the thieving stranger with the yellow beast, as though one had become the other. 'I'll write to Townsend,' she said. He was Mother's solicitor and Jasper Teague's before that; a family friend, back when Jasper still had friends. 'He'd know if there's something strange about the dog.'

'There's a poodle at work who plays the piano,' Ditto said. 'Pixie isn't exactly miraculous, she won't even scoff the mice. There was a nibble in the butter this morning.'

Rom spat. 'You didn't tell me.'

'Oh, I cut off the nibbly bit. She is a ratter, isn't she? Terriers are. Good Lord, Pixie, what do we feed you for?'

'What does darkmans mean?'

'Never heard of it. I should ask Ivy, she knows all the carnival parley.'

'I thought you knew how they all talk, the punks and Dilly boys. Ugh, don't eat that. You're vile, you do realise.'

'It's only a bit of mouse. Did you get your telegram?'

The jaunty yellow envelope had been shoved under the front door while Rom waited outside the shared bathroom down the hall, and she bolted down her toast to open it.

YOUR BROTHER IS QUITE SAFE PLEASE COLLECT GODALMING TODAY TELEPHONE TRURO

Which was absurd. Alec would have mentioned if he'd come south for a news story. Unless the telegram was for Ditto, but no: Andromeda Godden, it said, so someone knew her. The sender's name was nothing she recognised: Prideaux. What did they even mean, *quite safe*? Eleven words, they could have cut the *quite* and ducked the penny tariff.

Rom tugged her shoes on. She'd just have time to telephone before she caught her morning train. 'At least I can tell Alec about the beastly dog-thing.'

No milk bottles on the front step when she and Pixie descended to the drizzling street; the Greeners had nicked it again. Rain slopped down for the entire half mile over the tram-line to the post office. Their flat had no telephone, but that's the price you pay for Camden Town— a good price too, if you don't mind a terrace full of spinsters and Greeners.

The pavement was crowded with men, their shirts full of sawdust, and Rom shouldered through with Pixie following placid on the leash. She had to wait for a phone, watching the bobbing hats. *And then he said.* Rom read a woman's pink mouth. *And then she said.*

'Number, please,' said the operator, chirpy through the side-tone. 'That'll be the post office. Putting you through, miss.' More waiting. Rural line. Trying to hear anything on these sodding machines—

It connected with a click. 'Miss Godden, I presume.'

Behind her someone whistled and Rom pressed her palm to her left ear. 'You wired about my brother?'

'We only got hold of him this afternoon.' Now the voice was distinct, the only sound in the room. 'I rather fear he lost himself in the southern wilds.'

'There must be a mistake, my brother lives in Scotland, Mr—'

'Prideaux.'

'Yes.'

'I think not, Miss Godden.' A clean dry rasp of a voice. 'He's sitting in my parlour with his school trunk and a cup of tea.'

'Hell.' This wasn't about Alec at all. She wanted to kick herself. 'Do you mean Morgan?'

'The quarter doesn't commence for another fortnight. I'm afraid your brother can't stay here without signed permission—'

'Stepbrother,' Rom said. 'Morgan's my stepbrother. I can't help you, Mr Prideaux, I'm not quite sure why you thought I could. The school ought to fix this up with his people.'

The man's laugh was soft. 'I am the school. And I was under the impression you were his people.'

'You're a teacher?'

'Assistant master, fourth form.'

Of course. That voice. A cloud of chalk dust, the ghost of a thousand Latin exercises.

'The records inform me his father is currently in Egypt?'

'Yes,' she said, 'Harry's lived there for years. But you could call Morgan's aunt in Derbyshire.'

'Mckenzie asked me to contact you directly. He's been staying with a friend and appears to have run away. He walked to the station; with his trunk, I ought to add. His collar was still spotless.'

Rom felt suddenly tired. 'He ran away to Truro?'

'I can put him on the express tomorrow, if you can't make it down this afternoon.'

The phone line hummed. And this call was costing her by the second. 'I'm sorry he bothered everyone. I'm sure they'll send a chauffeur or something.'

'I see.' The man sounded expectant.

'So. Good afternoon.' Rom hung up with a bang. She tugged the leash and pushed her way out to the wet street.

Mckenzie. When had Morgan started using his middle name?

How like him to assume she'd help—now he wanted something and remembered she existed. He could damn well collect himself. Three years since he'd started boarding school and she hadn't even seen him for the last two; he spent all his summers with the swanky aunt and winters with his father in Egypt.

Rom splashed through the gutter. It'd be a clear day back in Cairo, blue shadows hopping with crickets. One of a hundred places she'd rather be.

Pixie snapped down and Rom felt her skirt rip. She hissed. 'Bad dog.'

Spray hit her boots as a car roared around the corner in a shrill of horns. The wheels barely missed her.

Rom unclenched her hands. Counting the cars, the slosh of wheels. A milk-cart driver shouted but the car was gone already, weaving beetle-green between the buses.

Pixie sat to scratch one ear. Rom eyed her. 'I would have stopped,' she said.

The dog sat immovable as stone.

'Come on,' Rom said, restless. 'Train's about to go.'

They walked on again in time with her own thumping pulse, which ought to be a comfort and never is because how bloody stupid—a step away from splattering in the streets and only the dog had stopped her.

Her heartbeat was a taunt. It wasn't a promise of anything.

2

It was cold this morning. I am tired of February. Townsend came by the house but I pretended I wasn't in. I cannot trust him, because he does not trust me; I shall leave my will with a different solicitor.

The noise is laughing in the trees again. My fingers are too stiff to work and only the stove in the kitchen stays warm; the fires have gone out. I have not lit them since Avery left. I shall finish my great work as I began it: no assistants, no encouragement, and only hope as sustenance.

The plums are rotting on the trees. It doesn't look like February.

JASPER TEAGUE, Journals, 8th February 1920

The apartment door slammed at a quarter past six and Ditto scuffed off her shoes. 'I'm late, I'm sorry, I know, but I got the shopping.' Her pink dress was spotted with rain and Miss Gwen's fur was draggled wet.

'I told you I'd get it.' Rom returned to her page. *The lion-headed figures of the Mithraic mysteries are shown with their bodies wrapped in one or more serpents, similar to the symbol of the snake-twined caduceus.* She bit her pencil. The Mithraic cults worshipped sun-gods, while the caduceus is a symbol of Mercury.

But Mercury got his staff from a sun god. He called a treaty with his brother Apollo, gave him the first lyre, and Apollo gave Mercury the caduceus—their most famous emblems, and they'd been gifts from each other. Even the gods had to call a truce sometimes. A loveday, like the old Cornish word.

Loveday. Like she and Alec used to yell through the garden when they were tired of hide-and-seek.

Ditto leaned over the chair and her kiss pressed soft at Rom's ear. 'Did you buy sardines?'

'Yes.'

'So did I.' Ditto pulled off her hat and rumpled her glossy cropped hair. 'I was marvellous today. Does that sound horribly pompous? Ivy didn't turn up at all, I think she's sore about losing the part. You look vexed, Rom. Are you vexed?'

'I'm not. How many rehearsals do you have left?'

'Twice a week till June.' Ditto flopped onto the sofa and began to towel Miss Gwen. 'Ruth Leary fell off the stage this morning and Anne hasn't learned a single step. Theatrical people, so unprofessional.'

'It's only cabaret, dear.'

Ditto's painted eyes were sharp. 'You are vexed, aren't you?'

Rom put down her notebook. And set the battered kettle on the gas hob and told her about the phone-call, Mr Prideaux, and Morgan.

Ditto settled her glasses on as Rom brought over the cups. 'I thought you didn't talk to the little one.'

'I don't,' Rom said. 'They'll call his family.' She pushed together the pages of her unfinished Mithraics and unpacked her sewing box. Dr Carr might be sniffy if she submitted a late paper but the ripped skirt hung insistently on the bedroom door.

She'd have to fold the whole hem up. It wasn't too tragic, everyone's skirts were short this year. She missed her old school uniform—no choice each morning, just a sailor collar and stout boots and nobody caring.

'Did you catch yourself in the door?'

'Pixie tore it.'

'Pixie has better taste than you do.'

'She stopped me crossing the road.' Rom pinned, and the shears glinted in the lamplight. 'I'd have walked right out in the traffic.'

'D'you think she knows about your ear? Like the blind soldiers who've got dogs to help them.'

Rom followed her gaze. Pixie had belonged to her grandfather, who'd written a volume on the dogs of European folklore—the Wild Hunt, the Hounds of Hell, vampire-hunting dogs in Roumania. The old man had made Pixie's collar, which hung like a filigree necklace across her broad chest.

'Perhaps she knows,' Rom said. 'She tells me when you're coming upstairs.'

'There you go, then. That car would have smashed you.'

'I was distracted. I'm not completely deaf.' Only her left ear, and the throbbing that crept up on her.

'I see.' Ditto picked up her newspaper again. 'So you nearly died.'

'It's fine.'

'You don't want a hug, do you?' Ditto looked over the paper.

'No,' Rom said, 'it's fine.'

'Good, because I can't always tell. What do you want for supper?'

'What have we got?'

'Sardines.'

'I'm going to have toast, I think,' Rom said.

The telegram boy knocked at half-past six. It was from Alec.

MORGAN NEEDS COLLECTING FROM WATERLOO STATION TOMORROW MORNING PHONE ME

'Damn Morgan.' Rom reached for her shoes.

'Is that what you call him? His surname?'

'Always have. He calls Alec *Godden*.'

'What does he call you?'

'I don't know. Umbrella?'

'Behind the door. You're not going out, surely.'

'Alec seems to think I will. I want to know why. Come along, dog,' and Pixie shook herself with a weariness Rom understood.

She had to hang on the phone line while somebody at the other end hunted up her brother in the newspaper office.

'Well,' said Alec's sharp voice at last, 'I've had a fine old time of it. Morgan ran away, would you believe—'

Rom leaned against the post office wall. 'I know, they wired me.'

'The little rat. Went off on a train to Cornwall, apparently. The school was hunting up his dad; they're welcome to phone Cairo if they fancy an earful. And his aunt's on holiday in France, nobody's about to fetch him.'

'Can't he catch a bus?'

'Not our little lordship. Buses are for plebeians. Anyway, can you collar him tomorrow?'

'Oz, you can't be serious.'

'The driver won't get to him till after lunch. School wants me to meet him like a bloody nursemaid. I think they want a responsible sort to stop him hooking off again and that's you, isn't it? Be a dear and grab him at the station.'

'Dear be damned, he's got a chauffeur.'

'Who's in Derby. It has to be you.'

The post office man was pointing at the clock. Rom chewed her cherry lipstick. 'Fine,' she said. 'But you're going to call his school, you've got free telephones at work. What am I supposed to do with him for half the morning?'

'Zoo? I must go, but I'll wire you Monday about the trip.'

'Coward,' Rom muttered, but she wasn't sure he heard before he hung up.

'Take him out for tea,' said Ditto, when Rom was home again and shaking out her wet linen jacket.

'I can't afford a kid's appetite. And the noise in a tea-house—'

'Zoo might work, then.'

'He's fourteen.'

'Everyone likes elephants,' Ditto said. 'Dear Lord, I haven't been through Regent's Park in ages, I'm always avoiding the out-of-towners.'

The Zoo was at the top of the Park, but the bottom led to the Strand if you had strong shoes and couldn't afford the Tube some weeks. Rom walked warily there even with the dog; things got messy in the Park at night, with the soldiers from the Barracks looking for the Camden Town apprentices, and the painted boys from the Strand looking for anybody, and the whole lot of them fighting or flirting or whatever else they did in the public toilets.

'Morgan can't come here, at any rate.'

Rom looked around at their living room—two sofas, one wicker garden chair, seventeen posters of Anna May Wong, and all their underwear strung up to dry. 'Nobody can come here. To think I could have had a place at the College Ladies' Hostel.'

'We're almost in Fitzrovia if you squint,' Ditto said.

'Can't you come along to the Zoo and distract him?'

'If I must. I'll duck over at lunchtime and meet you at the monkeys.' Ditto was already humming as she shuffled through her sheet music. Her voice had a nice warmth when she sang half under her breath.

'Is that for work?'

'It's Bessie Smith. She's quite wonderful and very famous. Do you ever listen to anything I tell you?'

'It's good. You're good.'

'I bloody ought to be if I'm to stay ahead of Ivy Munster. Little bitaine. Better lallies than any of us, but.'

Rom threaded the sewing machine. Bitaine was whore; she knew that much. She wondered whether to ask; curiosity usually got her in the end. She knew seven languages so far, three living and five dead— all more straightforward than Ditto, whose brisk talk came from circus folk and street walkers. At least she'd never be short on synonyms for dick.

Ditto was mouthing a melody. *The day you quit me, honey, it's comin' home to you.* Soft lips and poppy-red words. And it *was* poppy, the sneaky bitaine had borrowed her lipstick.

Ditto had plans. She was going to be on one of those Ziegfeld Follies posters. She was leaving next year, for Paris or Berlin or anywhere she could make it, and one day Rom would pin her picture beside the others: Ditto bold in black and pink, and red for the splash of her mouth. Maybe pinned in a tent—because Rom would be far away from London, with the flat thick smell of earth and her whole world shrunk as simple as the canopy overhead. As wide as the Nile.

And tomorrow?

Rom shook out her mended skirt. Good as new. Better, even.

Tomorrow.

Loveday.

It rained again the next morning.

'Sodding spring,' Rom said.

Waterloo Station roared with the ten o'clock rush and bitter smoke lay along the platform long after the train pulled in. Crowds and loudspeakers, the babble she hated most, and she picked at her fraying glove while she waited. A girl trailed past with a dog, her pumps clicking a flash of stockinged leg. Rom's hand closed in reflex over the leash she wasn't holding; Pixie was at home.

She shouldn't have bothered with gloves. Her College outfit was a skirt and tie and now anything else seemed a costume. When Mother had been young, trooping about being a poet and a lesbian and a model or whatever—that whole circle had all gone in for medieval gowns, blues like jewels and dangerous yellows. But everybody these days looked sharp and flat as paper dolls.

Ditto had nodded her approval over breakfast. 'You look nice in dresses.' Then Rom had pulled on her favourite hat and Ditto had stopped approving. Nothing wrong with leopard print, thank you kindly.

The crush of hats was already thinning before Rom realised Morgan wasn't there. She couldn't have missed him. He couldn't have changed completely. She knew she hadn't changed a bit; she was still as tall and solid and chestnut-coloured as Alec was russety scrawn.

'Blast,' she whispered. He'd come by first class.

Between the bump of elbows came a porter, shouldering a school trunk, and Morgan followed stiffly in his green flannel suit. He was small compared to the satchel over his shoulder. His cap looked new and his cuffs were too short across his wrists.

'Hullo,' said Rom.

'Thanks ever so,' Morgan said to the porter. There was a folded note in the hand he held out and the porter took it with a chuckle as he tipped his hat.

And Morgan turned at last to face her. 'Hullo,' he said. *L. M. Morgan*, said the red tin trunk at his feet. 'Couldn't find the gate.'

He sounded huskier but the stare beneath those level brows was just as she remembered. Would he want to shake hands? 'I didn't see you getting off the train, I thought you'd missed it.'

'I saw you,' Morgan said.

'We saw your Dionysian hat, anyhow,' said the man beside him; Morgan wasn't alone.

The man was finer than his hoarse voice, thin under his coat. Tall, bare-headed among the passing hats, his wave of dark hair held carefully in gloss. 'Miss Godden.' His gloved handshake was hard and brief. 'Prideaux.'

'So I guessed.'

'I was coming up to London anyhow, and I thought I ought to—'

'So I see.'

Prideaux sniffed. He took a rolled cigarette from behind his ear and bent to light it in the lee of Morgan's shoulder.

'Mr Prideaux was kind enough to bring me up this morning,' Morgan said.

'There was no need for Mr Prideaux to trouble himself,' Rom said. 'You oughtn't have let him. We'll be sure to pay for your ticket—' to the teacher, as he straightened and tucked the lighter back inside his overcoat. It was rough blue plaid, tied with a belt, buttons in woven brown leather. A country coat.

'I'm sure the school budget can cover a couple of train fares.' When Prideaux smiled his narrow face broke into deep parchment creases. 'I'm delighted to provide a favour.'

'I'm not sure it's a favour unless it's needed.' Rom looked back at Morgan. 'Fetch a cab, won't you?' She half-expected him to glare but he only paused to shake Prideaux's hand.

'Thanks awfully, sir.'

Prideaux gave a sort of bow in reply, turning to follow Morgan's sturdy figure as it ducked away through the crowd. The man's profile was startlingly pure. He blew a trail of smoke over his shoulder and returned to Rom. 'Your brother is an under-librarian this year.'

'He isn't my brother.'

'I know what he is.' Prideaux's tie wasn't even a tie, but a pearly silk ascot knotting his high collar. 'He's an exceptional student. A *rara avis* amongst the wasteland of fourth-year degeneracy.'

'One struggles to respect his intellect after seeing him walk into a closed door.' In fairness, Morgan had been ten years old with his nose in a book, but the point stood. 'If I don't wait here until he gets back he'll start daydreaming and never find me.'

'Your hat's rather unmissable.'

'Leopard skin was the robe of Egyptian priests, actually, thousands of years before Dionysus was worshipped.'

'A symbol of your priestly restraint? And not your Bacchanalian fervour.'

Rom looked at him. 'Sorry if Morgan caused you trouble.' A porter ducked between them to collect the school trunk and she stepped back. 'I'm afraid I haven't much sympathy to spare for him.'

Prideaux regarded her with tired dark eyes as though he were checking an index entry, and shuffled his shoulders beneath his coat. 'I imagine it's a finite resource.'

It wasn't quite cold enough for an overcoat this morning.

'I'm sorry?'

He'd said something else, lost in the passing rush. He leaned down to repeat it. 'Mckenzie has your cab, I think.'

There aren't many clever replies to that. 'Good morning,' Rom said stonily.

Prideaux dragged on the cigarette poised at his chin, but as she left he seemed to be waiting still. If she glanced back now he'd be watching her walk away, as he'd watched Morgan go.

She didn't glance back.

Behind the porter's bobbing cap she descended to the gusty street where Morgan waited, hands in his pockets by the taxi. His father's posture, Harry Morgan's, that straight-backed stance in a short man and both hands buried deep. He'd look like Harry too with that bony face. Deep brown colouring, the break in his strong nose. But he had only a touch of his father's softened Welsh sound and not even a suggestion of his humour.

'There you are,' Rom said. 'I thought we could go to the Zoo. Or something. Before tea.'

'If you like.'

'You're getting picked up?'

'Alec gave Bayliss your address in Camden Town.'

'It's closer to Fitzrovia, really,' Rom said. Morgan was waiting for her to get into the taxi but she waved him in; she couldn't relax with anyone on the left of her, and perhaps he remembered because he obeyed.

As they swung out into the traffic he settled his cap on his knee. 'You look well.'

Rom looked straight ahead. 'You haven't changed as much as I expected.'

'Lie. I'm as tall as you.'

'Lie. I've four inches.'

'You're wearing heels.'

Rom folded her hands over her purse. 'How's school? You're an Under?'

'Upper. Fifth Form next year.'

'Mr Prideaux's your teacher?'

'He's an assistant.'

'Odd sort of assistant.'

'Mhm.' They were dangerous, those sounds of Morgan's. This one could be agreement, or it could be *yes of course you'd think so.*

'You had a problem where you were staying?'

'Only a family thing. You needn't worry.'

'I wasn't.'

'No,' Morgan said.

They were silent through the long northern suburbs until the cab slowed on the Park Road. 'Zoo?' she asked.

'Tea at yours is fine. I brought books.'

And that's how she came to be standing at her own front steps, rummaging for keys while he gazed up at the grimy stone facade.

They couldn't leave his trunk downstairs because of the Greeners in Number Four so they carried it up between them. Rom kicked her toes twice. Ditto was home when she opened the door—mercifully, marvellously, eating toast at the breakfast table. Rom and Ditto looked at each other for a long moment as Morgan dropped his satchel beside the sofa.

'I'll make tea,' Rom said in her we-have-company voice.

'My name's Dido,' Ditto said in her watch-me-tapdance voice, and Rom hung up her purse and began to scoop stockings from the chairs.

'Is it too warm? We should open the windows.'

'Probably.' Morgan removed his gaze from Miss Gwen's dish of chicken necks under the table. 'It would help with the smell.'

Rom took longer than she needed to behind the shabby folding screen, hunting for clean teaspoons and lining them up on the tray. At least they had plenty of shortbread; kids could be relied upon to eat.

When she carried over the tea-tray Morgan's book lay open on his knee. He took a biscuit. Ditto shook the plate invitingly and he took another two without shame.

Rom plumped beside Ditto on the other sofa and took the biscuits with her.

'I suppose you'll be pleased to stop travelling,' she said, and Morgan looked up. 'You had to stay at the school last night?'

'Mhm.' He looked tired.

Ditto was refilling her cup. 'What's your favourite subject? Do you like sports?'

'Tennis isn't bad,' he said. Precise words, scissor-clipped. 'I don't mind maths. Don't like Latin. Rather pointless.'

'Probably,' Rom said, 'if you're not aiming for Classics. Greek too?'

'Both ancient and modern. Father said I should.'

'I'm not certain you'll need both; I suppose he thinks you'll travel.

How's history?'

'Dull. We do have a good science master.'

Rom balanced the tea-cup in her fingers. 'The one at the station?'

'No. The form master has been ill this year; Mr Prid*eaux* is his assistant.' Morgan said the name differently, a different emphasis.

'I hated school,' Ditto said. 'I only loved music. Do you play any instruments, Morgan?'

'None.'

'Chester Gill's jazz quartet is playing at the club this month, such a mess. The saxophonist broke his thumb and they had to get a local to replace him. But they're all French, you know, Continental C—they don't even play the same notes.'

'That's stupid,' Morgan said.

Ditto grinned. 'Come down and tell the band, I'm sure they'll be fascinated. Say hello, Miss Gwenevere. And that's Pixie, she belongs to Rom. D'you like dogs, Mckenzie?'

At the sound of her name Pixie emerged from under the wicker chair; she nosed against Morgan's ankle and retreated. Miss Gwen pounced onto the sofa and nuzzled his arm.

'Mrs Martin came up earlier,' Ditto said, 'asking about our milk. Hers is sitting rotten in the bottles.'

'Perhaps her refrigerator's broken.' Up here they all just shared the icebox in the hallway.

'Mrs Greener sets out a dish of milk for the faeries, and hers is always fresh. *Stop* that.' Ditto stood, startled to sharpness. 'That's enough.'

Morgan had Miss Gwenevere's scruff in one hard fist. 'It touched my food,' he said.

Ditto dived around the table. 'Let her off, she's only a baby.'

'You can't let it climb on the furniture.' Morgan tugged Miss Gwen from the sofa by her leather collar. The dog scrambled, her caramel fur shivering. He shoved her silky head against the rug.

Rom stood. 'Morgan—'

He released his grip; Miss Gwen darted whining under an armchair.

'You donkey.' Ditto glared back over her shoulder as she scooped up the spaniel. 'If you're scared of dogs we could have put them both downstairs.'

'My aunt has kennels,' Morgan said. 'You ought to keep them disciplined if they're inside.' He dropped his biscuit back onto the plate.

'We've never had a problem,' Rom said. But Morgan had returned to his book.

A waste of shortbread. He didn't even care to be here.

Rom leaned to scratch Miss Gwen beneath the chin. 'You're rehearsing this afternoon?'

'Writing a list of things to pack,' Ditto said. 'Though I ought to take Miss Gwen for a walk. If I just nip over to—'

'Afterwards. Later, Ditto. Please—'

Ditto sipped; Morgan turned a page.

'Shall I make another pot of tea?' Rom didn't wait for an answer. If only Alec were here; at least he could have talked to Morgan about tennis.

'Are there any animals you do like?' Ditto was asking him; her tone was rather pointed.

'Maybe,' Morgan said. 'From a distance.'

'I'd like a cat,' Ditto said. 'Rom wants a load more dogs but she's not even happy with the one she has.'

Rom leaned around the screen. 'Pixie's not mine. She belonged to my grandfather.'

'The writer?' Morgan said. 'Who believed in faeries.'

'Yes,' said Rom. It ruined his academic career. It was in all the newspapers. Does it amuse you, Master L. M. Morgan?

'One of his prints is over the sideboard,' Ditto said, 'spirit photography. Awfully Victorian, all that occult business.'

Rom saw his green suit on the edge of her vision.

'This was one of his clients?'

'He didn't have clients,' Rom said, 'and that's me.' Six years old, propped on a stool, just her and the draped black curtain and the wings.

'Probably a double exposure on the glass. This one was taken at St Veep, wasn't it.' Morgan unpinned the photograph beside it. 'Your aunt's place. I still remember the names of the apples.'

'Put it back.' Rom switched off the wailing kettle. 'It's private, those photographs.'

'They're right in your lounge room,' Morgan said. But he pressed the thumbtack in again and went back over to the sofa.

Rom glanced at the print as she spooned tea into the pot. Crisp as memory; a small girl in a muslin dress, her gaze sliding past the camera to her grandfather stooped beneath the camera's hood. A strange restless man, his hair entirely silver, though he couldn't have been much over fifty then. Already madder than mad, if they'd only known.

Perhaps Mother had guessed because they never went back to his little pink house by the reeds, built sandcastle-crooked. They didn't see him again before he died, two years ago now; he left behind a damp houseful of books, his debts, and a big white dog.

Perhaps Mother had been puzzled by the photograph he'd posted to them, months after the day it was taken: those wings. White span, black-tipped, blurred above the little girl's head. Double exposure on the glass, probably. Because there had been no bird in the room.

'Good book?' Ditto was asking.

'It's alright,' Morgan said. 'Are there any more biscuits?'

Beside that photograph was the other one, snapped by Aunt Minnie years ago—Rom and Alec in the orchard. Alec was twelve, wearing an air of freckled suspicion; clearly auburn, even in black and white. Which meant Rom was fourteen, with two long braids and a hole in her cardigan. The year Mother remarried and went to Egypt. The last year of the War. Fruit everywhere, and in the boughs above their heads a small foot dangling, glossy as an apple in its patent leather sandal. And that was Morgan.

Rom looked over her shoulder as she wiped her hands. His French had been better than his English when they first sent him over from Cairo to meet them. He'd been eight. He'd despised the cloudiness of Cornwall and missed his father. And on the long walk home from the riverside picnic he'd gotten tired and cried, and Rom had carried him on her back, her fingers hooked behind his warm knees, all the way home.

She brought the tea-tray over. 'Have you read the new one by John Buchan? You used to like *Greenmantle*.'

'I don't read Buchan now.'

'Only *Tarzan*?'

He cleared his throat. 'It's from my aunt. I had something else but I left it on the train.'

'Hard luck,' Rom said. 'I'm sure she'll buy you another.'

Ditto had buried herself in list-making and Rom gave up on conversation; she pulled out her abandoned Mithraics and settled in at the breakfast table. When later she glanced at Morgan he'd unpacked half his bag across their sofa with insular self-absorption. Pencil and pages, a pair of brass compasses; doing his homework.

Cat's Head. Pig's Nose.

She knew the names of the apple varieties too, striped pippins and russets. Bright afternoons and Alec writhing on the kitchen steps with a tummy-ache from too many plums.

Tommy Knight. Lady Sudeley.

In that photograph, the one in the orchard—she'd forgotten. Morgan had climbed the trees. He wedged himself between the branches, naming the apples, the song of his voice running fresh through the garden. It took him half the morning to get up; he hadn't even come down for lunch, once, just sat among the blossoms and the bees. Alec was impatient to play aeroplanes but Rom saw the set of Morgan's mouth. She couldn't remember how many days it took her to realise he was afraid of heights.

Gillyflower.

At half-past two Ditto went downstairs to let Bayliss in and Morgan gathered up his things.

The chauffeur, small and withered, ducked his head as he picked up the school trunk. 'All ready, Master Morgan?'

Morgan held out his hand to Rom at the doorway.

She shook it, slowly. 'So long, then,' she said. 'If ever you need us, Alec and me—just let us know, alright?'

'Alright,' Morgan said. 'So long.'

'Don't forget your compass.' The little brass tool had been dropped beside the sofa: she held it out. 'You wouldn't want to lose that too.'

Morgan dropped it into his pocket. 'My aunt would have bought me another,' he said, and followed the chauffeur downstairs.

3

Self-knowledge reveals to the soul that its natural motion is not, if uninterrupted, in a straight line, but circular, as around some inner object, about a centre, the point to which it owes its origin.

PLOTINUS

'So it went well?' Alec asked.

Rom huffed into the phone-booth receiver. 'Marvellous.'

'Morgan's got ages till school goes back. The aunt won't be too pleased to have him dropped in the middle of her tennis parties.'

'He'll have to hide in his room, then,' Rom said. Alec was silent, a long suspicious silence, and she shifted on her feet. 'Still there?'

'I told him he could come up on the train with you next week.'

'Oh, you wretch—'

'He called me and he was a bit upset, I think, he hates the Posh Aunty's place. He's rather lonely, Rom. I don't think he has a great many friends.'

'There's a reason.'

'Morgan said you offered. He's coming, anyway. You can meet him at the station. And it might do him good. Don't you think? He is family.'

'When it suits him.' The point of a holiday is to get away from botherations. All winter waiting tables at the tea-house, saving for a trip away. She sighed. 'You'd better warn him we're going third class.'

'Try not to stab him on the way up.'

'He played you, Oz.'

'I'm the one who has to share a flat with him once you get here. Look, Cartwright's growling at me, he wants the line clear. See you Thursday.'

They were useless as a family at saying a decent goodbye.

The deep streets were still shadowed as Rom reached King's College and its weather-bloomed face. The front steps jostled with students;

laughter inside, high and horsey.

'Somebody drew on Sappho,' a girl said as they got into the sudden cool. 'We're trying to get a look before the beaks wash it off.'

Sappho and Sophocles faced each other across the college foyer, life-sized in marble and quite proper, because a nipple doesn't count if it's classical. Rom would have missed the scrawl if she hadn't been looking for it. The thickened vein was neatly observed.

'What happened?' Some gawk of a boy.

'Somebody's gone and drawn a dick on Sappho.'

He flinched, the sap, as though a word could hurt him. From the stone staircase above fluted a girl's indignant voice. Meg Crawford in a fluster. 'It's indecent,' she was saying, 'you can be sure I'll be going to the Dean—'

Rom pushed past and up the stairs. Some people like to be outraged.

The lecture hall was already filling and she slid into the front row, unpacking her books in the wooden echo. She looked like a swot, but seated elsewhere in the rank of benches she'd lose any voices beneath the rustle of pages and her own thoughts. Here she had clear sound and a line of sight to Dr Carr's broad thoughtful face, or Dr Brackburn's choleric one, or Dr Marsden, damn him, who never trimmed his moustache and was an inveterate mumbler.

It was only Dr Carr today and he spoke crisply after a quarter century of booming to the backs of lecture theatres. He was alright, even if he was a Pottery Man; he had a liking for other Pottery People, and they all did a lot of Pottery in his class. He taught Assyriology, Rom's favourite, but he frequently managed to turn the subject towards sherd reconstruction or handbuilt versus thrown.

She squared her shoulders and tried to look attentive. The hall was cold, though; her hands felt slow as she took notes. And she couldn't focus on working when the relief of a holiday was rapidly collapsing into another sort of chore.

If I tease you—if I hold you—
  if I cage you like a bird and make you sing for me
Rom heard the words even through the apartment door as she unlocked it, Ditto's tender voice.
  will you leave me with any more than this—

a feather in my hands and a memory
She dropped her hat on the coffee table. 'I haven't heard that one.'

'I was singing it last night. There was an earthquake in Paris this week, destroyed half his hotel. Séraphin Desir? The singer.' Ditto put down her newspaper. 'I have spoken of him often.'

'You know I'm entirely deaf, dear. The Russian one?'

'No, the manager's Russian—she's got all the Votary girls who run seances. Half the dancers in her stage show were ballerinas before she put them into cabaret. But Desir's her star.'

'Ah,' Rom said. The poster pinned on their wall was all hot colours and restless feathers—*Madame Volkov et les Firebirds*. 'He was in the skiing accident.'

'And the riot at the Deauville races. It can't be a curse, that's just publicity, but he does have a reputation. Perfectly beautiful singing voice, he's everywhere this year.'

Rom leaned over Ditto's shoulder to see the newspaper. Desir looked slim, elegant in evening dress, his polished black skin crisp as midnight against his high collar. His eyes were lined with paint like a film star's. 'He's lovely. Doesn't look very cursed.'

'If I had the coin I'd go see him at the Folies Bergère, but I suppose he'll be around next year.'

Rom didn't tell her about Morgan and their holiday until she'd tidied after tea and was boiling dishwater.

Ditto took it fairly well, crossing her ankles on the sofa. 'At least Mckenzie's quiet.'

'Yes.'

'He seems clever.'

Rom dropped the spoons into the tin tub and the tea cups clinked. 'Quite brilliant, actually, at a lot of things. He used to sit in the garden and document everything. Plants and animals. He wasn't great at drawing. But he always had a sketchbook.'

'A good little swot like his sister.'

'When he was eleven he put nightshade berries in our porridge.'

Ditto sat up. 'Poisonous?'

'Deadly.' Rom held up a dripping glass to the light. 'It would have killed us but Aunt Minnie saw. She knew what they were.'

Ditto flopped back. 'Did Mckenzie know?'

'He always said he didn't. Said he'd seen the rabbits eating them so they couldn't be dangerous.' He didn't know the local plants, Aunty Minnie said. But belladonna grows in Egypt too.

'Bloody hell.'

'He got a ragging from his father, anyhow. Harry's decent. But I don't think even he knows what to make of Morgan.'

Ditto sighed. 'We can still do everything we planned. You can watch your swotty faerytale speech—'

'It's the Gifford Lecture,' Rom said, 'and it's about religion.'

'Same difference. And then we'll drink whisky and photograph sheep and whatever people do in Scotland.'

'I heard there's a good thing at Orkney. Early Celtic.'

'And that's why people assume you're a lesbian, dear.'

'Because I like history?'

'Because you don't like anything else.'

'History just sits there,' Rom said. 'You've got all the time in the world to figure it out.' She set the kettle over the indigo heat of the gas hob, and Ditto was singing again.

I'm held by a thread
but I remember you said
it was only a memory of fire

A quarter to ten in the morning, and Rom paced beneath the arch of King's Cross Station. 'If he's bloody late we're leaving without him.'

All down the platform people were buying last-minute magazines and she had to step out of the way for at least four women who sailed through the crowd with their hats pulled low, unless it was the same woman over and over. Tweed suits and felt hats, a trench coat, a hundred pairs of brown sports shoes, country boys in thick jumpers. Trunks and trolleys and nowhere Morgan.

'He isn't late,' said Ditto, who'd hopped through the steam to stand on the carriage step.

'Are you sure?'

'It can't be anyone else.'

Bayliss came first with his master's travel case, and Morgan followed in a belted Norfolk suit. He had cream-coloured spats buttoned over his chestnut leather boots.

'We aren't going hunting,' Rom said, as the chauffeur took his leave.

'It's Scotland,' Morgan said. 'Practically a safari.' And Ditto laughed, the traitor, as they stepped into the dim train and found their compartment.

Rom felt guilty in advance for the days Pixie would be left at home. But she'd be with Miss Gwen down in the landlady's flat. Mrs Martin loved dogs, and Pixie hardly loved Rom, so really Pixie was having a holiday too; it shouldn't be on her mind at all. But she felt she'd forgotten something, counting her bags and checking over her shoulder.

She settled back in her seat. 'You can't eat yet. We haven't left the station.'

'I'll save you some.' Ditto was unpacking her bag onto her lap.

'Dear Lord, tell me you didn't bring salmon sandwiches.'

'Do you eat salmon, Mckenzie?'

'Only fresh.' Morgan was gazing out the smudged-up window at the bustle of the rail-yard, his satchel sitting on his knees.

'Coffee then?'

Morgan pulled out his book in silence.

'Coffee, Rom?'

'No,' Rom said. 'Eight hours.'

'Yes,' Ditto said brightly, and she and Rom looked at each other across the faded blue compartment. 'Eight hours.'

Morgan had a bag of lemon drops and the crinkle of brown paper marked the morning as they hummed along. At lunchtime Rom went for a stroll. The train was mostly full of sporting people, noisy women and plump comfortable men. There were a few faded old ladies who didn't seem to approve of Rom's boyish hat and red lips, a scattering of children on their holidays, and one little dear of a boy who knelt on his seat to look at her through the sliding glass door. There was jam all around his chin. Rom winked at him, and he ducked back down.

It seemed cooler already but perhaps it was only the knowledge they were heading north.

Ditto met her in the corridor. 'He's finished the Agatha Christie and started something dreadful and illustrated.'

Behind Ditto's shoulder she could see Morgan through the glass of the compartment door. He sat silently with his knees together, taking up no room at all. 'Is it Emile Zola?'

'I tried not to look.'

'Well,' Rom said. 'At least he's keeping up with his French.'

They ate from the sandwich trolley as it passed. It was raining, and Rom went for another walk. Ditto found her leaning against the railing outside the back of the carriage and they hardly spoke for a while, just sniffed at the wet mossy smell as the train rumbled through deep green cuttings.

'We ought to go back in. With any luck Morgan will have been kidnapped.'

'Nobody's that mad,' Ditto said. 'They'd bring him back again.'

'Could we chuck him off accidentally?'

'No. Could we?'

Rom sighed. 'We ought to get soused.'

'We ought to get Mckenzie soused.'

They smiled briefly, and Ditto pulled her velvet hat lower about her ears. The gilt flower nodded in the rush of wind.

'At least he's staying over at Alec's,' Rom said. 'Serves him right.'

'Which?'

'Both,' she said, and tucked her arm through Ditto's as they headed back inside.

As they rattled towards Durham they bought coffee, and Ditto unpacked a parcel of waxed paper. The smell of boozy raisins swam through the dusty air between them all.

Morgan put down his book.

'We have fruit cake, Mckenzie.'

He ate it silently. Rom felt as though a wild creature had taken a crumb of bread from their fingers and skittered back into the bracken.

'Coffee?' she asked, but he shook his head.

It was cold and dark and the hanging smoke was ghostly in the electric platform lights when they stepped out into Scotland. The station was vast, a skeleton leaf of webbed steel above them.

'I should have brought my cape,' Rom said, 'I'm going to freeze.'

'I packed it,' Ditto said.

Alec was waiting under the glaring lights, in a vile orange bag of a tweed suit.

'Dear blessed Oz,' Rom said, 'I'm almost happy to see you.'

'Don't be theatrical.' Alec took her bag. 'How are you, Miss Hamilton?'

'I've been travelling for too long but I'm determined to be enthusiastic.'

His eyes slid to Morgan. 'You well, Mckenzie?'

'Pretty well,' Morgan said.

'Come along, then.' Alec nodded towards the street. 'I've got a cab waiting, and dinner.'

'And drinks?' asked Ditto.

'You poor little lambs. Drinks too.'

He took them to a busy modern hotel, and he and Rom rambled over their after-dinner whisky. Morgan seemed tired; he'd finished a second plate of lamb chops and sat quietly with his lemonade.

Alec was doing well. He looked more like Mother than ever with his freckles and whippet face and rusty hair swept over his high forehead.

'Since when do you smoke?'

'It stops me dozing off at work.'

'You oughtn't.' But he was the type, as Mother was. And that was her way of walking, a swift bound as Alec went to the bar and back.

Ditto had wriggled her way into a crowd of laughing girls and Rom caught glimpses of her hat in the next room.

'Do you want to go with her?' asked Alec.

'I want to talk to you. Has Townsend talked to you about the auctions yet?'

Their grandfather's finances had been a shambles, according to the solicitor; the clearing firm had managed the estate sale, at least, and the old man's books had brought in almost enough to relieve his debts.

'I wrote him last week about Pixie, because of the—' Rom put down her glass. She had no plans to spout about midnight monsters to Alec. 'The general oddities,' she said. 'He hasn't got back to me yet.'

'We know Jasper was hung up on alchemy and faeries. And paranoid about the War. Apparently he fixed an old ice-house to make a bomb-shelter.' Alec had seen it with Mother after the funeral; it was his property now, though Jasper had wanted to burn the place to ash. Rom hadn't been back since she was a child, since the dusty summer she'd been photographed; she'd nearly lost herself in the weedy garden.

'Townsend said the old man bought a cartload of gold bullion,' Alec said. 'Honestly, if we knew what he did with it all—'

'Dissolved it in sulphur, probably, looking for the philosopher's stone. It's a pity about the books. He had an early *Principia Mathematica*, it would have been fun to keep. I suppose the gardens have run wild behind the terrace.' Where she'd found the bird. Where the bird had found her.

'I didn't see it,' Alec said. 'But it was terribly overgrown. I wouldn't live on the edge of a marsh. Or is it a bog? I never know.'

'Does it have trees?' That was Morgan. 'Marshes have no trees.'

'Trees for miles,' Alec said, 'and then just a long slush of grass.'

'That's a swamp.'

'Thank you, Mckenzie,' Alec said primly, and his forehead creased. 'It's such a useless house, miles from anything but sheep.'

'Mother should be managing all this,' Rom said. 'It was her father.'

'Have you heard from her at all?'

'She writes.'

'Me too. They'll be over in September. Is that right, Mckenzie?'

Morgan drained his lemonade. 'If they say so.'

Then Alec was talking to him about the Olympic Games, and Rom sat back and sipped.

They hadn't been all together since Aunty Minnie's; their school holidays, porridge and warm milk for breakfast. Now Alec had a job, and Rom was at university, and Morgan was talking about the angle of reaction on a tennis racquet. Time had happened somewhere along the way.

When Ditto came in to steal her almonds, Rom tugged her dress. 'Are we grown-ups, darling?'

Ditto put her warm cheek to Rom's shoulder. 'I bloody hope not. Hush, they'll hear you.'

'My virtuous small brothers?'

'Everyone. You're loud when you drink.'

Their lodgings looked mercifully cosy as their cab pulled up; dark stone beneath a gabled roof. On a hill, like everything in Edinburgh.

'I'll ask a couple of chaps around for drinks tomorrow,' Alec said as she and Ditto hauled out their suitcases. 'They're rather decent. I thought I'd make cocktails.'

'When did you get so hideously worldly?' Rom patted his arm. 'It's good to see you, Oz.'

'I know,' he said.

The landlady was an old dear and their rooms were snug. There was a small rosy bedroom and a sitting room with a real fireplace, and Rom wiggled her toes on the carpet when she came back from her bath. She hadn't washed her hair and the smell of engine-smoke lingered as she brushed it out. Long hair, despite the bobbed crops of half the girls at the College; Mother always wanted her to cut it short. Perhaps that's why she hadn't.

'Tomorrow I need to buy a cardigan,' Ditto said, 'and then I'm blessedly free.' She was draped on her bed, staring at the dark-panelled ceiling and eating chocolates.

'Haven't you got a list?'

'Of course I have a list. And it says I'm free. Until cocktail hour; I hope they aren't all pansies, Alec's friends.'

'What do you care?' Rom glanced over as she pulled on her socks. 'You don't much like men.'

'I was being thoughtful. It's time I married you off to a decent fellow.'

'Hang that,' Rom said, 'a husband would never let me have a job.' She kicked her way into the tightly-tucked bed. 'I thought we could nose about Inchcolm Island while we're up here. It's a ruined church. Do you think?'

Sometimes you don't know how tired you are until you're curled up listening to late-night trains. Rom closed her eyes. The loneliest sound in the world, a train whistle going somewhere in the dark; except for bird-calls over the marshes, in Suffolk or along the Nile. The thrash of wings in the reeds.

She'd lost herself in their grandfather's garden once, the last day they'd gone to visit, in the twining paths and warm brown water.

Maybe she'd tripped. The water had been at her feet. Then behind her, she was deep in it and she kicked, panicked, her mouth stifled. Her nostrils shocked. Then hands caught her hair and she burst into sunlight, blinded, boughs above and a storm of beating wings. Her face pressed to feathers, musty sheaves.

Her arms stung with scratches when it pulled her onto the mud.

Mother cupped her face. *Rom, can you hear me?*

The bird, she said, crying, and they all laughed at her, and Father in his straw hat. The ibis lifted their heads, flashing the red stains beneath their wings as she squeezed her eyes shut.

She opened them.

Ibis, in her grandfather's garden.

How stupid. Rom stretched her shoulders on the mattress. It had been Egypt; the trees were date palms. The water was the Nile. She'd told the story for half her life but never realised, actually, it was the day she caught the river sickness.

The look on Father's face when the doctor told them—the French doctor with his lovely fine dark hands—he'd told them she'd never be able to hear again, not with the left ear, and maybe not the right one either. Her bed had rocked like a boat with fever. They'd sent her home to Aunt Minnie in Cornwall. And the next year she'd turned eight and started prep school there in England, only returning to Cairo for holidays sometimes, same as Morgan.

Rom blinked at the bedroom ceiling and closed her eyes. 'I'll pay you a shilling to put out the light.'

'Lazy quiff,' Ditto said, but she closed her magazine and hauled herself out to tug the beaded light-switch.

She must have been in a good mood because she stopped on the way back, and kissed Rom's hair in the dark.

4

*Townsend sent a letter. I haven't opened it; I know what he thinks of me. But if I
were as mad as he believes, I could never have survived this much pain.
He's a good fellow. I ought to send him some sherry at Christmas.
I worked today until the lamplight failed. I am making good progress since I
stopped visiting the creature; my health improves. My teeth ache, loose in their
gums, but this is the price of experience.
A year to make a fatal error. A lifetime to search for a remedy.*

JASPER TEAGUE, Journals, 4th Sept 1919

They were wonderfully idle the next morning. The marmalade was
very good in Scotland.

'Is this what it's like being rich?' Ditto asked.

Rom was digging through her travel case for a hairbrush. 'This is
what it's like being unemployed. Same thing, I suppose.'

After breakfast Alec met her out the front with a bright blue motor.

'It isn't yours, surely.' Rom ran her fingers over the dashboard as they
wound down through the city. The seats were buttoned leather like a
Chesterfield sofa. It was only a little two-door with its canvas hood up,
but it was nearly new.

'I borrowed it from a friend. Arts writer at the newspaper. He's
horribly wealthy; from his mother, of course, not from Arts.'

He drove well but took the hills blithely blind. Hills everywhere, this
pointed city tumbled like a toy town on a bed-spread, dark weathered
stone and spires sharp against the mountains. Ditto would moan
about her sore feet this evening.

'What's Morgan up to,' Rom asked, 'while you're out?'

'Reading.'

'*Tarzan*?'

'I think it was something about Pythagoras.' Alec changed gear,
swore, and changed it again with a clunk. 'D'you drive?'

'Tube for us. We really should find a place in town; maybe Soho.'

'We?' Alec's eyebrows arched as he swung the car through the dark streets.

'Ditto and me.'

'Yes. You had a boyfriend.'

'That was in January.' And that hadn't been his question. 'He was alright, I suppose. But I shall never marry.'

'I see.' Alec leaned out the window to swerve around a bus.

'You don't seem too shocked.'

'Half the office are queer as anything. We've got a sports reporter—I was *turning*, you ass. Cartwright keeps trying to move him to the theatre column but he'd rather interview rugby players. And Ditto?'

'I don't believe she's ever wanted anyone. She isn't fond of boys, though.'

'Oh.'

Rom smiled. 'You arrogant. She's older than you.'

'Have to keep my hand in, don't I?'

He deserved an elbow in the ribs, and got it.

Rom had dressed up a little, a linen dress in a fresh buttercream stripe, and she was glad of it when they stepped beneath the stone entrance to the Old College quad. It was hardly out of respect for the University people, who in any city stroll about the place like a man showing off his stables—she'd really done it for the building itself, the low strong facade with its regular arches. Darker than the stone of her own King's College, but all the buildings up here seemed to be bruised with gloom—the natural colour of the stone, or staining from the damp, she couldn't tell.

'Impressive,' she said, and Alec shrugged. He'd rather have a race-course.

They wound their way up the curving stairs to the Playfair Library and settled amidst the murmur of the gathering crowd. Rom tilted back her head to follow the long curve of the ceiling.

Stately as a temple, oddly long; like a hallway lined with marble busts, leading nowhere. You didn't see how vast the room was until you looked down again at the hats and fluttering programs of people pulling themselves into the seats below. Rows of bookshelves all caged carefully as though the books within were precious animals. Or deadly ones.

The lecture at the Old College was James Frazer's, the first time the university had invited somebody to talk about gods and not God. He wasn't the greatest speaker, but few scholars are; knowing something and knowing how to talk about it aren't the same. His white beard wagged at the far end of the library and Rom's mind wandered through the scrape of chairs and Alec's sniffling. She should have sat closer.

But she recognised the story. Worship of nature, respect for the dead. Tracking the moon and the slow wheeling of stars. The early animists believed every tree and every blade of grass was inhabited by a spirit: and then they forgot. The specific became general—a tree-god, a forest-god, a vaguer nature-god; at last a single creator as simplicity replaced chaos. But always belief in something.

The search for a hidden reality is utterly human, Mr Frazer said. Science hasn't clarified: atoms are invisible as goblins. Spring leaves will always look like magic. And perhaps that's what the Mithraics meant, worshipping a sun god, and what her grandfather was trying to understand before he waylaid himself with nonsense.

Mr Frazer didn't seem to see it that way; he laid out his anecdotes and prodded. But the world used to be full of miracles. What if you see something inexplicable? It's easy for believers; everyone else is left shuffling through clay tablets, reading monuments. Wondering if people have always wondered.

She followed Alec back down the curving staircase, watching the glitter of women's earrings.

'Everyone's here today,' Alec said, 'that chap's a professor from Hungary. And there's the mayor.'

'And that's the Director of the British Museum.' Rom leaned over the rail. 'I've seen him sometimes in the Reading Room, he can date a Greek manuscript by the handwriting. There, with the woman.' Who moved down the stairs, small and upright, her gown stitched in gold.

Her dark hair was clipped short. An extraordinary face, the puckish breadth of her cheeks and lush mouth, and people were raising their hats or moving out of the way as if they recognised a film star. Rom followed the shift of the silk gown over the woman's legs as she passed, a flash of gilt leather shoes.

'Evelyn Ash,' somebody said behind Rom.

His companion whistled. 'Miss or Mrs?'

Hard to imagine her as Mrs anything, that woman with her steady gaze.

'American philanthropist,' Alec said. 'Donates a heap of dosh to the University, I know a chap who interviewed her. Oh, look, it can't be Harper—' He was off and out the doorway already, seizing somebody's hand, a middle-aged sunburnt man in a shabby hat. Rom caught up in time to hear the tail-end. 'It is Harper, isn't it? We met at the Meroë dig. I'm Alexander Godden.'

The man said 'You're Harry Morgan's kids,' which was close enough. 'He was fairly a surgeon with a stick of dynamite.' *Feerly*. An Australian. 'What are you lot doing back in civilisation?'

'I work up here now. Andromeda's studying in London; archaeology.'

'Do you plan to come back over soon?' Harper asked as Rom shook hands. 'Cairo's buzzing. Everybody's sick to death of King Tut, but the Americans are digging the Valley next year. And there's a fresh thing in Ur.'

'I'm dying to,' Rom said, 'soon as I've got a degree.'

'With Robert Carr? I thought so, the pool of rabid Assyriologists is pretty small. Though it seems to be growing.' He tipped his worn-out hat at Rom. 'I'm actually heading his way to solve a bit of a riddle. A new find, think it's Hittite. It's a rum thing, you see.' Harper leaned forward. 'I found it up here.'

'In Scotland? That's far too old.'

'Just so. It was up near Inverness, Celtic tomb. Odd bones and a good bit of gold. I can't tell you where.' Harper's eyes crinkled into a smile, the gentle madness of a treasure-hunter.

'You two'll be here all day,' Alec said. 'If you're in town, sir, you ought to drop by for a yarn about Egypt.'

'I'm heading out tomorrow,' Harper said, 'but next time I'll look you up. I might call into the College when I'm down, Miss Godden. It's been grand to see you both.'

Rom called after him. 'Let us know how you get on with your Hittite tablet.'

'I shall,' he said from the stairs, 'but it's not a tablet. Not by a long shot.'

Alec looked thoughtful as he rumbled the blue motorcar back across the bridge. 'You always said you wanted to be an explorer. Or a detective. I suppose an archaeologist is a bit of both.'

'You forgot about the time I wanted to be an elevator boy,' Rom said. 'Those dear little hats.'

'How's that working out?' He swerved around a cyclist. 'I wonder if Mckenzie still plans to be a scientist.'

'Do you still want to be a soldier?'

'Sod that, it was only because of Dad.'

They were both silent, because it was hard to know what to say about their father. He'd been a good man and there had been a War and he died. Aunt Minnie was his sister; his sunny little seascape paintings still hung on the walls of her cottage, but Mother didn't often speak of him. Neither did they, these days, not to her.

Alec pulled up outside her lodgings. 'Should I ask Mckenzie? If he keeps his scientific journal, I mean.'

'Only if you want a kick in the shins.' Rom leaned against the car. 'You call him Mckenzie now.'

'Yes,' Alec said, 'when I remember. I think he might be trying to be less awful.'

'You know what he's like with new people. Tell him not to be rude tonight or we'll pack him off to bed. No, we'll catch a cab over. But first,' she sighed, 'shopping.'

It wasn't so bad, tramping around the cobbled streets with Ditto. The city was small and dark, not quite tame; a cool smell lingered in the angles—the sea mist, snagged in passing, and Rom sniffed as they strolled arm-in-arm. She could live here. Sitting at the tea-shops, working in the archives at the University. Trekking to find old cairns along the coast. Too many lives, and how are you supposed to choose?

But this was nice.

It would have been even nicer if Ditto carried her own shopping bags.

'Lovely,' Ditto said when they were home again.

'I have blisters,' Rom said.

Alec's place wasn't too awful for a boy's, though it looked as if he'd closed his eyes and jabbed wildly at a furniture catalogue.

'Fallen Angel?'

'Always.'

'I haven't any lime juice,' he warned, 'and the bitters taste like cough syrup.'

'It won't matter if I drink it fast enough.' Rom raised her voice over the rattle of his cocktail shaker. 'Five sorts of brandy but you can't afford another sofa?'

'Priorities; I never have important visitors. Do I, Tom?'

His lounge room was crowded. Tom Wells had arrived first, Alec's friend from the paper, a busy person in a striped jacket. And Mr Cretney, bland as butter; and Mr Mitchell, some sort of engineer. All three brought a bottle of something and Rom raised an eyebrow when Alec passed with the ice bucket. 'Just a small thing, you said?'

'Whisky's not drinking,' Mr Mitchell said, 'it's mother's milk.' He was a few years older than the others, a lean fair man with a slow Scottish catch in his voice.

'Spot the Glasgow boy,' Alec said. 'Another Grasshopper, Miss Hamilton?'

Morgan stood by the radiator in his dark suit, clearly struggling to keep his hands out of his pockets. But he held still when Ditto paused to straighten his tie. A glossy silk one, emerald stripes; he must have borrowed it from Alec.

Alec resided over the cocktail trolley in a velvet smoking cap. 'Do you have a little waistcoat too?' Rom asked.

'Perhaps he'll play the cymbals for us.' Cretney was leaning against the mantelpiece, toying with his rings.

'He'd make a perfect monkey,' Ditto said. 'But he does mix a nice drink.' She sparkled like cut-glass, shimmying across the room to play with Alec's gramophone.

'Actress?' asked Wells at Rom's elbow.

'Cabaret artiste,' Rom said. 'Is it obvious?'

'Blindingly.' He was the Arts reporter, of course. 'She'd be marvellous in Hollywood. We ought to ask Selwyn, he's our film star; aren't you, Sel?'

'Don't listen,' Mr Mitchell said, 'it was only a newsreel.'

'The picture theatres play it so often I know it by heart,' Wells said. 'Last week my mother made me watch *The Ten Commandments*. She kept dropping caramels under her seat and I had to crawl and get them. My mother—Sel's seen my mother.'

'She's nice,' Mitchell said.

'Oh, but old ladies like you. Either of you seen *The Sea Hawk* yet?'

'Marvellous,' Rom said. 'The battles were brilliant.'

'I thought it was rot.' Mitchell shrugged at their disgust. 'But the ship models were very fine.'

'You have to admit, though,' Rom said. 'Milton Sills dressed in black pantaloons—'

Wells would have danced, she thought, but she had a headache already. Morgan had the right idea, cross-legged on the rug, silent with his lemonade. He'd been packing up his satchel at Alec's table when they arrived tonight and she'd leaned over his chair to see. Maths homework, though it was more of a sketch; circles, his careful annotations, tidy lines dissecting. *Euclid? No, Kelvin's vortex theory. Kelvin was wrong, though*, she'd said, *atoms aren't made out of aether.* He'd shuffled back his chair. *Indeed.*

Rom leaned her head against the cool window and watched Ditto's glittering dress. Mr Frazer was correct in one regard: atoms are strange as faeries. Fifty years ago everyone thought an atom was a knot in the fabric of the universe. Father used to talk about it when he blew smoke-rings: *you can't cut a smoke ring*, he said. *It re-forms. If the room held still enough, the smoke would hang for eternity.* Now everyone knows atoms buzz together, livewire mosquitoes. Maybe in fifty more years the scientists would see something else again and this would all be quaint as pixies.

'Rom?' Alec's touch on her elbow. She hadn't heard him. 'Another for you?'

She swirled the dregs in her glass. 'Sod that, you'd need an undertaker handy.'

'Bloody ungrateful, the lot of you,' Alec said. 'I toil and I work—' He sipped. 'And still you all moan. What'll it be, Sel?'

Mitchell was looking at the lurid bottles on Alec's trolley. 'Well, I—whisky, I suppose.'

'Let me mix you something worthy. D'you like lemon?'

'A touch of ginger,' Cretney said, 'don't you think?'

'I'll be fine with whisky,' Mitchell said, but Alec thumped his shoulder.

'This will be your very own, and I shall name it the Raging Scotsman.'

'Alexander,' Wells said, 'why don't I get a drink named after me?'

'You're better off calling it the Diver's Dram,' Cretney said. 'Or perhaps—' he was picking at his jacket button— 'the Bachelor's Breakfast.'

Rom must have missed something because Wells laughed and then went silent. Alec was pretending he hadn't heard.

Ditto stood and held out her empty. 'Brimful, please, Alec. Do you dance, Mr Wells?'

'Like a legless goat. We can try, though,' as he fiddled with the gramophone.

The jazz roared bright and silver. Trumpets were never meant for somebody's lounge room—they were open skies, temples and triumph. The sound was too big for Rom's head and she wondered how soon she could escape without upsetting Alec.

Wells dropped into the window seat beside her and plunged into a chat about Scottish watercolourists. She expected Ditto to ask her to dance but she wriggled in too, and talk turned toward the beastly habits of theatrical directors.

Rom hadn't been paying attention to the gramophone but the melody emerged gleaming. A hard sweet voice, held like drawn steel. *It was only a memory of fire.*

Ditto had cornered Alec. 'You dance?'

'I do not.'

'You really are useless.'

'Kicking my ego works every time, Miss Hamilton; come along.'

Rom pressed her ear closed with one fingertip. Never quite silence. Knockings and odd pressures, the endless travels of her pulse like a vaunting ghost.

Not endless: marching somewhere.

Mr Mitchell leaned against the window seat. 'What about you, Miss Godden. You dance?'

'Not tonight, it's quieter over here.'

'You turned shy?'

'Disgustingly. It's my hearing,' she added, in case he took it for rudeness, 'I don't like music if there's people talking.'

Mitchell nodded. His sand-grained skin showed burnt pink above his shirt-collar. 'In France, after a round of shelling—well. There's still a ringing in my head sometimes.'

'Mine's a little like drums. My aunt taught me to lip-read so it's not too bad. Apart from the Flu, when everyone had paper masks—'

'And you can't read a thing.' Mitchell tucked his right hand into his pocket but she'd seen it already; blunt fingers stained yellowish, pitted with scars. The tip of his thumb was missing. 'Your brother said you all lived in Egypt for a while?'

'We travelled once, North Africa before the War. And then holidays, because of our step-father's job.'

'Mckenzie's father?'

'He's in the railway, civil engineer, but he works with the digs sometimes. Did you ever get near Egypt in the War?'

'The sandflies were bloody murder.'

'Say that again.'

'I said it—was bloody murder. You heard me, though.' Uncertainly.

'You say it so beautifully. *Murder.*'

'Hook off,' Mr Mitchell said, but he was laughing. 'I was mostly in France.'

'Infantry?'

'Ordnance. Munitions delivery and supply.' He sipped, his gaze moving to the others dancing on the rug. His eyes were pale grey. Clear as water. Shadowed by the brows above them, and Rom thought about the world behind his words, a place between midnight trenches on a plain of mud.

'Pity you didn't see the living side of Egypt,' she said. 'The villages and the markets. And the ancient bits. I can't wait to go back.'

'You can't find enough bones in Britain?'

'Rom, the poor dear man.' Ditto leaned over them. 'Don't ask her about dried-up mummies or she'll turn you into one. Alec's looking for you, by the way.' She busied herself with the devilled eggs as Mitchell excused himself. 'Say what you will about your murderous brother, he does look like a little gentleman. I'm going to tell him his tie's delightful.'

Rom shuffled over to make room. 'What did Mr Cretney say before? I didn't hear.'

Ditto cackled. 'He called Mr Mitchell ginger. Ginger *beer*, Rom, as in queer.'

'Is he?'

Wells settled beside them. 'I plan to find out.'

Ditto raised her eyebrows in a mimicry of Alec's glare. 'Well, you really are too much.'

Wells choked on his cocktail and hauled himself back off the window seat. 'You never said you did impressions. Alec,' he called, 'pay attention. You're about to be horribly insulted.'

'I can't just do it on cue,' Ditto said, following him over, but she was already shaking out her shoulders and sizing Alec up. 'Alright,' she said, 'here.' And she did it again, the narrowing of Alec's eyes and the arch of his brows, and then—light, nasal—'You going to finish that drink, old goat?'

Alec sat up straight. 'Brilliant,' he breathed. 'Do it again.'

'No,' Wells said, 'do me, I'm bloody begging—'

For half an hour Ditto mimicked them all without mercy. Wells and his awful posture, Cretney's drawl. Mr Mitchell got his turn, that soft Scottish dragging of the r's, and he shook his head in helpless recognition.

'Now Rom,' said Alec, and Ditto rolled her eyes.

'I copy Rom all day and she doesn't even notice.' There it was: the lean of Rom's shoulder, conspiratorial. One hand on her hip, contrary to the irritable angle of the head: a leaning-in to listen, not reveal. Is this what she was?

Ditto pursed her lips: 'Stop fussing with your hair, dear, you know they'll only be looking at your tits.'

Rom's laughter joined the rest but she caught Ditto's wink.

'You're rather good.' Morgan put down his glass. 'Could you do me?'

'You're pointless material,' Ditto said, 'not nearly ridiculous enough.' But she pulled off her loose scarf and cleared her throat and straightened an imaginary collar, and the field of her presence folded shut. She held her shoulders level. Crossed her arms. 'Well,' she said, and a flatness settled in her voice. 'You're wrong. But I don't have time to argue.'

And they were all dissolving with laughter again and Wells said he'd be hanged if Ditto's name wasn't up in lights by Christmas.

She was good. Superb, really. She draped the scarf around her neck and fluffed out her hair and there, she was Ditto again. Rom's chest felt gin-warm and sleepy. Ditto was born for the stage; she never tired of company like Rom, who in odd moods only wanted silence and a locked door. But this was a holiday. Rom didn't mind watching them ramble until Wells left for a theatre show and Cretney went to dinner, finally, and the others stormed downstairs to see them off.

Rom leaned against the sideboard and got herself another drink, keeping an eye on the level as it rose. She slurped in triumph. Not tipsy in the slightest.

She'd thrown her jacket in Alec's bedroom and now she flicked the lights on, hunting: Alec's bed, unmade and despicable, and her purse on an armchair, and a neat camp stretcher under the window which must be Morgan's. And Morgan's satchel. Rom scooped up her jacket and paused.

She shouldn't. But his sketchbook was sitting beside the satchel, so she did.

Morgan still drew things.

Wild plants and squirrels, things he saw at school, all firmly pencilled; every page was incised with ghosts. The animals looked stiff. He tried too hard and the care made it difficult to look at. The dates showed he didn't draw often. And he hadn't attempted human figures. The most recent page was just a pattern, meandering curves, the kind that spills when you're thinking of something else—repeated down the page in double waves. Something like a temple frieze; maybe he'd copied it from a building.

But he'd be good one day if he kept it up, which he probably wouldn't. He had an eye for beauty. At what age does it become a liability?

A door slammed. The others were trooping back.

Rom put the sketchbook down, and switched off the light when she left.

5

Alec was pouring a final brandy when Rom returned.

Morgan had curled in an armchair with his chin on his folded knees.

'Tired?' she asked him.

'Probably just the Cointreau,' Alec said.

'Oz, you didn't. He's just a kid.'

'Old enough to know when to stop.'

'Thank heavens somebody is.' Ditto stretched her back luxuriously. 'We ought to call a cab.'

'I can take you.' Alec was already hunting for the keys.

'You can hardly walk,' Rom said.

'Doesn't matter, it's only Tom's car.'

Mr Mitchell pulled his hat on. 'I'll drive. We'll fit.'

'Excellent,' Alec said, 'we'll go the scenic route and you can see the lights. Grab your coat, Morgan.'

They did fit, just about—Mr Mitchell, and Ditto beside him, and Rom and Alec and Morgan squeezed on the bench behind.

Alec wasn't as wobbly as he should have been; perhaps he often swilled bad drinks on a Thursday evening. Rom asked as they hummed through the darkened city, but he grinned. 'I'm not soused enough to discuss whether I'm taking care of myself.'

Mr Mitchell pulled the car up, and Ditto squinted. 'Rom, I do believe your dog's here.'

'So it is,' Alec said as he stepped out. 'Looks just like Pixie.'

Rom glanced up at the lodging house steps and kicked her toe on the gutter. There was a white dog sitting at the door.

Morgan followed them up. 'It can't be. It's hundreds of miles.'

'Four hundred,' Mr Mitchell said. 'Is she really yours, Miss Godden?'

Rom didn't even want to look at its collar, the golden knotwork chain and the white-lashed eyes. She reached across the dog to get the door open and went up the carpeted stairs.

The dog followed at her heels.

Rom switched on the lights and Pixie sat on the rug.

'It's her,' Ditto said.

Mr Mitchell whistled. 'Gem of a dog.'

Pixie's eyes were chips of ice. Rom wasn't sure if she wanted to touch her. 'How did you find me?' She crouched and put out her hand. The dog's fur was stiff and cold.

'But what on earth for?' asked Ditto. 'Why'd she come after you?'

Pixie pushed her head into Rom's hand, butting her knees.

'Good girl,' Rom said, though she didn't know why. 'Good girl,' and Pixie huffed a long sigh.

Her stiff tail thumped the floor. She closed her eyes, and it looked for all the world as though she was smiling.

Pixie's flank showed dark with mud in the electric light. They washed her in the bathtub, Ditto soaping and Rom rinsing the fleece of suds from Pixie's eyes.

'She looks normal enough,' Mitchell said in the doorway. 'The breed, though...'

'We first heard about the will from Mother,' Alec said. 'She said it was a terrier and we all expected some foxy little thing. And when we went to pick it up—'

'At least I got a dog,' Rom said, 'you only got a rotten house,' because they all seemed to find it as funny as Alec did.

Pixie didn't smell like dog, not even wet. She was heavy; solid in the shoulders, of course. Clear-eyed, too. She must be old. Mustn't she?

Pixie yawned and shook herself wetly across their dresses.

'More drinks,' Rom said. They settled in the sitting room, Pixie flopping in front of the radiator. 'No more dog-talk.'

'Not a chance,' Alec said, 'this is bleeding brilliant. I should write it up for the papers.'

Mitchell was running thoughtful fingers over his chin. 'Has the dog ever been up this way? Sometimes they walk miles to return home. Or to family.'

'We've never been this far north,' Rom said. 'And she's not exactly fond of me.'

Mitchell's laugh became a cough, muffled in his sleeve.

'It's too impossible,' Alec said. 'If you're certain it's the same dog—'

'Oz. You know it's the same dog.'

'It isn't impossible,' Morgan said from his corner of the sofa. 'It clearly just happened. But she can't have walked.'

'Alright then, Mr Morgan,' Rom said, 'what's your idea?'

'She caught the train.'

'Sneaking aboard and hiding all the way here?' Alec said. 'I hardly think so.'

'Because a magical dog is much more likely.'

'You'd be surprised how many people are sure of magic,' Mitchell said. 'I had a captain who'd never touch a white horse. He was convinced they were devils. And my grandmother, when she was small, saw a giant rabbit walk through the kitchen door like a ghost and drink up the cat's milk.'

'I don't mean to rag on your grandmother,' Alec said, 'but kids see all sorts of things.'

'Do they?' Morgan asked.

'I should think plenty of adults see only what they expect.' Mitchell ran his rough fingertip over the rim of his glass. 'There's peculiar things in the world.'

'Did you ever see an oceanic monster? Sel works on Orkney,' Alec told them, 'diving in the bay.'

'Not this summer—bronchitis, never the same after the Flu. I'll get back soon, though.'

'Diving for what?' Rom asked, and Mitchell smiled.

'Battleships. Team at Scapa Flow's raising the scuttled German fleet, there's a fortune in the materials.'

'They made a few news reels of it,' Alec said. 'He dived during the War, too.'

'Navy?'

'Not exactly, but I grew up around boats.'

'He's still not telling you,' said Alec. 'Selwyn engineered the punt they run the pumps from.'

'Adapted from a German floating dock,' Morgan said. They all looked at him, and he shrugged. 'It was on the news film.'

'You weren't Navy, though?' Rom asked, and Mitchell reached for his glass.

'Munitions. We went all over.'

'Decent crew he's got,' Alec said. 'One of the salvors worked for Damant, diving U-boat wrecks for the cipher machines. To break the codes. I wonder what kind. We used to run ciphers at school to sneak notes—fairly simple, z's instead of a's, but we fancied ourselves wildly intelligent.'

'We had a code at school too,' Mitchell said, 'but everyone kept forgetting it. Some fool wrote the key in his notebooks and couldn't understand how the beaks cracked the damn thing.'

'We have a code nobody can break,' Morgan said. 'The monitors stopped trying.'

'What sort?' Mitchell asked.

'Beaufort cipher. There's a tabula recta for decoding and we keep a copy in our workbook. One of the masters figured it out. But he said the cipher's remarkably clever and whoever came up with it should be rather pleased with themselves.'

'Who did come up with it?' Rom asked.

Morgan didn't appear to have heard. 'He started giving us ciphers to work on if we finish early.'

'They shouldn't encourage note-passing,' Mitchell said, 'bad for discipline.'

'He's only the assistant,' Morgan said. 'I don't believe he cares.'

Likely not, Rom thought, if you're a rara avis. You can pass notes under the master's nose and he'll still deliver you to London like a first-class parcel.

She leaned across the sofa while Mitchell and Ditto were refilling their glasses. 'Was Mr Mitchell a spy? He's cagey about the War.'

'Everyone thinks everyone was a spy,' Alec said. 'Somebody must have done the actual fighting.'

'Munitions inspection.' Morgan sat down with a fresh glass of lemonade. 'Mr Mitchell was in bomb disposal.'

Alec put down his whisky. 'He didn't tell you, surely. Did he?'

'His hands. Father works with explosives too.'

'Sure you're not the spy, Mckenzie?'

But Morgan was right, of course. Blast damage and acid burns, the joints taut and bleached.

'Mr Mitchell,' Rom said when he returned to his seat, 'did you ever consider a job in archaeology?'

Ditto flopped her head into Rom's lap. 'God, don't start.'

'I'm not sure I could survive too far from the sea,' Mitchell said. 'Have you got any pirate hulls to raise?'

'There's always engineering work involved, that's all. Earthworks and pumps. And sometimes there's treasure. If you're ever keen, there's been talk about excavating at Orkney. The Skara Brae settlement.' Rom smoothed Ditto's glossy hair, and Ditto was sleepy enough to let her. 'Older than the Pyramids.'

'Odd place to live,' Alec said. 'What did they do all day? Looking at the sea.'

'It doesn't take much to make a good life,' Mitchell said. 'Water, food. A strong roof. Something to mess around with when you're bored.'

'Lonely,' Rom said.

He smiled. 'Someone to mess around.'

'The problem with you,' Alec said, 'you're not nearly ambitious enough. You could take your helmet and dive the Pacific for pearls. Beaches and everything.'

'Also sharks,' Mitchell said. 'I'll take my chances with the westerlies.'

They spoke of the boats on the Nile, and the divers on the Japanese coast where Ditto's father had been born; and the ancient crannogs in the lakes up here, whole villages built on struts above the water. 'The fish-divers in the marshes of Sumer still do it,' Rom said. 'Floating villages made of reeds.'

'Wherever there's water, there'll be people,' Alec said.

Something thumped and scuffled on the other side of the wall.

Rom sat up. 'Where's Morgan?'

She got to the door first and flung it open. Halfway down the carpeted stairs Morgan was sprawled with his boot wedged in Pixie's jaw.

'What in all of Christendom,' Alec began.

Morgan glared. 'Tell your dog to let me go.'

Rom cannoned down the stairs. 'She won't stop if you pull. Let go, Pixie.'

The dog growled around Morgan's boot.

'What were you even doing out here?' Alec asked.

'Fetching my bloody coat from the bloody car.'

'Oi,' Alec said.

Mitchell ducked around Alec and came down the stairs. 'What's the matter?'

Morgan kicked with his other heel and caught Pixie in the throat. She drew back with a snarl and snapped onto his ankle.

Morgan brought his fist down between the dog's eyes. 'You fucker.'

'*Pixie*,' Rom said, but the dog was rumbling and Morgan made a small terrible sound. He hit her again.

'Stow that.' Mitchell caught Morgan's wrist. 'Easy on, kiddo,' he said less roughly. And over his shoulder to Rom, 'Tell her again.'

'Drop it, Pixie,' Rom said, low and hard.

The dog heaved a sigh and opened her jaws.

'Outside.' Rom tugged Pixie upstairs by the scruff. 'Bad dog,' she said when they got to the bathroom, but even to her own ears it sounded weak. She closed the door harder than she needed to.

When she came back Ditto was dabbing Morgan's bared foot with a damp napkin. It looked like a proper bite, a puncture above the pale nub of his ankle bone.

Alec gave a grunt of sympathy. 'Nasty enough.'

'Morgan.' Rom didn't know how to begin. 'How did you upset Pixie?'

'You think it was something I did.' His mouth was a white line. 'Your dog bloody bit me.'

'Oi,' Alec said again, uneasily.

Mr Mitchell was sitting on the step beside Morgan. 'She hasn't done this before?'

'Never, I wouldn't keep a dog who—'

'She's a bulldog,' Mitchell said. 'Isn't she?' He didn't look at Ditto's busy hands or the bloodied napkin. 'They don't let go once they grip.'

Ditto sat back cheerfully. 'We'll get this wrapped up for you,' she said, 'it's only a sprain. I've danced on worse.'

Morgan leaned against the wall in silence.

'Keep it elevated, do you think?' Mitchell stood and brushed his jacket down.

'I'd say so. No weight, no walking. No stairs,' Ditto added, and Alec lent a shoulder as Ditto helped Morgan to his feet.

They got him upstairs and settled onto one of the beds. Alec brought the ice bucket while Ditto darted down to the landlady for bandages.

Morgan was in a vile silent mood. He didn't look anybody in the eye and was clearly relieved to be left to Ditto's ministrations when she returned and shooed them out.

'Well,' Alec said when they collapsed in the sitting room. 'What was that about?'

'Buggered if I know,' Rom said.

The bedroom door was open, and Alec sighed. 'Is it you two he learned his awful language from?'

'Probably school,' Mitchell said. He stretched out his legs towards the fire. 'They pick up all kinds of rubbish.'

Alec grinned wolfishly. 'When can we expect your treatise on modern childcare, Dr Mitchell?'

'Well, what was your school like?'

'We never sullied ourselves with such wickedness.'

'Bullshit,' said Rom and Mitchell together.

Ditto flopped across the sofa's arm and Rom wriggled over. 'Is he alright?'

'Only a little twist,' Ditto said. 'You'd think he'd broken it, the sulk he's putting on.'

'My grandmother was from the Islands,' Mitchell said; 'when she was a kid they tied knots in a thread and wrapped it around a sprain. Binding the body whole, I suppose.'

'Thread has always been magic,' Rom said.

'She used to draw a sort of maze pattern on the steps of the dairy, too, to keep out the witches.'

'Trapping a monster in a labyrinth?' Alec asked. 'Worked on the Minotaur.'

'We never had a problem with minotaurs either.'

'She might have been right,' Rom said. 'The Babylonians did the same thing; magic knots. Threads and ropes. You know the cartouche around a pharaoh's name? It's a double cord, an amulet for luck.'

'Sel, you know ropes and things,' said Alec. 'Make the kid an amulet and fix his bloody ankle.'

Rom stretched her shoulders and knelt to scoop coal into the steady crackle of the fire. 'He deserves his bloody ankle.'

'You think he provoked Pixie,' Mitchell said.

Ditto answered. 'Pixie's a calm sort of dog. And Morgan—'

Rom closed her eyes against the heat. Morgan is Morgan.

Ditto went to check and leaned back around the doorway. 'Nearly asleep,' she said, 'or pretending.'

'Should we leave him here tonight? Ditto and I can sleep on the sofas.'

'Less stairs back at Alec's,' Ditto said. 'He'll be shaky for a few days.'

'Righto,' Alec said, 'I'll play nursemaid, shall I?'

Rom's neck eased. She'd rather step on a thumbtack than face that level stare across the breakfast table.

Alec carried Morgan's jacket and buckled boots. Rom held the front door open to the night air, and Mr Mitchell carried Morgan downstairs to the car.

Morgan looked resolutely sullen, his head turned away from Mitchell's shoulder, and ignored Rom's goodbye.

But she shook Mitchell's hand when he and Alec came back up to collect their coats. 'I'm sorry; Morgan can be rather rotten.'

'He is, isn't he? Bit of a sulker.'

'He did just get bitten by a dog,' Rom said. 'He's always been quiet.'

'Probably needs to get outside a bit more.'

Quite clever, Mr Mitchell was, but not the most observant.

They left Pixie to sleep in the bathroom when they went to bed, and the dog seemed subdued the next morning. You'd never imagine she could bite anyone. Rom watched her, though, when she fed her some livers, which she barely touched, and when she put down a dish of milk; Pixie licked it clean.

Rom's temples ached. She didn't allow herself to think until after breakfast. Not until she was getting dressed, rummaging in her travelling case—she couldn't find her other kidskin shoe and went hunting for it, kneeling to peer under the floral bedskirt. And she found it.

One shoe. Three hairpins. Dark blood on the carpet, and the broken body of a snake.

6

Rom called Alec from the landlady's phone downstairs.

'Are you sure it was a snake?'

She didn't bother to answer. 'Ask Morgan what it was doing in the house.'

'Can't you?' And then, more steadily, 'We ought to all be here when we talk about it.'

She showed Alec the snake when he arrived, and he looked quite sick. Perhaps he hadn't believed it until then. They'd scooped the dead thing into a bundle of newsprint and it sat in the bathtub, a bloodied mess. Its head was nearly bitten off.

'Is it an adder?'

'Why don't we ask Morgan?'

'Rom. You don't think it was him.'

'Pixie must have killed it. And she bit him. Has he said anything today?'

Alec peered into the bathtub. 'He went straight to sleep last night and I've barely seen him this morning.'

Ditto seemed tensely optimistic. She stood in the doorway, chewing on her thumbnail. 'How strange it is,' she said for the fifth time, and Rom looked at her.

'I've had enough of strange.'

Pixie had nosed about the snake's body before they'd moved it, but wouldn't come near it again. They left her in the lounge and hoped the landlady wouldn't come up to tidy while they were out.

Rom barely spoke to the others on the drive to Alec's. It was maddening. No point asking Pixie what had happened and less point, probably, in asking Morgan.

He was in Alec's little lounge room when they arrived, sitting on the sofa in his dark green suit with his bandaged ankle propped on a cushion.

He marked his place in his book with one fingertip. 'Something wrong?'

It was Ditto who told the story of the thing they'd found in the bedroom, and Rom watched Morgan's face as he listened.

His brows creased. 'Five foot long? Not an adder. They're the only snakes in the British Isles; that would have made more sense.'

'So an adder would have been perfectly fine,' Rom said. 'Up the stairs and inside a house. In Scotland.'

'Any markings?'

Alec's face was tense. 'Don't give us a biology lesson, Mckenzie. Did you do this?'

'Is this why Pixie bit you?' asked Rom. 'You put a snake in the house and she bit you.'

'Don't be ridiculous.' Morgan winced as Alec caught his collar.

'You think we're going to believe it was a coincidence?'

'Come off it, he's injured,' Ditto said.

Morgan wrenched himself from Alec's hand. His cheeks were flushed. 'Why would I do something so bloody stupid?'

Alec glared. 'Why do you do anything? I don't bloody know.'

'Why should we believe you?' Rom folded her arms.

Morgan looked from Rom to Alec. 'You can't possibly—' He stopped. His nostrils flared like a horse's. 'I hate you,' he said distinctly, and turned his face towards the window.

'None of that,' Alec said, 'apologise at once.'

Morgan didn't move.

Alec made a sound and stepped forward but Rom slapped at his hand. 'None of *that*,' she said, and pulled him into the kitchen.

'I'll have his guts.' Alec was in a sort of shock. 'He as good as confessed.'

'What if it wasn't him?' asked Ditto.

'Rom? You know it was him.'

Rom had known it as soon as she saw the snake. Certainty until the moment Morgan looked at her. He'd expected her to help. Something in his face had changed when she hadn't. 'Snakes don't just appear in Edinburgh,' she said. Nor do dogs. Things were not where they were supposed to be. 'I'd call Mother and Harry but there isn't any point. They'd only laugh, they pull snakes out of their boots before breakfast. They'd think it was an odd story and wouldn't see what we mean at all.'

She asked Alec when he dropped them back to their lodgings. 'Has Morgan got any friends? Did he talk about his school?'

'We had the chat. What he'll do when he finishes school, things he likes. Harry wants him to go into the military. Something strategic. He's clever enough. Did you say he was a librarian at his school?'

'Yes, though that doesn't make sense either. When has he ever cared for helping anyone?'

'I do think he's grown up. He talks a terrific amount when he's in the mood; don't ask him about atoms. I think he hated last year because of the third form monitor—Morgan was stuck fagging for the pompous ass. I had one like that in Under School.'

Perhaps that was it after all. 'And this year?'

'This year he's working in the library. He's exempt.'

'How very convenient for him,' Rom said.

Alec whistled. 'Clever little beast.'

'He's good at getting what he wants.'

Ditto shook her head. 'It doesn't mean he's not telling the truth.'

'We can't know,' Alec said. 'We likely never will. But I'll be keeping an eye on him.'

Just after breakfast the next day the landlady of their lodging house came up to their door, looking puzzled. 'There's a lady wants to see you.'

Rom went down to the street door. On the front step was a fizzling type of woman, tall in her sporting togs, with a flop of fair hair. Thirtyish? A quick voice. 'I was hoping to catch you.' She had a camera on a strap around her neck. 'Miss Godden, is it? My name's Penelope Lloyd. Glad to meet you.' She held out her hand.

Rom didn't take it. 'How did you get my name?'

'Newspaper. Perfectly marvellous article about your dog, did she truly walk to Scotland in a day? I was hoping I could ask a few—'

'Oh, bloody Alec. Sorry. No questions.'

The woman peered. 'Is she a bull terrier?'

'She's a nuisance.' Rom snapped her fingers at Pixie, who'd wandered downstairs behind her.

'I like a good mystery. The unknown and all that.' The woman stood with her feet braced, like a sailor looking out to sea. 'Her name's Pixie?'

It's hard to ignore a direct question. How did Morgan manage it? 'Yes,' Rom said.

'Faery hound, eh? You're lucky we're all quite modern. A few thousand years ago that dog would be a god. That's my thing, you see.'

'You're a historian?'

'Doctor,' the woman said. She worked at a convalescent hospital, apparently, investigating the effect of sunlight on tubercular patients, and intravenous injections of gold and silver. Electrical healing beds. Concentrations of healing energy created by pyramid shapes. She seemed to believe a lot of knowledge had been lost through the ages, from the ancient Arabs and Greeks and everybody.

Same story as usual. A fanatic, and Rom interrupted. 'Thanks for your interest. I must go.'

The woman's smile was sunny. 'Where did you find her such a marvellous collar?'

Pixie headed upstairs and now Rom was alone, Andromeda marooned on the rocks. 'No clue,' she said, and this time pulled herself straight. She stared, and kept staring, and the woman faltered.

'Have a good day.' Rom closed the door.

'Nice to meet you,' the woman said from the other side.

'You rat.'

'Be fair, it's a good story,' said Alec. 'Cartwright put it on page two. Somebody in Aberdeen telephoned about his cat who once came back after three years away; we could start a series on Wonder Animals.'

Rom closed the car door and leaned back through its open window. 'I'm not here for a good story. This is supposed to be a holiday.'

She'd brought Pixie along to town, and the dog followed calmly while Rom rummaged in bookshops and did shopping of her own. Quiet, uneventful. And Ditto was taking a nap so Rom went alone to Inchcolm Island, taking Pixie on the smoky little ferry, and clambered up the beach to the broken Abbey.

The island was a green crescent in the grey sea, and the old ruin sat solid, bleached pale as a seashell. Nice enough to draw, if she only knew how.

'The Scottish buried their dead here for centuries,' a German tourist said to her, 'and Vikings also. Ghosts do not cross water.'

'Perhaps that's why they have rivers in the Underworld stories.' Rom looked at the blunt spire against the sky. 'The Greeks and Egyptians.' Always something to guard the waters, a ferryman or standing stones. The keepers, Hades or Hecate or Anubis, all the black-dog gods. And somebody to measure the deeds of the dead. The Greeks called him Thoth but the Egyptians called him another name: Tje-hut, he-who-is-like-an-ibis.

The cry of sea-birds was everywhere. The lift of their wings reminded Rom, as all birds did, of waterbirds restive in the heat of Egypt; cranes, egrets.

And ibis; a shambling bird with a certain austere beauty. She'd noticed them first in the Museum at Cairo, when she was seven or so, the vivid dead and sculpted, paint and stone. Beaks a moonish crescent; for stirring the mud, Mother said. Only afterwards, emerging into the dry blue daylight, Rom had looked again at the river and seen the living birds. They'd always been there but some fancy made her think they'd lifted from the boxed exhibits to populate the reedy riverside. She'd recalled the hidden colour of their underwings as if it was their secret name when she tried to draw them later.

Artists have a chance at catching something, like Morgan's sketches. But a line on paper isn't the bird. And she couldn't draw, only scribbles. What are you supposed to do with this desire?

All the way back on the ferry Rom thought of it, with Pixie at her feet and the salt smell in her nose.

'Home again.' Ditto sighed as they packed their travel cases. 'I did find a wonderful cardigan.'

Alec drove them to the station, and helped Morgan step up into the carriage.

Rom paused with him on the platform. 'He's still limping. He has to be back at school on Thursday.'

'I doubt he can manage the train to Surrey on his own. Shall I call the aunt?'

Rom bit her lip. 'I can take him down,' she said. Only a couple of hours there and back. This feeling was almost certainly guilt. 'We don't have coin for a hotel, though. He can stay at ours tonight.'

Morgan seemed unconcerned when she told him. She wondered how much of his silence was apathy and how much was resignation.

They left Pixie sulking with the porter and his assurances the dog would be quite comfortable in the guardroom. Their compartment was busier this time; apart from Morgan in the corner, they had a shy Scottish girl in a dark-grey dress—her name was Aggie (soft little voice she had) and she was travelling to visit her brother in hospital. Ditto shared their sandwiches and had to fetch more.

She came back in triumph. 'No beef, only beastly potted fish.' Rom growled but Ditto stood in the doorway, pleased and heedless. 'Look, I found somebody. Well, she found me, didn't you?'

'I do hope you don't mind.' The woman leaned her smooth fair head over Ditto's shoulder. 'May I join you?'

'I already told her she must,' Ditto said. 'We got talking in the dinner cart—Dr Lloyd nursed in Malta, would you believe? Where your brother was, Aggie. So I thought we could all eat our Beastly Sandwiches together.'

'I can't say no to that,' Rom said slowly.

'Call me Pen, truly. *May* I have a Beastly Sandwich, please? Too much talking and not enough chow this week. Ought to confess, I recognised your dog on the platform. I was hoping I'd run into you.' Dr Lloyd looked at Rom. 'I was up here for work. Trying to get some funding, but millionaires aren't keen on sun-lamp theory.'

She seemed quite knowledgeable about European folklore and knew the Mithraic legends Rom mentioned. She'd spent time in Serbia during the War. There were sun cults there, as always where people farm and follow the seasons.

When Aggie asked about Malta, Pen said, 'We had the whole lot of boys from Gallipoli. It's very likely I patched up your brother. Encephalitis is a nasty thing, though. Damn that Spanish Flu.'

The worst is how it reappears long after you've gotten the all-clear— Mother hunting the warmth in Egypt, and Mr Mitchell coughing over his whisky. The weakness lingers when it should be a memory.

'Go on,' Ditto said to Pen, 'ask her about the faery hound.'

Rom thought she heard a rude sound from Morgan's corner.

'Four hundred miles overnight,' Ditto said. 'What do you call that, Dr Lloyd?'

'It isn't the first time I've heard of it. In Serbia—may I tell you?' Pen brushed sandwich crumbs from her lap. 'It was behind the Front. We'd heard tales about a fox hanging about the trenches at night, and some of the boys were trying to shoot it.' She caught Ditto's look. 'They were hungry. It was a long winter. Nobody could hit the thing and we didn't have bullets to waste, but an Irish lad managed to nab it with a snare.'

Even Morgan appeared to be listening, though he didn't raise his head.

'It only had three paws, this fox. When the boy went to break its neck it screamed, as foxes do—' Aggie shuddered— 'and so the boy let it go. Swore the fox had spoken to him in his head, told him its name and begged to be spared. Tertius, the fox called itself. That boy from Dublin was my x-ray assistant,' Pen said. 'A practical sort of lad. But he stuck to his tale.'

'Horrid,' Aggie said, counting a row of knitting stitches.

'At least Pixie hasn't talked,' Rom said. 'Did anybody get marks appearing on their hand?'

Pen glanced over. 'What sort? Like the plague?'

'Not quite. Just a pattern; my grandfather collected animal folktales, I think there were a few like that.'

Pen shook her head. 'No, but that's just half the story. A few days later we had a visit from a French battalion. One of their lads in post-op told us this three-legged fox was a sort of camp mascot; they put out clean water, and would have left food if they had any—and they'd named it Tertius.'

She was gazing past Ditto at the flat yellow fields.

'Best of all, though, was the French captain who told me they'd seen the fox at the mess-tent, the morning they were bombed. The thing is, my lad freed the fox on Monday night, and the French captain saw it on Tuesday, a few hours later. Two hundred miles.'

Ditto looked at Rom, and Rom shifted on her seat.

'Is it possible?' Ditto asked.

'Odd things happen,' Pen said. 'Only a story, of course. May I? Thank you.'

'Sandwich, Rom?'

'I don't like potted fish. You believe it, though.'

To Pen, who sniffed. 'I believe what I see, and I've seen strange things. I haven't even told you the strangest one of all, about the Polish lads who killed a wolf and dragged it back to camp. They got it to the firelight, and it wasn't a wolf. It was a man.'

'Did they—they—' Ditto stopped.

'He was naked,' Pen said, 'and his hair was long and grey. But the oddest thing of all, they said, was something he was missing. Something nobody's ever missing.'

'What was it?' asked Morgan.

'An umbilicus,' Pen said, and took another bite of sandwich.

Rom folded her arms. 'His navel?'

'Precisely. The Polish lads said it was unborn and undead, and wanted to burn the thing. I think they did, in the end.'

Ditto's hands were wrapped tightly around her coffee flask. 'And what happened?'

'What do you mean?'

'Oh, I—thought you were going to say it came back to life or something.' Ditto laughed weakly.

'My story isn't thrilling enough? No, it didn't come back to life, not that I heard.'

'We've finished the sandwiches,' Rom said. 'Morgan, have you any lemon drops?'

He didn't look overjoyed to share. The Scottish girl took hers with a blush; she was only a year or two older than Morgan.

'Rom,' Pen said. 'Is that short for Andromeda? I'm Penelope, you see. And I wonder if Ditto—'

'Is Dido.' They all smiled wearily. 'You were lucky with your names,' Rom said. 'Dido and Penelope were heroines; Andromeda just sat on a rock and waited to be rescued. And my mother calls herself a suffragette.'

Ditto was powdering her cheeks. 'We still aren't as glamorous as some of the ancient queens at work.'

Pen laughed. And even Morgan's mouth twitched, but Aggie didn't get the joke at all.

'She was fine,' said the guardsman as they disembarked. 'Wouldn't touch her meat, but I gave her a bit of my sandwich.'

'She's usually a picky eater,' Ditto said, 'well done you.'

Rom took Pixie's leash. 'You little rat, you're just being contrary.'

The dog licked herself complacently.

'I say, Miss Godden—' Pen's head bobbed over the sea of hats. 'Wasn't sure if I'd catch you, but here.' She handed Rom a card. 'If ever you have a problem with that Pixie of yours. A most peculiar dog.' The stripes of the woman's blazer dipped away like a flag.

'A most peculiar person,' Rom said.

7

I have been working but it is difficult with the hot buzz of flies and the marshland stench.

The nights are the worst, when I am too tired to sleep. I thought the situation would be better now the house is empty but the garden is full of birds and wild things. I think they all come to hear it speak. They know how hungry it is.

JASPER TEAGUE, Journals, 26th June 1918

'At last.' Ditto dumped her bags. 'I nearly missed the smell of our mice.'

Marvellous, to take off hats and hang up coats and drink tea from their own cups, even if it didn't feel quite home with Morgan seated in the living room. He'd ascended the staircase while Ditto cajoled the cabbie into carrying the trunks, and now unpacked his books beside him on the sofa.

'Will you be alright to sleep there?'

'If you saw my dormitory you wouldn't need to ask.'

They left him at his usual occupation; reading, or pretending to, and went to buy sausages, tramping through the evening streets. A bone for Pixie, too; Rom had to reassure Mrs Martin downstairs that the dog was quite well, and it was nobody's fault she'd run away, and no, they'd never heard of a beast walking out of a double-locked courtyard.

In Ditto's room they fell onto the bed, half-exhausted. Ditto unlatched her suitcase with a grunt. 'I'm sick to death of my own clothes.'

'Who's going to tell his majesty there's only toast for breakfast?'

'When I have kids they'll never complain about their meals. I shall employ a chef especially.' Ditto tugged off her muslin dress and slid off the bed, and tap-danced in triple-slow time, her necklace swinging against her pink girdle. For somebody who didn't like being touched, she was very good at being looked at. 'I'd be a darling mother.'

Rom sat up. 'I think you would be.' But she hadn't imagined Ditto would ever want to. Babies would be fun if you didn't need husbands

66

and such. Ditto teased Rom, though, about her little affairs at College, about marrying a dentist and knitting booties or buying Tudoresque houses in the suburbs.

'My mother never planned to be a mother,' Rom said. 'She was going to be a vestal or something. Perhaps she found a man who didn't bore her.' Perhaps she'd wanted a baby too, and that was the end of it. 'When Father died she said she'd never marry again. She managed two years alone. These days I don't pay much attention to what she says.' Rom unhooked her stockings and rolled them off. 'You wouldn't marry, would you?'

'And get my own bank account? Maybe. I could always marry a pansy. *You* will have thirty-eight children,' Ditto said. 'You'll marry a man who plays golf. You'll make him dinner every night.'

'I can't cook for tuppence.'

'*Golf.*' Ditto slithered out of her silk shorts. 'And you'll adopt at least a dozen cats, the manky ones that bite. You always want the miserable type.' She plumped onto the bed, her naked legs flopped loosely. Polished ivory, and the sleek dark hair between them like a splash of black paint. Nobody's legs would ever be as lovely as Ditto's.

'Of course they'll be manky.' Rom climbed in and pulled the covers over them both. 'That just means they need a lot of extra petting.' She settled her head on the pillow, and bumped Ditto's bare shoulder gently.

'I'm not a cat,' Ditto said.

'You do like sardines.'

'That's just necessity,' Ditto said, but Rom twitched her arm under Ditto's warm waist. She kissed across her shoulder. Rubbed her nose over the tiny silken hairs on the back of Ditto's neck.

Ditto pulled Rom's hand across her hip and tucked it close between her own. Warm curled fingers. 'Silly,' Ditto said.

Darling. So silly herself, pretending to be a doll. Pretending she wasn't as soft as anybody else. Rom nestled her cheek into the sleepy crook of Ditto's neck, feeling the slow weight of Ditto's body settle against her own, and she thought it was almost enough.

'Where did the porter get to?'

Godalming Station churned with schoolboys and Rom frowned

across the herd, but here bobbed only the hats of fond parents come to say farewell.

'There's Mr Asherford,' Morgan said. The man's bright tie flashed amidst the uniforms. 'He'll have the school car waiting.'

A boy pelted past and his swinging satchel caught Rom in the shoulder. 'Ass,' she muttered. Morgan followed her with manufactured caution.

This morning had been easy enough; Morgan had made himself toast before she and Ditto even woke and solemnly set the kettle to boil again as they scrambled for shoes. But Ditto had gone straight to the theatre, and only Rom rattled down here to Surrey. Her eyes stung with train-smoke. Commencement of the bloody quarter and not a bloody porter in sight.

'Good morning, Miss Godden.'

Rom whirled. Under the station clock she located the iron bench and the dark eyes watching her over a newspaper.

'Minus the Dionysian halo today.' Mr Prideaux laid the paper over his crossed knee and tilted his head, that shapely head she'd somehow recalled in profile.

'I didn't know you had a dog.' Morgan knelt to touch its neck. Under the iron bench the animal closed its eyes contentedly. 'Foxhound. It is yours?'

Prideaux lifted one wrist to show the leather leash.

'Nice-looking,' Morgan said.

The dog was, actually, the very image of what a dog should be: bright-eyed and soft-eared, russet patches over its creamy coat. But Rom was in no mood to agree. 'I thought you weren't fond of dogs, Morgan.'

Prideaux had half an eye on his newspaper again. The blue plaid overcoat was slung around his shoulders and the dark suit beneath was tailored snugly. He was barely broader than Morgan, for all his height.

'Aren't hunters kept in couples?' Morgan asked.

'Perhaps that's my dog's problem,' Rom said, 'she might be lonely. But just imagine having two of them.'

Prideaux raised one brow in a shorthand of surprise. 'Not the doggish type?' He tucked his left ankle onto his right knee and resettled the newspaper. His trousers were cuffed rather high over a slim column of dove-grey ankle. 'Dogs forgive most frailties; cats, I find, have a tendency to regard one with such abysmal contempt.'

'They're marvellous judges of character. Morgan, you're sitting in the dust. See if you can fetch a porter.'

Morgan stood, wincing carefully, and she just as carefully ignored it as he left.

Prideaux growled. 'No running on the platform—' and two boys scuffled to a halt behind Rom. 'It's Wentworth, isn't it?'

'Walters, sir,' said the taller boy.

'No running.'

'Yes, sir.' They walked away with ceremonial stiffness until they'd passed the ticket booth.

The fox-hound bent its soft head towards Rom's ankles. Prideaux whistled, a quick liquid sound, and the dog settled again.

The leather soles of Prideaux's narrow shoes had been patched. There were deep creases worn into his dark trousers. A glint of buttons behind the flies, straining slightly.

Rom looked away.

Morgan's hat was moving away beyond the postcard rack. A porter's pert cap paused and nodded.

'I do believe Mckenzie is limping. Nothing serious?' Something about the man's stoneground voice made sudden sense. He wasn't native English; each word and punctuation mark was pressed like steel print.

'My dog attacked him. Apparently.' Rom turned. 'To be quite honest, I'd believe anything about Morgan.'

'I remember,' Prideaux said, 'sympathy is short.' He was scanning the Financial page.

'Yesterday I spent eight hours on a train with him.'

'Not a born traveller, is he.'

'Oh,' Rom said eventually, 'you brought him up to London last week.'

'Hardly eight hours but enough to fray his temper.'

'Did he misbehave?'

'He bought lemon drops at St Austell and round about Reading he attempted to seduce me.' The man raised sleepy eyes. 'He wanted his desk moved to a spot beside the window. He thought I might enjoy a permanent position. His uncle is on the School Board. Did you know? I wasn't aware.'

Morgan would be limping back through the crowd. She had to stop herself from turning to look for him.

'He didn't get very far,' Prideaux said, 'though he could hardly have known who he was dealing with.' He returned to his paper. 'You might want to watch him closely.'

'Morgan's not a baby.' The arrogance. 'I never see him anyway.' As if it was her fault. If it was even true.

'You'd prefer I kept an eye on him, then?'

'You shouldn't have to, he shouldn't behave so dreadfully.'

'I look at what is, and don't waste much time on what ought to be.'

Morgan was returning with a comic rolled up under his arm.

Rom turned to him. 'Alright?'

'Asherford's about to head off again.'

She didn't glance at Mr Prideaux. 'I'll go for my bus too. See you later then. Morgan—'

'Mhm?' He was tucking the comic inside his jacket.

'Telephone if you need us, won't you? For anything.'

'Alright.' He shook her hand before he went. Off to find the car, unhurried, weighted by his satchel.

Prideaux had disappeared behind his newspaper. The dog peered around his polished black shoes and licked its nose.

Rom's steps echoed in the concrete tunnel back to the street outside.

Morgan, who hasn't read comics since he was ten—oh, he's clever. Comics are currency at boarding school. He always carries sweets. He's very good at getting his own way. To accuse him, though—

Rom was in the windy cobbled street and halfway to the bus stop before she realised what was stuck in her memory. She stopped. And held her swinging purse against her hip as she ran back to the station.

The tunnel, steps, the concrete platform almost empty. Boys clustered at the far end, bags abandoned, crouched over marbles as they waited for the car.

Prideaux stood with his dog beside the hissing train. He looked over at the sound of her heels.

'You were in Cornwall,' Rom said, 'when I telephoned you.'

Prideaux shuffled his shoulders. 'Of course.'

'But you said Morgan returned to school.'

'I don't believe I said that, exactly.'

'What happened when he ran away? Exactly.'

Prideaux looped the dog's leash over his arm and reached inside his coat. 'Mckenzie had a row with the boy with whom he was staying, and caught a train to Truro.' He flicked open a yellow cigarette tin. 'So he told me, though I can't vouch for anyone's words but my own.'

She'd asked this before. She was talking in circles. 'What's in Truro?'

'He had my address in case he got himself into trouble. As I gather, his mother's sister is rather unpleasant.'

'You didn't tell the truth.'

Prideaux felt for his lighter. The dog growled softly and he glanced at it as he patted down his coat. 'It was factual,' he said. He fished the lighter from his trousers and lit the cigarette. Entirely wrong, everything, his starched white collar and worn-out suit, the gaudy watch chain, the coat too short across his long legs; that country coat. Those city shoes.

Everything was wrong.

'Did Morgan really try to bribe you?'

'Have you found something about him you won't believe?'

'You shouldn't have let him run away.'

'He had nobody better to call.'

'How dare you,' she said, wonderingly.

Prideaux blew a smoke ring. 'You have a bus to catch.'

Rom's head was thick, a nest of wasps. She barely heard her footsteps as she crossed the endless platform, down through the tunnel to the wince of sunlight below.

When she got home her shoulders were stiff. Ditto brimmed with other things—the show, the costumes, Miss Gwenevere, and it was a relief to listen. But things revolved in Rom's thoughts when she woke and watched the light on the ceiling.

She glared out the window on the Tube. Her thumbnail was bitten to flesh. She could talk to Ditto about Pixie; Ditto knew Pixie. But nobody knew Morgan at all.

'Miss Godden?' The lecture hall was nearly empty. Dr Carr was wiping his glasses on his tweed jacket.

Rom closed the book on her knees. 'I was somewhere else completely.'

'First Dynasty of the Amorites, I should hope.'

'Have you seen Mr Harper, sir?' Rom paused by his desk on her way to the door. 'He was at the Gifford lecture last week, said he planned on coming by.'

'He'll be in next week to give a talk,' Dr Carr said. 'Fresh off the digs, forging new territory—' He put his glasses back on. 'The things he found in Scotland. Did he mention them to you?'

'Possibly Hittite. He's looking for a cuneiform man in London.'

'Horstmann at the Museum, probably. How are you getting on with that assignment?'

'I've been held up with a sort of family problem,' Rom said from the doorway, 'I'll bring it next week.'

He was probably cross, she thought on the train home, because Harper hadn't brought the thing to him instead.

She was hunched at the table, elbow-deep in her essay, when the door thumped open at half-past five.

'Ivy—the little bitch—'

Ditto was shedding scarves and shoes like a tornado, and Rom sighed. 'What's Miss Munster done?'

Ditto slapped the poster down. 'They're actually coming to London. Really truly.'

It was the same blazing artwork as the music-covers tacked above the sideboard; black and lurid yellow, a bird-cage in flames. Or was it wings? *Séraphin Desir*, it said. *Le Phénix*.

'She's holding auditions, Madame Volkov—three nights only at the Silver Slipper. And Ivy Sodding Munster's going for it, and half the girls from *Ducky Dear*, and Mr. Tyson said if anybody ditches him for that French arsehole we'll lose our parts.'

'Oh, Ditto. Dear—'

'Sodding old sod,' she finished violently.

'If it's what you really want,' Rom said, 'can't you make it somehow?'

'The Phoenix thing's for three nights only,' Ditto said. 'Slave-pay. And *Ducky*'s a full season. I can't ditch a job, I might never get another one.' Her mouth was set. 'What a fucking nuisance.' She bent her sleek head and let Rom kiss her.

'I'm sorry, dear.'

'I'll manage,' Ditto said, and Rom knew it wasn't to be mentioned again.

She went back to writing. Ditto vanished to the bath; and she was smiling when she came back, full of news about Sally Corditch who got herself pregnant and is still turning somersaults even though she sicked up her lunch behind the faery woodland scenery.

But Ditto didn't sing as she put away the tea-things; and when she did, it wasn't Séraphin's song, not that night or the next.

Alec rang on Friday afternoon and Rom stood in a glass box on the Strand with her brother's voice, scuffing her toe into the telephone stand as he rambled.

'Sel Mitchell sends his regards. And Tom wants to know if the dog has done anything else extraordinary. Has she? I wonder if Pixie caught the train after all. If Morgan got it right he'd be unbearable.'

'Oz,' Rom said, and Alec stopped mid-sentence. 'You know people, don't you? I mean you know how to investigate people.'

'That sounds ominous.'

'It's about the teacher at Morgan's school—the one who gives them ciphers.'

'Mckenzie said something?'

'No, but I don't like it.' She explained. And heard the rustle of Alec's notepad on the other end.

'Prideaux. Is that A-U-X? I'll get Wells to look him up.' Alec's voice held a professional terseness. 'It shouldn't be difficult, the man will have a War record. We'll find something.'

Rom felt a little better when she hung up. 'We'll put Alec's brain to good use,' she said to Ditto when she unbuckled her shoes upstairs. 'Oh, my darling, what is it?'

Ditto's painted eyes were smudged with tears. Rom didn't have time to get her coat off before warm arms flung around her.

'Ivy,' Ditto said. 'Ivy Munster's gone.'

Rom held her, breathing greasepaint and violet perfume, and they curled together on the velvet sofa.

Ivy was quite missing and hadn't been home to feed her cat. No family to speak of; a carnival girl.

'Sure she isn't just on holiday? Perhaps if she found a boyfriend—'

'She missed all her rehearsals,' Ditto said. 'The orderly daughters didn't care either. Said the same as you.'

Her misery twisted Rom's stomach. 'I didn't know you were so close to Ivy.'

'She's naff as pants. But if I ever went missing—'

'Your parents would go to the police and we'd get you back.'

'A Japanese man and an Irish washerwoman? The police wouldn't even talk to them. We're invisible, us and Ivy. You haven't a clue.'

Rom's cheeks felt hot. 'I was trying to help. I'm sorry.'

'If you want to help, do it. Ask your brother.' Ditto shoved her hanky away in her pocket. 'I'll go around the dance halls, and Jenny's brother's a copper in Marylebone. I'm going to find her.'

That afternoon she came home from rehearsals briskly focused. 'I got the name of someone who can help.'

Rom was frying eggs. 'Like Alec's journalists, you mean?'

'Better. I think this one's in a gang.'

'Ditto—'

'He hangs about the dockyards and apparently knows everything worth knowing. We'll see what coin he's after, and we might learn something.'

Rom turned off the heat. 'We?'

'You're coming. I need Pixie in case Mr Kingsley's a murderous nutter.'

'This is a terrible plan.'

'I've agreed to meet him tomorrow.'

Rom groaned. 'Rendezvous in a backstreet?'

'Don't be silly,' Ditto said. 'He's meeting us at the Lyon's Tea-house.'

Alec whistled over the phone when he heard. 'Missing girl? That's a long shot. I don't know London well, and this type of thing—' He sighed. 'They vanish, and we can't even write it up because nobody knows anything. She's probably gone for good.'

Rom prickled at his resignation.

'Your teacher fellow, though.'

She pressed her ear close. 'You dug him up?'

'He's horribly overqualified to be teaching Latin to school kids. I don't know what he's doing there unless it's very temporary indeed.

74

There's a couple of degrees, politics and modern history, and he studied at Oxford after—'

'Oxford?'

'Doctorate in Philosophy, and another in Linguistics, though I can't see where he found the time. And listen to this: run out of Balliol last year after a nasty bit of blackmail over a senior researcher's wife. *Very* senior.'

There was scope for a mind like that at a school like Morgan's. 'Manipulation,' she said. 'Is that his game?'

'Oh, he wasn't running the blackmail, he was the one with the wife. Faculty threatened to tell the papers, and he didn't care if they did, and the researcher was horribly mortified. You've no idea how hard I had to wriggle to get anybody to talk. But it never did get to the papers and Dr Prideaux left quietly, so money may have changed hands somewhere. Which is,' Alec said, 'a kind of blackmail after all.'

'Bad news, then,' Rom said.

'It gets worse. That's the only thing I found. He told Oxford he served but he doesn't have a War record. The only Dr Cranach Prideaux lived in York in 1892.'

'Thirty years ago? Bastard. So who's this one?'

'No clue.' Alec's sigh was sharp as shaken paper. 'The school employed him after a recommendation, no help there. He should be gone by the end of the year. But it's trouble.'

Rom turned up her collar in the cold phone box. 'We ought to take Morgan this summer. We could go to Aunt Minnie's. His aunt won't want him.'

'He deserves a break, anyhow, he's been studying like mad. Harry said he's doing well, at least. Quite a head for numbers.'

'And ciphers,' Rom said slowly. 'Even his teachers said so.'

'The assistant master. Who lied about War service.'

'The assistant master, who doesn't have a record. Perhaps his department removed it. The sort of department who doesn't use names.'

'The sort who'd be keen on a kid who likes numbers.' Alec paused. 'If you wanted to recruit a kid you'd pick one without much family around, wouldn't you? The kind who'd rather stay with a teacher than his mother's people.'

They were both silent.

'Morgan won't tell us,' she said. 'But we need to get him out of there at term break.'

'I'll call his aunt,' Alec said.

Ditto perched on her chair, craning her neck to watch the tea-house doorway.

'He'll be a pick-pocket,' Rom said, 'with an old top hat and somebody else's waistcoat.'

'That's pantomime, don't be stupid. He'll be the slimy type who sells cocaine at nightclubs.'

But the man who found them at their table was barely twenty-five, a soldierly sort with a vivid mouth and bold fighter's chin. His eyes were quick and clear and he shook hands with curious gravity. And he was not entirely a stranger.

Beneath his tweed jacket he wore a red woollen jumper.

'I'm Kingsley,' he said.

Rom sat forward in her seat. 'We saw you at Gordey's.'

'And you're the one with the English Terrier.' He gestured to the doorway where they'd left Pixie.

'You were poking around the club that night,' Ditto said. 'You're a copper?'

'Not I.' Under the table Mr Kingsley's boot-heel bounced. 'My job's simple. People go missing and it's full time work turning them up again.' He had a lilting mixed-up accent, American probably, a clear tenor bell of a voice. His eyes flitted over the room; he didn't seem to miss much. Maybe a docker's gang kept him to track their debtors. But he had an openness about him; odd to imagine him as anybody's hard-man. 'I've spread the word about Miss Munster.'

'What have you found?'

'Nothing,' he said. 'No trace at all. And that's a rare thing. Tell me what you know.' He listened in silence, his eyes lowered. 'This Russian woman; did your friend Ivy ever meet her?'

'I'm not sure Ivy even made it to the audition,' Ditto said.

Mr Kingsley twitched his nose. 'Or ever made it back.'

'You think there's something funny going on,' Rom said. 'You've heard something.'

'You know the Votaries of Light?'

'They work for Madame Volkov. Cabaret performers.' Ditto shrugged. 'Running seances and flouncing about at parties.'

'I've been watching Volkov since last November, New York to London. Backstreets and theatres and nightclubs. By my count there's twenty-eight souls gone missing.'

Ditto drew a long breath. 'There's always stories going around, talent scouts and *film* producers and such.'

Rom had heard the stories. Most girls had. 'Where's Madame Volkov now?' Their posters covered London already, pearls and flames and bird-cages.

'Munich,' Kingsley said, 'touring around with the Phoenix. No point going at her; nobody can get close enough. If you truly want to track Miss Munster, you'll come at it from the other side. Do you truly?'

'Whatever it takes,' Ditto said.

'Well, then. Miss Munster worked in the carnival a few years back; Corbin Quinn's Aurelian Circus. Do you know it?'

'We went as kids,' Rom said. 'Everyone's heard of it.'

'Do you know it?' he asked again, exactly the same tone, but she felt he meant something different.

'Not really,' she said.

Kingsley sat back in his chair. 'We can try, anyway. We can go this week if you like.' He looked at Ditto, and away again. He didn't seem to meet anybody's eye for long. 'Saturday? Quinn's camp was close at last report, just past Cheltenham.'

'That's hours,' Ditto said. 'I suppose we can catch the early train.'

'I can meet you at the station with a car.'

Rom hesitated. 'We haven't a lot of money to pay you.'

'I was already on the case. A friend owed a favour to a friend of a friend,' Kingsley said. 'Relix is between them. Payment, I mean.' He stood. 'Can you bring the white dog with you? It might help with Quinn's people.'

'I hope this works,' Ditto said. 'Someone's bound to remember Ivy; they might know where she'd hide if she got in trouble.'

'Or they might be sore at her for leaving,' Kingsley said. 'They've got their own ideas of loyalty. Don't be expecting a welcome.'

8

Some nights the creature weeps. I would give the world away to be rid of this thing. The earthworms come up from the soil and squirm naked on the garden path; I know they hear it too.

There is no gold left anywhere; the newspapers say we are at War with the Kaiser. I had wondered why there was no fresh milk.

JASPER TEAGUE, Journals, 16th Dec. 1916

On Thursday there was a Cairo postmark among her morning letters. *Rom dear,* said her mother's rapturous writing. *You haven't told me yet how Frazer went. We'll be over for Christmas hols—Minnie's been bullying me and I suppose I should. You're going to hers in June? How perfect. You'll be able to bathe in the river. We're well; I hope you are too—get your degree and hurry over, Rom dear, I miss you.*

Not enough to write more than three times a year.

It's gorgeous you'll have the summer together. Mckenzie said you're taking him too—he seemed pleased, poor darling.

And then a rambling two pages about the Hallorans, you know, with the German Shepherds? Who'd come to stay and wouldn't eat eggs for breakfast.

Rom read it again. Mckenzie. *Did* he sound pleased about a holiday? Now Rom was the only one left who called him Morgan.

The next letter was from Aunt Minnie: spring-green paper bordered with buttercups, not her style, but it had probably been a gift. Aunt Minnie didn't waste things. She'd be pleased to have them all for the summer, she said. Hadn't seen Alec for a year, nearly. How was Rom's last assignment on the currency of ancient Britain? Aunt Minnie liked Celts, and a pre-Roman coin got her quite excited in a quiet Aunt Minnie way.

It was going to be a nice holiday, actually.

Rom sifted through the stack. Townsend the solicitor had responded, on a snowy sheet of linen paper, to her vague query about Pixie: he'd had met the dog years ago and thought her a well-behaved beast. Leaving her to Rom was almost reasonable compared to the wilder excesses of Jasper's mental state. Any strange behaviour on Pixie's part was probably due to colic; had Rom tried giving her some lean beef? A polite two paragraphs that amounted to *Your grandfather was mad as a blue goose and you might be too.* Rom used the letter to mop a drip of tea.

Among the advertisements sat one last envelope, thin yellow bond paper, return address Godalming.

The pages crackled under an indecipherable scrawl. The words barely varied except for the deep loops and high ascenders, dashed out with the haste of a doctor's prescription.

Miss Godden.

Your brother was involved this week in a small Incident with a boy from Fifth form. There were no serious injuries, altho the other boy managed to stab himself through the hand with a pen: the steel nib passed between the second and third metacarpal bones.

Regrettably neither Monitors nor Masters were present at the time; the exact—was it 'circumstances'?—are yet to be established. Your brother sustained a broken nose but the nurse assures us any damage will heal quickly.

There's every chance the Incident was due to carelessness on the dormitory staircase. Considering this probabilitie, the school has no intention to discipline either party beyond the usual charge of disruption.

I believe the Head Master has contacted Mckenzie's father regarding the above but given our recent conversation and your ongoing interest in your brother's academic year, I deemed it pertinent to contact you.

Regards,

C M Prideaux

The man had a Victorian fondness for indiscriminate capitalisation. The spelling was uneven; didn't he teach English?

She needed to write to Morgan. But there was no easy way to put it. *Your teacher isn't what he says.* Morgan wouldn't take advice. *Don't speak to him.* And she couldn't simply drop it in a note. *Mr Prideaux. You know the one? Either he's seventy years old or he's stolen somebody's name.*

Rom put this letter beside her tea-cup and debated whether to reply.

Not worth the ink. But she slipped a single line into one of her own sky-blue envelopes—*thanks for your exemplary concern*—and posted it off.

She took Hieroglyphics today in the clattering lecture hall. And Dr Carr after; she was looking forward to Mr Harper and his news from Scotland, from anywhere other than rainy London, where the rest of the world seemed distant behind the drizzle.

'Mr Harper will not be in attendance today,' Dr Carr said. 'Time is apparently of no concern to him; perhaps he's spent too long amongst the primitive camps of the Oxfordian dig teams.' He was a Cambridge man, of course. 'A previously undiscovered species, yes? *Feris oxfordia.* Family *Perfossores.*' That earned him a scattered laugh. Perfossor means digger; not his worst pun.

At least Oxford gave their female students proper membership. At Cambridge you could do all the work in the world and they'd never let you graduate. It's not about what you are, only how they see you.

'Miss Godden,' he said when everyone else was surging for the doorways afterwards. 'It seems we're to learn more about Mr Harper's find, at least. Horstmann completed his translation and it's Hittite after all.'

'In a Celtic burial site? A bit impossible.'

'Perhaps not Celtic.' Dr Carr lowered himself into his chair. 'Bronze Age, I believe. But we've never found a skull exactly like it—Neolithic, covered in painted clay, which is certainly not characteristic of British tumulus culture.'

Rom stopped. 'But cuneiform hadn't been invented yet. It has to be more recent.'

'Not necessarily. The skull could be millennia older than the words. The cuneiform was engraved on a gold plaque in the skull's mouth. Apparently it describes a river of gold beneath Babylon.'

Rom snorted. 'Koldewey's excavation team would have noticed if there was.'

'It won't stop an avid hunter,' Dr Carr said. 'We shall have plenty of questions when Mr Harper decides to grace us with his presence.'

Rom made her way into the windy Strand. Wrong thing, wrong place. Hittite cuneiform in the cold hills of Scotland. Somebody had been very far from home.

But strange things happen every day, and it still wasn't the strangest thing she'd seen this week.

She stopped outside the Tube station at the phone booth. The connection to Godalming hummed like a distant windstorm. 'I was hoping to speak to Mr Prideaux. He's an assistant master, Fourth form?'

'I see,' said the woman's comfortable voice. 'Who shall I say is calling?'

'Andromeda Godden. It's business.'

'I shall let him know,' said the rounded west-coast voice; the housekeeper. 'If you don't mind waiting, miss.'

Rom waited. Past the point of irritation, well into wondering if she should hang up and send a telegram instead; but saying what?

The ear-piece clicked. 'He's gone, I'm afraid,' said the woman.

'When will he be in?'

'He's left the school, miss, he was only temporary. If you send a note we can forward it.'

'I'll write,' Rom said. She wasn't going to write. But she had a question. 'What's the best time to talk to the students? I need to speak to my brother.'

During evening study, the housekeeper said. She'd have to call after dinner.

Rom did, out in the cold that evening, from the phone box on the Camden Road, waiting for somebody to hunt up Morgan. A long hold, cursing the cost of seconds.

He sounded slightly out of breath when he picked up. 'Andromeda.' Rolling the *r*, emphasis on the *e*. Greek, correct; not her name.

'Hello, Morgan. Are you well?'

'Of course.'

He was there. Perhaps that's all she'd wanted to know. 'I heard you were injured.'

'An accident. It's fine.'

'I tried to call Mr Prideaux about it, but he's gone already.'

'Yes, this week.'

'Has Alec asked you about coming down to St Veep? We'd be happy to have you.'

'He did. Thanks. Sounds good.'

That was the polite conversation spent entirely.

'I'd like ask you something,' she said. 'I thought you'd probably know better than anyone. It's about ciphers.'

A pause. 'Alright,' he said.

'If I found a coded message, where would I begin if I needed to figure out how it worked?'

'Patterns,' Morgan said. 'Frequency recognition. Look at how often the symbols show up and if you're lucky, it'll be simple and not run through too many shifts.'

The same symbol surfacing from the chaos. A line, a name. 'Like Sherlock Holmes, *the most common letter in the English alphabet is e*, and all that. But what if it's completely random?'

'Nothing's random. There'll be a key. Kerckhoffs's Principle says even if all the information is made public, it must be secure without the key. You can hide a secret in plain sight. I can't be much help without seeing the cipher itself.' Morgan's voice was distant. 'I'd better go, it's banco and the monitors will come looking.'

'Thank you, Morgan.'

He paused again. 'Of course,' he said.

'Plimsolls, d'you think?'

'It's the countryside, Ditto. There will be mud,' Rom said.

They got to the station eventually; Pixie seemed jumpy as they settled her into the guard's carriage. The train was nearly empty. Apparently there weren't a lot of people heading towards the Cotswolds on a showery Thursday.

Rom pulled off her coat in their compartment. 'What about your rehearsal?'

'I can turn cartwheels in my sleep, I'll catch up next week.' Ditto unbuckled her shoes and stretched out on the seat. 'What about your studies? You've been whingeing about that essay.'

'Dr Carr's hardly going to fail me; we've had some marvellous chats about Grooved Ware.'

'Oh? Clever.'

'It isn't like that,' Rom said. 'I work hard.' She rummaged for her toffees. 'Sure you can't come to Cornwall next month? St Veep, our aunt's place. It's rather nice.'

'The show starts at the end of June and Mr Tyson'll flay me if I skip rehearsals.'

'Not even for a few days?'

'I do wish I could. Morgan had a fine go at ruining the last holiday.'

'Actually,' Rom said, 'I asked Alec to bring him. May I tell you something? Quite seriously, dear. About Morgan's schoolmaster.'

Ditto put her magazine down and listened. 'What a mess. Is he the smiling handsy type? All my dancing masters were crawlers.'

'At any rate, we should keep an eye on Morgan.'

'You do care after all.' Ditto was unwrapping a tomato sandwich. 'About the little rotter.'

Rom rested her head against the dusty seat. 'It's like Ivy Munster,' she said. 'Somebody has to,' and they were quiet as the train rumbled on through the damp green valleys.

Outside Cheltenham station Mr Kingsley was parked against the leafy hedges in a touring car, a glorious chocolate-coloured Packard. Rom eyed the trim as she opened the door for Ditto and Pixie.

When Kingsley slid into the driver's seat he paused, breathing in the scent of the hedgerow. Rom leaned forward to speak at his shoulder; his thick jacket held the smithy-scent of metal. 'Rather a nice car, Mr Kingsley.'

'It does the job,' he said.

At every crossroads he pulled up and stared at the sky. Down the side roads he leaned out the window to read farm gates. 'Next right,' he said finally, and turned towards them as he spoke. Rom could just hear him over the idling engine but she had a feeling he knew she was lip-reading.

The road brought them to an overhanging tree where they parked. The high hedge shook with sparrows. Rom and Ditto followed Kingsley on foot, over the stile, and Pixie seemed pleased to be off her leash in the fresh smells. Tents and flags blazed at the bottom of the field. A main road ran past them on the right, where the faded red-and-yellow Big Top squatted like a storybook toadstool.

Ditto glared. 'We could have parked down there. Good lord, the horse shit.'

Kingsley looked back over his shoulder without a break in his stride. 'We're coming in downwind. Wiser, all things told.'

'Stalking,' Rom said, and he smiled.

'Always, Miss Godden.'

The smell of a circus unfolded, horsey with trodden straw, damp canvas, and the drift of smoke and sausages. Caravans clustered with canopies and a pair of tethered goats watched with sharp yellow eyes as they passed. Children juggled between the caravans, where women sat with their mending baskets in the canvas shade. Rom half-expected Pixie to cause a fuss over the unfamiliar place but the dog kept at her heels.

They were being ignored as they halted at the camp's edge. Kingsley waited without concern.

It wasn't long until a small man in shabby leather ducked out of a tent. 'Can I help you?'

'Hoping to talk to the lady herself,' Kingsley said.

'Not 'ere,' said the small man, 'only Corbin.' His ears were prominent, delicate; the sunlight glowed pinkly through them. He tucked his thumbs into his vest. 'Hard luck.'

'When's the lady returning?'

'You know how they are, the fine folk.'

'That helps us precisely not at all.'

'Can't we talk to Mr Quinn?' Ditto asked Kingsley. 'He'd know, wouldn't he?'

'He's a contrary bastard.'

'That he is,' said the small man, and stared as if he'd just realised Kingsley wasn't alone.

'We haven't time to trot around the countryside,' Ditto said. 'Will Mr Quinn talk to us, sir?'

The man shrugged. 'Soon know,' he said, and slipped away.

'Be careful in there,' Kingsley said as they waited. 'Keep Pixie close to you.'

'You're not coming in? But you brought us here,' Rom said, 'you know what to say.'

'To the lady, on a good day. Not Quinn, not ever.'

Ditto looked properly annoyed. 'That's not quite fair, Mr Kingsley.'

He pulled off his flat linen cap and rumpled his hair. 'I'm not allowed. Quinn's people and my people, some time back. If word gets out I'm nosing about, you see—there are loyalties.'

Ditto looked at him keenly. 'Between gangs.'

'Sort of a long-time disagreement. It's nearly over, anyhow. Forgotten,' Kingsley said. 'Make sure you tell them Pixie's not yours.'

'What? Why?'

But the small man was back and beckoning them to follow, and Kingsley strolled away with his hands in his corduroy pockets.

Behind strung lines of washing, the tents gave way to meadow between the encampment and the treeline. Horses everywhere, cropping at the grass or rolling in the churned-up pasture.

People had gathered down on the slope to watch a great dark mare go through her paces, but the creature wasn't tethered as she circled her master. The wind caught the horse's tail and flapped the jacket of the man with the whip; and Rom realised the jacket was a tailcoat, and the man was Corbin Quinn.

He gestured with his riding crop. Somebody stepped forward to the horse, who dropped her head at rest. Quinn strode up the field toward them, the gloss of his black boots twinkling, and stopped a few paces away. His face was painted mask-white. His pointed beard looked as though it had been inked onto his chin. 'Who sent thee?'

'Nobody. We're here for ourselves,' Ditto said. 'Looking for my friend.'

Quinn's eyes settled on Pixie. 'Dimber wee dog,' he said. Pausing on the last word: dog-ge.

'She isn't mine,' Rom said warily. 'She was left to me by my grandfather.'

He tapped his crop against the square toe of his boot. 'Collared, but nish o' thy collaring.' He loosened his own tight collar and set his fist on his hip with the poise of a stage conjurer. He wasn't quite as tall as Rom, a muscular block of a man. His greasepaint glistened with sweat, smudging his black-rimmed eyes, but it only seemed to deepen the hostile lines of his face. 'Business?' he said abruptly.

'We're looking for Ivy Munster,' Ditto said. 'She's a friend of mine at the theatre and she's missing. Nobody will help us but we want to find her, Mr Quinn. She used to work for you.'

Quinn twitched his nose. 'Miss Ivy Ava Munster. Aerial act, trapeze.'

'Yes, sir.'

'And who are you?'

'Dido Hamilton.'

'I'll be trined an I shred my own kinchin.'

Ditto frowned. 'You prefer not to betray your people?'

'Aye.'

'She's missing, Mr Quinn, and the cop—' Ditto paused. 'The harman-becks won't help us, she could be mullered and they'd never care. I know she had no family, but she had you.'

Quinn's eyes narrowed. 'Come away,' he said, and they followed through the mud.

Rom ducked beneath the tent flap into the dim canvas heat. There was grass underfoot but it was neat as a room; two folding deck-chairs with ocean-liner stripes, and a stack of tin travel chests. A narrow camp bed was set up in one corner. Everything was clean and sparse and ancient.

Quinn paced with his white-gloved hands folded behind him, tucked beneath his tailcoat. His savage chin jutted and he looked for all the world like an irritable bird. 'Where is the hunter?'

Rom glanced down at Pixie's placid head. 'Who?'

'The one as brought you.'

'By the stile,' Ditto said, 'but he wanted to stay back.'

'Likely.' Quinn leaned out of the tent and shouted. 'Eho!' And a brisk patter Rom couldn't catch. He looked back at them. 'What binds him to thee? What's his relix?'

'He said somebody else is paying him.'

'Naught's for naught,' Quinn said. 'Ivy was kinchin, and ye'll be helped, but the hunter—' He hissed. 'I'll whip him beneshiply an he shred me.'

Rom hoped she was catching most of his meaning. 'I don't believe Mr Kingsley's looking for trouble.'

Quinn's gaze was direct. 'Do you know him?'

'We've met him before.'

'Do you know him?' Quinn asked again, and again Rom felt it wasn't the same question at all.

'No,' she said firmly.

Quinn smiled. 'Trust none,' he said, 'and cry blackfriars on the dimber words of bird, beast, or bookman. Wiser, all things told.'

He dragged one of the tin trunks into the square of sunlight that slanted into the tent. He appeared to have forgotten them as he carried over an enamel bowl and jug and set them on the trunk.

Something scuffled outside the tent. 'I can walk, you silly prick,' came Kingsley's welcome voice, and he stepped beneath the canvas. He was rubbing his shoulder.

A muscular red-haired woman loomed behind him, with a slim boy in a black velvet doublet who had ears cropped close against his head. Movement shivered at the boy's neck and a mouse peered over his collar. The boy blinked; his eyes were yellow.

Kingsley pulled off his cap. 'Ben lightmans, bird.' He put one hand on his chest as he bowed his head.

'Ben lightmans, beast,' said Corbin Quinn.

The two men looked at each other across the tent, and Rom knew as if she'd seen it written that she and Ditto had found the camp of the Crow's People.

'How goes it?' Kingsley asked.

'Gloves off.'

'No need for games, Mr. Quinn, that's between yourself and—'

'Pax,' Quinn said. 'Gloves off.'

Kingsley glanced behind him. 'Call off your people, then.'

'Shut your gleeking muzzle. One chance more.'

'I'm doing it, aren't I?' Kingsley pulled the brown wool mitt from his right hand and wriggled his fingers. 'Glove off, Mr Quinn.'

The boy in black velvet crossed to the trunk and filled the waiting bowl with water.

Kingsley stepped over to it and dipped in his bare right hand. 'Satisfied?'

Something tightened through Rom's stomach. She leaned around the woman to see Kingsley's hand. The pattern marked his skin, fine and dark as threads—up his wrist and banding every finger in tangles.

'Do you see it?' whispered Ditto.

Rom's chest was hot and damp. She rubbed the back of her own hand as though she might feel something.

'Vallick's People,' Quinn said, bent over the bowl.

'You knew about that. You know all that I am. Are we done?'

Quinn stepped back. 'Aye.'

Nobody seemed to have a towel ready so Kingsley dried his hand on his red wool jumper. 'Bloody told you,' he said.

'Other hand, beast.'

Kingsley pulled his right glove back on. 'No chance.'

'Are you still bounden?'

'I'm here in my own name. You can't ask that,' Kingsley said with rising sharpness.

'This is my camp.'

'You can't ask that,' said the red-haired woman softly.

Quinn spat on the grass at Kingsley's feet and turned his back, straightening his bow tie. His painted eyes settled on Rom and Ditto. 'Ivy Ava Munster, is it. Others have gone. Others will go. She is free to do as she pleases.'

Ditto huffed. 'You won't help us?'

'Miss Munster auditioned for a stage show,' Kingsley said, and Quinn turned his head. 'You're in the gig, Mr Quinn. You've not heard of Séraphin Desir? He's a jazz singer, goes by the name *Le Phenix*. His manager put advertisements in the newspapers.' Kingsley's eyes were steady. 'She's looking for Votaries. Twenty-eight souls missing.'

'Ivy went to them?'

Ditto broke in. 'She planned to, anyhow.'

Quinn wiped his face on his sleeve. 'We will look, and we will tell you what we ken.'

'Splendid. Many thanks, Master Crow.' Kingsley stuck his hands in his pockets. 'Shall we be going, my ladies?'

'Relix first,' Quinn said. 'Or are ye faithless?'

'Half an oriole sounds fair for a scrap I could rummage myself.'

'My bargaining is with the kinchin,' Quinn said.

Kingsley made an odd sound in his throat. 'Don't, Miss Hamilton. It isn't money he wants.'

Ditto's hand paused on her purse. 'How do you take your payment?'

Blood, thought Rom. Secrets. A bargain with a witch—

'Have you a garden?'

Ditto laughed nervously. 'Only the manky courtyard in our flat.'

'It is enough.' Quinn stepped up to her. 'You both have care of it?'

'Rom's name's on the receipts, too, but really Mrs Martin just hangs her washing down there,' Ditto said. 'Nobody else does because the Greeners in Number Four steal our—' Ditto stopped. Quinn waited, hands behind his back. 'Yes,' she finished.

Quinn turned to Rom. 'What is your name, kinchin?'

'Andromeda May Godden.'

Quinn was tugging off his white cotton glove. His bare hand was roped with sinew, the same warm brown his face must be under the greasepaint. 'For as long as you live, your gardens shall be wildered by the Crow's People. Air and earth and aqua shall be free to our folk. Do you both agree?'

Kingsley shrugged at them. 'Birds and such. You'll hardly notice.'

Ditto let out a breath. 'I agree.' Quinn extended his hand, and Ditto shook it.

He turned to Rom, who pulled off her duck-blue glove. A crunching grip. His thumb pressed into her wrist. 'We helped you,' he said. 'Do you accept our words?'

'Yes.' Rom tried to tug her hand away. A frosted ache was seeping to her nails.

'You accept the price?'

'Yes.'

'You'll not shred nor seek to split upon it?'

'He means you aren't to go back on your—'

'I know,' Rom said to Kingsley, 'we said we agree.'

Quinn released her hand. Rom shook out her fingers. They were mottled purple with his grip.

'Fare thee well on the high road,' Quinn said, 'and the low road, and the maze between where no roads be. And you, beast?'

Kingsley raised his chin. 'What?'

'Don't come back,' Quinn said.

'Could have been worse,' Kingsley said as they clambered over the stile. 'He's a cockered old sod.'

'We *saw* your hand.' They reached the car and Ditto perched on the running board. 'Tell us what you've got us into.'

Kingsley was checking under the hood, leaning into the oily dark of the engine. 'What do you think it was?'

'I think it's magic,' Rom said. The word didn't sound as silly as it should have, with the wind in the chestnut tree above. Even with the sleek motor beside her. Even in the twentieth century.

Kingsley wiped his fingers and slammed the hood. He didn't answer, and Rom rubbed her right hand. Her wrist ached dully. 'But there's no such thing as magic, is there, Mr. Kingsley?'

He started the engine and didn't look back at them. He whistled, though, under his breath, the whole drive back, an aimless wandering noise that wasn't a melody.

When he opened the car door for them at the bus stop, Ditto didn't budge from her seat. 'Is the Crow a magician?'

'Will you please get out?'

If he hadn't said please Rom might have gone. 'Is Ivy one of them?'

'She's mortal. Quinn takes in all folk, as the Pavees and the Romani once took in his people. He cares for his own and few others.'

'And you?' Rom eyed him. 'Can humans have those marks?'

'They can.'

'What do they mean?'

'I'd have to ask relix for the knowledge.' Kingsley kicked the car tire. 'Look, can you go? I'm supposed to be somewhere this evening.'

'If you don't answer,' Ditto said, 'we'll march back and ask Quinn.'

'Do you want your skins eaten?' He fished out a battered pocket-watch. 'If you've got questions next time, you'd best be ready to pay.'

Ditto climbed out of the car. 'And how do you take your payment, Mr Kingsley?'

He closed his watch with a snap. 'I'll send news by Crow's People.'

'We don't know any,' Rom said, but Kingsley smiled crookedly.

'You're about to have a garden full of them. Ben lightmans, mistresses. Ben lightmans, dog.' He tipped his cap.

There was a telegram waiting under their apartment door as they unlocked.

PHONE IMMEDIATELY WILL WAIT

Rom didn't even take her coat off. She took Pixie with her to the post office.

The phone whirred when Alec picked up. 'Are you alright?' Almost angry. 'Did you see the papers?'

Rom scrambled back through memory, Mussolini and Irish rebels and civil war in Greece.

'Mr Harper's dead,' Alec said. 'Somebody killed him, we heard it from London this morning. They found five snakes in his bedroom.'

Rom pulled her coat closer. 'Oh, Alec—'

'We spoke to him and it was the next day, Rom. There was a snake in your room the next *day*. Don't go anywhere,' he said. 'Don't let the dog out of your sight. I'm going to ask Cartwright if I can come down and cover the story.'

'What? How—'

'Harper's place was ransacked. He found treasure, didn't he? There's gold behind all this, and somebody was after it. I'll telephone when I have news. Yes?'

'Yes,' she stammered. The dial tone wittered.

She walked home with Pixie, briskly in the cold, and cold all over. A random dart of fate is sting enough; she could bear it. But now she wasn't sure if it was chaos she was looking at, or the wildest and most terrible design.

9

'In the beginning was the Word.' No line so clearly illustrates the dilemma of the translator.

How does one convey the meaning of the original Greek, when 'λόγος' doesn't simply mean 'word'? It means reason, argument, speech, proportion; a living discourse, and a rational account.

In the beginning was not a word: it was a spoken sound. A manifestation of an idea, an expression of perfect order. Language cannot hope to convey everything that must be reconstructed to form a complete picture of a culture. It's a useful relic but lacks the purpose of a physical object, such as a weapon or pot.

DR ROBERT CARR, Lecture notes, 28th March 1924

They were quiet over breakfast. Rom had gone out early for the Sunday paper and now it lay open between her and Ditto. *Archaeologist found dead after Cairo expedition.* And beneath, in cheery square font: *Coincidence or mummy's curse?*

'How stupid,' Rom said coldly. 'The reporters won't look in the right places if they're spouting that kind of rubbish. They're saying it's Lord Carnarvon all over again.'

Ditto was reading. 'A cobra was found in Carnarvon's house the same day he opened King Tut's tomb.'

'In Egypt,' Rom said. 'It has plenty of snakes. London doesn't. I don't believe there's any curse at all. Somebody murdered Harper and they aren't even doing him the justice to investigate.' Her head felt dense. 'If we only knew why—'

'Not everything has a reason,' Ditto said.

'People don't just die.'

But they do. Father in France, a bombed-out trench behind a nameless town. Half her friends' fathers and brothers, taken by the War. Or the Flu, like Morgan's mother; pointless endings. 'Alec seems to think it's about the gold Harper found,' she said.

'What do you think it's about?'

Rom pushed away her cold tea. 'I don't know. But Hittite writing doesn't belong in Scotland.' Nor do snakes. Patterns don't appear on people's hands and conjurers don't wander the countryside in circus tents. She'd spent too long, lately, worrying about what shouldn't be. 'Grab your hat,' she said.

'Alec said not to go anywhere.'

'He's just worried we'll get murdered. But we need to talk to somebody who understands oddities.' Rom shook her purse over the table and pulled out the tattered business card. 'We're going to see the doctor.'

Dr Lloyd's Institute was in Hackney.

The address was in Hackney, anyway, and Rom stood dubiously with Pixie on the steps.

'Don't be a snob,' Ditto said, 'she's got a plaque up.'

But the plaque was for a *Music Teacher From the Continent with Many Years Experience*. The other door was down a flight of steps in the sodden courtyard.

'You can't have a research facility in a terraced house,' Rom said as they descended. 'Does this feel normal?'

'We're here to ask about a poisoned archaeologist and a magic dog,' Ditto said. 'They don't have special buildings for that.'

Rom knocked.

Pen answered, bustling in a black rubber apron. She pulled off her gloves and grinned. 'Hullo, you lot. And Pixie.' She nodded. 'Come through.'

They followed her into a basement parlour, solidly Victorian with its damask wallpaper and old piano, while unmistakably a laboratory; the bookshelves were crammed with files and cloudy jars and a rack of x-ray prints leaned in the empty fireplace. 'This is my base of operations. Rather humble, I'm afraid. Has your dog done something else strange?'

They'd agreed in the cab not to mention the mark on Rom's hand, or Mr Kingsley and the Circus; they didn't know what the doctor wanted, and Quinn wouldn't approve of sightseers. But Harper's death was already in the papers and there was plenty of oddness to tell about Pixie, about snakes, and Hittite writing thousands of years out of time.

'I don't know what any of it means,' Rom finished. 'Or if it's at all connected. But there's too much strangeness all at once and we thought you might at least know something.'

'Queer story. I'm glad you came.' Pen knelt on the rug beside Pixie. 'May I take a closer look at her?'

She sniffed at Pixie's fur. She didn't touch her, but she gazed at the gilt collar as Pixie nosed warily at her hand. 'Did she come with the collar?'

'From my grandfather.'

'How much does she weigh?'

'She's a lump; I can't lift her.'

Pen's questions were brisk. The dog's diet, habits. Temperament. She hooked a stethoscope into her ear and felt gently across Pixie's chest. She pressed down in the centre and waited, and her face twitched as she stood.

'Let me turn on my lightbox.' She was pinning x-rays against the backlight above her desk as they pulled up their chairs. 'I got hold of some prints from Germany last year. This one's a cat,' she said. The stretch of the narrow chest was clearly feline. 'And this one's an adult human.' The x-ray on the right. 'Human, apart from an unusual malformation; the heart is too large for the body. And it skips two out of three beats. Slow as an elephant's. And your dog—' She paused. 'Pixie appears to have the same.'

'Is she ill?'

'Not exactly. The problem is, both those x-rays are from the same person. The cat and the human. Taken at different times, but the same test subject.' She folded her hands on the desk. 'I think we have the same situation here. Pixie isn't a dog.'

'My dog's a werewolf,' Rom said flatly. 'Is that what you're trying to say?'

'Of course not. Werewolves are superstition,' Pen said, 'but perhaps it holds a bit of truth. These creatures seem to be something extraordinary. They speak to animals, control them, and sometimes take their form. Pixie happens to be mimicking a dog but some have other shapes; cats and birds. Foxes,' she added. 'I haven't seen many up close, and I've never seen one like Pixie.' She opened a folder and pushed it across the desk.

Clean-edged medical photographs, shot with professional

steadiness. Animals and humans and some, Rom thought, were corpses.

'I've collected these for years,' Pen said. 'Hunting around Europe for other doctors who've seen odd things.'

Rom didn't touch the spread photographs. A double pupil in the eye of a little girl. An old man with long pointed teeth. A tufted goatish tail. Clawed fingers. Gills. And the last ones showed human torsos, all bare, and they all showed the same thing.

'This is what you were talking about on the train,' Rom said. 'The wolf those soldiers found—'

'These creatures were never born,' Pen said. 'We don't know what the marks are, but you might recognise them.'

The pattern was raised on the skin where a human navel should be. Diamond-shaped, ink-black, twined from knotting lines. Each subtly different, marking every body.

A compact variation of the mark Rom had seen on her own skin.

'They look like Pixie's collar,' Pen said.

Ditto's face was serious. 'Are they faeries after all?'

'We don't know what they are,' Pen said. 'I call them fey, but I can only guess. Perhaps what people call faeries have only been these people all along.'

It made a kind of sense that sat on the edge of understanding. Too much sense to be ignored. 'You've seen this?' Rom said.

'Only once. In Serbia. I saw an old woman turn into a goat.'

Rom leaned forward. 'How?'

'There was a woman. And then there was a goat. Just blue fire and it happened.'

Rom glanced at Ditto and met her quick dark glance. 'Haven't you just asked them what they are?'

'They don't give much away,' Pen said. 'Only one was happy talking; I got a vial of her blood by exchanging it for a pint of my own. There's quite a long history of fey creatures who are nourished by human blood,' she added reasonably.

Rom sat back in her seat. 'Why hasn't Pixie ever changed?'

'I think it's her collar,' Pen said. 'Gold seems to affect the creatures. And the design looks like a fey seal, I think it's binding her somehow. Somebody had the knowledge to make it.'

She pushed the file over. Tucked inside was a little illustrated page, cups and vines and trumpeting cherubs. The border pattern twined exuberantly. Familiar. 'It's from a book called *The Nest of Amoury*. It's only poetry, but the illustrations seem to reference alchemical formulas. See here, the sun in the corner? And this cup has the symbol for iron. They used to hide these things when everybody frowned on magic. What if they were hiding a secret even better than gold?'

'This book explains what Pixie is?'

'I'm hoping it will, when I find the damn thing. There are stray pages in antique shops but I can't get a full copy. One's coming up at auction next month but I don't have much hope; I never had a chance last time, the price it went for. Three hundred pounds, I could buy a car for that.'

'There must be a way,' Rom said. 'Whoever bought it might let us borrow it.'

'Tried that. Unknown buyer at a deceased estate. Somebody's library got sold off, a heap of good things on alchemy and Celtic cults. Even had an early edition *Principia*.'

Rom curled up her hands. 'Oh?'

'Old writer chap. It's a pity he died, we could have asked him all about it.'

Rom sighed. Long, unsteady. 'His name was Jasper Teague,' she said. 'He was my grandfather.'

The room was silent.

Ditto laughed weakly. 'You mean you could have had the book? You sold it.'

'Alec sold it.' Rom's chest burned. 'We didn't know.'

Pen erupted into laughter. 'I was looking for his book and found his dog instead. Marvellous. Do you believe in coincidences? I don't. That sounds like fate to me.'

'It's not a coincidence,' Rom said. 'It isn't fate either. There's a bloody clear causal link, and it's Jasper. Alec can ask the solicitors.' She must have begun to take Pen seriously, this woman and her shabby home laboratory, if she was still sitting here listening to this absurdity. 'We'll track the buyer, we can ask them. But lord, what a mess.'

Pen closed the file. 'Talk to your brother if you must, but I think the less people who know the better. We aren't the only ones looking for *The Nest of Amoury*. Perhaps somebody came for your friend Harper.'

'Who's looking?'

'Her name's Evelyn Ash. American woman. I'd like to sound her out. Undercover; just imagine if the government were to get hold of this. I know bureaucracy.' Pen shuddered. 'I'll never have a chance if they classify the whole thing.'

A sprawl of thought. 'You think she's after the fey?'

'Anyone would be, if they knew. In Italy only the witches were brave enough to approach them. But it seems your grandfather knew how to bind one into animal form.'

They looked at Pixie dozing in front of the radiator. 'He knew, but we haven't got him,' Rom said. 'Not even his books.'

'Can't we just break the collar?' Ditto asked.

Pen shook her head. 'These things aren't human. They aren't tame, I mean. If there was a reason your grandfather collared her—'

'We need the book,' Rom said. That was it. Their only plan. Ridiculous, though, all of it, and she hesitated. 'Are you sure? About all this?'

Pen smiled, bright and shy. 'I'd stake my life on it. This will change medical science. That's why I'm stuck here on a Sunday, researching things that make no sense. For no money. Without nearly enough proof. I wish I didn't have to believe it, but here I am.'

Rom and Ditto didn't speak much in the cab home. It seemed impossible; the bustle of cars and wet sky and faeries, apparently, all around them, and quiet at their feet on a leash.

'Are we going to believe it?' Rom collapsed onto the sofa when they got inside. 'It could be bosh. Kingsley could have been faking. Dr Lloyd might be a nutter.'

'We don't know anything,' Ditto said. 'We don't know why the sun comes up. I mean I *know* why the sun comes up, but I just learned it at school and it makes sense, and I believe it now.' She looked at the dog. 'I'll believe Pixie's a shape-changing fey until I find a better explanation.'

Atoms are no more visible than goblins. If the whole thing was magic you wouldn't even know.

'Alright,' Rom said, 'just until we find somebody who knows what they're talking about,' and Ditto nodded as she handed down the yellow-painted tea-cup. 'I wish we could just ask Pixie.'

Ditto snorted into her tea. 'Go on, then.'

Rom knelt on the sofa. 'Doggo,' she said. 'Pixie dear—' which felt wrong. She never called anyone dear except Ditto. 'We don't know what you are, and it would be bloody marvellous if you could tell us.'

Pixie raised her head, her clear eyes unblinking.

Ditto's grin was a tease. 'I don't know what we could possibly be doing wrong.'

'Maybe we have to have the right words,' Rom said, 'the right name.'

Pixie settled her head on her paws with a sigh.

'I'm writing to Alec,' Rom said. 'He won't believe a word but it wouldn't hurt to see if he's got any ideas. And tomorrow I'll check the College library for *The Nest*. There must be another copy somewhere.'

Apparently not, said the clerk at the College. Rom spent a busy and horribly costly afternoon at the post office between phones and telegrams, hunting up antiquarian bookstores, but some hadn't heard of it and none had a copy.

'Chap at Cambridge wants £20 for a single page,' she said to Ditto. 'Imagine the price of piecing a whole one together.' She bit her lip. 'The library at the British Museum has millions of books. It can't be as rare as all that.'

She marched up the Museum's colonnaded steps the next afternoon and into the breathless cool. Past the wide clean stairs, where she'd usually head to the Egyptian and Assyrian rooms, and straight to the courtyard and curved facade of the Reading Room. It was a vast place, silent under the gilt white dome, warm with books and whisperings.

She had to apply for a Reader's Ticket.

'It isn't a study room,' the clerk said absently. 'You can't use it for exam research.'

'I know,' Rom said. 'I'm looking for a rare book. If you could just have a squiz before I fill out the form—'

'Ticket first,' he said.' Do you have a recommendation from somebody?'

'No.' Rom bristled. 'I have a job here at the Museum, actually, over in conservation.' No need to tell him it was twice a month, unpaid. 'I work with Dr Carr, he's in Assyriology at—'

'Wonderful,' the clerk said. 'You can get a recommendation from him, then.'

'The cosmology of the Egyptians was more than an explanation of natural phenomena, where most religions begin,' Dr Carr said, 'and more than a vehicle for political dogma, where most religions end. It was a structure for their understanding of life and all that comes after it. The unseen world existed very close beside the visible.'

Rom looked down at her scribble in her notes. Wolf-snouted Anubis. Thoth and his scribe's palette. The gods walked between the animal world and human forms, fluid as the Nile. Just as simple to believe in a hundred gods as one, if you're going to believe in something, and even the Greeks—who questioned all things seen and unseen, space and time and existence—they sat down to eat, and bowed their heads to the household shrine.

You have to believe something, even if it's only for a moment.

She hesitated as she handed over her assignment. 'May I ask a favour, sir? I need a ticket to the Reading Room at the Museum. I don't suppose you could give me a recommendation?'

'If there's a text we don't have in the College, I can check my own library.'

'It's not exactly ancient history.' She might as well tell a half truth, in case he wrote it on the note. 'I'm looking at solar symbolism for Dr Marsden.'

'I see.' Not quite listening as he scribbled.

She needed to ask. 'Did you hear about Mr Harper, sir?'

'I did, yes.' Dr Carr looked up. 'Terrible business.'

'Theft gone wrong, I think they said. Would anybody kill a man for just a rumour of gold?'

Dr Carr handed her the note. 'Merely a lot of talk. Although I believe there was something interesting about the bones he found.'

And there it was, the pattern in the chaos. 'Not quite human,' Rom said.

Dr Carr's gaze was steady. 'Harper mentioned this to you?'

Think. Quickly. 'In passing. Is it Hittite after all?'

'The text is, but not the context. Mr Harper showed it to Horstmann, who consulted several scholars of early script, including myself. He needed a Bronze Age specialist, too. And an Iron Age chap; the decorative knotwork on the skull has a decidedly Celtic appearance.'

Rom swallowed. 'Knotwork?'

'Painted on the clay. Clearly not Sumerian in origin.'

'Tumulus culture has never given us painted skulls,' Rom said. 'Perhaps—'

'I can assure you it is not my theory alone, Miss Godden.' He pulled a crease of pages from his jacket. 'The specialists are in agreement. I marked the main points.'

Various notes, tidy or illegible, starred with Dr Carr's indications. The historians' conjectured dates were all wrong—either the pattern on the skull was a few millennia too early, or the tomb was too late.

But Rom nodded as though it made perfect sense. 'Not Babylon, then.'

'The cuneiform on the gold disc mentioned Babylon. But it could just as easily be the literal translation, 'the gate of heaven'. I taught you that last year,' Dr Carr said. 'The malformed skull itself is curious but not unique. A physical disability was frequently seen by ancient cultures as being the touch of fate; the hand of the gods, so to speak. It was probably the remains of an early Celtic priest or witch-doctor.'

'And the gold disc?'

'An ancient cult object.'

Perfectly reasonable. All of it. He made sure of that. Rom breathed out carefully. 'The trade routes must have been more complex than we considered. Your man at the Museum has the skull now?'

'He does, thank goodness. He's sending it to me for analysis.'

Rom looked again at the pages in her hands; Dr Carr's sketch, the specialists' notes. One of the sheets was sheer and crisp with sepia ink. A slant scrawl, and she turned the page over. She looked at the name for a long time. 'Cranach M. Prideaux,' she said. 'Archaeologist, is he?'

'Linguist,' Dr Carr said. *'The golden tongue will speak*, do you see? He hasn't translated it literally; he says 'golden' meaning blessed, or god-like. *The blessed tongue will speak, and the house of dust will echo.* But his research seems sound. Although he references several German archaeologists; an amateur would be unaware of the political niceties of scholarship.'

'Do you know him?'

'He did write an interesting piece about the angularity of early scripts being linked to the available writing materials.'

'I'll take his word for it.' There was a London address on Prideaux's letter as she handed it back: Great Queen Street. 'Thanks for the recommendation.' She gestured to her assignment. 'Sorry it's rather late; I'm not entirely sure of some of that bibliography.'

'I'm sure it will be fine, Miss Godden.'

She went out into the damp spring streets.

A fey's bones would be a most incendiary treasure. Mr Harper had found something impossible, and Dr Carr knew more than he was telling. But didn't everyone?

Rom's fingers were icy in her pockets. Great Queen Street was barely half a mile. She could walk.

She turned left instead of right on the College steps, down the windblown Strand and through the odd place in between—Holborn's dusty law courts on one side and Covent Garden on the other. You couldn't pick if a shop would be full of clerks or hungover actors. It was tough to tell them apart. Into the narrow theatre streets and out again; taverns, hotels. Past a decorator's window full of fabric samples, and there it was: number 55.

Royal Sovereign Pencil Co, said the sign. *Falcon Pencils. Stationery Novelties.*

A shop.

Then a wide warehouse driveway, and the next window along was empty; *to let*, the faded sign said: *magic lantern screens made to order.* A decade out of date; nobody wants Victorian games when they've got films.

She walked back to Number 55 and peered through the window. It looked busy, a harried boy behind the counter and clerks buying notepaper. Or *Wolff 'J' Pencils: trade rates available for law students.* Or *Indelible Ink.*

Rom blew her nose violently and walked onwards.

Prideaux was stuck in this mess, but he'd never been here. Just a parlour-trick projection. Magic lanterns, paper and light, long gone.

10

The creature broke another glass this morning. I found it painted in blood across its skin, over all the walls and door. No words, just patterns like a bird's tracks.

I took the china dishes from its room. Now it must drink from a leather flask.

I need to strengthen its bonds. It will bleed its filth and let the stuff eat through the floor. I need more gold.

JASPER TEAGUE, Journals, 12th Oct. 1916

'Faeries,' Alec said on the phone. 'You aren't being serious.'

'You got my letter, then.'

But he sounded grim when Rom told him about Dr Carr and the translation. 'This could be linked with Mr Harper. He was digging alone, it wasn't an official excavation. But what if he found something he wasn't meant to? Cartwright won't let me cover this, said I'm not experienced. You honestly think it's magic bones?'

'The doctor believes too. I saw the Circus myself. Our courtyard's full of sparrows, out of nowhere, crows and starlings—there was a hawk this morning. And yesterday I went hunting for this alchemy book, *The Nest of Amoury*. Finally got a ticket to the Museum Reading Room and they had a copy. Early eighteenth century.'

The clerk had carried it over to the padded desk. The grand crowded room was almost silent; shuffling seats, a stifled cough. She'd held the thing in her own hands: a slim volume, cream leather speckled with age. Her throat tight with the nearness of truth, and when she opened it—

'The book was blank. Somebody stole the pages and left the cover.'

'Hell,' Alec grunted. 'Dead ends all around.'

'Not quite. I asked the name of the last person to borrow it. Damn cross they were too, having a theft; they even let me look at the ledger. Turns out nobody's touched it in thirty-three years, and the last was Jasper Teague.'

'Oh, I say—'

'I didn't mention he was our grandfather.'

'I should bloody hope not. If he had to steal it, though.' Alec was muttering. 'We could try an antique shop—'

'Nobody's got it. I borrowed a stack of other books from the College library, though. Alchemy and faerytales, anything I could find with shape-shifting animals. We might find some clues while we're looking for *The Nest*.'

'Oh. *Oh*—'

Rom knew that rising inflection.

'Jasper's house,' he said. 'If the old man was researching this all along—'

'We sold his books.'

'No, but he had papers, I saw it with Mother. If I can tell Cartwright my grandfather was researching the same thing as Mr Harper—' Alec's voice was a buzz. 'I'm going to Hollesley. There must be something we haven't thought of.'

'You believe it now?'

'Of course not. But Jasper did, enough to steal from the British Museum. And somebody believed enough to murder Mr Harper. I'll wire you when I get there.'

Ditto came bolting back from putting Miss Gwen out in the courtyard. 'It's just like a spy story. Look what I found in my pot of marigolds.'

A tiny scroll of crackly paper, written in waxy pencil. *II: 21.5 10.30*

'Did crowfolk bring it?' Rom looked up from her open books. 'It has to be Kingsley.'

'The 21st of May is this Wednesday.' Ditto pursed her lips. 'Half-past ten is the time. What's the eleven for?' She drained her glass. 'It looks like musical notation. A repeat sign.'

'Does he seem the type who'd read music?'

'He seems an odd type, I don't think we should make guesses about the things he might know.' Ditto smoothed the paper between her fingers. 'Repeat. He means the same place again.'

They smiled at each other. 'The tea-house.'

'When Alec calls, I can tell him we're better investigators than he is.'

Rom had started taking notes as she scanned through her borrowed books—ideas, anything she could garner about faeries, and Ditto leaned in to see the scrambled writing.

'What have you got?'

They guard gold. They don't like talking about themselves. They guard their names. They demand payment for services. They hinder as much as they help. They aren't from here. Like djinn they could fly and disappear at strange times. Like Greek dryads, they sometimes lingered in favourite forests or rivers.

'I've been in the middle of Welsh folktales for four hours,' she said.

'Faeries don't sound too bad,' Ditto said. 'Singing birds, buried treasure. Lots of feasts.'

'Keep reading.'

The next bit she'd found was about Maeldun, who tried with his crew to leave the Queen of Fae's island. The Queen stood on the shore and threw a ball of magic thread, and one of the men caught it and it stuck to his hand, and no matter where they sailed it led them back.

'Do you know the old word for a ball of thread?' Rom asked. 'It's clew.'

'How did the ship escape?'

'They cut the sailor's hand off.' She shrugged. 'The fey aren't kind.'

'And you think Pixie's one of them.'

The white dog whimpered at the sound of her name.

'Possibly. I'm not sure what Jasper was doing.' Rom opened another book. 'Alchemy is something altogether different. The four tools, the four stages of purification, the sacred marriage of the Red King and White Queen—that's a blend of sulphur and mercury. But it seems to be philosophy as well as practical science, and there's thousands of years of ideas. The point was to be mysterious so nobody's exactly being clear. I found something, though.'

Ditto leaned over her shoulder. 'Phoenix?'

'It's mentioned everywhere, but it's not a person; it's another name for the philosopher's stone. One of its symbols is the sun. And entwined snakes. And the initiates of alchemy, the sorts of gatherings they held—'

Ditto whistled. 'The Votaries of Light?'

'If Madame Volkov knows something about alchemy, and the fey know something about Desir, maybe we've got some questions for Mr Kingsley.'

It was another night before Alec's wire arrived.

AT GODDEN HOUSE BAD NEWS KEEP PIXIE CLOSE PHONE IMMEDIATELY

They walked down together in the dark, and took Pixie with them.

Ditto squeezed into the phone box too. 'You're not leaving me on the street,' she said as Rom dialled.

Rom hardly breathed until she heard the phone click. 'Alec—'

'I had to drive into town to telephone,' he said. 'I could have wired but I wanted to—you know. Make sure you're alive.'

'I'm alive. Are you staying at the house?'

'Sod that. No electricity. And the place is an awful mess—but all wrong, cups and chairs and spoons laid out in rows like a collection. Townsend said that's how the estate people found it. I've had a look through Jasper's notes, though—'

'Anything about Pixie?'

'Not yet. I got his bunker open; it's empty. But the cellar—' Alec stopped, and Rom felt it was the thing he'd been circling around. 'Well, you see—his notes mentioned a weapon.'

He'd gone down to the stone cellar, half dark-room and half laboratory and entirely unlit. 'If I could only switch on a light,' he said. 'But there was a machine there. Something set up. Haven't a clue what.' Alec's laugh was brief. 'Big as a travel case, with a vat full of water. Or something. Didn't get too close, actually. Wires everywhere, and a generator, I think. The whole place stinks and burns your eyes and—well. What would a weapon look like?'

Alec was alone in Suffolk with only his scepticism to protect him, and it was failing fast.

'Should we come up?'

'I wired Sel, actually. Sel Mitchell. He's here.' Alec sounded sheepish. 'We'll look at the house in the morning. If it's a bomb or something he might actually have a clue. He's mad with boredom while he's off work, and I think he's quite interested.'

'Alec. What have you told him?'

'Everything, obviously.' That was a proper laugh. 'I needed to talk to somebody normal. He thinks I'm a nutter but he hasn't said it, at least.'

'Good,' she said, and realised she meant it.

'The old man had a couple of gas-masks hanging around; they'll come in handy.'

'Jasper really was holding out for the War.'

'God knows. Oi, Sel—'

The phone scuffled and Rom heard Mr Mitchell's voice. 'Evening, Miss Godden. I'm sorry, Alec's thrown me in it.'

Damn you, Alec. 'Mr Mitchell. What do you think will be up at the house? Alec said it's rather nasty.'

'Certainly a danger, by the sound of it. Apparently there's a case of nitro. Crates full of ammonia and cyanide salts; alcohol, mercury.'

'That's toxic, isn't it?' Rom asked, and saw Ditto's painted eyebrows arch.

'It could mean anything, dark-room chemicals, but I think—' Mr Mitchell hesitated. 'Do you believe Alec's right? About a government plot?'

Rom looked at Ditto and Pixie huddled against the glass. 'I wish we knew. How is Alec? He sounds skittish.'

'Skittish.' Amused. 'He's fine. But there'll be trouble tomorrow if he tries to touch anything.'

'If you can get him to sit still it's more than I ever could.'

When Alec got back on his voice was sharp. 'You were laughing about me.'

'Of course. You're entirely ludicrous. Keep yourselves alive.'

'I'm trying. And what are you doing?'

'We're going home to write a list.'

They did, after dinner; Ditto plumped on the sofa and opened her notepad with a flourish.

Rom poured tea. 'I wonder if the truth isn't collective after all. If enough people believe it—' She folded a cushion beneath her head. 'At least Alec's investigating.'

'Better him than me, stuck in a dead man's house.'

'Everybody's house is a dead man's house eventually,' Rom said. 'Anyway, he's got Mr Mitchell helping.'

'Aren't you envious?'

'Don't start, please.'

'No, he's not your type, is he?'

'Blond?'

'Decent.'

'I've liked plenty of decent people.'

'You admire them at a distance and end up with rotters.'

'You're not a rotter.'

'Thank you, dear. But I was *thinking* of the girl from your College last year.'

Rom sipped. 'She knew a lot about Roman British settlements.'

At least Mr Mitchell wasn't an utter child like the boys at the College. Or the ones she'd known when she was in school.

Sarah Blaney had the sweetest eyes in Fifth Form and they'd all been mad about her, but it was Rom's bed she climbed into after lights-out. Rom never thought of wanting a boy until she stayed at Katey-from-Leicester's.

Nicholas was Katey's brother, eighteen, a year older than them and not a child, although he seemed to think Rom was; he talked to her about polo and Kipling and not much else, and she'd lost her temper, probably.

She'd found him in the stables, slim and careless in his high field boots. He smelled of dry hay and warm horse and damp boy—a new smell, sharp and sour as green apples. She sat on the stall rail and swung her legs until he stopped working and looked at her.

He was different from a girl. He barely said a word as they did it, only to apologise for the hay under them, and he didn't laugh at all. He wasn't sure if he was supposed to kiss her but they were in the middle of everything by then, and the hay tickled her back and she wasn't thinking about kissing, only the summer heat of his body and the little noises he made against her neck as he finished.

Nicholas was the first boy. But she'd still never seen a man quite naked; the fascinating frankness of their shape.

Rom glanced at Ditto's downcast lashes. It's a longer thing to please a girl; they look at you with that wry sort of patience. Even Ditto—who never wanted it and only liked to touch herself—even she had that same quiet look in her eyes sometimes when Rom kissed her. Nowhere to hide, a good sort of honesty.

'There.' Ditto pushed the page across the coffee table. *The Odd List*, it said, and it was underlined.

bad faeries

madame volkov and her etceteras
Circus of Weirdness
snakery
Pixie?
Doctor Lloyd and the Grand Werewolf Conspiracy
Mr Harper RIP
suspicious skull
Nest book
whatever the devil Jasper Teague was up to

'Do you feel better now?'

'Very much so.' Ditto yawned luxuriously.

Rom did too, just at the sight of Ditto's wide-rambling writing. There's something about the written word, something clever it does between the abstract and the concrete, and now it was only another page awaiting translation.

'If Mr Harper was murdered by snakes, too,' Ditto said, 'ours couldn't have been from Morgan after all. You'll have to apologise.'

'I know.' But there had been no way to guess. What else was she meant to think? The fey had power over animals—but that would mean fey were following them. Unless the danger was Pixie. But Pixie had killed the snake. Hadn't she?

The edges of reality soften and the whole world liquifies; mercurial, uncontained.

'What are we going to do about *The Nest*?'

'Alec will probably find something in Jasper's notes,' Rom said. They could find the missing words by the margin of their mention—like the page in front of her, with its absence of another odd thing.

She wrote it. *Prideaux*. This time the word didn't make her feel better. 'Kingsley finds people,' she said.

'And?'

Rom began to unpack her notebooks. 'Alec's journalists didn't have much luck, but Kingsley might. I'm going to ask him about Mr Prideaux. There's something going on there.' She dipped her pen and squeezed. The reservoir swelled, the pen filled. She wiped the nib clean. 'Sanctimonious prick.'

'Oh?' Ditto raised her head from her magazine. 'You didn't tell me he was nice-looking.'

'I didn't,' Rom said, 'because he isn't.' She bent over her notes. That discontented mouth. The grand nose, a square-edged curve. Nice was not the word.

'Ben lightmans, all.' Kingsley stood outside the tea-house when they arrived. 'D'you fancy a walk?'

He led them down the busy Strand. The wet street was refreshing, even if Rom had to strain over the traffic to hear him, but he looked sombre. 'I've had news from Mr Quinn. Three more people disappeared this week. I'm afraid we won't find much trace of Miss Munster.'

Ditto's face was tight. 'Dead?'

He didn't want to answer. 'Madame Volkov and Desir are dangerous people. They'll be in London next month, and I plan to dig around their show and see what they're stirring.'

Rom and Pixie kept pace beside him, and Ditto fell into step on his right.

'We have a few things to ask you,' Ditto said. 'How did Ivy Munster die?'

'Can't say.'

'Is it magic, that mark on your hand?'

'Mortals would call it magic.'

'Fey are immortal?'

'Your words, not mine.' He frowned.

'Is the mark on *my* hand magic?'

He glanced at Rom. 'Yes.'

'What's it from?' she asked.

'You made a bargain with Crow.'

'It was there before I ever met Crow.'

He looked straight ahead. 'Interesting.'

'Do you know why?'

'Can't—'

'Can't or won't?' Ditto asked.

'We can pay in blood,' Rom said, 'if that's what you want.'

'We could come to an arrangement.' Kingsley turned down an alley toward the colourful mess of Covent Garden and they followed through the market crowds, Pixie sniffing the dampish air, stepping through fallen lettuce to a flower stall.

The girl among the buckets of daffodils didn't even glance up, but an old man peered out. 'Mr Kingsley.' His voice was a kind of whistle. 'What are you nosing after?'

Kingsley pulled off his cap. 'I'm looking for the Circus, Mr Gurden. Where is it at, d'you think?'

'West.' Mr Gurden sat back on his stool. 'And heading westerer. There's a storm coming from the north.'

'I hadn't heard.'

'Teb you a couter it's a dab lot of swen. The birds and beasts are taking cover. Are you not?'

Kingsley shook his head. 'I'm not afraid of bad news, Mr Gurden. I'm hunting up the stormbirds themselves.'

The old man felt his waistcoat for his pipe. 'Where there's crowns, the law follows. He's in a right state.'

Kingsley stood very still. 'Who?'

But the old man flapped his hand. 'Git out, now,' he said. 'I'm packing up.'

Kingsley ducked under the hanging flower baskets and they had to trot to catch up with him. 'You know the Strand, Miss Hamilton? Place called Cartouche behind the Hammonds theatre.'

'It's the Midnight Palace now,' Ditto said.

'New management, same wallpaper.'

Nile-green wallpaper, as it turned out, a sharply different class from the cheerful squalor at Gordey's. Rom looked around the club as they entered. In a few hours' time, when the lights dimmed on the sofas, the place would gleam with sly charm.

A sad-eyed barman was stacking glasses behind the counter. The shelves behind him glittered with decanters and a row of painted globes, something lifted from a library, scrolls and oceans and faded night-skies.

'We're looking for somebody who can read a map,' Kingsley said.

'We're closed,' the barman said. 'Is that a dog?'

Rom had no intention of leaving Pixie anywhere out of their sight.

'Mr Gurden said there's a storm up north,' Kingsley said. 'Can you show us?'

The barman put down his dish-towel and folded his arms on the counter. 'I don't do favours.'

'Put it on the tab.'

'Hang that, darling, Zinn owes half of London.'

'We'll pay.'

'He owes *florins*, Mr Kingsley.'

'You'll have it. By crux, string, and bone you'll have it. Will you read for us?'

The barman blinked his mournful eyes. 'I'll fetch a dish,' he said. 'You draw blood.'

'How much?' Rom turned to Kingsley as the barman vanished into the back room.

'You needn't fuss, he doesn't want yours.' Kingsley dropped his pocket knife on the bar and tugged up his sleeve.

'That was one of them.' Ditto's voice was a whisper. 'Fey.'

'His name is Mr Claker,' Kingsley said. 'Got the stuff?'

The barman set down a glass platter, which glistened sluggishly with a fingerful of something clear and oily. He unfolded an awkward sheet of paper, an Ordnance Map, and slipped it underneath.

Kingsley nicked his forearm with his knife and drew a bead of blood onto the tip. He stirred it into the waiting oil.

Mr Claker tipped in a golden drift of powder from an envelope and rested his fingertips on the edge of the dish.

'What are we looking for?' Ditto asked, but her voice sounded tight. Something was happening in the dish. Stirred like a cup of tea, the surface swam with living stars. The map beneath was visible through the oil. An entire constellation gathered on the left of the dish, along the west coast, Rom realised. 'They're all fey?' More than she'd ever imagined, in every city, scattered through the towns. Along the rivers. 'There's a heap in Ireland.'

'Those are little people. We're looking for solid spots.'

A nugget where the glitter drew together; one in Dublin. And a scant few others; London, the Midlands. And west, the heart of the Circus. 'What are they?'

'They're Coronets,' Kingsley said. 'Move it north.'

Mr Claker pulled the dish across the map, and the oil slopped and re-formed.

'They're fey, too?'

'Aye,' said Kingsley, 'they're captains.'

Mr Claker laughed, a slow strange sound. 'It isn't a war anymore, Mr Kingsley. Forget sodding *captains*.' He looked at Ditto and Rom with a sort of contempt. 'Coronets have names. They have crowns. You don't want to meet one.'

'They already have,' Kingsley said. 'They visited Crow's People.'

'Crow's out of bounds.' Mr Claker shifted to the other foot. 'I shouldn't be talking to you.'

Rom rounded on Kingsley. 'You took us to a faery king and didn't tell us?'

'Not a king these days,' he said. 'Anyway, he's different, Crow's People bargain with anyone who pays. Who's this, north of the Wall?' He pointed at the pulse of gold, large as a thumbnail over the coast of Scotland.

Rom leaned forward. 'That looks like Inverness, where Harper—'

'Go on.' Kingsley was watching her with bright eyes.

'Somebody we met in Edinburgh, he was there last month and found something. Bones. And then he was killed.' She paused. 'By poisonous snakes.'

'Snakes. Dear me.' Mr Claker began to pack away the dish. 'Somebody's going to get their little arse slapped.'

'Phoenix would never do this,' Kingsley said. 'Appearing so openly. Using that name.' He kicked his boot-heel into the floor. 'I have to go.'

Mr Claker coughed. 'Reporting home?'

'You need to warn your master. If Volkov sets a Coronet loose, we'll all of us burn.'

'I take care of my own game, Mr Kingsley.' Claker called after them. 'Aren't you forgetting something, my love?'

Kingsley leaned back around the doorway. 'You know where to send the bill,' he said, and clattered down the stairs.

11

How absurd these words are, such as beast and beast of prey. One should not speak of animals in that way. They don't pretend. They are as they are, like stones or flowers or stars in the sky.

HERMAN HESSE

Down on the street Rom stopped. 'Does this have something to do with Mr Harper?'

Kingsley surveyed them with sudden focus. 'You can have three questions, but I'll take you up on your payment. Relix will be a pint of blood. From each of you, please.'

'A sodding—'

'It's only half a litre,' he said, 'it won't harm an adult.'

'Do you need it immediately?'

His smile shouldn't have been quite so pleasant. 'Leave it in your garden. I know where you live. Two questions left.'

'We're not falling for that shite,' Rom said. 'You didn't tell us when the questions would begin.'

He clicked his tongue. 'Can't blame me for trying.'

Ditto looked ill. 'Do you—bite the neck?'

Kingsley's back stiffened. 'I'm not an animal, Miss Hamilton. I'll take it in a clean jar, fresh venous blood. Venous means from the vein—'

'We know,' Ditto said.

At least he'd answer them, but Rom didn't have the faintest notion what to ask. They couldn't afford to babble the first thing that came to mind. Her stomach turned over. 'I think I need lunch.'

Ditto bought fish and chips. They found an empty shopfront with a clean front step and sat with the steaming paper bundle, and Pixie beside them. Kingsley sat too, his elbows propped on his knees.

Rom leaned to whisper at Ditto's shoulder. Ditto nodded. 'Alright, Mr Kingsley.' Rom pulled off her gloves and picked out a chip. 'First question. Did the fey kill Mr Harper and Ivy?'

L.B. Hazelthorn

'It sounds likely.'

'Why would they do it?' asked Ditto.

'That's another question,' Kingsley said. 'Are you sure?'

Ditto's eyes narrowed. 'You're getting two pints of blood for three questions. You can jolly well elaborate.'

He shrugged. 'Ivy went to an audition for Votaries and didn't return; she and many others. Madame Volkov is feeding something hungry. Crow thinks she's an Acatour, a food collector. As for Mr Harper, he opened a tomb that didn't belong to him. That's on his own head. But whoever killed him broke Law to do it. Mr Gurden's right, a storm is brewing.'

'And what about the snake at our place? Was it sent by the same person as Harper's?'

'I could say, if I knew.'

Rom licked salt off her thumb. 'Question number two. How do we free Pixie?'

Kingsley's face gathered. 'This is something strange. Even Crow has no answer. She can't speak nor shift, and it seems to be tied to the collar.'

'I've taken it off her plenty of times,' Rom said. 'Can we break it? That's an associated question, by the way.'

'That's not a thing I ever knew.'

'Also associated: does Pixie have something to do with the mark on my hand?'

'I can't comment on another's Skein.'

'It's still there, then.' Rom rubbed at the blank skin.

'Oh, aye. Blood bound, in blood revealed. It's always there.'

'Does she need anything?' Ditto bent to give the dog a chip, and Pixie swallowed it whole. 'Is it hurting her?'

'It doesn't seem to be. I'd smell if she was ill.' Kingsley didn't seem as strict on the rule of three as he liked to appear.

'Those missing people,' Rom said, 'you really meant their souls.'

'Fey eat a lot of things.' Kingsley looked away.

Ditto's face was hard. 'Ivy was murdered.'

'Relix cannot be taken without permission, the Law ensures it. She must have offered.'

'She'd never.'

Rom shivered. 'Nobody would.'

'Mortals do odd things. They have odd desires. And not many can refuse the Phoenix if he asks.' Kingsley's heel bounced. 'He's giving a show at the Waldorf Hotel, invitation only; millionaires and royalty.'

'Report them,' Ditto said. 'You've got your own law, you can turn them in.'

'There's the Law,' Kingsley said, 'but it isn't justice. By the time it arrives it might as well be death.'

'Dr Lloyd said fey couldn't die,' Rom said. 'Deathless and unborn. Is that the case? I did see a child in Crow's tent; he must have been born from something.'

'Not a child,' Kingsley said. 'Maybe the form of one. There are no fey children.'

Ditto was munching chips, staring at the shops opposite. 'So they're not immortal. Somebody could shoot this Phoenix and his body would die?'

Rom elbowed Ditto. 'We aren't killing anyone. Can we stop him, though? That's a conversational question, not a paid one.'

'I can't approach a Coronet in my own name,' Kingsley said, 'but I might be able to speak as Quinn's emissary. Ivy was one of Crow's People. And Phoenix has always been more reasonable.' Kingsley rubbed his nose. 'They'll see me coming a mile away, but you'd be allowed in.'

'Just like at the Circus,' Ditto said, 'you need us.' But she looked at Rom. 'We might find out what's going on. Maybe about Mr Harper too.'

Rom watched Pixie nosing around Ditto's hand. 'We need to talk to a powerful alchemist. I wonder if Volkov would use this kind of magic.'

'Either way,' Kingsley said, 'she knows enough to summon one of us.'

Rom and Ditto looked at each other. 'Question three,' Rom said. 'Who's *us*?'

He blinked. 'What?'

'We know you're not human.'

'Well.' He shuffled on the step. 'Before the Rain and the Law and the Knife, there were Arbiters. They were pen and sword. I was with the Leopard's folk, but her ranks are destroyed and her People scattered. '

'That's not an answer,' Rom said, 'that's just metaphor. You can do magic?'

Ditto's eyes were wide. 'There were hundreds on that map. Nobody could hide that kind of secret.'

'We'd be stupid to tell,' Kingsley said. 'There's always some mortal who wants thrones or wars. Some are afraid and some are cruel. They build us shrines and burn us alive. Only the Coronets were strong enough to reveal themselves, and even they're wary now. I keep my head down. I get by.'

'Is Pixie one of your People?' Rom wasn't sure how their allegiances worked, but the dog seemed content with Kingsley's presence.

'She's a minor rank amongst the Numbered,' with that sideways smile; 'much like me.'

'Can you grant wishes?'

'If you don't mind losing a finger.'

'You're not faeries?'

'By whose definition?'

'What about satyrs? Or dryads?'

'End of question time,' he said. 'Leave your relix in the garden, yeah? It'll be collected.' He stood, brushing off his trousers. 'I'll leave a note once I get a way into the Phoenix's show, and we'll plan. It'll be dangerous. The first time Desir walked in mortal form, he was a god. Last time he overthrew an empire. Mr Claker's a cockered little piss-prophet but he's right about Coronets; they've got names and crowns. They'll drink your blood like wine.' He tipped his hat. 'Ben lightmans, mistresses. Ben lightmans, dog.'

He laid one hand on his chest, a sort of bow, and sauntered into the crowded backstreet before either could protest.

The next night there was a knock on their apartment door, well after dark.

It was Alec's voice through the door. 'Rom?'

'Did something happen?'

He looked feverishly tired as he pushed past them and dropped his travel bag, rummaging in his pockets. 'Look here.' He unfolded a bundle of paper on the table.

'It isn't—'

'Gold,' Alec said. Three teaspoons and a small fork.

Ditto whistled through her teeth. 'So that's what everybody's after. Jasper really did it.'

'No.' Alec dragged out a chair and sat. 'It's fake. I took them to a jeweller's—they're gold on the outside but it's pewter underneath.'

Rom picked up a spoon. The handle had been acid-dipped, showing dull grey metal.

'Why the dickens would Jasper do it?' asked Alec. 'He said his work was successful. I read his notes.' He pulled a notebook from his jacket. 'And he said he had an assistant. He made a bargain with some sort of a—thing.'

Rom sat down. 'He knew what Pixie was. He bound her?'

'I don't know. He doesn't give them names, he—' Alec rubbed his forehead. 'He calls them beasts. Or *chasma*, like they're some sort of scientific event. They taught him what he wanted but there was a price to pay. Jasper called it something, the payment—' He leafed through the notebook and held it out.

Their grandfather's writing was precise in faded pencil.

On days like this, when my solution smoulders in the crucible and the beast watches from the fireside, I am tempted to believe the relix was too high. When one is young, no price seems too high for the fulfilment of our dreams. Now I am old and the gamble sickens me.

Rom had to clear her throat. 'What did he give?'

'I don't know. But he created something that frightened the daylights out of him, and he went and built a bunker in his garden. What happens when we release her?' He stared at Pixie's dozing bulk. 'What if he bound her for a reason? Remember the Arabian Nights— the fisherman let the djinn from its jar and thought it'd be happy. But the djinn was so mad about being sealed up that he wanted to kill the fisherman anyway. If we release her, Pixie might not care who we are.'

'If she was angry she could have let me die, any of half a dozen times. And they can't all be monsters. Mr Kingsley's a darling.'

Alec looked startled. 'You saw him again?'

Rom explained, but he seemed too restless to listen properly.

'Of course this Phoenix *would* perform at the Waldorf. They'll get all the bored nobs investing in their mystical trash,' he said. 'It stinks of a scam. Jasper too. He kept a journal—this was the only volume I found, but it's all rubbish. He was mad as a bat.'

'You *saw* what he had in his house,' Ditto said, 'you saw the dead snake we found—'

'Why fake the gold? It's just the same as his photography. Idiotic games.'

'He didn't try to scam anyone,' Rom said. 'This pewter's hallmarked, he didn't hide it.'

'Exactly,' Alec said. 'I asked the jeweller. Do you know what sort of equipment it takes to plate metal? An acid bath. Cyanide salts to diffuse the gold, electric current to bind it.' He laughed shortly. 'Generator and a vat. That's what he had in the cellar.'

'It wasn't a weapon?'

'Not a bit. Selwyn said the place was dangerous enough, black powder and nitro. But nothing else.'

'Those are ingredients for alchemy, too.'

'Oh, I'm sure they are. It's pointless,' Alec said. 'We haven't got gold or answers.' He pulled on his coat and began to button. He missed one and started again, viciously.

'We've got a few answers,' Ditto said, 'Mr Kingsley said Phoenix is behind the missing people.'

'He's the chap who took you to a circus and showed you a trick? I'm not exactly overwhelmed with confidence.'

'What about my hand?' Rom said.

'Have you seen that mark again since?'

She didn't have a good answer. 'Dr Lloyd is very serious about all this.'

'You don't even know what she's after. If she wants cash to buy this book, she can go ask her millionaire woman. We haven't a cent.'

'We have,' Rom said, 'you just don't want to spend it.'

'Ask Mother, if you need some.'

'It isn't hers, it's Harry's. I'm not asking Morgan's father for money. And how are we going to explain a couple of hundred pounds? You've got the cash. We need to finish what we started.'

'Jasper Teague started it.' Alec looked at her. 'And I'm finished. Sel and I will find out what we can about Harper and then I'm going home.' He growled. 'I should have asked Morgan about the stuff in the bloody cellar, he knows his science.'

'Mr Mitchell didn't recognise the electroplating vat?'

'He learned about explosives from the other end.' Alec leaned against the table tiredly. 'Sel's a mechanic, not a chemist. I don't think he finished school. He knew what all the chemicals do but he could hardly read the labels.'

'I didn't know.' Rom hesitated. 'He must be good at his job on the boats.'

'He's clever as anything, but he's not the book type.' Alec was collecting his bag.

'You're really going?'

He stopped at the door. 'There's no point staying. I'm starting to see why Jasper went batty.'

Ditto's face crumpled as Alec's steps died away. 'It can't be rubbish. We saw.'

Rom picked up Jasper's notebook, a slim worn volume. 'The old man might have been deluded, but he wasn't lying. At least we've got his words now. Let's make some tea.'

They skimmed impatiently through descriptions of Jasper's health. They read again, impossibly slow, inspecting every sentence, transcribing anything that felt like a clue.

He rambled. He was vague. There were traces, though, of his assistant; the creature. *It was bad-tempered today and threw a jar of acid over my notebook. We finished early. I think it might be hungry again.*

'Jasper couldn't have been more than sixty when he died,' Rom said. But ill; long lists of his pains. There were flashes of his personality; at his best he was curious, thoughtful. He had a dry sort of wit and she sometimes glimpsed his younger, more hopeful self.

There were entire pages about ingredients, costs and sourcing, the irritation of cleaning up after his small disasters. He wheedled chemicals from university laboratories and ordered poisons from chemists, tiny packages from multiple shops across the country. There were folktales and dreams, paranoid ramblings.

The reading public is charmed by faery stories but nobody wants an intimation that some strain of higher science might approach the realm of the magical. The seeker is considered worthy, but the one who purports to be a finder must walk alone.

No name at all for the chasma he'd summoned, the beasts who walked in his house and seemed to weigh on his mind and worry his dreams—not until the last few pages.

It's done. The collar has been tied in place; Pixie's form will remain fixed. Not even the Law can break it now, and I hope she will be guarded for as long as she must guard.

Nimue charmed her faery teacher and learned the secrets of his power. She bound Merlin in a cave of stone, tied by his own words, and have I not learned from this?

Rom jumped. Pixie's cold nose bumped her elbow and pushed into her lap. Sniffing at the notebook, and she stroked the dog's heavy head. 'Do you remember him?' she asked. 'What did Jasper do?'

Pixie made a bright whining noise and turned away. She circled around the room, restless, keeping against the wall, as Rom and Ditto read late into the night beside the wavering lamp.

Rom felt her own thoughts still pacing in the morning. 'He shouldn't have bound her like this,' she said at breakfast. 'It was his decision to work with the fey and if he agreed—if he knew what kind of payment it would take—he should have freed her when he was finished.'

'Maybe he didn't get to finish.'

'Or he did and turned coward. Pen might make sense of his notebook. Alec's right, we haven't a clue what she plans to do if she finds the fey; we don't need to tell her everything. But she might know what Jasper was doing with those chemicals.' Rom flexed her fingers. 'And we need a doctor, anyway. We have to bottle two pints of blood by Friday.'

Pen flipped through Jasper's notes, her brow gathered. 'Chasma. That's what he calls them?'

'It's usually used to describe a hole torn open in something,' Rom said. 'Or a meteor.'

'A natural phenomenon.' Pen nodded. 'He mentions alkahest, one of his materials. I thought the stuff was pure myth.' She sat back from her desk. 'Your grandfather was very dedicated. The gold might have been a hoax but this work looks complex. Must have had quite a laboratory.'

'What was he looking for?'

'Transmutation. Isn't that what everybody wants?' Pen was unpacking her medical case, hunting for sterile needles, and eyed them curiously as she drew her chair up close.

'Mr Kingsley said venous blood,' Ditto said, and Pen shrugged.

'Nobody opens an artery, too dangerous.'

Rom bared her arm, turning her head away as Pen pressed the hypodermic needle gently into the crook of her left arm.

'So you've found yourselves a fey who'll talk,' Pen said.

'When he feels like it.' Rom winced through the sting. 'He only gave us three questions, and some of it we'd already guessed.'

'He doesn't think much of humans,' Ditto said. 'And he said Séraphin Desir is fey, too. The singer.'

Rom tried not to shudder at the runnel of her blood from the silver tube to the waiting jar. A pint looked rather more than she'd expected, now she was sitting here. And Kingsley hadn't exactly been fair in answering their last question.

'Why do you think they drink it?' Ditto peered at her own bright blood. 'Are they vampires?'

'They take all sorts of payments, but they certainly don't eat human food,' Pen said. 'They must find some value in blood, considering the effects of their own. I haven't discovered much about their diet in my research.'

'What research?' Rom asked. 'Exactly?'

Pen searched amongst her folders. 'I did some tests on a fey blood sample last year, and the stuff's quite remarkable.' She pushed a photograph across the desk; a jar with a transparent shard inside, something like amber. 'It dries hard as resin and you can grind it into powder. It's a golden colour. Dilute in saline and inject into the site of a wound—the effect it has on mortified flesh is unprecedented; the body appears to regenerate itself. Even from the point of death.' Pen's fair brows furrowed. 'It isn't just medicine, you understand. There's no trace of infection and the patient's health is guaranteed.'

'You've seen it?' asked Ditto, a sort of croak, and Pen nodded.

'The value of this material is beyond calculation, as you can imagine, which is—well. Why I'm only showing you a picture.'

Rom put down the photograph, cautious not to jerk the needle taped into her arm. 'It sounds impossible.'

'I can assure you it's not. I saw a child undamaged after an accident that should have killed her. And I met a nurse in France who gave up one of her feet in exchange for something that cured her septicaemia; she made a bargain with a woman who could speak to bees.'

'Pixie's blood is made of this stuff?' asked Rom.

'The Ancients call it panax. The panacea.'

And that was what it reminded her of, that piece of blood like a jewel in the glass bottle. 'The philosopher's stone.'

'Exactly,' Pen said. 'It's terrific stuff, but the blood I've found since isn't quite the same; it's red, useful for sterilising wounds but nothing close to the pure gold. That's the true treasure of alchemy.'

'Did Jasper know?'

'He must have,' Pen said. She removed the needle gently from Rom's skin and let the last dribble of blood funnel into the jar. 'Not just the metaphors of the Great Work, the spiritual concepts of the adepts, but the chemical equivalents. Once we have *The Nest,* we'll be able to recreate it.'

'We'll bid at this auction,' Rom said. 'We'll get it back. Although Jasper had the fey to help him with his work.'

'We might yet, too,' Pen said. 'Do you think your Mr Kingsley would talk to me?'

'He might. If he turns up again. He'd need a lot for it. I wonder what Jasper paid for everything he knew.'

'I'd pay any money.' Pen tucked the photograph away. 'For panacea? The perfect medicine? People have burned cities for less.'

12

The illness lies so deep I shall never be free of it. I have no strength left. The beast shall not have another drop of my blood.

I bear my life some days with a stoic fortitude I am nearly proud of, and other days I sit at my desk and weep. This victory is worth nothing. Less than nothing, for the cure is my disease.

I have finished the hidden room. It is warm and golden as a fire. It should be safe in there.

JASPER TEAGUE, Journals, 2nd Oct. 1915

'So many people,' Rom said. 'Ridiculous to think we have a chance.'

'Nonsense,' Ditto said, 'we either get it or we don't.' She tapped the bidding paddle against her chin, eyes darting over the crowded auction hall. 'Lord, the beards on the old coots, you'd think it was the nineties.'

'Where shall we sit?' Pen asked. 'I'm not getting stuck behind anyone taller than me.'

They squeezed along a row of tweedy knees, close enough to the front to hear the auctioneer's voice. Everyone here was a rival today.

'There's at least twenty lots before ours,' Pen said.

'Nineteen,' Ditto said as the hammer came down.

Rom shuffled on the wooden seat. They were lucky to be here at all. Last week Alec had relented on the cash; they had some left from Rom's last birthday but most came from the sale of Jasper's library, which seemed a horrid irony. Alec had been bitter enough when he tallied it up. 'You could almost buy a house for this. If you throw it away on a book—'

'A supremely rare one,' Rom said. 'If it's not what we're looking for we'll just re-sell. No risk.'

Pen had put in fifty of her own. And Ditto, wonderful Dido, had frowned over her biscuit tin of coin and put in a handful. They had three hundred pounds today and only grim hope it would be enough.

They hadn't heard back from Kingsley, though they'd left their jars of blood in the courtyard and found them gone at dawn. He had no news, then, or had moved on. Or found himself a better meal.

Rom rummaged in her bag for her fan. Summer had unfolded like a yellow umbrella upon them. She gazed over the hall, skimming hats and heads. 'I wonder if they're all here for books. Or if it's the paintings.' There were dozens of estate sales, Victorian furniture and fussy watercolours. 'This really is our only chance,' she began again, but Ditto interrupted.

'I need to listen. We can worry later.'

Rom flopped back against the chair and fanned herself. 'Stinking hot,' she said.

Pen ignored her. Everyone was either craning or buried in their catalogues or lounging, affecting nonchalance; it felt like an examination hall at school. Noisier, though. Like a church, if churches were any fun.

'Good afternoon, Miss Godden,' said the voice behind her shoulder. 'How's your luck running?'

She snapped her fan shut and turned in her seat. 'Fine,' she said.

'Glad to hear it.' Prideaux leaned forward in the row behind them, dangling an auction paddle in grey-gloved fingers. 'You're bidding today?'

If she wasn't careful she'd say something rude and truthful. 'Are you?'

'If possible. A teacher's wage is not impressive.'

'Temporary assistant teacher. You left the school.'

'Have you been checking up on me, Miss Godden?'

'Quiet.' Ditto moved up a seat with a huff.

Pen turned. 'And who do you work for?'

'I don't work for anybody.'

'Lot thirty-one,' Ditto hissed across the empty seat.

'You wrote to Dr Carr,' Rom said. 'What do you know about the skull Harper found?' She had to turn sideways to hear him and his shoulder nearly touched hers as he leaned in.

'I wrote to Horstmann, actually. The skull is a mystery, and thus it ought to remain. It's no business of any Museum.'

'It's entirely their business,' Rom said, 'preserving history. And researching. What's your real name, by the way?'

He looked down at his hands. And up again. 'You've come here for *The Nest of Amoury*.'

'What makes you think so?'

'I've heard the Museum sent a representative to bid. I doubt your people have the funds to match them.'

Rom felt herself flush, a creeping heat above her linen collar. 'We're here, aren't we?'

'You and a few hundred guineas? Not a chance.'

'Pipe down, this is us,' Ditto said.

'—fair condition,' the auctioneer said, 'minor foxing—' The book on the podium was small, a neat dusty-blue thing. The auctioneer gestured. '—book-block is complete, edges gilt. Re-bound as usual—'

Usual for a three-hundred-year-old volume. Or one that had been stolen from its original binding by somebody's grandfather.

Rom clasped her hands on her knee. 'You're wasting your time if you expect us to give up.'

'I'm not attempting intimidation.' Prideaux's cool sigh brushed her neck. 'I'm suggesting a truce. If we pooled our resources we might have a chance.'

'And share the book?' No point pretending they were here for anything else. Ditto was poised in her seat, ready to bid.

'—eighty pounds, looking for ninety, any advances on eighty—'

'I don't want the book,' Prideaux said. 'I want access to your grandfather's library.'

'It's all gone. We sold it.'

'Even the notebooks?'

'—one hundred and sixty pounds now, bid rests with the gentleman in the red tie—'

'No deal,' Rom said.

Ditto flourished her paddle and the auctioneer nodded.

'—one-seventy from the silver hat now, any advances now—'

'It won't go for less than four hundred,' Prideaux said. 'How much do you want it?'

'Not enough for that,' Rom said. It was a lie. Pen would know it.

'I see.' Prideaux flashed his gloved palm at the auctioneer.

'—one ninety five from the blue coat—thank you, sir, do we have two hundred pounds—'

Ditto glared. Prideaux didn't seem to notice.

'Why do you want his notes?' Rom asked.

'Why do you want *The Nest*?'

'We're all researching.'

He bid again over her head.

'Two-fifty-five,' the auctioneer said.

'I'm sorry?'

Prideaux twisted closer. 'I said you may refuse if you'd rather. I wouldn't dream of influencing your decision.' His gloved finger tapped her elbow. 'You're out.'

'—and three hundred from the gentleman with the red tie. Do I have three-twenty?'

Ditto plumped back into the seat beside her. 'Bloody bastard,' she said. 'Rom—'

Pen shrugged. 'Why not split it?'

'We don't know what he wants it for.'

Prideaux was looking past them at the auctioneer but he raised his eyebrows above a hieroglyphic smile.

'No,' Rom said. 'You can't do this to us.'

'—four-twenty, now. If there are no more bids at four-twenty—'

'It's your funeral,' Prideaux said.

'—bid rests with the gentleman in the red tie. Four-twenty, ladies and gentleman—'

Rom turned back around in her seat, fixing her blurring eyes on the podium. 'Prideaux offered to go in with us.'

'Do it.' Ditto's eyes were wide. 'Rom—'

'—no advances?'

'Five hundred,' Prideaux said clearly.

'Five hundred, sir. Thank you, sir. Any raise on five hundred?'

'Sodding sod,' Ditto said.

'—no advances on five hundred now? Going once, going twice—'

'Hell,' whispered Rom.

'—and sold, for five hundred pounds, to the gentleman in the blue coat.'

'Now what?' Ditto elbowed her. 'Now what, little miss clever?' They didn't look behind them.

'Now we go home,' Pen said.

When they slid out of their row Prideaux was gone. Nobody spoke a word until they got to the musty echo of the foyer and Pen stopped. 'That was our chance,' she said mildly. But her eyes were bitter.

'What could I do?'

'Take the bloody offer.'

Ditto shook her head. 'We can't without knowing what's involved. These people know something.'

'Exactly why we need to talk to them. You could have bought it.'

'He didn't even need our money,' Rom said. 'Teacher's wage my arse, he knew we couldn't afford it.' She pushed through the crowd and down the steps to the rushing street. She stood on the footpath, breathing in the smell of horse and heated engines.

A cobalt flap of coat dashed between two buses.

Rom dived around an old soldier on crutches, and straight over the road. Nipping through traffic. Past a postboy on a bicycle. Onto the footpath opposite, and she pulled up short.

Prideaux leaned against an open car, veiled in cigarette smoke, thin as a twig in his beautiful worn suit. The coat was draped beside the gilded crook of a walking cane.

He saw her. He didn't move.

'Haven't you got a book to pay for?'

'I'm waiting for somebody to make me a better offer.'

'Not us,' she said.

'Not you.' Prideaux untucked his pocket-watch and glanced at it. 'That man in the red tie was a buyer for the Museum. I expect he'll be quite interested in its provenance.'

Ditto's heels were loud on the footpath as she and Pen caught up. She didn't even pretend to be friendly. 'So you're him, then.'

Pen's face was set. 'What do you want the book for? Really?'

Prideaux tapped ash from his cigarette. 'I've heard the illustrations are quite charming.'

'Are you a spy?' asked Rom.

'Is that what Morgan said?'

'You lied, you're not a teacher.'

'That's an unpleasant accusation. I could be quite offended.'

Rom tried again. 'What do you know about the chasma?'

Prideaux flicked away the ruins of his cigarette and reached inside his jacket for another. 'Is that what you're calling them?'

'That's what my grandfather called them.'

'Chasma is what they call themselves,' he said. 'Humans usually called them spirits. Or *uttuk*, Miss Godden.'

'From the Sumerian, *udu*.' Clay tablets she'd cleaned and documented, cuneiform lists of ancient protections. 'Demons.'

'*Zi dingir nindul-azagga kanpa*.' Some kind of Babylonian, impossible to tell with the way he said it, rolling the r and cutting the syllables. A proper academic would translate flatly and correctly, so any scholar could understand.

But one of those words she knew. 'Exorcism, exactly. They saw illness as a curse, they use just the same word for darkness. Or a godly voice—'

'No,' Prideaux said, 'I mean demons. As detailed in many well-preserved Iron Age texts; I presume you've read the Bible?'

Rom searched his narrow face for any speck of mockery. Faeries she'd accepted. But she couldn't begin to explain why this was so much worse.

Pen said it first. 'They're dangerous, then.'

'Only as dangerous as knives,' Prideaux said.

'I've been researching,' Pen said, 'I know what their genetic material can do.'

Prideaux shifted on his feet. 'The things you know could be engraved in 24-point Baskerville on the back of a penny.'

Rom's voice felt thick. 'My dog walked six hundred miles to kill a snake in our bedroom. Somebody needs to explain what's going on.'

'She didn't walk.'

'I beg your pardon?'

Prideaux dragged shortly on his cigarette. 'She would have caught the train.' Something scuffled in the car behind him and the foxhound peered over the door. Prideaux's hand settled between its soft ears, scratching. 'I want the notebooks,' he said. 'You want some clarity. If you're ready to make an exchange—'

'We're considering it,' Pen said.

'No,' Rom said, 'we're not.'

'You won't find another copy,' Prideaux said; 'I'm sure you've realised your search is over. And no chasma will tell you how to break your

Skein.'

'Who told you?' Rom stared, aware of Pen's stiff curiosity. 'We didn't tell anyone, only Alec. Apart from Mr Kingsley.'

Prideaux smiled, his fingers curling behind the dog's ears. The dog blinked up at them. Warm brown eyes, jaunty red collar.

Ditto made a faint sound. 'You little prick.'

'Mr Prideaux,' Rom said. 'What's your dog's name?'

The fox-hound whined and ducked back into the car.

'I'd best be going.' Prideaux pulled out a card-case. 'Hunt me up when you decide you need me after all.'

Ditto pulled the card from his fingers, took hold of Rom's arm, and started off down the street.

'The dog.' Rom stumbled. 'His bloody dog.'

'I know. But it can't be.'

Pen caught up. 'What's wrong?'

'Mr Prideaux has a fox-hound. A hunter, just as Quinn said, and I never even realised—'

'His dog's a chasma?'

'His dog is Mr Kingsley,' Rom said. 'Conniving sod.' Clay tablets, rows of them, incised with curses. Would it work? If she rained vexations on a wandering schoolmaster?

She groaned. 'What does his card say?'

'Nish,' Ditto said, 'of course.' The paper was thick linen but there wasn't a name, just a phone number crisply engraved.

'We can't give him the notebook,' Rom said. 'Can you imagine what he could do if he bound a whole lot of fey at once?'

'He already knows about them,' Pen said, 'we'd be giving up scraps in return for something better.'

'There must be another copy of the book somewhere.' Rom tucked the card into her purse. 'We aren't calling Mr Prideaux until we're absolutely desperate.'

The train roared like a headache as she and Ditto rattled home. She sagged on the shabby seat. The tunnels flickered and her dull reflection hung at her left hand, an eyeless ghost, but it was better than glancing over at Ditto's face. Because there was nothing to say. No book, no plan. They were desperate already.

'This is pointless,' Ditto said. 'Mr Claker didn't even like us.'

Rom started up the stairs. 'I don't think Mr Claker's the one we ought to talk to.'

The Midnight Palace nightclub was nearly empty, a few tired businessmen snared at the bar before the Tube ride home, but as she and Ditto looked around the evening stir was beginning; a waiter folded napkins; the brass band dragged their drum-kit across the stage.

Mr Claker leaned over the bar to glower at Pixie. 'Hello again. And humans. I don't read for free.'

'I don't expect you to.' Rom eyed the licensee sign by the front door. 'We're looking for the owner.'

Claker wiped a glass in silence and hooked it into the overhead rack. Then he nodded towards a booth by the shuttered windows.

They found a small solid man bent over a beef pie and a pint.

'Mr Webster?'

He didn't put down his fork. 'Who's asking?'

'My name's Rom Godden. I was wondering if we could ask you about—magic and things.' It seemed strange to use the word aloud. Here, of all places, with the distant street-roar and lazy voices from the band.

The man leaned out to look at Pixie. He wiped his handkerchief over his moustache. 'She yours?'

'My grandfather's.'

'Righty-o. Take a seat.'

Rom shuffled in beside Ditto, her palms hot inside her gloves. 'You're the manager here. And Mr Claker's master?'

'I am.' Webster sat back and folded his hand over his belly. 'Nice gig it is, too. Used to be a cargo rigger.'

Ditto sighed. 'Not a sorcerer, then.'

"Course I'm a bleeding sorcerer. Aren't I, Claker?'

Mr Claker bowed, a silent apparition beside the table. 'True enough, sir.'

'It's just book-learning,' Webster said. 'A bit of reading. I'd rather be memorising the twelve names of Barbas than hauling shipping crates in Wapping drizzle.'

'How did you find them?' Rom nodded at Mr Claker. 'What did you have to pay?'

Webster sniffed wetly. 'I had a fair bit owed around the place. The docker's boys were after me and my life weren't worth pigeonshit, begging your pardon. Claker found me. He made an offer, we struck a deal. The club runs a profit and the dockers stay clear.'

'Why are you here?' Ditto asked. 'You know magic. You work with demons. Why are you running a bar in Soho?'

'Why not? It don't cost much, just the odd bit of blood. We live quiet and comfortable. If I wanted to be a millionaire, he'd be asking all sorts of nasty payments; wouldn't you?'

Mr Claker ran his tongue over his teeth.

'Shifters can't create something out of nothing,' Webster said. 'They've got their laws, same as us.'

'Aren't you worried people will find out?' Rom glanced at Ditto. 'You're telling us, for one thing.'

'And I could stand on that bar and swear I'd seen God. Who'd listen? The world's full of wildness. The ones listening are the ones as already know.' Webster gestured to Pixie. 'Like that one; her collar's a shifter seal and no doubting. What's it for?'

'No clue,' Rom said. 'We don't know why my grandfather made it. Or how to break it. Or why I've got a fey mark on my hand.'

'You've got a Skein, but you don't know what you're paying?' He raised his sparse brows. 'There's a tale.'

Rom looked at Ditto. He'd just given them more information in two minutes than anything they'd pulled from Jasper's books.

Ditto nodded.

So they told. Everything they knew, the whole Odd List, while Mr Webster finished his pie. He hadn't heard of the Circus, though he'd seen crowfolk around London. He'd read about Séraphin Desir in the papers.

And he frowned when they explained the auction. 'Mr Kingsley I have met; good lad. But Prideaux—I don't know the name. You mean Mr Argent?'

'Built like a stick,' Ditto said.

'Blue coat,' Rom said. 'Snide bastard.'

'That's the one.' Webster drained his pint glass. 'We call him the Magician. He's been tracking shifter movements all winter, hangs about the West End like a bloody plague. He's offered you a deal?'

'We think he's a government spy.'

'Could well be. There's not many nobs as wouldn't want a pet demon. No offence, Claker. I've never heard of collars, but then I don't dabble in hard magic; you get what you pay for, see, and you pay for what you get.' Webster shook his head. 'You've got a Skein you didn't make yourself. Your grandfather sold you out.'

'So we guessed,' Rom said. 'What was he playing at?'

Webster looked at Mr Claker. 'Go on.'

Mr Claker shuffled. 'Only one knot can bind a bloodline. Your grandfather forfeited a human soul.'

Rom's head thumped like something mechanical. 'Mine?'

'Must be,' Webster said. 'Mr Claker doesn't make mistakes.'

Laughter brayed from the distant street.

'Nobody can do that,' Rom said. 'Jasper couldn't promise somebody else as payment. Could he?'

'If the descendant is yet unborn,' Mr Claker said. 'A theoretical existence has no say in the matter.'

'But I do now,' Rom said. 'I'm here.'

Mr Claker looked at her, and away towards the ceiling. Perhaps for him she was already gone.

Rom leaned back in the booth, trying to drown the chatter from the band, the stench of spilt beer. How stupid that her fate should find her here in a faded nightclub.

But fate had happened years ago. Far from here, out of her reach.

'Real question,' Ditto said, 'will freeing Pixie mean instant death?'

'Depends on the contract,' Mr Webster said. 'Some are short; some might be a life-term. Sounds as though the dog's taking care of you, rather than not. There's precious little else I can tell you. I'd not be taking chances, though.'

Rom began to gather herself slowly. Gloves, purse; dog leash. Her ears were seething. 'Is there anyone else we could ask about this? Another magician somewhere? Anyone who isn't Prideaux or Mr Kingsley,' she added, tired.

'Not as I know of,' Webster said. 'Shifters keep themselves close. If you've got the trail, you'd best be chasing them.' He stood and leaned across the table to shake their hands.

Ditto stopped by Mr Claker. 'Is there any way we can explain things to Pixie?'

The demon refolded his hands. 'I can't comment on another's Skein. You must unbind her first.'

'We're bloody trying,' Rom said.

There was nothing to say on the train home. Her thoughts swelled in all directions. The afternoon clung humid to her limbs; the stairs to their apartment trooped endlessly.

'Rom,' Ditto said when they got inside and leaned against the door. 'What will you do?'

'I haven't the faintest.'

They wired Alec's hotel and he arrived in a huff, shaking out of his jacket. 'Selwyn's gone to visit his sister somewhere, I need to ask him about Whitehall. I don't expect the government to tell any kind of truth but if there's a spy ring—' He stopped. 'What's happened now?'

Rom opened her mouth. She shut it again. She turned to boil the kettle.

Ditto explained.

'Jasper.' Alec was wide-eyed as Rom brought the tea cups over. 'He bloody what?'

'Too chicken to sell his own soul, I suppose,' Rom said. His horror cut her nerves. It was too hot for tea, she didn't want it now, and she began to slice oranges.

'This can't be allowed to happen,' Alec was saying, 'nobody has that sort of power—'

'If Prideaux's correct, if we're dealing with demons—'

'We're going to believe him?'

Rom slammed down the knife. 'Mr Webster had no reason to lie. Nor Kingsley, we paid him.'

Alec rubbed his eyes and collapsed in his chair. 'Are you alright?'

'No,' Rom said. 'But we have time.' She swept the bright quarters onto a plate. 'I don't plan on dying this week.'

Probably she was supposed to feel something. Maybe she would tomorrow—everything that showed on Alec's face; confusion, anger. But there was only a keen silver pain through all her mind as though something had set a string humming. An agonised impatience.

This was not the end. A knot can be undone. She could read her way through the whole Museum if they only had what she was looking for. 'We need to talk to Pixie.'

Ditto nodded. Her warm eyes said the rest.

That meant the book; and the book meant Prideaux.

They came with her the next day: Alec anxious in his orange suit, Ditto fluttering in the wind, and Pixie like iron between them.

Rom stared at the red-painted phone box door. 'It's useless,' she said, 'he only shows up when we don't want him.'

'I'd certainly like to never see him again,' Ditto said.

Rom stepped into the close metallic air, the business card pinched in her fingers as she dialled. Somebody on the street turned to look; she was on display in here. Caged in glass.

The brassy ringing stopped. 'What is it?'

Rom stood up straighter. 'Who is this, please?'

'Who do you think?' Tinny, distant. Unmistakable. 'You called me.'

It was actually his number. The simplicity was overwhelming. 'It's Andromeda Godden. You gave us your card at—'

'Yes,' Prideaux said. 'What is it you want?'

'We'd like to talk about the book.'

'Shall I send someone to make the exchange?'

'We haven't agreed yet. We need to see *The Nest*.'

'As you please. I can meet you Friday afternoon.'

She wasn't about to play it on his terms. 'Thursday morning,' she said. 'The student library at King's College.'

A pause. 'It ought to be neutral territory. Don't you think? Robert Carr is your professor. Would he be a satisfactory witness?'

'I suppose.' Thinking furiously. 'Yes, that's fine. I'll ask him.' At least she'd see if Dr Carr reacted. He wouldn't want her talking to his amateur Hittite translator about anything skull-related. And it wouldn't hurt to have somebody else present. 'I'm bringing my brother,' she said.

'I shall come alone. Good afternoon, Godden; I look forward to doing business with you.'

The dial tone swelled like a bee.

13

Though I am so wary of the stronger acids, my fingers ache and burn. I have managed transmutations that would astound a magician or a chemist—but this panax eludes me.

I need a steady source of alkahest. It will involve magicks more complex than I have yet attempted and I will not be able to rely on anyone's help. I cannot write it here: I think the creatures read my notes. There is nothing safe.

JASPER TEAGUE, Journals, 18th Feb. 1913

Rom trapped Dr Carr in the hallway after her Wednesday lecture.

Apparently Prideaux had sent him a note. 'Quite right too,' Dr Carr said, 'you're a student without an available guardian, and I have previously been in correspondence with him; his request was entirely proper.'

'I'm a legal adult.'

'But not, I think, married.'

She smiled tightly. 'I plan to bring my brother. But I do appreciate it. Apparently Mr Prideaux has a history of blackmail.'

Ditto wasn't going to be free; her show was a fortnight away from opening. 'And that's just when the Phoenix will be in London,' she told Rom that night, propping her feet on the sofa. 'Are we going to investigate?'

'I'll be at Aunt Minnie's. Anyway, we won't need Madame Volkov. We're going to work it out alone.'

Alec agreed. 'We can't trust anyone,' he said, 'only ourselves.' He was sour about the whole thing but mostly seemed relieved they hadn't had to pay for the book. So was Rom, they couldn't afford it, but this was a different kind of bad—handing over Jasper's notes to anyone, and Prideaux worst of all.

On Friday they arrived at Dr Carr's office early enough for Rom to introduce Alec, stare at the cabinets full of earthenware, and begin to feel a restive heat.

The place was sullen with summer rain; Dr Carr opened a window but the air that flooded in held no relief. Alec, always inquisitive, had a lot of questions about Dr Carr's collectables, the delicate curves of raw or painted clay, and their relative values on the open market.

Rom had been here once or twice before and couldn't have focused even if she'd been interested; she stiffly settled into a chair.

She'd read the entire notebook, inspected each word and looked up every material Jasper mentioned, every reference to myth or history. She'd copied out the entries in case they proved useful. Now she wondered if she should have cut it open and checked for invisible ink, but she forced herself to relax. Stop tapping her foot. Some of Jasper's entries hadn't even been coherent; unlikely he'd been organised enough to hide anything important. Maybe Prideaux wanted something else completely.

'He's late,' Dr Carr said.

'He's going to throw us over,' Rom said, but Alec shook his head.

'He wasn't hanging around for nothing.'

There was a sharp rap on the door. Alec dived to open it.

'Morning,' Prideaux said. He tucked his gilded cane beneath one elbow. 'I kept you waiting.' No hat. Loose grey suit, tight gloves, and a silk scarf softly knotted. His shoulders seemed gathered against a chill. 'You must be Dr Carr.' He offered his hand with fastidious care. 'And Goddens, times two. Have you been well?'

'Brilliant,' Rom said. 'How's Kingsley doing?'

'He's such a help to me,' Prideaux said. 'A little headstrong, but he really is a very good boy.'

She sat, fuming. He wasn't going to mention demons. Or any kind of magic—perhaps he didn't trust Dr Carr. But now she couldn't mention it either.

'I have to congratulate you, sir,' Dr Carr said as they all sat; 'your translation for the tumulus disc was immensely useful.'

Prideaux tilted his head. The hair was clipped short across his nape, high and oddly monkish. 'Glad to assist.'

'I was shocked to hear about Harper,' Dr Carr said. 'I don't suppose you have more news than we do?'

'I suspect he told the wrong people what he'd found and they got in before the government could.'

Dr Carr eyed the jingle of fob charms on Prideaux's watch chain.

'You work for an agency?'

'I'm impartial.'

'A teacher?'

'Occasionally.'

'What do you do when you aren't teaching?'

Prideaux considered. 'I spend a lot of time in the bath.'

Dr Carr looked over his glasses. 'So you do not specialise in languages.'

'I specialise in nothing at all,' Prideaux said. 'Specialisation leads to the emaciation of the intellect. I never trust an expert.'

'There is a reason for the questions, Mr Prideaux.'

'Curiosity.'

Dr Carr frowned. 'Caution.'

'Not even just the littlest bit of inquisitiveness?'

'Why did you leave Oxford last year?' Dr Carr had done some homework of his own.

'They disapproved of my politics,' Prideaux said. 'Don't underestimate the implacable pettiness of bureaucracy.'

'I see. So the story about the—the business arrangement—'

'Oh,' Prideaux said in a different tone of voice. 'No, that was quite true.'

Dr Carr cleared his throat. 'You wish to return a book to Miss Godden's family.'

'No, I am offering to lend it. For a period of three months, I think, renewable.' Prideaux pulled the slim book from his breast pocket and laid it on the table. 'In exchange for Mr Teague's papers.'

Rom's neck prickled. 'That wasn't the agreement.'

'We've established that you have no other access to the book, Miss Godden. This is the agreement.'

Alec leaned forward. 'Why do you want Jasper's notes?'

'He was researching Celtic burial mounds. I like Celtic burial mounds.' Prideaux laid his hand over the little book of poetry. 'Why do you want to read this? If I'm not mistaken, it's the same copy your grandfather—'

Don't say stole, thought Rom, don't you bloody dare.

'—left you.'

Rom tried not to glance at Dr Carr. 'I want it because I'm studying the alchemical view of solar cults.'

'Fascinating.' Prideaux slid the book across the desk.

It was the same edition as Pen's single page; there were similar drawings scattered throughout. Rom checked the spine, the page numbers. The weight. Then she passed it over to Alec. She expected Prideaux to be offended by their close examination but he waited, drumming on the table-edge.

'Fine,' she said.

Alec pulled out Jasper's shabby exercise book and handed it over. Prideaux flipped through the pages in one sweep. Ran his thumb over the spine. 'Is this all?' He sniffed the back cover thoughtfully and put it down again. 'The deal was for his complete notes, not the selected works of his middle-aged depression.'

'That's all I found,' Alec said. 'If there's any others, they weren't in his house.'

Prideaux shrugged. 'So this is our agreement? His private papers, every word he left behind.'

'Yes,' Alec said.

Rom shushed him. 'No. We might discover something new, and we don't plan to let you claim it.' She didn't care how rude Dr Carr might think her; clarity was too crucial to be tidied for an audience. 'This notebook, nothing else. That's the deal.'

Prideaux blinked, heavy-lidded. 'In writing, please.'

'I'll draft it up,' Dr Carr said.

'Awfully complicated,' Alec said, filling the silence over the scratching pen. 'I suppose our word isn't enough for you.'

'Judicious use of paperwork is a simplification, not a complication. The alternative is sharing the book.' Prideaux folded his hands. 'You could pay for half.'

Two hundred and fifty pounds. And where would it be kept? Who had the first right if everyone was in a hurry? It would mean endless negotiation. 'No.' Rom tucked *The Nest of Amoury* into her purse; hers and not-hers. It would have to be enough.

Mr Prideaux stood, reaching for his cane. 'And that is why we have contracts. Cleaner, isn't it?' He was looking at the glass cases behind Dr Carr's desk. 'You have quite a collection of crockery.'

Dr Carr winced. 'It's earthenware. And the smaller pieces are

Egyptian faience, some interesting perfume bottles from the Late Period.'

Prideaux didn't appear to care for pots. 'Ah, the specimen in question. Is this the original condition?'

'I suppose so.' Dr Carr passed the page to Rom. She signed her name, and tipped back on her chair to see what Prideaux was examining. A globe of yellowed ochre sat cushioned beside the ranks of faded ceramics.

She came over to the cabinet and knelt. The thick baked clay had been moulded delicately around the skull beneath, glazed and painted; twining knots in faded red still crowned the brow. Hollows had been pressed into the remnants of the eyes.

Rom laced her hands tightly. Two long slanted eyes like a cat's, and at the corner of each, a second smaller eye-socket. The open mouth was a cavernous little slit; within it gleamed the edge of gold.

'It's very probably a sculpture,' Dr Carr said; 'at this point nobody is certain if there's any bone under that.'

'I seem to recall reading an article,' Prideaux said. 'Something comparable was excavated several years ago in the Sumer.'

'Some cultural beliefs do appear to develop simultaneously,' Dr Carr said.

'This article said it was a guardian relic—an ancestor, or something meant to signify the apkallu. Does that sound accurate, Miss Godden?'

Rom looked up, surprised. 'The apkallu are the gods. And their half-mortal children.'

'This scholar believed the skulls were used for witchcraft; divination and necromancy.' Prideaux leaned his hip against the case as he felt for his cigarette tin. 'Perhaps even the teraphim mentioned in the Bible, the disgraceful objects condemned by the priests.'

'Perhaps,' Dr Carr said. 'However, the remains found in Sumer have quite a different context from this Scottish find—'

'Do they?'

'—and professionals tend to warn against drawing hasty conclusions. If somebody is determined to find a link, they probably will.'

'No doubt.' Prideaux rolled his paper between deft gloved fingers. 'Perhaps Horstmann knows. You mentioned he was a friend of yours?'

'Colleague,' Dr Carr said. 'Acquaintance. I worked with him during the War. In France, mostly.'

'Active service?'

'The Graves Commission. Monuments for the fallen; we had a team of historians as consultants.'

Mr Prideaux paused. 'Adjutant General's Office.'

'You're familiar with our work?'

'Run out of Whitehall, I believe.'

Dr Carr's face tightened as he pushed the waiting page towards Prideaux. 'Many things were. Centralisation of information.'

'Yes,' Prideaux said. 'Many things.' He left his signature, a looping scribble beneath Rom's. 'What's your theory on this skull, Dr Carr?'

'It appears to be a cult object.'

'But what do you believe it was used for?'

'It doesn't have a use. Symbolism is inherently arcane, Dr Prideaux.'

Prideaux slid the cigarette behind his ear. 'Arcane means unknown. Somebody knew. It clearly isn't you.' He smiled. 'You have some very nice tablets here.'

Dr Carr stood, smoothing his jacket with an air of completion. 'Not many; a London office is too damp. These were from the excavation of Sippar. Miss Godden's class has been translating them.'

Prideaux began rolling a second cigarette. 'Anything interesting, Godden?'

Rom slid back into her seat. 'We'll be working on Gilgamesh later this year. I'm looking forward to seeing those; so far it's just ancient receipts and temple accounts.'

'A civilisation can hardly be expected to function without receipts,' Dr Carr said.

'Indeed,' Prideaux said. 'And clay is always for records, things people have no desire to recall.' He tamped the cigarette tightly and licked the edge of the paper. 'The important things were in their heads. *Lingua vivit in lingua*; language lives on the tongue, in the mouths of the priests and poets. Bound into memory and revived each feast day. Or composed in fancy, teased out by some whim of the attendant genius and set loose; passing like wild birds. Fired like a golden lance at a lover in one brief burning climax.'

Dr Carr polished his glasses and replaced them. 'You are a poet, Dr

Prideaux?'

'Unfortunately not. Poetry demands sincerity. It was nice to meet you in person, Professor, after our correspondence.' Prideaux held out his hand. 'I should thank you for taking the time this morning.'

Dr Carr shook it. 'I was already considering a meeting when you wrote about your business with Miss Godden; I took it as a sign.'

'Everything is full of signs,' Prideaux said. 'Everything depends on everything else. All things breathe together.'

'That's inconvenient,' Dr Carr said.

'That's Plotinus. Don't read Plotinus, you'll see where I get all my jokes.'

Alec was gathering up his umbrella. Dr Carr looked as though he wanted to wipe his hand on something but was restraining himself. Prideaux was taking his leave, already fiddling with his lighter, and this time he used his cane.

His left foot dragged. He was limping. Not tenderly, nursing an injury, but stiff on a familiar wound. Rom followed. Had she ever seen him walk?

She stopped him the top of the stairs. 'You have some knowledge of teraphim, Mr Prideaux?'

'Well.' Prideaux lit his cigarette and heaved a sigh. 'I have a Curiosity.' He said it with a capital C, a source of irritation and great pride.

'We were told you're a magician.'

'They're free to say what they please.'

'You know very well why we wanted this book. Mr Kingsley must have told you.' It didn't matter what she said now; they both had what they wanted, and he'd slip back into whatever half-world he made home. 'I don't suppose you ever considered being helpful.'

'It crossed my mind.'

'My grandfather—' She ought to say this. Prideaux was going to read the notes anyway. 'I think he did some terrible things. I'm trying to fix it.'

'Altruism, is it.' His flourish was nasty. 'What did he do, Godden?'

'He tried to control demons. My dog, Pixie.'

Prideaux leaned on his cane. 'He sounds a thoroughly unpleasant man.' He was smiling, a thin kind of contempt, and she wondered how exactly he'd gotten Kingsley to work for him.

'It's a bit of a coincidence,' she said. 'Don't you think? Everywhere we go we've managed to run into you.'

'Hardly coincidental. There aren't many linguists in Britain who also have an interest in—'

'I'm sure you have explanations.'

'Then you understand.' He shuffled his shoulders, the movement close to quivering satisfaction. 'It's no more a coincidence than looking up and seeing the moon. In Italy or New Zealand; it's never far away.'

'Of course it's always there, it's in orbit. That's not the same.'

Mr Prideaux was peering out the hallway window. 'Delicious weather we're having.' He folded up his collar before he strolled downstairs.

'Whitehall,' Alec said outside. His cheeks were two bright spots. 'The War Graves Commission was a branch of the War Office, the same building that organised intelligence. It's not impossible.'

Rom felt lightheaded. 'Dr Carr's a spy?'

'It's brilliant cover. Lawrence of Arabia did it. Imagine, old men doddering about Europe, designing graves and looking at body counts and surveying damage and oh bloody hell, Mr Harper must have told them. He told the man at the Museum what he'd found. And then he died.'

'Does the Museum know about the demons?' The monstrosity of this, an alchemy textbook disguised as a volume of poems. An alien beast disguised as a white dog.

'Prideaux knew an awful lot about it. Is he one of them?'

'Dr Carr doesn't trust him,' Rom said. 'That has to be a good thing.'

'Nobody trusts him,' Alec said, 'it doesn't count for much.'

'Does it matter?' The book in her purse seemed better than an ingot of gold. 'We've got the source itself.'

She'd had late nights pressing out the last of an essay. She knew how to handle this one. As soon as she and Alec were home Rom kicked off her shoes and spread everything on the table, with tea, and the lamps blazing, and all her borrowed books of magical history lying open.

The title page of *The Nest* held a hymnbook flavour: heart, palm leaves, piercing arrow. The contents were far from holy—romantic poems tangled in quaint metre and pastoral airs, shepherdesses and wild satyrs.

But the illustrations were wonderfully strange. The delicate etchings carried symbolism far older than the Restoration verse.

Ditto swept in at dusk, desperate for news. 'Perfectly gorgeous.' She looked through Rom's magnifying glass. 'Everyone got what they wanted, then.'

'More or less.' Which is to say nobody got what they wanted and the book wasn't theirs, but that's how a compromise works. Rom had a stack of tracing paper and Alec was making copies of the decorative borders. 'Dr Lloyd will want to see. And it's practical conservation. If the primary source is damaged we still have a facsimile.'

'You museum men make good spies,' Ditto said. She was too tired to speak after a day on her feet and when she went to bed, Rom dimmed the lamps and continued with Alec.

She laboured over the musty pages long after midnight. Sometimes she felt things falling into place as she recognised symbols of serpents and doves, the crescent moon and the firebird.

And sometimes she felt as though she'd lose herself in twining branches. Jasper had collected hundreds of books; maybe this one held nothing. Pen thought it was important. But Pen hadn't even known these things were demons. The truth was still obscured, arcane.

Somebody knows, Rom thought, but it clearly isn't me.

It was dawn when Alec fell asleep on the wicker chair, and she flopped onto the sofa. Some of her optimism guttered with the smoking lamp. She didn't know what she'd been expecting—something clear, definitive. Instructions, preferably. But this could have been any book in the world if it wasn't for these illustrations.

All week, each night, she worked on *The Nest of Amoury*. At the College she sat tensely through her lectures, resenting the minutes spent on early Hittites. Ditto had rehearsals every day and dragged home on swollen feet. She listened with good humour as Rom ran through the latest detail she'd discovered or some odd reference. Alec ducked in and out, camping in his hotel or their sitting room; Cartwright had given him leave to investigate Harper, and he was digging through records. Mr Mitchell was visiting his sister in

Brighton but he sent inquisitive telegrams.

The four alchemical Humours seemed a good starting point, Rom thought. Sanguine might mean demonic blood, with Choleric for sulphur; Pen was setting up her laboratory to begin testing things.

She was looking for something else, though, among the knotwork borders. The only books she'd found on summoning demons had long instructions on how to make them appear and obey. It took magic rings and scattered salt, libations to the planets. No mention of a collar, and all those demons seemed to be famous ones, kings or dukes. Coronets, she guessed.

She could only return to the book.

She soon knew each page by heart. But did sulphur mean the chemical element or the spirit of fire? An ingredient? A method of heating? Was the crescent moon beside it an indicator of time? A moon could mean common silver. But here with sulphur it could be a symbol of living silver, a sacred marriage that might mean mercury sulfide or simply a philosophical commentary on consciousness.

Shapes and patterns reappeared. Four elements. Four seasons. Anything could be anything, a maze of metaphor. Some of it was clearly impossible, like the alkahest Jasper mentioned, a perfect dissolving agent which couldn't exist or else it would eat through its storage jar.

Rom felt the truth could be assembled, though. A dig progresses in layers; careful brushing, gridding her finds on paper. Jasper's shadow lay over the path. At odd hours of the night she nearly sensed the confusion pulling together.

'Have you got the secret to eternal life yet?' Ditto leaned in to kiss her cheek. 'That looks worse than Shakespeare.'

Rom sighed and pushed the book away. 'English spelling wasn't standardised for centuries. No wonder everyone spoke Latin for the important things.'

'Rare birds,' Ditto said.

Rom followed the pointing finger. 'Where?'

It was the title of a poem. Rom scanned the illustration, a hooded traveller beneath a sky full of wings. The scrolls held a faded litany: *The Waking Night, The Burning White, The Sleeping Gold, The Darkest Bright*. Four birds in the corners; a crow and a dove. A long-legged crane. And one, spread-winged, that might have been a phoenix.

'It must be the stages of alchemical purification,' Rom said. 'The raven is nigredo, unpurified metal. Then it's heated and refined; albedo the dove, citrinitas and rubedo. The idea is to end up with gold. Or it's a sort of mental pilgrimage, and you end up wise. Don't know if it ever worked.'

'The poem's talking about owls and albatrosses.' Ditto lost interest. 'Not the same as the picture. Not rare, either.'

'Albatrosses are uncommon, at least,' Rom said. 'My father said so.' He'd known all the funny ways of birds. He kept a little notebook and wrote down when he saw them.

She went and brushed her teeth, rubbing the ache in her neck. And buried her face in her pillow. It's bad luck to kill an albatross. They mate for life, all those birds in the poem; the survivor would be left adrift. Did they seek each other across the lonely sky? You could search forever. Or you could find another right away. Like Mother. What's replaceable?

The drawings were puzzles; they might have a key one day. But the poems were indecipherable: only love.

Kingsley stood at the bottom step of the College.

'You. Did you follow me?'

'Of course.' He caught up with Rom as she pushed down the street towards the station. 'I wanted to talk to you. I didn't lie, you know.'

'You didn't tell us who you were, either.'

'I really am looking for Desir. I have a plan, but I can't do it on my own.'

'Go and ask your master for help.'

'He's not.' Kingsley sounded pained. 'I work with a lot of people. I'm hunting. It's what Arbiters do. And if they're all gone, it becomes my job.'

'He was petting your head.'

Kingsley shoved his hands in his pockets. 'He does that to everyone.'

'Why do you want Desir?'

'I don't, I wish he wasn't here. The Golden has the gift of vision. Sometimes he can see straight as an arrow, and the others will come to him, they'll want to know what he's seen.'

'Which others?'

'Crow thinks he might be working with another Coronet. She's been at all his shows. Have you heard of Mrs Ash?'

Rom didn't break her stride, but her expression was probably answer enough.

'By the time everyone realises what they are,' Kingsley said, 'it will be too late.'

'I want to see him do real magic.' Mrs Volkov must know more practical alchemy than Jasper ever did. And maybe seeing them would make sense of the things she'd been reading: the Phoenix, living fire. The voice of the gods.

'I can get you a ticket and you can walk right in.'

'Ever so kind, you want bait for your trap.'

'They took your friend.'

'Ditto's friend.' But she was calculating. It might be useful to have Kingsley's help as long as they didn't discuss anything important in front of him. 'It won't be safe if they find out why we're there. How do you fight a Coronet?'

'You can protect yourself, lots of ways,' Kingsley said. 'I'll come with you. Will you help?'

'You want Desir more than we do, you should be paying us.'

'You want to know about demons. Showing interest is dangerous, it gives us something to work with.'

She was thinking of Jasper's faerytales, the blood-drinkers of Bulgaria, and something slid into place. 'You're not allowed to enter if you're not invited. You need to go with somebody human.'

His ruddy brows gathered. 'Are you coming or not?'

'I will,' she said. 'And Alec.' An insider eye at the Waldorf would get his attention. 'We'll be your cover. But I want to talk to Mrs Volkov.'

'Deal,' he said.

They shook on the street corner.

THE

NEST OF AMOURY,

being a *book* of *verſes*

treating on themes

paſtoral, romantick, & philoſophickal

by

APOLLINE de FLORENT;

in a *New & Modern* Tranſlation from the *French* by

VICTOR ARGINTIU

with Sundry *curiouſly* graven

COPPER PLATE ILLUSTRATIONS

of a *Detailed* kind.

"If thou but ſetteſt foot on this path, thou ſhalt ſee it everywhere." *Hermes Triſmeg.*

LONDON:

Printed at *St Bride's Lane* by *J. Cobbin* for V. ARGINTIU.   1721

14

'This is the high life,' Alec said. 'Do you want another drink?'

'It's eleven in the morning. We're supposed to be focused.'

'I'm paying a glorious amount of attention to this martini.' Alec was flushed but it might have been excitement. The Waldorf's smoking lounge was crowded and he craned his neck. 'Half these cads are probably Peerage. I do believe that's a Rothschild.'

Rom carried half a glass of champagne for camouflage. She'd pulled out her best dress for the occasion—a navy chiffon thing—and Ditto had clucked at the ankle length, outdated already: *You can't.*

Can and will. She'd taken up the hem and wore one of Ditto's long necklaces, and looked fairly presentable and nothing like herself. And they weren't themselves tonight, if anyone asked—Alec was a columnist from a Spiritualist magazine, documenting the wonders of Madame Volkov's seances.

'Not that she's given one,' Alec said. 'Shoddy dodger.'

Madame Volkov had been holding court for an hour, a dry little woman draped in jet beads and surrounded by Votary maidens in vaguely Doric tunics. There was nothing remarkable about her theatrical accent, or her circling of the room with a brazier of incense while the aproned waiters hovered by the doors, exchanging glances over the drinks trays.

But there was a growing excitement among the tuxedos and jewelled gowns, the reporters outside and the new arrivals.

'Desir's about to come down for a pre-show introduction,' Kingsley said behind them; he'd been patrolling from the upper floors to the kitchens. He'd walked in easily with them at the grand street doors, through the gleaming foyer; Kingsley took Rom's arm as they crossed the threshold of the lounge, and nobody had looked twice at him.

'It's that easy?' she'd asked, as they handed over their coats.

He'd downed a glass of champagne and set the empty on the tray. 'Don't invite a demon unless you're certain you want them.'

She'd expected him to turn up in a dinner suit, but he wore his usual corduroy trousers with a tidy dark jacket. Quite at home, like somebody's attendant chauffeur.

'This is the part when you give us weapons,' she said. 'Isn't that appropriate for a spy mission?'

'This is recon, we're not attacking anyone.'

Rom narrowed her eyes. 'You said there were lots of ways to fight off chasma.'

'I did. There are. I never promised to tell you any of them.'

She swore, ignoring the glare from a frizzled man beside her.

Alec put down his drink. 'You bally thing, I said we shouldn't trust you.'

'We didn't.' Rom hefted her purse. 'I brought Jasper's book with me. Partly to show Madame Volkov, mostly so Prideaux can't steal it back and make us pay for losing it.'

Kingsley's wide mouth tipped into a smile. 'Wise,' he said. 'Look, no chasma can touch you without breaking Law. But there's something rum going on. I know Desir's in the building, I can scent him. The way he showed up on Claker's map—he's incarnate. Volkov made him a body when she summoned him, it's not just some poor sap under possession. He's going to be powerful.'

Alec sipped. 'Not dangerous, though?'

'Into the Palm Court, please,' one of the Votaries said in a charming voice, and Rom and Alec followed with the crowd.

Rom had seen it in newspapers, pictures of the hotel's tango parties, busy socialites drinking tea, but she hadn't expected the fluid quality of the light in here. Green walls and white marble, glass above. Potted trees and gilded balustrades. The grand glass doors had been hung with banners, coiled snakes and palm leaves.

Alec whistled. 'They've turned it into a bloody swimming pool.'

Down the marble steps, where the courtyard should be packed with tables, the pale stone lapped with water.

'Everyone will take their places in the Golden Pool.'

'No bathing suit?' Rom stood on her tiptoes to see. 'I'm not undressing in front of a load of tipsy wankers.'

The Votary waved her hand towards a pavilion tent. 'We have robes,' she said, in her maddening soft voice.

They were white linen things, and a wreath made of glossy leaves, and all the women shuffled into the pavilions, tugging off their shoes and stockings.

'At least they've got clothes,' somebody said. A nervous whispering laugh. 'I thought they were going to make us bathe naked like the ancient Greeks.'

Rom snorted as she pulled the gown over her head. A river's worth of Spartans would be easier. Modern people don't know how to be naked.

Alec had been rigged out in robes too when she returned, a white tunic and a bit of drapery over his shoulder. His laurel wreath was pulled low over his forehead.

'You look nice and classical.'

'Shut it.' He rubbed his ankle against his bare calf. 'This is the biggest load of rot.'

Rom braced as they descended the steps, but the water temperature was neutral. How? Calf-deep on marble. A breeze moved within the glass room, spiced air stirring the palms.

Alec sniffed too. 'Cinnamon?'

There was something keenly wonderful in the room. One of the Votaries played a harp, brushing the strings with her hands, and the hum ran through their lowered voices. Mrs Volkov swept to the stairs and in this opulent chamber even her vaudeville manner seemed mysterious.

'Thank you, my friends, for joining us this morning.' She bowed and her velvet robe swayed. 'Perhaps you are wondering why we are gathered so early in the day.'

A man bellowed on the left. 'Missing the damn cricket for this.' His wife hushed him.

'She's here,' one of the Votaries said, her voice clear and glad.

Rom turned. They all did.

Mrs Ash's cream silk gown was nearly sheer, her heavy necklace strung with red coral. Her scarlet belt cinched in a curved knot beneath her breasts and Rom felt the shape of it burn her, something forgotten or waiting to be known. But the other thing she wore was worse: a living python twined over one shoulder and nestling her throat.

'We are honoured to welcome you,' Mrs Ash said. Low warm voice. 'Whether you believe or not.' Her delicious eyes enclosed them. 'Whether you belong or not. The seekers of truth have not always gathered in the shadows. Why must things be hidden in the night? That is for dream and for sorrow.'

She spread her hands, and her pale gown shimmered in wide folds. Through the silk shone her gilded nipples. 'Belief asks for a leap of faith, a fool's step. But there's no brink of doubt here. We only invite you to turn your faces to the light. There's nothing to believe. But there is everything to see.'

'Her belt,' Rom said quietly, 'I've seen that symbol.'

'Everything's a bloody symbol,' Alec said, but he was wrong. Everything was itself, so full of thingness Rom could nearly hear it.

The light moved first. Her vision speckled with a shoal of gilt, shifting fish through the water and air. Murmurs, splashing as people stepped aside or reached out.

Then sound. It hummed in Rom's hands and throbbed in her teeth and she tried not to clench them. A second note, and more just below hearing, lapping through her. In the water—filling the walls, vibration edging into the windowpanes and the atrium ceiling.

Nobody announced him, but everyone knew Desir had entered. They turned and found him in their centre, silent in the middle of the pool. His dark hair was dusted with gold and wreathed in laurel. Eyes rimmed in paint, warm basalt black. A sweep of linen over bared shoulders. His fingernails gleamed.

'Good lord,' somebody said behind her, and it felt like a prayer.

Something tugged Rom's feet. She shuddered, afraid to look, but it was the pull of water as Desir walked toward the steps. The pool sank and rose again, deep unsettled waves in unison. Curved and dipping backs of crystalline fish. Lazy tails, fins heaving in his wake.

He took his place beside Mrs Ash at the top of the stairs as the waters settled.

'Welcome,' Desir said. His voice rang with clarity from the corners of the room. 'You came today to listen. That is all I shall ever ask of you. Perhaps you wanted singing, and you shall have it—and perhaps you like to see the golden rain, the dancing, the manifestation of all joys. You shall have this too. But first, you will listen.'

He turned, surveying the room. 'There are some points about the year that serve to show us where we stand. Your earth is a glorious clockwork and its machinations are pleasing. And a point approaches soon whose signal light will show all standing shadows. The gates of Heaven have been closed, but this is the age of change.'

Sound reached Rom's bones without impediment. It left flashings on the floor, the water, the harp in the corner. The champagne glasses. Resonance, and she breathed deep. Light splintered from the demon's skin.

'There is monstrous injustice in the heavens,' Desir said, 'and upon the earth, and through the facets of the Circum. In some years, very soon, such a battle will come upon us as cannot be yielded. I do not seek to persuade you. This is no more than declaring a movement of the weather. Truth makes no claim upon you. Truth merely is, with the radiance of light and the strength of an anchor.'

Rom's chest felt tight. And loose, unravelled, and she swayed. Idiotic to be so affected. She didn't even believe. Belief means clawing at things unseen but this was in the air, it was everything. And the only madness is denial, if the truth strikes you like a lance, and everything you are says yes.

'When the press of war descends, I hope you will stand at my side,' Desir said. 'There is only one injustice, as there is only one crime: to close one's mind against the world; to think oneself isolated. Have just a little patience, now. Keep watch and know yourselves to be witnesses to the dawn. Truth will cut open the midnight of the world, and we will find a new freedom.'

Alec's face was tight. One of the women began to sob, an ugly sound.

'Some may choose to dedicate themselves to the Golden. You are welcome to join the Votaries. Some of you may choose to continue onwards, finding the light in your own lives: may health and truth follow your footsteps. The choice is always yours.'

Wind moved around Rom's limbs, touching her hair, cool and keen. The sobbing woman clung to a Votary's arm. 'You have to take me. It's everything I ever wanted. Please—'

'The Law will burn in revelation,' Desir said. 'The sky will break. We will sing ourselves the darkest bright.'

He turned away. A ripple moved through the crowd and another man splashed to his knees as if the sound had been the only thing holding him.

The Votaries were passing towels around and Rom rubbed down her shivering legs. There was a different sort of murmur when they all returned to the lush stuffy lounge. The waiting canapes felt unimportant. Some things are more real than reality.

The Darkest Bright. The opposite of a star, she thought. Or a star turned inside out, a poisonous constellation. A falling sky-full.

Life in death,

    end, beginning,

        and—

'Egg sandwiches,' Alec said. 'You'd think they'd at least give us salmon.'

'He's the Golden,' Rom said. Clarity passed but she was sure of this. 'Dr Lloyd is looking for demon blood to make panax, but what if it's only Coronets who've got the right sort?'

Alec dabbed his chin with a napkin. 'You believe Desir?'

'I don't even know what he's trying to tell us.'

'Truth isn't a fact,' Alec said. 'It lives. Everything afterwards is translation.'

'Bullshit, Oz. That's not how you talk.'

'Probably because I can never think of the words.' He frowned over his sandwich. 'If that was magic—'

'It's magic.'

'But if this was always—if everyone knew. Couldn't it be wonderful?'

'Don't tell me you want to join the Votaries.'

'Hang that.' But he was watching Evelyn Ash. She shimmered in a crowd of admirers, the least invisible person Rom had ever seen. In the lights and swinging music she was the hot atomic heart.

Madame Volkov and her assistants moved amongst the crowd, enquiring quietly, ushering a few people back through the doors. Going upstairs, the whisper seemed to be, and Alec smiled uneasily. 'Is it soul-eating or an orgy?'

'Go and find out.' Rom rubbed the condensation on her glass. 'This is how every cult works, same as the Mithraics. Or the Eleusinian

Mysteries. A charismatic priest, and everyone happy or scared and wanting to believe—'

'I could laugh easier if I didn't know how they felt.'

People used to build temples for them, Kingsley said. But things are different now. A hundred years ago no hotel had telephones in every room. And now? A car outside: to an airport, train to Russia or steamer to Egypt, the whole world big as a dream and small enough to put in your pocket. The impossible happens every day. Magic might stand a chance.

'There you are,' Kingsley said, as though he could possibly have lost them. 'Come along, you've got your five minutes.'

Alec emptied his drink.

Desir had returned, sharply-cut in a black tuxedo. He loomed, a mountain coming into focus, and beside him Madame Volkov looked frail as a wooden doll.

'Madame,' Kingsley said. 'Mr Desir—'

'This is a surprise.' The Phoenix didn't look surprised. 'I don't believe we gave you an invitation.' His voice was low and resonant and distinctly French, a shock; Rom hadn't even noticed when he spoke in the other room.

'I'm here in Quinn's name,' Kingsley said. 'This is Miss Godden. She's requested a breath of your time.'

Madame Volkov's mouth thinned. 'Gorgeous to meet you. Would you like to know your fortune?'

'No,' Kingsley said. 'Miss Godden is the white dog's owner.'

Desir's face was fixed like rock. 'Is it true—'

'She doesn't know,' Kingsley said tiredly, 'none of us do. The maker is gone.'

'That's what I want to ask about,' Rom said, and dug out The Nest.

At Desir's nod, Madame Volkov left them silently.

Desir took the book in careful hands.

'Does it say how to break the collar?' Alec asked as Desir leafed through it.

'It reveals many things,' Desir said, 'none of which should be printed on paper and sitting on a human's bookshelf.'

Across the room Mrs Ash turned. She smiled at whoever she'd been talking to and sauntered over to lay one hand on Desir's arm. 'A charming convocation, and you didn't tell me?'

'We're discussing the collar,' Desir said.

Mrs Ash sighed at Rom. 'You must make allowances for my brother. He is entirely graceless when he talks shop.' Her eyes gleamed. 'That collar can bind anything, beast or bird, or the very Kings of Hell. It's made of bittergold.'

'Conjecture,' Desir said, 'you have no proof of that.' But his face shadowed.

'Can it be broken?' Rom asked. 'Is anything strong enough?'

'A bind like this has no relation to potency,' Desir said. 'Nor skill. It's the mutilation of the magical arts. It's like spearing a falcon and stitching its wings to a grindstone; no thing in existence should be anchored thus. The maker had this book,' he said to Mrs Ash.

She opened the front cover. Closed it again. Handed it back to Rom, and the way she and Desir looked at each other was a disturbance at once wonderful and troubling. You could shout and they wouldn't hear. They looked nothing alike. They were undoubtedly siblings.

Mrs Ash turned back to Rom. 'Séraphin will speak with you about this. Today.'

Rom's heart was hard and tight. 'Thank you.'

'This is not a kindness,' Desir said. 'The collar is not supposed to exist. Morax will kill you for it.'

Rom heard Alec's little sound. 'Are we in danger? Somebody attacked us here in London, months ago. A wolf-thing.'

'He was just a scrounging war-dog,' Kingsley said.

'And the snake?'

Mrs Ash blinked her liquid eyes. 'I only wanted to look around. It wouldn't have hurt you.' She turned to leave, her movement a slink of pale silk, and Rom itched to kick her square in her insolent spine.

But Alec said, 'Did you mean all that? About living with magic in the open.'

'Do I look as though I lie?' Desir asked.

'No, sir,' Alec said. Stumbling. 'I just wondered what would happen if the existence of the chasma came out. It would be chaos.'

'Chaos is finite,' Desir said. 'Something always resolves itself.'

Mrs Ash nodded her head. 'Give my regards to old man Crow.'

She seemed to be leaving the hotel, sweeping into the foyer to collect her coat, and a rush of guests followed her. Probably taking advantage of the press cameras outside to get written up in a society column tomorrow. 'They're not going to close the bar, surely,' a Baronet said, but the waiters had settled in for a long afternoon; the main performance wasn't for an hour or so. Madame Volkov had vanished with the Votaries and her volunteering guests, and Desir was retiring upstairs behind them.

'Probably an orgy after all,' Alec said. 'I wonder how much Cartwright would have paid for pictures.'

Rom had a sandwich and was munching fiercely. 'Mrs Ash sent a snake to my house.'

'He'd probably pay for the story alone. *Exclusive show dazzles London's finest—*'

'And *you* never said.' She glared around for Kingsley but he'd disappeared again; they found him chatting to one of the trim young waiters by the buffet table. 'Oi, it's not a holiday,' she said to him. 'We need to find Ditto and Pixie. Our home's not safe.'

'It is,' Kingsley said, 'technically. You can fetch them if you must.' He waved vaguely at the ceiling. 'I don't think that lot will be finished any time soon.'

'Not a chance,' Rom said, 'you'll slide out a back door the moment we look away. Alec will go.'

'I should be phoning Cartwright—'

'You're eating salmon toast and ogling. Take Kingsley's car.'

'Take a cab,' Kingsley said, 'you don't know London roads.'

'Probably a good idea,' she said as Alec left, 'he doesn't exactly respect a brake pad.' Although she wasn't sure if the car was even Kingsley's. 'Does your master know you're here?'

Kingsley swirled his champagne glass.

'You shouldn't have another, you'll be stone-drunk.'

'They don't work on me,' he said, 'I just like the bubbles. This is a nice party.' He rocked on his heels. 'I thought it might be a mess when Lady Tyet turned up, her plans aren't always in harmony with Desir's. But they were here together, not even fighting.'

Tyet. Rom could picture the shape now, Mrs Ash's red belt. She'd only ever seen it in stone, as an amulet or hieroglyph. 'What's her real name?'

'You can't ask that.'

'If I looked in the demonology books, would I find her?'

'Yes. Maybe. Look.' Kingsley scruffed at his neck. 'It's best not to get too close to Captains. They're good at gathering things around them, they can't help it. Don't ask too much about them.'

'I'm not afraid of Lady Tyet. I just need to know what I'm dealing with.' Maybe saying the name did it. Or maybe it was the flare of memory. 'In Crete there was a goddess of snakes.'

'Wonderful,' Kingsley said into his glass.

'Some scholars think she might have been a version of Ishtar, from the Mesopotamians. The Hebrews called her Astoret.'

'Oh?'

'Like the demon Ashtoroth.'

'Oh.'

'Ishtar's brother was the sun.'

Kingsley stood on tiptoe, eyeing the waiters. 'Bee's Knees would be nice. Do you think they make cocktails?'

The slice of light blinded her. The room shuddered. Somebody screamed and Kingsley shook himself muzzily. 'Lightning,' he said.

Rom laughed anxiously as everyone steadied themselves. 'I thought it was an anarchist chucking bombs.'

The chandelier trembled under the wall of soundless thunder. Kingsley made an odd high noise. 'Idiots, they're going to be caught.'

The waiters were ushering everybody to the foyer but no-one needed encouragement; the guests surged for the door. Kingsley's hands tensed in fists as though he wasn't sure what to hit. Or whether to run.

'Management will chuck them all out if they start a riot.'

'But if it's not on purpose—' Kingsley was trembling. 'Crux. Stay here.' He ran for the stairs.

Rom gulped down her sandwich and bolted after him.

15

It's difficult to sleep when can I hear the beasts in the garden and all down the stairs. The house feels full of their breath and the sounds of their obscene pleasures. But they cannot help their sin. They only have each other.
I cannot blame them, not when I have sins of my own.

JASPER TEAGUE, Journals, 4 Sept. 1912

Kingsley knew exactly where to head, hovering at the end of the corridor before plunging left. Doorways everywhere, plush stairs as they scrambled to the next floor. One of the doors flung open but it was just a man in a dressing gown, clammy with fright as he ran for the elevator.

Kingsley was walking soft and poised in his heavy leather boots, and he was listening.

The room door at the very end of the hallway was closed. He shouldered it open.

A haze of incense stung Rom's throat. The little room was crowded with people draped on sofas and cushions, limp in sleep or an opium fug. The smell of charred honey drifted down. She's seen some of these faces downstairs, men in tuxedos and women beaded like dolls, Votary maidens. A hanging brazier choked out smoke.

'Sod,' Kingsley said. 'Sod sod sod,' and he crouched beside one of the Votaries. Rom looked again at the lax faces, the moist half-open eyes. A blankness too hollow for sleep. 'Crux fuck it—' He stepped over cushions and Rom followed to the next room.

A lofty hotel suite hung with green velvet, the modern furniture slim and elegant. This seemed to be the sitting room, pale carpets and fresh lilies. It was cloyingly hot. A heavy smell of burning. The noise still rang in the room around them—keening, spinning, and Rom shook her head to clear it. One of the sofas smouldered and the flames licked towards the broken window.

The room wasn't empty. Two people sprawled face-down on the carpet, a heavy man and a Votary. The girl's limbs was blistered red.

Rom looked back at the window. She was going to be sick.

'Who are you?' Low, rough behind her.

She spun.

A young woman staggered wild-eyed, her sequinned dress wet with blood. 'What are you?'

'Visiting,' Rom said faintly, but the stranger seemed to be addressing Kingsley.

'Quinn knows I'm here,' he said. The woman snarled. She swept a jade-green vase from the table and swung it.

'Stop,' Kingsley said, 'stop that or I'll—' He grunted as it shattered against his shoulder. 'Bloody thing.' His eyes were hot and nasty. 'What are you, then?'

The woman's teeth were broken, bleeding. 'The Law.' She settled low as though she meant to leap on him, a strange stance in her heeled shoes. 'Your Law, in this world and any other.'

Kingsley raised his voice. 'Sir?'

The sound from the next room was a subterranean crackle. '*Ka-ma.*'

Kingsley growled as the woman clawed him. He threw her, reaching for the shards of porcelain, and pinned the thrashing creature down.

Rom knew she should close her eyes. She didn't.

Kingsley jerked the woman's head back and slashed.

When Rom looked again it seemed too quiet and Kingsley was wiping his hands on one of the curtains. The woman's body was face-down but the bright pool under her seeped to reach Rom's shoes.

She tried to focus on the window in front of her, the door they'd come through. The scorch marks on the walls. The bodies. The keening sound made it hard to think.

Kingsley leaned cautiously into the next room. 'I think they're all—' He jumped back as a thump of liquid fire hit the door-frame and slumped smoking down the wallpaper. 'It's only me, sir.'

That aching voice. '*Who?*'

'Captain's Tracker, 985. What happened?' Kingsley peered in again, and this time stepped in properly.

'*He. Sent. Law.*' Each word was hot, distinct.

Rom wrapped her arms around herself and followed. There was a man's body on the floor of the lavish fire-scarred bedroom, but Kingsley addressed the collapsing canopy of the bed. 'May I approach?'

No reply. True silence, and Rom hadn't understood the hum's penetrating volume until it released them.

A great thing nestled on the slung drapes, making the bed sway with its weight. A massive bird, the span of its wings pressed against the ceiling, crested and white. Not white—when it moved the room refracted, shimmering like the edge of your vision when you close a glass door.

The wings slid violet as they shifted, crimson and lemon-yellow, mirroring the colours in the room. Or carving up the light.

'Everyone's dead,' Kingsley said.

'I. Burned. Them.' The bird raised its wings in a stir of smoke, a fanning multitude of wings. 'They. Hurt. Me.' Jewelled black eyes. The curve of its neck reached serpentine. The Phoenix leaned down.

Kingsley swore and dragged Rom into the sitting room. Behind them the bedroom creaked and flared, and the light in the doorway flickered hotly blue.

She wasn't sure what had happened. Or what was about to. 'Someone should call the police.'

'You think that'll help things? We have to go, sir,' Kingsley called.

'Stupid dog.' Séraphin Desir's voice came sharply from the other room. 'I've been clipped.'

'The Carnifex came?'

'Not in himself. He took hold of the mortals and they turned on me.' Desir was at the bedroom doorway in his trousers and dress pumps, easing himself into a starched white shirt. Rom stared. She tried to find some shape of the creature she'd seen in the other room. Sourness rose in her throat as her thoughts caught up with her. 'These people were possessed?'

'Easier than making a body,' Kingsley said, 'if you want to step in and out fast.'

She felt limp. 'Out of where?'

'Here,' Kingsley said. 'Space. Aether. This lot would have been vulnerable, opening up their minds. Already preparing to—' He clicked his tongue. 'Advertising for Votaries, that was madness.'

'They offered themselves,' Desir said. 'I broke no Law.' His clean shirt was already staining across one shoulder with a strange metallic blue.

Kingsley sighed. 'You won't get far.'

'It will heal,' Desir said. But he allowed Kingsley to inspect his shoulder with quick hands. The edges of the wound were translucent. The slick indigo blood had a sheeny subtle fire, gold as luminescent stone. The flesh seemed to quiver and Rom looked away.

'Getting yourself in the papers...'

'Have you never tired of hiding, little dog?'

'I notice Lady Tyet left before things went nasty.'

Desir pulled his arm away and moved it, a delicate rotation as he tested his body, and the light spun again.

Rom felt dizzy. She gazed at the broken corpses on the carpet. They gave their last moments to a demon, and found themselves seized by another thing completely—helpless, attacking without compunction. 'Where's Madame Volkov?' She paced shallow breaths, trying not to smell smoke and flesh. 'I have to talk to an alchemist.'

'And I'll need a well-bound door tonight,' Desir said. 'Who are the adepts in London?'

'Let's get out of the building first,' Kingsley said.

'You have a car?' The Phoenix was tugging on a pair of white kidskin gloves. 'I need an air ticket. I'm returning to the Americas to find Dire-wolf.'

'Do you need medicine?' Rom asked. 'We know a doctor.'

'No.' Desir pointed to the sofa, his black velvet opera cape, and Kingsley wrapped it around the Coronet's shoulders.

'Mr Desir's the Golden,' Kingsley said, 'he doesn't need much to keep body and soul together.' His warm eyes were rather flat. 'He doesn't need to take mortals at all, in fact.'

Desir didn't appear to be listening as he started for the door. 'Bear and Tyet will be coming with me.'

'Bear hates cities. It's safer if you return.' Kingsley fell silent as they passed through the hushed outer room, hung in death and incense, and Rom wondered whose safety he meant.

He didn't speak in the hallway either, walking a few steps ahead of Desir. Two flushed men in suits hurried by, maybe managers on their way to investigate, and one stared at Desir as they passed.

'We'll go through the back,' Kingsley said. 'Once they find the bodies there'll be a mess.' He paused on the way, opening doors and peering into the press of people in the halls and lounges. There was a distant sound, a babble of panic. 'Is anyone left? How many Votaries did you have?'

'I wasn't counting,' Desir said.

Kingsley led them into a maze of service hallways, the seamy underside of the grand hotel. Housemaids darted and shouted. It sounded as though the place was being evacuated, or the guests were stampeding, and somebody had lost their diamonds and everyone wanted their car brought around.

Rom's feet felt numb and foolish in her heeled shoes. It would have been better to go with Alec, fresh air, instead of wheeling through the corridors like rats. The maids and bellboys glowered as they pushed towards the kitchens but nobody tried to stop them.

On the ground floor Kingsley hesitated. 'I can't sense her; too many people. Should I come back?'

'We find her first,' Desir said.

They turned back to the guest quarters of the hotel. Kingsley stopped where a set of gold-panelled door hung dragged off their hinges, and he peered in. He said something muffled.

The smell coiled in Rom's nose, bitter and foul and sweet. She stepped in behind him.

The empty ballroom blazed in cold electric light. The floor gleamed wet. Something heavy was hanging from the chandelier, red flesh slung raw from a chain like a butcher's slab. Amidst the torn meat stuck a few yellow bones, ribs and a stump of limb. Where the chain was hooked through the chandelier the flesh was intact, the skin still attached; a curl of fingers.

The room was silent except for a small wet dripping.

Rom drew back. 'Is that—' Madame Volkov. She wasn't even sure of that. 'Mortal?'

'It was.'

The floor was scattered with beads. Black jet winking. Rom pressed her hand over her mouth.

'Her name,' Desir said, his voice a resonance of bronze—'her name was Boleslava.'

Kingsley dragged shut the ballroom door. None of them spoke until they'd returned to the service halls. 'If Morax is after you, nobody will assist.'

Desir's teeth were pointed. 'I shall burn him too.'

They clattered into the kitchens and the shock of afternoon rush. A cook stood shouting from a chair but apparently the panic hadn't spread this far. Rows of ranked benches, steam and the great clash of pans and Rom couldn't hear anything, although Kingsley's lips were moving. She followed the rough tweed of his jacket as they pushed through to the exit and the sudden cool air.

The arse-end of the Waldorf Hotel was like every other London terrace, sunken steps up to a narrow street. Stained brick, square windows, the same thing opposite. Cars everywhere, crowds dawdling from the theatres either side, and hotel staff smoking on their break. Rom shivered.

Nobody seemed to notice them. Maybe it was one of the few corners of the city where nobody would look twice at Rom's torn gown or the blood on Kingsley's trousers, or Desir in his top hat and cape.

Kingsley was speaking. 'If you can just get to a way-station—'

'Vallick has one,' Desir said.

'Burned out in the Popish riots. You've been gone a while.'

'Is Junius still in the East?'

'Allied with the Cat's people and won't see you.' Kingsley arched to check the crowd.

Rom didn't feel sick any longer. Fear is angry if you hold it right. 'That. In there. Is that going to happen to us?'

Kingsley didn't look at her as they started down the street. 'It's a quarter hour each way to your house. If your brother doesn't get here soon—'

'Are they in danger? Somebody could kill them. Or possess them—'

'Morax can't possess them,' Desir said, 'unless they permit it. And we will be safe until nightfall.'

'That's only a few hours,' Rom said.

'It's midsummer.' Desir smiled, a glorious thing. 'We stand on the edge of the solstice. A long day, and all of it mine.'

'They're here,' Kingsley said, and Rom was about to ask who when she heard the dog's bark. She saw Alec's hair. And Ditto's glittering hat on the street corner, and some of the ache in her stomach unknotted.

'Bloody hotel's on fire,' Alec said. 'What in heavens happened?'

Ditto saluted like a sailor. 'You've all been busy.' She eyed Desir, drawing herself upright. 'I've heard of you.'

Rom hugged her. 'This is going to be dangerous.' Her voice was muffled in Ditto's shoulder. 'Are you alright?'

'Don't be silly, I brought Pixie.' She pushed the lead into Rom's hand and the creature reached to nose at Rom's hands. Rom let her, gently, smoothing Pixie's head.

'We stopped on the way back.' Ditto nodded toward Mr Mitchell, who shrugged apologetically.

'Alec said there might be trouble,' he said. 'You found the people who set the snake on you?'

'Yes,' Rom said. But that problem seemed a thousand years ago. She didn't know where to begin.

'Truth gets people killed,' Mr Mitchell said. 'Tell me what I need to know.'

Kingsley pointed. 'This is Mr Desir.' The Phoenix inclined his head, eyelids slick with gold dust. 'There are some people who want to catch him.'

'People?'

'You'd call them monsters.'

'I see.'

'So we're moving him somewhere safer.'

'I see.'

'Any questions?'

'None.'

Kingsley shook his hand. 'I can work with soldiers,' he said. They were pushing deep into the crowded theatre quarter, the grubby gleam of Drury Lane, and Desir strolled as though he hadn't a care. Perhaps he didn't. He was the most dangerous thing on these streets.

Mr Mitchell glanced around. Theatre, café, picture theatre. 'Are we going far?'

'Less than half a mile.'

Ditto slid her arm through Rom's. 'You're getting rescued after all. Aren't you simply ecstatic?'

'Delirious.' Rom's eyes ached. But it wouldn't hurt to have Mr Mitchell along. He dismantled sea-mines for a job. His hands would be steady.

'Did somebody really die?' Alec asked.

Rom didn't want to explain. It felt hot and stoppered stiff inside. She told enough for Ditto to squeeze her hand, and Rom didn't let go of it. Pixie flanked her other side and they were safe here. The rest could wait.

Kingsley led them down Drury Lane until the theatres became shabbier and there were crowded taverns everywhere, and then they turned right. The long pillared facade of the Freemasons Hall lined the bend of Great Queen Street.

Desir stopped. 'What's this?'

Kingsley cleared his throat. And again. 'We're going to see the Magician.'

'If he knows I'm here—'

'Everyone's read the papers,' Kingsley said, 'you weren't exactly subtle. You want something secure? It's the best-tied house this side of the Wall. If he agrees to take you under his roof we'll have time.'

'That's hardly encouraging,' Alec said.

'We don't have a choice,' Rom said, but it wasn't true. There's always a choice. She could go home if she wanted to.

'Don't they know we're coming?' Mr Mitchell stood as tense as Kingsley. 'Should we ring ahead?'

'Unwise,' Desir said. 'We don't want him running away.'

The stationer's window jostled with customers, just as Rom recalled it. She trouped with the others into the shop. Kingsley ignored the staff and the crowded counter, and they paid no attention either, to six people and a dog; one of the clerks nodded briefly.

A door directly ahead seemed to lead to an upper store-room. Ditto sniffed as Kingsley unlocked it. 'Come here often?'

Kingsley ignored her. Echoing stairs, a square flight boxed back on itself. They stopped at the top in a whitewashed portico fitted with an incongruously fresh black telephone. A heavy linen curtain hung opposite. The air blistered with an engine-room smell, dry and hot.

'You lot stay here,' said Kingsley, and ducked through the portiere curtain.

'We should have rung ahead,' Alec said, 'this isn't right.'

'Mr Kingsley seems to know what he's doing,' Mitchell said, but he was listening at the portiere and stepped back just before it opened.

'Come in and wait,' Kingsley said.

Rom stepped in with Pixie bumping at her knee.

This was certainly a storage area. A big room; shelves and cabinets were loaded with books and crammed again with jars and boxes, enough pottery to dazzle Dr Carr. Paperwork lay everywhere, piled on the floor. But it gave the unsettled sense of standing in some back entry to a country-house; maybe because of the walls, shabby Brunswick green, and the pale coir matting—the sort of place you hang umbrellas.

Stone slabs and broken limbs of statues leaned in corners, shoved on top of the shelves, gesturing empty hands.

The only island of organisation was a slim central desk lit by windows to the street. A fire roared on the left beside an iron day-bed hung with stripes. On the right, a staircase wound upstairs above a closed door.

Two leather armchairs flanked the fire. A grey suit jacket hung on the desk chair.

And now Rom saw as though with a different sense the rumpled day-bed, the half glass of water, the whole place so lived-in she didn't want to touch a thing.

Desir slung his cape over one of the leather armchairs. Pixie slunk to the fireside with her muzzle directed to the stairs.

Alec sat in the other chair, ignoring Kingsley's pointed look, and cupped his ear tenderly. 'Somebody's blowing a dog-whistle.'

Kingsley glanced over as Rom pressed one hand to her pulsing temple.

'I'm sorry,' he said, 'the house is afflicted if it holds another Coronet.'

Alec stood abruptly. Rom turned.

'Hullo, children,' said Mr Prideaux.

16

Avery's assistance has been useful. But I cannot trust him any more than I trust the tide. He undoes my work as I sleep, I am sure of it. He burns my papers. He twists my words.

I must do something about him.

JASPER TEAGUE, Journals, 6th Dec. 1911

The Magician stood above them on the staircase landing. He wore no jacket, only his grey waistcoat over a white-striped shirt, and a tie like amethyst smoke.

'I ought to say I'm pleased to see you. But I'm not.' He came down slowly, his cane tucked behind his back, a creak on the wooden stairs. He stopped in the middle of the room.

'May I approach?' Kingsley asked.

'No.'

Kingsley straightened. 'Every traveller's got the right to claim shelter at a way-station. It's only for the night—'

'You,' Prideaux said, 'you've earned a rating you won't forget.' He looked at each of them. 'Godden and Co? I am acquainted with you. Miss Hamilton; the white dog.' He turned to Mr Mitchell. 'You must be the hired gun.'

Mr Mitchell moved restlessly. 'And who are you?'

'Dr Cranach Prideaux.' He didn't hold out his hand.

'That suits well.' The windows shuddered as Desir spoke. 'Prie-dieu. Or is it *pré d'eaux*? Fine choice.'

Too many names. What others did he hide? Like knives, titles, curses.

'I should be getting along to work,' Kingsley said.

'Nobody's going anywhere,' Prideaux said with extravagant good humour, 'until I find out why there's a Coronet bleeding on my rug.'

After a day of horrors Rom felt only fury. 'Somebody killed Mr Desir's Acatour.'

'Nasty, I'm sure. I hope you weren't expecting any dinner. There's hot water in the boiler and a room beneath the eaves and that's about the limit of my hospitality.'

'It's enough,' Mr Mitchell said. He seemed to be losing patience. 'Kingsley said it would be alright.'

'Kingsley is not the master of this house.' The room was very quiet. Prideaux turned on his heel to Desir and Rom's head spun as though she'd tilted upside down. 'What brings the lord of noonday to the western isles?'

Mr Mitchell almost staggered. It wasn't her ears at all: the room. Twin points of gravity.

'I came over to visit Bear,' said Desir.

Prideaux cracked his knuckles. 'How thrilling.'

'But now I hear about this bittergold, this thoroughly bad piece of alchemy. Have you seen?'

'It wasn't me.'

'I have not accused you yet.' Desir looked around at the worn coir matting. 'This is your Nest? It's humbler than you ever were.'

Prideaux's smile was dazzling. 'Even a rose has roots in cow-shit.'

Desir said something, quick and dry, a sound Rom didn't know.

Prideaux spread his hands with expansive modesty. 'It's a living.'

Desir switched to English. 'You behave like one of them.'

'Do I not look well?'

'No,' said Desir. 'You look old.' He tipped his head, hair glittering with gold in the afternoon light. 'Older than I, even. You have not been eating. What are you hiding from?'

Prideaux seemed to hover tensely on his tiptoes, the cane clasped behind him. 'London has been the world's largest city for a century. Seven million people, and I'm in the heart of it. Do you know where we are? Within the mile I have West End theatres and Holburn law courts. Fleet Street and Piccadilly Circus. Where else would I be?'

'I asked Mr Kingsley to find me an adept,' Desir said. 'I didn't think to find you starving yourself in silence, no more than one of Quinn's roadlings.'

'I am invisible.' Prideaux's voice ground like grit after Desir's. 'I'm not in the mood for travels.'

'I don't like this humour on you,' Desir said. 'You'd do well to shake it off. Eat something. Sleep. Go for a long walk. I'm returning to the Americas with Bear. Do you know what's coming?'

'The end of your homily?'

Desir stood. 'Hold your tongue, for once in your hollow life.' He was nothing near Prideaux's height but he was powerfully built. 'You are an unfortunate interval in a difficult day and I have nothing to say to one who refuses to hear. But you know how the stars align. Things are moving, *êkhos*. Things make a shape sometimes.' Desir picked up his cape and smoothed it over his arm. 'I don't need supper. Good evening.' He went upstairs.

Prideaux turned to watch, his body a tight curve of inquisition. Nobody spoke.

A door closed distantly.

'Alright.' Prideaux shivered like a cat coming in from the rain. 'Approach.'

Kingsley's shoulders softened. 'It was a bloody wreckage, sir, Morax seized his mortals.'

Prideaux sank into the chair behind his desk. 'Did any of them see Pixie?'

'No, Rom said, 'Alec picked her up while I was talking to Mrs Ash.'

'So you've met the Children of the Golden Throne.' Prideaux tipped the chair back on two legs. 'Aren't they exquisite? If Desir's got a plan, there'll be a proper bit of fuckery. Quinn's People will guard every field and road if you lot can get him to the coast and out of the damn country.'

'I thought crowfolk weren't going to help,' Ditto said.

'They'd do it to keep reins on Séraphin. And Quinn owes me a favour. Everyone owes me a favour, but he's a genuinely useful debtor to have. Also there's the nepotism.'

'You're his—'

'His well-beloved nephew.'

'Have he and Desir always been enemies?' Rom asked.

'What a silly question,' Prideaux said, 'we can't afford enemies any more than we can afford friends. Quinn and Desire are simply between alliances. Tyet worries me infinitely more; she's got her eye on the bittergold.'

Rom had one good question. 'How do we destroy the collar?'

'You don't,' Prideaux said. 'You go home.'

'Do we need a different book? What else would Jasper have used?'

'Your grandfather had exactly the resources you've got, except he happened to be clever. Stop nosing about. There won't be a problem, as long as you remember not to have seen what you've seen.'

'But if this Morax finds out—'

'That's fallacious panicking. Do you not think I'm fascinated? I can't touch the collar. None of us can. But they've got you running scared with a little bit of rhetoric: break the collar and risk hell knows what, or keep the collar and risk Morax. It's called a chiasmus, Godden. You think you have to choose, but there's always another way.'

'Which way?'

'I haven't finished thinking yet.'

'How are we meant get Mr Desir to safety?' Mr Mitchell said. 'Do you have a plan for that either?'

'True,' Alec said, 'we can't just pack him on a train. He's going to get attention.'

'What's more dangerous,' Rom said, 'Morax, or a train station?'

'To us or Desir?' Ditto asked.

'There's a sea-demon down Wapping way,' Kingsley said. 'He thinks Mr Fornello might be in local waters.'

Prideaux set his chair down and laced his fingers over his folded knee with an expression of didactic patience Rom was already labelling *teacherly*. 'Even Morax would baulk at baiting an Ancient.'

'It'll take some negotiating, sir. He'll want to talk to you.'

'This place might as well be open if I'm not here to hold it,' Prideaux said. 'But you can tell Fornello we'd be willing to drop that little debt of his.'

'Me?' Kingsley looked horrified.

'No, I need you to run some messages before nightfall. Mr Godden's going.'

Alec stood up. 'Oh, I say. I'm not exactly qualified.'

'You're a reporter. You'll do fine,' Prideaux said. 'And you can take your friend with you, Fornello likes soldiers.'

Alec bristled. 'I'm not leaving the girls here alone.'

'I can take care of myself,' Ditto said.

'And we have Pixie.' The dog was on her feet at once, alert over squared paws, and Rom dropped to pat her. 'I don't think we'll have any trouble.'

Mr Mitchell turned back to the Magician. 'What about you?'

'I'm going to smoke half a tin of cigarettes,' Prideaux said, 'and count the seconds until I get my house back. In the meantime I'll speak with Tyet.'

'You can talk to other chasma,' Rom said. 'From a distance?'

'Yes, Godden. It's called a telephone.'

Kingsley sighed. 'I'll show you lot where to put your things.' The others followed upstairs but Rom didn't move from beside Prideaux's desk.

She tried to think of him as a demon, a Coronet like Mrs Ash or something like Kingsley, but she couldn't grasp it. She only had the sum of his appearances. 'You're a sneaking slimy liar, aren't you.'

'Not a liar, surely.' But he looked as though he knew what was coming.

'Who are you? Why did you want Jasper's notes?' Oh, questions. Too many. She gritted her teeth. 'You knew the entire time who our grandfather was. Even when you took the place at Morgan's school?'

Prideaux settled himself deeper in his chair. 'Your family's the only reason I'm still moored on this hell-forsaken island.'

'Did you tell Morgan who you are?'

'That would be an unspeakably dangerous thing to tell a child. Do I look like a fool? I've got a civil war to defuse. Run along and play with the others.'

She went upstairs slowly.

Two cramped rooms under the attic roof, stuffed with crates and furniture and the odd sweetish smell of mice. Pixie nosed into the corners. More statues everywhere, splashed like the floor with limey dobs of bird droppings. There were nests in the low rafters. Each room had just enough space for the camp beds and travel chest tucked like an afterthought beneath the high windows. Phoenix had claimed one room already and didn't seem inclined to share.

Alec surveyed the other. 'This is us, I suppose. I don't fancy the rats.'

'No rats,' Kingsley said, 'I keep the windows open and crowfolk get them all. There's the other bed downstairs if you want it.'

Mr Mitchell looked at Rom. 'Do you trust these creatures?'

'Not as far as I can kick them,' she said, and Kingsley made a wounded sound. Her legs felt like water and she sat down hard on the camp bed. 'But the stuff at the hotel—whatever Morax is, he's worse.'

'The Bull of Heaven has no mercy,' Kingsley said. 'We'd better tackle Fornello. Follow me, Mr Godden. Mr Mitchell. Do you know how to crank-start a Packard?'

Ditto rolled onto the camp bed as the others filed out.

'Dear lord, I'm tired.' The tension in Rom's throat was threatening to turn into tears. 'We're in danger as long as the collar exists.' That reminded her, and she tugged the little book from her purse. Ditto's head bumped hers as they lay peering up at the pages. 'I think I know how panax is made. We need to talk to Pen. And Morgan; how much does he know?' She dropped the book on her chest. 'We should go and get him. He'll miss the last week of the quarter but he was already coming to us for the summer.'

'You're going to kidnap him from school?'

'It's not kidnapping if he's already ours.'

When Alec and Mr Mitchell returned just before evening Rom was hungry enough to eat some of the limp sandwiches they'd brought. They all sat cross-legged on the attic floor.

'Fornello was away but we talked to one of his People in a pub,' Alec explained, as calm as if he did this on a daily basis. 'Salty little chap. They'll have a boat waiting on the coast. Kingsley said we ought to go with them, too, the car's safer than any train. I suspect he's not keen on being stuck alone with Desir for half a day.'

'Could we do it?' Rom asked. 'Kingsley could drive us to Aunt Minnie's after. Big house, plenty of quiet. We can sort out the damn collar. And grab Morgan too.'

'We could,' Alec said. 'And Sel can come. Mr Prideaux should be off the phone by now, I'll call Aunt Minnie. Anyone having that last sandwich?'

'I don't think there's any real food in this whole house,' Ditto said. 'I wonder if Prideaux keeps a pantry full of blood.' Kingsley was downstairs; if he could hear them it was his own fault for listening.

'Mr Desir said Prideaux wasn't eating at all,' Alec said. 'Can the damn things die?'

'That's another list we need to make,' Rom said. 'An encyclopaedia of chasma.'

By the time the attic was growing dim, Alec had wrangled half a plan. 'Aunt Minnie said we're welcome early, if Sel and I don't mind sleeping in the picker's sheds. And I've got a few days' leave from Cartwright if I cook up a tale about the Waldorf attack.'

'And Morgan?'

'I told the school it was a family emergency.'

'I can't go anywhere.' Ditto stretched out her legs. '*Ducky Dear* opens next week, I've got rehearsals.'

Rom sat upright. 'Can't you come? Even for the drive?'

'You won't be gone long, anyhow, I've got you tickets for opening week.'

Rom looked at Kingsley. 'Is she going to be safe at home?'

'Certainly, if you take Pixie with you. The collar's the only thing Tyet wants.'

Rom tousled the stiff white ears. 'Nasty job you got, doggo.' Did Jasper know what he'd made? It couldn't have been simple. Nor safe. One day, when she wanted to scare herself, she might ask why he'd risked it.

'What are you hoping to do?' Mr Mitchell asked.

Rom stood and brushed down her dress. 'There are three demons in this house. One of them's going to talk.'

At the bottom of the stairs she stopped. 'Kingsley,' she said, 'where is he?' In the absence of a proper name that would have to do.

'I wouldn't bother,' Kingsley called from the telephone, 'he's got a headache.'

The panelled door beneath the staircase stood half-open. 'In here?'

'Miss Godden,' Kingsley began, but she pushed through the door. The small wooden room was bare-windowed and filled with the last golden light. Gleaming with green plants, potted ferns and mossy things. Beneath the window sprawled copper pipes and a green enamel bath.

He was in the bath, of course.

'I thought it was you,' Prideaux said. 'I heard stomping.' His dark wet head was propped at one end of the tub. He didn't even open his eyes.

Rom stepped back towards the door. 'It can wait.'

'Unlikely, I don't plan to emerge any time today; sit.'

There was a wooden chair in the middle of the room. She sat. It was only marginally less awkward. 'i need to ask you. How can we break the collar?'

'You're operating under the assumption I'm here to assist.' Prideaux flopped one dripping hand over the edge of the bath and she gave up trying not to stare. His skin swarmed with delicate blue-black knotwork around each finger and up his wrist. Over the skin and sinking under, merged with venous traceries.

She dragged her gaze back to his face. He was looking at her. Which was precarious, but possibly the safest place to fix her eyes. 'You must be curious. You want to know how Jasper did it. If you help us we'll let you examine the bittergold.'

'Will you? Will you permit me? I'm not touching this mess.'

'But you know how to?'

'I could take a guess. But I wouldn't, if I were you.'

'Pixie's stuck. Even a demon shouldn't be kept locked up.'

He smiled. 'Noble Andromeda.'

'I have a conscience,' she said.

'Against all the opinions of the earth you'd set your conscience? The arrogance.'

'What did you offer Morgan?'

'I don't make contracts with children.'

'Nice try. Alec's been on the phone to his school today.' Which wasn't a lie, just misdirection. 'He stabbed a boy with a pen and you covered for him. You wouldn't have wasted your time.'

'Nor did I. He can't pay relix.' Prideaux sighed. 'British law doesn't recognise your brother as an adult in any capacity.'

'Stepbrother,' Rom said.

'Except for criminal responsibility, but that's hardly a wise plea.'

'I thought you'd have demanded blood at least.'

'You're failing to observe. Mckenzie's family is writhing with fascinating people. His godfather's in Parliament. Great-grandmother's a millionaire. Uncle in the Home Office. And he's very clever himself, which doesn't hurt.'

'Clever enough to be useful to you?'

'I've been a teacher for too many years to underestimate the value of a blank slate. *We turn clay to make a vessel, but it is on the space where there is nothing that the usefulness of the vessel depends.* Lao-Tze was quite correct. Once Morgan comes of age he'll be a formidable ally.'

'You're just a spy,' she said. 'You want information.'

'The word is mightier than the sword.'

'Pen,' she said, 'not word.'

'You'll find you're mistaken.' He leaned back his head to stare at a hanging fern. 'Do you think we use force? We're the stumble in the dark. The suggestion of doubt. Quietly and inevitably, humans decide we're right. And we must be, if they decide it. That's truth, isn't it?'

Rom's hands felt cold. 'Something has to be absolute.'

'You're going to talk about your conscience again. Kingsley, get the towel.'

The floor creaked as Kingsley passed. He must have been right behind her.

'You have to tell us everything you know about bittergold.'

'Don't order me,' Prideaux said.

'Please, then. We can pay, if that's how it works—'

'Andromeda bloody Godden.' Bathwater surged and Prideaux stood to reach for the towel in Kingsley's hand. Rom looked away. And looked back, but the lines were already fading from his skin. Elaborate knots across his shoulders and hands and hips, disappearing beneath the surface. Tangling in a star before running down into the dark hair of his body.

'Pay?' His voice was steady. 'You can't afford me.'

She didn't trust her voice to answer. She turned back to the door.

17

Mine is the spear and yours the word that guides it—
Yours is the aether and mine the star that sings—
Lost is the key, and pain the price it fetches,
Memory's merchant thieving the coin it brings.

Wingéd the step and burnt the blade you gifted—
Hornéd the moon who guards the heaven's gate—
Lonely the road and wounded the one who walks it—
Cunning the hands that knot the clew of fate.

Fire and sky-hold, sing of the listening word—
Whisper of hunger, and curse in the house of dust:
'Kiss of the wanderer mazes the feet of the foolish—
Scale of the Arbiter reckons the heart of the just.'

A Rhyme for the Road, Apolline de Florent;
transl. V. Argintiu. From The Nest of Amoury, 1721

In the outer room, Rom slumped in a fireside chair and hardly felt the blaze.

Kingsley brought her tea. 'I did tell you not to.'

'*Thank* you, Kingsley.'

When Prideaux finally came out he'd dressed himself, mostly; his silk robe hung open over dark trousers and starched white shirt—a poisonous yellow silk bordered in black velvet flowers, ornate and upright. He dropped into the other chair. 'Haven't you seen Skeins before?' he said. 'You must have seen Kingsley.'

'Not naked.'

'How very restrained of him.'

She was certain she shouldn't ask. 'That pattern you have, the diamond one?'

He didn't look over. 'Go on.'

'What is it? I've seen photographs.' And the borders of her book. His book, if she was going to be particular.

His book. It always had been: a jolt like nausea.

'Probably it's a humanoid thing,' Prideaux said, 'a maker's mark. Which is, if you think about it, both the highest and lowest form of irony.'

The others were coming downstairs. Pixie nudged her knees. Too many things to ask and she didn't dare stop asking. 'It's a seal?'

'A name.'

'Your name.'

'Apparently.' His polished shoe bounced against the chair-leg. 'Wouldn't you assume? Seeing as it's upon me that it happens to be emblazoned.' He turned. 'Back for more?'

'We're leaving at dawn,' Mr Mitchell said. 'Is the government involved in this rubbish? I should like to know if we're going to be shot as we leave.'

Prideaux tilted his head. 'Pretty coloured hair,' he said. 'Are you a true blond, Mr Mitchell?'

'I don't like this,' Alec said, 'travel won't be easy if there's somebody following.'

'You're taking my car,' Prideaux said. 'I can assure you, nobody will see it unless you want them to.'

Dusk had settled and Kingsley turned on the lamp beside the desk. Rom saw now that the desk was hinged at the joints with brass, like the polished chair behind it. And the curtained, book-strewn day-bed in the corner, where Rom moved to sit beside Ditto—its iron frame latched neatly. Campaign furniture, centuries old, made for a captain's war-tent.

The portiere drape was closed. The windows blinked with darkness, reflecting their shifting gestures, and the room didn't feel like a hallway now. It felt like a hearth, or a high place in a tower.

'Is Tyet going to come back for the bittergold?' Rom asked Prideaux.

'Ask Séraphin, he's the one with Sight.'

'No,' Desir said, poised on the staircase. 'No; this story is yours, I think.'

Prideaux's face gathered as Desir settled into the vacant wing-backed chair. He cleared his dry throat. *Êkhos*, the Phoenix had called him—echo, apt but perhaps unfair. Anything next to Desir was empty noise. 'We sit on the rim of the summer solstice,' Prideaux said, 'and that's a winter's tale. It's all cunning and treachery.'

'I want it,' Desir said.

Prideaux rubbed his hands together. 'Alright,' he said. 'Alright, you children. There once was a king.' He didn't raise his voice but Alec stopped pacing. 'We shall call him the Bull-king: a great, fierce, obstinate man. He ruled his islands by means of shrewdness and rigour, and a dazzling alliance with two chasma—a prince of stars, and a queen who rose from the sea. These two could walk as lions, as dogs, as sea-beasts: they flanked his chariot and accompanied his fleet, and though his fleet was the greatest in all the isles, there was little need for war. None dared attack. So he had leisure to turn his mind to magic and the great arts, and his most precious tool was the mind of his cleverest craftsmen, the architect Daidalos.'

'I know this one,' said Alec.

'It was Daidalos who first forged an impermeable metal, a chain of subtle and dangerous gold. The Bull-king realised he could overpower even his allies, the sea-gods, and so he did. In their rage the chasma betrayed the Bull-king to his enemies and his palace burned. Daidalos escaped, though, with the alchemical secret.

'Perhaps it was a seal of this alloy that stoppered the pythos of Pandora. It could have been a bittergold ring upon King Suleiman's finger. The world hasn't seen its match in three thousand years. Now a little white dog is wearing an extraordinary collar, and we would like to know why.' He looked at the Phoenix. 'Yes?'

Desir raised his brows. 'You did not speak of the Bull-king's adversary, or the labyrinth beneath his palace.'

'My story,' Prideaux said. 'You said I could tell it.'

'Nor did you mention his halfstar children. Nor the traitor who first revealed the gold to Daidalos.' Desir turned back to them. 'The Bull-king's architect made something else with his stolen knowledge—a knife, a tiny thing, such as a king might use to cut his fruit, but it was a blade which does not forget. It could wound a chasma's flesh through all eternity and bite every form they take. The Bull-king used it to kill the greatest amongst us, the captain of captains. My father.' Desir's breath shuddered his chest. 'If the tricks of Daidalos return to common knowledge, there will be trouble.'

Mr Mitchell leaned against the desk. 'Can we use the stuff to fight Morax?'

Prideaux didn't move his eyes from the fireplace. 'Have you listened to a single fucking word I've said?'

'You're all afraid,' Desir said. 'That is no fit state for wisdom.'

'They'd be a sight less frightened if they had a stash of panax,' Prideaux said. Desir stirred in his chair and Prideaux rounded on him. 'No society ever collapsed from an excess of knowledge. If humans are going to learn these things again—if now is the time—it's preferable the information be widespread, reliable, and free.'

'Very philanthropic,' Alec said. 'Why haven't you told the world yourself?'

'I'm not suggesting anyone stand up in daylight and announce our existence.' Prideaux's narrowed gaze slid over him. 'You need to be very sure of your plan. Who is the first to suffer, if the notion of monsters gets tossed about? Who's the first to be suspected?'

It might have been rhetorical but their silence appeared to irritate him.

'*Anyone*. Is that too hard for you? Anyone too weak, female, inexplicable—wrong colour, wrong gods. Your government will sort you all like vegetables and the bury the rejects. They're only ever waiting for the opportunity. I thought you read history, Godden—one whisper of chasma and they'll burn out the country, looking for Jews or witches. We can protect ourselves. We *cannot* prevent every mewling bitch with a grudge from overturning the stones of society and poking whatever he finds. Make the panacea,' Prideaux said. 'Finish what your grandfather started. When you're ready to test and publish, when the time comes due, we'll find the means to assist. Until then—' He drummed his fingers on the arm of his chair. 'If anyone inquires about Pixie, refer them to me. Consider yourself allies of my house.'

'Who?' Mr Mitchell asked. 'Who the hell are you?'

'Yes,' Rom said, 'which of your many names should we wave at them? Is Magician a name or title? The map-reader at the Midnight Palace called you Mr Argent. Is that one real?'

Prideaux's eyes glittered. 'They're all real. But if you like the classics, you can refer to me as Naberius.' He stood, reaching for his cane. 'Captain of Legions, Limina Silentii, and Marquess of the Outer

Declensions. I also answer to *sir*. What the fuck are you smirking at?'

To Desir, who spread his hands calmly. 'I just came down because I was hungry.'

'Good luck, I don't think any of this lot want to be eaten. Don't touch my desk. If anyone needs me, I'll be on the phone.' Prideaux swept under the portiere curtain, his yellow silk robe a hiss in the doorway.

'Do you think he was joking?' Ditto whispered.

'I'll know when I get hold of a library,' Rom said. 'I should grab my books when we drop you home tomorrow.'

The two of them curled on the day-bed under the tent of striped drapery. It was late—there didn't seem to be any clocks around the place—but neither had managed to sleep yet.

'Pack some clean clothes too,' Ditto said. 'Your dress has blood all over the front.'

Somebody was rattling with the fireplace beside them and Rom twitched the curtain open; Prideaux again, poking the coal shovel around and returning to his desk. The room was already sweltering. Maybe demons like their ambient temperature reminiscent of the Seventh Ring of Hell. Or maybe he didn't want to run out of bath water.

'Stop wriggling,' Ditto muttered at her shoulder.

Lord knows she was trying. Her cushion was too thin for a decent pillow and everything smelled of dust and cigarettes, but she was too tired to care. If only Prideaux would leave. But then he'd be somewhere else in the building. Better he stayed where she could see him, something between the door and the night.

Pixie flopped over heavily on the wooden floor beside them, and Rom sighed. She should be able to fall asleep like *that*. (An elaborate finger-snap in her mind.) Ditto's hip dug her back and she closed her eyes.

She must have slept because something woke her. The fire had sunk to a sullen glow. That sound again; the squeak of the staircase. Not even footsteps, just a movement of the house. Shadows, shifting air, and even through the curtain she saw the glint flick off the midnight windows. Desir was coming downstairs.

She pulled the curtain open a fraction. Past the arc of firelight sat Prideaux at the desk, his elbows propped on it.

Desir crossed directly to the fire. He warmed his hands, head angled to scrutinise the books along the mantel, and moved quietly around the room—observing everything, his left arm clasped in his right, unhurried in the almost-dark. The air had this sense again of glassy rotation, gleams sent out to chime against the jars on shelves. His black tuxedo glistened visible only when the silk caught firelight.

Prideaux rummaged in his tray for another pen but didn't look up.

The windows trembled. It might have been wind. Rom couldn't hear it.

Desir completed his circuit; he crossed to the desk. He sat himself on the corner of it, at Prideaux's left elbow, his back to Rom. He shrugged his suit jacket back from his shoulders and shuffled it neatly off.

Prideaux pushed it aside from his pages and continued writing.

She wasn't going to watch. Hadn't meant to all, but she'd been tensed for a noise, some disagreement as soon as they spoke, but neither did. Desir was unfastening his collar. He moved like a man undressing alone, eyes fixed on the ceiling, tugging open the high placket.

Prideaux put down his pen. He stood.

Desir hooked him by the tie and shoved him back in the chair. And continued unbuttoning his shirt and eased it away from his wounded shoulder, meticulously; the cloth seemed to have stuck to the flesh. It glowed dim with luminous ichor.

The Magician stood again from his chair, slowly. This time Desir waited.

Prideaux pressed a careful thumb to the wound, gauging something, depth or severity. Maybe he found what he was looking for because he leaned close. He bit down deep into Desir's broken skin with all the delicacy of an animal dropping its lips to water.

Desir's fingers curled around the nape of Prideaux's neck. He pressed his cheek to the smooth dark hair. Maybe he spoke. Nothing she could hear. Nothing she'd understand.

When Prideaux pulled away at last he leaned against the desk, his head hanging slack. He pressed his shirt-cuff to the dark drip of his mouth.

Inexactness then in his movements, feeling for a handkerchief. He cleaned himself; he came to the fireside and slumped into an armchair. He crossed his outstretched ankles and rolled a cigarette.

Desir had buttoned the shirt again, smoothed the collar, slipped on his tuxedo jacket. He sat on the desk-edge, dreaming, or watching something near the ceiling.

Rom didn't know how long the silence rolled like a spinning coin as the cigarette burned down to a hot little eye.

Prideaux seemed to have forgotten he was holding it. His eyes were fixed on the fireplace. The cigarette flared and dimmed, and he flicked away the end.

Desir stretched his shoulders and stepped across the rug.

The Magician didn't glance up. He uncrossed his ankles as Desir settled onto his lap, straddling his narrow legs, and his gloved fingers drummed the silver lighter on the arm of his chair. Tapping like rain.

Desir's fingers moved to his neck; the length of the amethyst tie untucked. And then the studs of his collar. Desir bent his head to the bare curve of Prideaux's throat and Prideaux closed his eyes. He arched against the touch and when the lips moved over the hard line of his chin to meet his mouth, Prideaux stilled his hand, and uncurled it, and the lighter fell.

Rom turned her face to the pillow. A dog was howling in the street. Beyond the window, the traffic on the high road was a distant roar.

'Toast,' Ditto murmured.

'Hm?'

'But I don't suppose there's any chance of that.' She rolled to kiss Rom's shoulder, and Rom hauled herself out of sleep.

Still dark; Kingsley's boots were clumping somewhere upstairs. 'We'd better get dressed.'

'In a moment,' Ditto said. 'You're going on holiday. Have you got a list?' She hung over Rom, her sleek hair slipping into a halo.

Rom touched her shoulder. 'What should I write?'

'You're going to eat plums,' Ditto said. She held very still as Rom stroked down her arm. 'You're going to swim. Demons don't exist and we're pretending the world is normal.' Ditto kissed her cheek. Brief, sweet. The day-bed shook as she slid off, and Rom growled.

'Bloody—' Grasping too late for Ditto's arm. The curtain swung shut. 'Tease.'

Rom pulled on her dress.

When she climbed from behind the curtain into the morning grey, Mr Mitchell was surveying the room like somebody at a murder scene; the bookshelves, the polished glass bottles. He examined a tray of bronze pieces and straightened quickly.

'It's not as bad as you think,' Rom said behind him. 'That's a Roman door-chime. The phallus was a talisman for good luck, they put it on kids' jewellery for protection.'

'I see.' Mr Mitchell laughed softly. 'So that statue, then—'

It was a grand herm lodged in the entrance, holding back the portiere curtain. Pale stone, worn bearded face. An empty smile intact above a foursquare pillar detailed only with pert genitalia.

'Quite acceptable at the time,' Rom said, 'for marking roads or springs.'

'And that's some kind of fertility festival, I imagine.' Mr Mitchell waved at the framed engravings between the windows.

Rom peered closer. 'No, that's definitely obscenity. Are they tentacles?'

'Morning all,' Kingsley said. 'Ready to go?'

Desir was waiting in a chair already, fitting his gloves.

A door slammed upstairs and Prideaux's voice vaulted in the stairwell. 'Where the fuck is my coat?'

'I don't know, sir,' Kingsley called pleasantly, 'I'm not a fucking retriever.'

They were halfway down the steps toward the shop when Prideaux's voice floated after them. 'Try not to get eaten, children.'

'Will do,' Alec said.

Prideaux appeared on the stairs, severe in his dark suit. 'Be nice to Mr Fornello,' he said, 'or he'll have your head off.'

'Aye.' Kingsley pushed his hands into his pockets.

'See you in hell, Séraphin.'

Desir didn't even turn his head as they descended to the stationer's shop and the cool street below.

Kingsley's chocolate-coloured car was squeezy once they all piled in. He drove, and Mr Mitchell sat in the front bench seat with Pixie on his lap and Ditto tucked beside him.

Behind them Desir settled his top hat on his knees and returned to sleep. Rom claimed the other window. Alec got stuck in the middle, by virtue of being the scrawniest, but they weren't going far; just Camden Town.

When Ditto got out she stopped at Desir's window. 'Is Ivy Munster really gone?'

Desir's closed eyelids didn't move. 'Like last summer's flowers,' he said. 'She was not unappreciated.'

'She was my friend.' Dittto's painted mouth gathered. 'I'm not sure I can forgive you, Mr Desir.'

'Do as you will,' he said, 'it is your birthright. But give your friends the same freedom.'

Ditto was silent as she and Rom climbed the stairs to their apartment.

'I wish you were coming with us,' Rom said.

'We can't have everything,' Ditto said. 'I wish I had a solid diamond house. No, I don't—that sounds useless.'

Rom packed quickly, shedding yesterday's beaded dress and pulling on her travelling gear, boots and riding breeches. She tipped all the demonology books into her trunk. 'We won't be more than a week. I know.' She paused to press her lips to Ditto's hair. 'Your show. I'll come back to see it.'

'I'll wire you if there's any trouble. And you too.' Ditto's eyes were keen.

'I'm not putting up with any nonsense. From demons.' Kicking her trunk shut. 'Or from Morgan. Take care, dear.'

Ditto didn't come back down to wave them off. Rom didn't mind. She hated goodbyes too. When she got to the street the taxi had arrived already, and Mr Mitchell loaded her trunk.

'Sure you'll be right?' Alec asked him.

'Fine,' Mitchell said. 'You can get me from the station. And I'll keep an eye on her.' He shook Pixie's leash.

Kingsley peered from under the car's bonnet. 'You're going by train?'

'Taking the luggage down. There's a hunt on for Mr Desir and the collar,' Mr Mitchell said. 'It's smarter to split up.'

'You learn fast,' Desir said from the car's back seat, his eyes still closed.

The early morning traffic was rumbling when they set out again. Just the four of them, roomier now, and Rom could lean out to wave at Ditto at the window as they pulled away.

Alec stopped Kingsley as they headed into the suburbs. 'Left,' he said, 'we're going to Surrey first.'

'Crux. What for?'

'We're taking Morgan with us,' Rom said. 'Desir doesn't need to arrive at the coast until this afternoon. Sorry,' she added to Desir, who shrugged. Probably he was used to this, thousands of years of being dragged around in coaches, chariots. Litters.

Kingsley sulked. But he turned left.

The Phoenix curled into his corner, his beautiful head crowned by the window. When Rom glanced at him later he was writing tersely in a crowded notebook. He seemed to be in perpetual motion, his gaze fixed on some horizon. An arrow; a boat. Maybe for an immortal the world spun so fast they could never be at rest.

'Mr Desir.'

He lifted his brows but didn't stop writing.

'We want to destroy this bittergold as much as you do. If there's anything at all you can tell us—'

'This matter is now under the auspice of Nido Naberius. It's not for me to comment.'

She sank back against the seat. 'You mean nobody's allowed to help us now.'

'They could,' Desir said. 'But they'd have to be willing to talk to Mr Prideaux.' He spoke like a clean incision, an inflection that might have been French and might have been mockery. He returned to his work.

It wasn't that he didn't have anything to say, she realised. He simply had nothing to say to her.

There wasn't much hope of conversation anyway. The engine was probably costly and impressive but it was hellishly loud for talking. And there was something penetrating about Desir's eyes. That look of his. So brief, as though he had no need to see any further. It was a relief to turn away.

Around them were just roads. Fields. Long hours of dust and nothing, hot when the sun struck her window and cold on her ankles, Desir writing beside her and Alec trying to smoke cigarettes in the shelter of the windshield.

Mid-morning they rumbled into Godalming and Alec braced himself. 'Here we go, then. What do we tell Morgan?'

'Nothing,' Rom said. 'He'll make his own deductions, we'll see what they are. And then we smack him with questions.'

18

New Year's Day. I have been at this work for ten years now. Sometimes it feels like the merest few months; at others, it seems I must have laboured for many centuries. Time always moves oddly when I am distracted.

Avery has been with me since the beginning, despite his comings and goings, so today has been a celebration of sorts. We sat beneath the early moon and made a toast—to us, to my work. I have grown accustomed to his presence, more than I imagined possible, despite our great differences and his difficult nature. I could not bear to be without him now.

What a thing to say. I should not have had that second brandy.

JASPER TEAGUE, Journals, 1st Jan. 1910

The school was behind the village, tucked around a winding road that climbed damp bends and opened onto a great airy lawn. It was spired and sprawling, long red roofs like a town's worth of churches tacked together. The grass was very green. The sky was very open.

Kingsley parked beside a demure long hall that was the size of Rom's entire prep school and was probably the gym room.

'Jolly for some,' Alec said without malice. He vanished inside and returned with Morgan buttoned up in full uniform, and the school trunk bumping between them.

Morgan looked well enough, his nose apparently none the worse for having been broken. Clearly Alec hadn't explained because he stopped when he saw the car with Kingsley at the wheel and Desir in the back seat. 'I'm going to assume there was no family emergency.'

'We thought you'd want a few extra days off school,' Alec said cheerfully. 'Hop in.'

'Nice motor.' Morgan eyed the white-walled spare tire on the running board as he stepped up. 'No train?'

'Detour,' Alec said, 'we're driving Mr Desir to his boat.' Desir raised his fingers from the pencil, an abbreviated greeting. 'We'll be home by dinner.'

'Mhm,' Morgan said. He settled into the front seat, avoiding

Kingsley's glance, and disappeared at once behind a book. Only when they were back on the road did Rom realise it mightn't be clever to give him a day's silence to compose his story.

The sun had risen fiercely and the fields steamed as they passed. She'd never been through this part of the country; railway, river, knobbled hill. The roads were busy and they slowed often to pass horse-carts or little country cars. The Packard was wide and rumbling but nobody turned their heads. Rom wondered how invisible they were in this car. Maybe Prideaux had just said that to make them feel better.

It would be more awkward to attract curious stares, though, and downright dangerous if anyone recognised Desir. But invisibility held a certain emptiness; this long noisy car and the kick of dust were nothing more than wind in someone's vision.

As they wound toward the coast, sparse scrub and houses, she saw a child perched on a stile, a tiny boy in a brocade jacket. Then, a few miles later, a gentleman with pointed mustachios saluted from a bridge as they rolled across.

And later, a woman beside the hedge, pulling a handcart; her feathered hat and flouncing skirt were a century out of style. Crowfolk were on the road, before and behind.

The air sang already with the keenness of the sea. Kingsley pulled up at last in a busy village where the street became a promenade and the grass ran down to the ocean. He got out and stretched beside the dunes. The scrub stirred with countless small birds, finches and sparrows. He dropped to a crouch, speaking with something in the waving grass: a long-eared hare, leggy and wild-eyed, that caught Rom's stare and darted away.

'All's well,' Kingsley said as he rejoined them. 'Mr Fornello will meet us here. Lunch, yeah?'

Alec was shaking out his leg. 'God, we've still got a whole afternoon before St Veep.'

'Ah,' Kingsley said. 'It might be longer; Fornello can't bring the skiff in till high tide. Not more than four hours,' he said over their groans.

'So we can't get Selwyn until nine at least,' Alec said.

'I didn't know other people were coming.' Morgan picked up his satchel. 'You didn't say.'

They trooped through the village shop while Kingsley refuelled.

There wasn't much to choose besides wilted ham and lettuce sandwiches. Rom got some chocolate too.

Morgan was hanging around the newsstand and she wondered if he was buying another comic. When he came to the counter he had a newspaper, and ordered a pennyworth of peppermint sticks.

On the grass between the road and the ragged dunes Rom sat with her sandwich, feeling both impatient and deflated. She wanted to drive on, skimming the low flats under the sky. She wanted to get to Aunt Minnie's and unpack.

Alec craned his neck. 'Where's Morgan?'

Over at the car, apparently, one foot on the running board, chatting to Desir. Who'd put down his notebook and was listening.

Alec called. 'Lunch, Mckenzie.'

He half-turned, waving; he'd heard. But he lingered, and marched back eventually with the newspaper and a paper bag of sweets. He ate his sandwich with a certain abstraction.

'What were you two talking about?' Alec asked.

'I was asking Mr Desir how he's enjoying his holiday.'

'What's it to you?'

'I'm not stupid.' Morgan unrolled the newspaper over Alec's knee.

Singer missing after eight die in hotel explosion. Renowned performer Séraphin Desir is believed to have escaped the accident, which killed his manager and seven others—

'I see,' Rom said, with hot discomfort. 'What did Mr Desir say?'

'Not much.' Morgan said. 'But he must be important. Kingsley's transporting him; that's Mr Prideaux's car. Did somebody find out Desir's a demon?'

Rom put down her sandwich. 'The Waldorf was attacked last night. I was there. A lot of people died. We might even tell you about it, if you explain what you know.'

'How did you all find out about them?' he asked. 'Was it your grandfather?'

'Morgan,' Alec said. 'Say it now, please.'

Morgan shook open his bag of sweets and fished out a peppermint stick with infuriating care. 'Your dog is supposed to be able to change her shape.'

'We know what they are,' Rom said. 'They give wishes. They don't like questions, and they're paid in blood.'

'They're not faeries,' Morgan said with quiet scorn. 'And they despise questions; they aren't allowed to lie. Isn't that so?'

Kingsley was silent, frowning at the ground.

The notion was staggering. If the demons couldn't lie. If everything they'd been told was reliable—

'It isn't always blood they want, but it's always a sacrifice,' Morgan said. 'I believe they absorb radiant energy; they don't eat human food. And they don't grant wishes. They're paid in full for every service rendered.'

'How did you find out?' Alec asked. 'Did Prideaux tell you?'

'He told me about Kingsley. Enough to know they aren't human.'

'You believe they're magic,' Alec said.

'Yes.' Morgan looked around at them. 'Don't you?'

Alec shrugged. 'I'd have picked you for a sceptic. You didn't even see Desir's show.'

Morgan didn't seem anywhere near concerned enough. 'It sounds like a typical spiritual revelation. Spiritual in the largest sense of the word; purely energetic. The creatures have indescribable abilities, so we might as well classify it as magic.' He waited. 'You can tell your story now.'

'And what about you?' Rom said.

'What about me?'

'Are you a human?'

Morgan's eyes narrowed. 'Of course I bloody am.'

'Rom. That's a bit harsh,' Alec said, but he looked relieved.

'You'd better start talking,' Rom said. 'How long have you known about all this?'

'Since March.'

'Last holidays,' Alec said, 'when you ran away to Prideaux's digs—'

'I wouldn't have bothered if he was ordinary.'

'Did you know they eat souls?' Rom couldn't stay quiet. 'You should have dropped it the moment you found out.'

Morgan's cheeks were darkening. 'Like you did?'

She bit her sandwich in silence.

Alec didn't like arguments unless he started them. 'Cheer up, we're at the sea-side. I'm going to buy an icecream.' He cricked his neck at the car. 'Is Mr Desir sleeping?'

'Probably.' Morgan had sucked his peppermint stick to a stiletto point. 'Brains too large for their blood volume means extended sleeping patterns. There's a chance they're cold-blooded.'

'I suppose you've got a whole encyclopaedia.' The last bit of Rom's patience sizzled to pieces. 'I can nearly believe Prideaux might cover for you at school. But there's no chance he'd tell you what he was.'

Morgan paused for so long she wondered if he was ignoring her. Then he shrugged. 'Mr Prideaux had a puzzle he wanted solving. I agreed.'

Alec was ablaze. 'Are you quite mad?'

'What did you get out of it?' Rom said. 'How can you expect us to *trust* you if—'

'Silence.' Morgan said. 'I just wanted silence. That's what I got. Spare time working in the library and a seat away from the others in class. I said yes. I'd do it again.'

'You helped a demon. So you could get a better seat in class?'

'In exchange for a puzzle I'd solve for nothing? It was a fair trade. I won't explain myself again.'

'What was the puzzle?'

'I haven't figured it out yet.' Morgan stashed his bag of sweets. 'What happened at the hotel yesterday?'

'Rom saw more than I did,' Alec said. 'And we're still not sure—'

'Don't.' Rom stood.

'Come on, he's in this too. He ought to know. And the danger, you saw it yourself...'

Rom was out of hearing, slithering up the dune and down to the scudding beach. The wind whipped her hat and she had to pull it snug around her ears.

It felt wrong to wear shoes at the beach. There were plimsolls in her trunk. But that was somewhere on a train, in the care of Mr Mitchell and Pixie. Rom slipped off her boots and stockings and left them with her hat in the lee of a rock. Under the breeches her legs prickled in the sudden chill.

The sea was cold, even ankle-deep. She retreated to the sand and began to walk, her toes crumbed with grit, far up the long sweep of the beach. And back again, her jacket flapping.

Alec had come down onto the beach too, hunkered on the tideline. He was patting the sand up into a heap. His chin was tucked into his collar and he looked about eight years old.

Rom crouched at his side. 'We made such a good one, that time on your birthday.'

'The one with the moat was better. Moats are always better.' He shuffled on his knees.

'Remember Father's?'

'We found all those feathers for it. And Mother put the last wafer biscuit on top of the tower.'

Rom scooped at the sand. Carving long grooves, packing along the side. 'What did Morgan say when you told him?'

'Not a lot.' Alec wiped his cheek on his sleeve. 'He seemed a bit horrified about the bodies and thing. He really mightn't have known how dangerous it is.' Alec slapped the mound higher. 'It's good to have him along. Better than having him nosing around on his own.'

It might be time for another truce. 'We can't afford enemies,' she said, and it was true enough that she didn't care who she was quoting.

The sandcastle spouted two spires now. She'd dug half the moat.

Morgan's school shoes stopped beside her. 'Are you building a canal to the sea?'

Alec sat back on his heels. 'Perhaps, if we're feeling energetic. But canals always break their banks. And if you build them too wide the water doesn't move.'

Next time Rom looked up, Morgan was kneeling beside Alec and had begun a slim channel down to the waterline. He held his cap in his left hand, digging with his right, and the wind dragged his hair across his eyes.

And much later, when they'd finished the castle and were fiddling with pushing a doorway into its heart, Morgan cut the channel with dips along its length, a series of little ponds like pearls on a string. He was nearly at the water's edge.

They could humour him. He was humouring them, after all, digging the wet sand without a word about its pointlessness. And it was quite stupid, making a sandcastle. But here in the gull-blown silence it felt like a thing worth doing.

Alec stretched up on his toes, waving to Morgan at the waterline.

They saw Morgan kneel at the hem of surf to make his last scoop. 'Here it comes,' Alec said.

The surge pushed up the channel and lapped the moat, darkening the sand and disappearing in a tracery of foam. The next wave left it brimming, a ring around their fort. The ripple shivered from bank to bank.

Rom looked down the plumb-line length of the channel, its mouth already softening into a delta. The pools were full, slowing the tide up the narrow passage, controlled and contained.

Morgan wasn't even hurrying as he walked up the beach to them, brushing off his hand against his shorts.

'It held,' Alec called down to him. 'Pretty damn good if I do say so. *Ponds*, Mckenzie, well done.'

Rom caught Morgan's eye across the towers. 'Brilliant,' she said. 'It really is.'

'We should have done this with Selwyn,' Alec said, 'he'd have appreciated it.'

'He'd have turned it into a five-storey aqueduct or something,' Rom said.

Morgan was rolling down his shirt-sleeve. 'We wouldn't have built it if he was here.'

Alec grinned. 'Likely not, Sel takes his games too seriously.'

'He is a grownup.' Morgan tugged his cap on.

'And we're not?' said Alec. 'I don't suppose you were ever a proper baby.'

'Because I didn't sleep with a stuffed rabbit?'

Alec clapped him on the shoulder. 'Brutal little chap, aren't you.'

'Probably.' Morgan stepped carefully over the moat towards the dunes. 'I'm not an idealist.'

He had to be though, Rom thought, to squat in the wind and build his canal as solemnly as his father might carve a railway through a mountain range. Maybe he didn't understand what idealists are. They're not always dreamers like her own father, like Alec's friend Tom with his unfinished watercolours.

She watched him climb the dune beside Alec, his half-skid and his sturdy stance at the top. Idealism isn't blindness; it's vision. A lonely sort of clarity to have.

They got ice cream after all. Rom ate hers in the dunes with *The Nest of Amoury* on her lap, and by the time the evening tide had drowned their sandcastle and swallowed the beach, she thought the day had been redeemed.

The air was greying when Desir emerged from the car, looking like a prince of vampires with his dark cape. Kingsley roused them all and led them far down the beach, away from the twinkling lights of the promenade.

The wind was rougher now, and the five of them stood in the growing silence, watching the silvering sea.

Alec must have been getting hungry. 'Is Mr Fornello far away?'

'Somebody's coming,' Morgan said.

Someone humming in the twilight, deep and wobbling and not quite sober. A big old man rounded the point, bearded, grand in his grubby trousers and dark pea-coat. His knitted cap was low over his eyes. A tattoo wound high around his neck, inked with dragon-scales. He was loping crookedly over the uneven rocks and Rom blinked until she saw the little white cap at his side, the boy half-propping up his heavy arm.

'Kinchin,' the big man greeted them.

'Mr Fornello?' Never had Alec sounded so high and uncertain. 'Mr Prideaux sent us to—'

'Gad.' Fornello roared over him. 'Argent's fucking lucky to have me. Follow on; follow. Boat's on the shingles here. Halloo there, sunshine. Still like to sing?'

'Still,' Desir said.

As they wobbled over the rocks they reached the boat pulled up in the lapping tide, an open wooden dinghy, and Alec frowned. 'I thought you said there'd be a ship.'

'Beyond the point. Even our muscle-man here couldn't row all the way to Ireland, could you?' Mr Fornello scruffed at the boy, who straightened his cap in silence. 'Hop over, sunshine.'

Desir settled his top hat under one elbow and turned back to them all. 'I'm obliged,' he said. 'Though this is not the day that would have been; I missed seven consultations.'

'Yes, a lot of people got murdered yesterday,' Rom said. 'Sorry it wasn't how you planned.'

'I don't plan,' Desir said. 'I only see. You may hear your fortunes now; each who assisted me is owed this much.'

'We don't go in for divination,' Alec said. 'Thanks anyway.'

Desir's eyes fixed on him, unblinking. 'Fate hangs over us like noonday. We walk in its light and can see no shadow. But it tracks us, regardless. Fate is fickle and many-faced; one finds it only by the echo.'

Rom stirred and Desir's gaze moved to her.

'It is joy, and a feast of emeralds. It is despair, and a knife of mercy. It weeps in the heart of a labyrinth, a fool to its own mind. It sleeps like a snake in a lover's heart. It unwrites Law itself to break the old vows of bone. And loyalty it rewards with a tongue of fire. Until death comes at last, an old friend, and greets you under the painted stars.'

'That wasn't necessary,' Kingsley said.

'This is the form of fate,' Desir said. 'I have given my seven omens.' He turned to the wooden boat lodged in the tide, and stepped unwavering up to the dancing prow as if he walked on dry land.

The froth of the surf showed creamy. Mr Fornello waded in. The boat crunched and rocked and he whistled shortly. 'Jump in, mauvey. The Siren's folk are sweet this evening; we'll have no troubles crossing.'

'Oh, I'm not going,' Kingsley said.

'Oh, you are.' Mr Fornello reached and grasped Kingsley's collar. 'What we like to call security. You want Arbiter on your scent if something happens to his Golden?'

Kingsley hissed and pushed a key into Alec's hand. 'Crowfolk will come for her.' It took Rom a moment to realise he meant the car.

'Make yourself small,' Fornello said, 'this lad takes up the whole gunwale. On, then. On, lads. Benedixi, kinchin.' His hand flashed in a salute, and the oars slapped.

Rom was already back on the dunes when she heard the sea-demon's song, and the whistle of the white-capped boy.

Hold his tail, boys, and bind him fast—
take him along, my stormy
the devil's own teeth will have you at last—
take him along, my darling

She looked back, but she could only see the distant lighthouse; glancing, rounding, extinguished.

It took Alec six tries to start the Packard. He navigated the darkening roads with painful care. When the three of them made it to the train station they found it closed; Mr Mitchell was smoking sleepily on the steps with Pixie and two trunks. 'The station master's wife brought me dinner. Hullo again,' as he shook hands with Morgan. But he couldn't hide his smile. 'How are you enjoying your holidays?'

'Haven't decided,' Morgan said.

It was only half an hour of road after that. Pixie curled on Rom's feet in the car, and she wondered if the dog had missed her after all. Not-dog, she reminded herself, as her forehead hit the rattling window.

Coming home isn't what you expect. Sometimes it's a train between morning hedges, the high white house with its pointed roof and Aunt Minnie waiting at the door.

Sometimes it's a late-night slink up the driveway.

Alec stirred Morgan's shoulder and shook himself as they collapsed out of the steaming car. 'Good grief, I don't want to drive for weeks.'

'You've got to be at the train station on Tuesday,' Rom said.

He rubbed the bridge of his nose. 'What?'

'Collecting Dr Lloyd. This isn't a holiday, we've got work to do.'

Alec groaned like a bull-calf, and they all hushed him on the kitchen step.

19

Rom recognised the bedroom before she opened her eyes. The kitchen door thudding downstairs, the old stable's distant clatter from across the garden. Memory tastes like mothballs. Open and see: slant whitewash, sunlight over Pixie's back, the spare bed's crocheted coverlets in apple green.

This was the room she'd dreamed of when she was stuck at school, homesick or lonely, groaning over her monthlies. This was the view. Damp lawn hemmed by glossy shrubbery and an angle of the clothesline; orchard dark under the folded hills.

Aunt Minnie was cooking eggs when Rom trooped down with Pixie and found Alec and Mr Mitchell at the table already. 'Morning, my pet.' Aunt Minnie's quick embrace smelled of coffee. 'I hope you slept nicely. You all got in very late.' She'd waited up for them last night with the resignation of those who live without telephones.

'It was rather a mess yesterday,' Rom said. 'The train was late and we had to borrow a car.'

'Alec said the car broke down.'

'Did he?' Rom glared at him over the table as they sat down.

Aunt Minnie bustled, her apron tied over her riding trousers. Bobbed hair a mess of waves. Well over forty, tanned with gardening and showing a myriad of crinkles radiating from her eyes and her busy mouth; very like Father, who'd been her older brother. Rom in childhood had never noticed the similarity, but now Father was only a photograph in Aunt Minnie's parlour and maybe Rom looked for him. It felt disloyal—Aunt Minnie should be loved for herself, flicking stems from tomatoes with deft fingers. The same absent smile Father had always worn, but Aunt Minnie's hazel eyes were rather sharp.

'We have another friend coming down from town this week,' Rom said, 'if you don't mind. Just for two or three days—we can cook everything. She's researching Celtic graves and things.'

Aunt Minnie was chopping parsley. 'Anything I should worry about?'

'Of course not,' Alec said, but Aunt Minnie wasn't smiling.

'You'll have to do a bit better than that, Alexander. Get your story straight.'

'It's not a lie,' Rom said. 'Somebody was in trouble yesterday and we had to give them a lift.'

Aunt Minnie scooped scrambled eggs onto her plate. 'Is it your trouble too?'

'There won't be any problems,' Mr Mitchell said.

'You seem old enough to know better.' Aunt Minnie dried her hands. She glanced at Rom and Alec. 'And you two are always getting into scrapes. But you must behave yourselves in front of Morgan, I don't want him mixed up in your adventures.'

Rom bent over her plate. No point explaining that it was too late.

She followed Alec to the garden while he fed the chickens.

'Will Aunt Minnie ask questions?'

'Lucky for us, Mr Mitchell has a trustworthy face,' Rom said. 'She'll be iffy about whoever comes for the car, though.'

'What car?'

The driveway was empty. Only a tire-track in the mud; crowfolk move silently.

When they went back in Morgan was slouched over his eggs at the kitchen table. He raised his eyes to nod and returned to eating. Not a morning person.

'I've been lazy with my pruning this year,' Aunt Minnie was saying. 'But it does look nice. We should have lunch out there tomorrow.' She draped Morgan's plate with a slither of bacon. 'Peas on the bench, Rom, if you want to shell them.' A suggestion that would bear no objections. Rom grinned as she settled at the table. 'Mr Mitchell, you're a northern boy? Lantic Bay's worth a look if you're sightseeing.' Aunt Minnie was no fool. She didn't believe a word they'd said.

Morgan had finished his bacon and his gaze wandered over the kitchen, the yellow gingham curtains and the egg-blue mixing bowl in Aunt Minnie's hands. The slate floor, tinted with a silver bloom. Low ceiling; whitewash; thyme strung in bunches.

Familiar to Rom. Hard to know how it looked to Morgan. But she wondered if it was true after all, what Mother said in her letter, if he was happy to be back here—if he liked the wet garden and the bee-noisy orchard and this kitchen. It was part of his childhood too.

'Your arm, dear.' Aunt Minnie put down her knife.

Morgan was cradling his left elbow. 'It's fine.'

'What have you done?'

'Cricket.'

'I can take a look if it's giving you grief.' She'd been a veterinary assistant before the War, and a volunteer nurse when the hospitals had filled.

But Morgan shook his head. 'I've had worse.'

'May we set up some things in the parlour?' Rom asked. 'If you're not using it. We don't mind eating dinners in the kitchen.'

'You've got nice weather for it, anyhow,' Aunt Minnie said. Whatever she thought *it* might be.

Rom paused at the kitchen doorway as they left. 'Morgan. Are you coming?'

He set his knife and fork together on the plate. 'Is that a good idea?'

Rom wasn't certain either. 'We could use your brain.'

He wants to, she thought, as he followed her into the parlour. He could listen to everything they'd learned and give away nothing.

Alec was strutting in the parlour like a military general. 'What's the order of business?'

Rom laid out the library books with her sheaf of notes. 'The Magician said we've got everything we need to replicate Jasper's work.' She set *The Nest of Amoury* on the table. Morgan opened the paper-wrapped book, leafing gently. He knew he wasn't entirely trusted.

'This is the alchemical textbook?'

'The drawings are ciphers,' she began, 'probably chemical signs,' but he was already scattering through the stacks of her research papers.

'What have you got?'

He dropped into the window seat, pulling a cushion onto his knee without taking his eyes from the book. 'Ask me after supper.'

Rom whistled Pixie over from the door. 'Come along, doggo, you're going to help us.'

Alec looked uneasy. 'Can't we make panax without her blood?'

'Hang the panax.' Rom unbuckled Pixie's collar and laid it on the table. She'd handled the basics of metallurgy at the College, field tests for artifacts. 'We're going to figure out this metal. Let's start with vinegar.'

Assisted by Alec's deft shorthand, she and Mr Mitchell worked through the morning to make a satisfactory summary. 'It does appear to be genuine gold,' Mr Mitchell said. 'Doesn't tarnish.'

'The weight's maybe on the heavy side.' Rom replaced the collar around Pixie's neck. 'Prideaux said it's an alloy.'

'Can't we just get a crucible?' Alec asked. 'Melt it down?'

'Maybe,' Morgan said from the window. 'It could be that easy, if it were guaranteed the power was in the form and not the materials.'

When they trooped into the hallway for lunch he still looked thoughtful. 'What's the source of a demon's magic? What is it we're dealing with?'

'Wish we knew,' Rom said. They took the plate of ham sandwiches out to the shady back garden. 'If we knew about demons' lives, where they come from, we might get an idea how they work.'

Aunt Minnie returned with a bowl of peaches and a coconut cake and they all searched for safer subjects as she sat on the grass beside them. 'I'm just nabbing some cake before you gobble it,' she said. 'I'll be going to town if anyone's got letters.' She started taking notes on everything Alec wanted from the shops. 'This isn't a boarding house, Alexander, if you want a cooked breakfast you can make it yourself. I'll be over at Victoria's tomorrow, will you need me terribly?' That was the neighbour, whose orchard carried on along the other side of the river. 'I'm a useless spinster aunt,' she said to Mr Mitchell. 'I can't knit and I'm no good with children. I've no earthly clue why my sister-in-law keeps sending her infants to me.'

'You make a fine cake,' Alec said.

'You caught me at a busy time of year. Picking season. No, I shan't need the huts, the pickers all stay at Victoria's. But listen. Polly will send me rude letters if any of you die so please keep your heads on. Don't make me chaperone you.'

'May I come to the post office?' Morgan asked. 'I need to send telegrams.'

'If you like.' She plumped him another slice of cake. 'Alec says you're going to join the military. Army?'

'No,' Morgan said.

'Navy? Brave kid.'

'No. Not joining.'

'What the devil do you plan on doing, then?' Alec asked. 'It would suit you perfectly. Wearing a uniform, shouting orders.'

'The military would be a waste.'

'Of your brains?' Rom said.

'Time; effort. Living and dying for somebody else.'

'What about for your country?' Mr Mitchell sat back against the beech trunk. 'If there's another Great War.'

'The arguments of millionaires aren't really a matter for patriotism.'

'I joined when I was seventeen.' Mr Mitchell's pale eyes were rather cold. 'What would you have done if you'd been old enough, and your conscription came through?'

'It wouldn't have. My father works in railroads. Essential wartime profession—'

'If he wasn't.' Shortly. 'If you were like the rest of us, Mr Morgan.'

Morgan paused. 'I don't know.'

Rom wasn't sure she'd ever heard him say that.

Mr Mitchell brushed off his trousers and marched back into the house. They all seemed to realise he'd been politer than he wanted to be, and not for Morgan's sake.

'Now you've done it,' Aunt Minnie said mildly. 'You mustn't speak to people like that.'

Morgan put down his empty plate. 'It isn't personal.'

'It is for some of us.' Alec followed Mr Mitchell inside, and Rom was left mashing her cake crumbs.

'I'm washing linens this afternoon,' Aunt Minnie said. 'Rom, pet, go and check on the copper.'

Rom reached the laundry door before she realised why she'd been packed off.

She stirred the steaming tub, hauling the slop of hot bed sheets over to the mangle. Aunt Minnie had no real right to scold Morgan; he was more guest than relative. But he'd get a proper earful.

Alec came out and helped her hoist the sheets onto the clothesline in the garden, wrestled between them.

'How's Morgan been with you?' she asked.

'Still grouching. Still calling me Godden as though we're school chums.'

'He wasn't entirely rotten when he was ten. Was he?'

'You're just mad he doesn't need us anymore. Are you coming down to the village? We ought to get ice cream.'

Rom went along to post a letter.

Fri 20th June

Dearest Ditto—

I hope you're keeping well. Mr Desir and Mr Kingsley went off safely with a most tremendous pirate type and now we're twiddling our thumbs until Dr Lloyd arrives. Morgan's being a pest but that's old news. I'm doing my best to have a holiday, there's plenty of cake at least.

Good luck with rehearsals—I wish you could have come for a rest but I'm glad you're having fun prancing around and being magnificent. Please put your feet UP when you sleep.

Ever yours-

Rom

Next morning Morgan cornered Rom and Alec in the parlour as they assembled all their notes. He wasn't content with their reports, apparently.

'Describe everything you saw. How did Mr Desir do it?'

'Is it relevant?' Alec asked. 'Pixie's the one stuck in a collar.'

'Everything's relevant,' Rom said, 'that's why we need to make this encyclopaedia.'

Mr Mitchell poked the length of twine beside Morgan's notes. 'What have you been measuring?'

Morgan's brows gathered. 'What makes you think it's for that?'

'You've put knots here at intervals.'

'Checking to see what these patterns actually looks like,' Morgan said. 'You couldn't measure with it, there are no numbers.'

'That's only needed for comparison,' Mr Mitchell said, 'keeping track so you can recreate it. Half the time I just use my hand-span or a pencil length.'

'The architecture of the ancients began like that,' Rom said, 'intervals on a string. That's probably how the harp got invented.'

'That's not what magic is, though.' Morgan ran his fingers over the twine. 'The priority should be locating the source of the demons' power.'

Mr Mitchell shook his head. 'Don't you have any curiosity?'

'Once I control things, I can ask the chasma any question I like.'

'He's got you there,' Alec said. He nodded to Morgan. 'It was clever, though, trying something practical.'

'If I had to guess about their magic,' Rom said, 'I'd think it was a kind of radio-wave. Desir's singing shook the windows.'

'How would that work?' Morgan said.

'I don't know, how does a telephone work? We all use it anyway.'

Morgan blinked. 'That's a terrible example. Don't any of you know? Not you,' coldly to Mr Mitchell, 'the others.'

'Of course we don't,' Alec said.

'Then you ought to shut up. This isn't electricity. It's not radio waves, it's something bad enough that your grandfather made a bunker to escape it.'

'Alright,' Alec said, 'do you have a better idea?'

Morgan diminished slightly. 'The borders of those illustrations do seem to represent demonic seals. And Prideaux told you those represent a name. The most efficient kind of name, since they can't be changed or hidden. Probably it's intrinsic to their power.'

'What language would it be?' Alec asked. 'It must be horribly ancient.'

'I plan to check every library when we get home again,' Rom said.

Morgan folded his hands on the table. 'When was writing invented?'

'Millennia,' Rom said, 'as far as we know from cuneiform. Maybe seven thousand years?'

'What language?'

'An early kind of Babylonian.'

'And before that?'

'Clearly we don't know,' she said patiently, 'because it wasn't written down, was it.'

'But you think you're going to find their true names in a book.' Morgan's eyes were contemptuous. 'This will be another form of communication, probably without words. Kelvin believed each element made a knot, with a starting point of helium.' He waved one finger. 'A circle like the sun, helios. And this is carbon—' His hand moved, a trefoil loop. 'Perhaps there's a chemical formula for every chasma.'

'What have you got so far?' Mr Mitchell asked.

'I separated Mr Desir's seal into various design components.' Morgan flicked through his sketchbook. 'Here's one.'

Rom sat up straighter. She'd seen it once before, his pencilled lines. Interlocking curves. Now she pictured the designs she'd seen in Pen's photographs. And the other one, on the Magician's naked flesh, pale and venous as marble. 'Where did you see it?'

'I was shown a drawing of Desir's seal. And asked to solve it.' His mouth relaxed, almost a smile. 'This was Mr Prideaux's puzzle.'

Rom leaned over the book. 'A demon's name would be valuable to anyone.'

'Nice pattern,' Alec said, 'I get the same thing when I stir my tea.'

'I'm analysing Pixie's collar the same way,' Morgan said. 'Maybe Jasper used an element of her name to bind her. But I need a proper library.' He rubbed his hand over his eyes. 'Theory's not finished. It's possibly erroneous—'

'Morgan,' Rom said, 'we're doing what we can. We're all making it up as we go.' She touched the page. 'You've been working on your puzzle all this time? I thought it was a running dog design, like a Greek key. I never imagined something like this.'

Morgan took his hand from his face. 'You've seen it before.' Rom didn't answer, and he sat back in his seat. 'You looked at my notes.'

'Well, I—yes. I saw it.'

'When?'

'Edinburgh.'

He didn't move. He didn't even look angry, but his expression shuttered closed.

'Rom, you beast,' Alec said. 'Much good it did, anyhow, none of us could have solved the thing. I don't know if any one person could. That's the point of this, isn't it? Dr Lloyd will help us on the biology side of things. Unless we're prepared to melt the collar down we can't do more. Good work, Mckenzie.' Alec pushed back his chair. 'I'm going swimming.'

'Good idea,' Mr Mitchell said.

Alec stuck his head back around the doorway. 'You coming, Captain?'

'Don't have swimming things,' Morgan said from behind *The Nest*.

'Don't need 'em,' Alec said.

Morgan lowered the book. 'That was a no. I was being polite.'

'Well, don't be, it gives me the creeps. Swimming, Rom?'

'I've got letters to write.' She hesitated at the doorway. 'Sorry,' she said to Morgan, but it's tough to find an excuse when there isn't one.

Morgan turned another page and didn't lift his eyes.

It was going to be a bad few days.

20

Saturday June 21

Hullo Rom,

*Work is gorgeous and dreadful. My stage costume is silver spangles all over with
a cape of feathers and it's rather fetching. My heel's got a blister the size of New
York. How's things in sunny Cornwall? I do hope you've found the philosopher's
stone because there's at least half a dozen dolly scarves in the window at
Liberty's and I think we should buy them all.*

*Miss Gwen sends her love and hopes Pixie's having fun chasing rabbits. Do
demons chase rabbits?*

Ever yours,

Ditto

On Monday the afternoon kitchen seethed with heat. The house was
quiet, apart from the occasional whack of shuttlecock and racquet
from outside in the humming garden.

Aunt Minnie looked up from the chopping board. 'How long has Mr
Mitchell had that cough?'

'As long as we've known him.' Rom was rolling pastry and trying to
ignore an itch on her neck. 'Months. Bronchitis, he said.'

'Bloody soldiers. They don't seem to know the medical definition of
bed rest.' Aunt Minnie tipped the tomatoes into her bowl. 'He's Alec's
friend?'

'Yes.'

'I thought you might have invited him down.'

'No.' Rom gave the pastry a solid slap. 'I wanted to bring Ditto, I told
you about her when I wrote. But she's stuck in London with work.'
Best friend, she'd written. She could tell things to Aunt Minnie, but
there were divides.

Aunt Minnie probably guessed anyway; she had Victoria-next-door,
and neither had ever married. But if Rom began to explain she'd have
to decide where to stop. Her chest dampened as she put her weight
behind the rolling pin. She had things she wanted to say. Too much,

flooded with formless meanings, but they got sidetracked before they found a vent.

She dropped the rolling pin and scratched her neck. 'Do you want those peas now?'

'Good thinking.' Aunt Minnie was shuffling coal into the wood stove. 'Off you hop, I was half a minute away from sending you out to play.'

Rom was rustling through the delicate pea-vines by the clothesline when she heard Alec's whistle. He had his jacket bundled under his arm. Mr Mitchell was with him, freshly dampish, hair wet and shirt hanging open. They'd been swimming.

'Cold?'

'Not a bit of it,' Alec said. 'The river's in sunlight. Are you going down before dinner?'

'Not I,' she said. 'I don't swim.'

'Not even in midsummer?' Mr Mitchell seemed to recall his shirt, moving to button it, and she caught his smile. 'You grew up here, Miss Godden?'

'Yes. Mostly. And it's Rom, please.'

'But you never jumped in the river? What a waste.' His fingers reached the top buttons and the raw strong collarbone. The paler skin below it, fine and freckled.

'Dinner's at seven,' she said. 'And Alec's on dish-washing duty. Even Morgan can tidy after himself, I'm sure you'll manage.'

'Morgan's in school training,' Alec said in protest. 'I'm a free man. Or ought to be,' but she didn't stay around to listen.

She and Aunt Minnie pulled the old potting table from behind the stable and set it for dinner in the cobbled courtyard by the back door; chintz tablecloth in the wide blue shade of the rhododendrons. 'She,' Aunt Minnie said, and dusted off her hands in satisfaction.

Rom was carrying chairs from the kitchen. 'Who?'

'St Necessity; the mother of invention.'

'We could have had another picnic,' Alec said when he arrived, dressed and combed.

'Not with my knees,' Aunt Minnie said. 'The parlour's been commandeered and the kitchen's too warm.'

'You ought to get an electric stove,' Rom said.

Aunt Minnie was whisking salad dressing. 'You can when it's yours.'

'I didn't mean it like that,' Rom said, but Alec hooted.

'Bossy little heiress.' The old place became Mother's, after Father died, but she had no time for a cottage in Cornwall. Aunt Minnie lived here as she always did, and one day it would be Rom's. 'Room for half a dozen children,' Alec said as they all sat.

'Don't be stupid,' Rom said. 'I only need about three.' That's another life; children might fit somewhere, a place like Aunt Minnie's, with plum trees and chickens. But it's not a tent along the Tigris River. And not Ditto, either; she'd be in Berlin, dancing for somebody else's eyes. Life is too short. The world's too much.

'I suppose three's enough,' Alec said. 'I need to be an uncle; Morgan's too old to be impressed by card tricks.'

The little table was piled with food—bright sliced tomatoes, pickled onions, egg and bacon pie with the pastry Rom had hefted against Aunt Minnie's marble-topped counter. She was always hungry at home too, but the making of food was another chore. Here the minutes added up to something better. Cooking on a proper stove made the difference, maybe, or cooking for more than herself. She wished Ditto could be here too, eating pie.

'You ought to have kids yourself,' she said. 'Christmas would be fun again.'

'I don't see the point of marrying young,' said Alec, who couldn't boil a potato or endure his own company and would certainly have a wife by the time he was twenty-five.

Mr Mitchell laughed, half-muffled. 'I don't see the point of marrying at all.'

'How about you, Mckenzie? Damn him, where's he got to.' Alec grinned. 'He'll get through Oxford at seventeen, inherit Harry's mining shares, and marry a film star.'

'Cambridge,' Morgan said from the kitchen step. 'They have a better science department.'

'They've got the best archaeology projects too,' Rom said.

Morgan seated himself at the table. 'Why didn't you study there?'

She hadn't expected him to reply. He'd been ignoring her presence strenuously. She sifted through several retaliations before she settled on the truth. 'I'm not a boy,' she said.

Morgan paused. 'Unfortunate.'

Aunt Minnie was in and out, serving vegetables, and it seemed wiser not to talk too deeply. 'I wonder if anyone's planning to excavate Harper's tomb at Inverness,' Rom said. 'If I don't end up in Egypt after College, that'd be a fascinating dig. How's the winters on Orkney? I imagine the excavation season would be short up north.'

'You ought to come up and take a look either way,' Mr Mitchell said.

'They might uncover anything, a tomb like that. At Knossos they found the golden mask of Agamemnon and two new languages. It changed the entire Minoan history.'

'That's why your encyclopaedia is pointless,' Morgan said. 'You assume it will make a recognisable form by accumulating details. You'll never know the important detail you've missed.'

Rom refilled her glass with lemonade, willing patience. 'Which?'

'I don't know. But there will be something. Knossos might have been important, but nobody discovered that for thousands of years. I'm not sure you can afford to wait.'

'Plenty of important things get discovered accidentally,' she said, 'they found King Tut's tomb under the diggers' tents.'

Morgan put down his glass of water. 'You mean to trust in luck.'

'Details are important,' she said. 'Scientists are used to noting everything.'

'A lot of scientists get interested in things that appear to break a rule. The thing they should look at is the rule itself. Mathematicians are aware of this.'

'You don't think we've discovered anything? Archaeologists might dig for months, a few centimetres a day, but every pot sherd makes up a greater picture of a whole civilisation.'

'All it tells you is the civilisation used pots.'

'Don't talk about things you don't understand. An archaeologist—'

'You're not an archaeologist,' Morgan said. 'You're a student.'

'You're not a mathematician, you're a petulant little prat.'

'The terms aren't mutually exclusive.' Alec must have kicked him under the table because Morgan glanced over. He waited until Aunt Minnie returned to the kitchen. 'Nothing in the assembled facts explains how chasma work. Examples are a distraction. We need to find a mathematical proof.'

Rom didn't look up. 'Every example says something.'

'Your button.'

'What?'

'Your top shirt button is missing and you've replaced it with a pin.'

She heated. 'I didn't have time for sewing.'

'It doesn't reveal anything historically significant about clothing manufacturing in the early twentieth century,' Morgan said. 'Nor anything useful about humans as a species. It's a pointless detail, and a chasmeric encyclopaedia will be full of things like that.'

'It says a bit about humans,' Mr Mitchell put in. 'We're impatient.'

'Apparently archaeologists aren't,' Morgan said.

Rom cut her sausage savagely.

'More water, Captain?' Alec topped up Morgan's glass. 'I call him Captain Blood,' he said to Mr Mitchell, grinning wide as a cat. 'The Welsh pirate, you know? Henry Morgan.'

'Henry Morgan is my father,' Morgan said.

'But you've got the same name.'

'Mckenzie is his middle name,' Rom said, because Mr Mitchell looked lost. 'Or one of them; he's named after half his family tree.'

'I was named after my uncle,' Mr Mitchell said. 'He was a horse-thief. Pirates are better.'

'Oh, nobody's ever called him Henry,' Rom said. 'We always called him something else.' Alec looked across the table at her, brief and dangerous, and Morgan didn't look up at all. 'His first name. Didn't we, Morgan dear?'

No reply. If Aunt Minnie had been there Rom would never have continued, but Morgan had been vile all afternoon. And anyhow, he had it stamped on his school trunk: *L. M. M.*

Rom leaned across to Mr Mitchell. 'We always called him Loveday.'

Morgan put down his knife and fork.

'Family name,' Alec said, 'Cornish. Not so common for boys, though. Is it, Captain?'

Rom shrugged. 'I was surprised to see you'd started using Mckenzie. I suppose the alliteration's nice.'

Morgan picked up his glass of water and drank half of it, his eyes downcast. The table was quiet. Aunt Minnie came down the steps with the coffee things and Alec launched into some semblance of cheery conversation but Morgan didn't speak again, and excused himself as soon as he'd emptied his cup.

'We shouldn't have.' Alec muttered as they cleared off the table. 'Now he'll be a perfect beast all week.'

'He already was,' Rom said.

Mon. June 23th

Lady Dido,

All's well apart from Morgan not speaking to me for three days. He's trying to figure out the pattern of Pixie's collar but he won't show us a thing. We did find a mention of a demon called Naberius in one of our books, a Marquis of Hell. Phoenix and Ashtoroth are in there too. The information is centuries old though—maybe those names are too public to hold power. Dr Lloyd arrives tomorrow so at least we'll get to work then.

Alec ate too many plums and thinks he's dying.

I'm so glad the show's up and roaring, dear—I can't wait to see you in your costume. I miss you. Best of luck.

'Here he is,' Aunt Minnie said. 'Did you get past the roses?'

Alec had managed to snag himself and was quite vocal about the idea of planting roses along a driveway.

But he'd taken the horse-cart and collected Pen, who looked keen and sparkling as she shook hands all around. 'How truly jolly. Thanks ever so for letting us invade your house.'

They carried Pen's suitcase up to Rom's room, and Rom was fairly sure she caught the doctor sighing. She didn't like having anyone in her room either. Not even Ditto, sometimes, but here there wasn't much choice.

The heavy trunk went into the parlour, where Pen seemed eager to set up a miniature lab. She winked at Rom when she saw the sofas squared around the empty hearth. 'I can kip in here tonight.' She was setting glass flasks and scales on the mahogany table where they played cards in winter. 'You said you've had some ideas?'

'Better than that,' Rom said, 'we found more demons.'

She and Alec told the story in bits. It was clear they were all straining in different directions—the doctor was all about panax and they'd have to set the rest aside for now. They said nothing about the bittergold or its properties. Pen was a fidgety sort of listener, asking questions out of order, but her eyes blazed.

'If the answer's in that book, we'll have it. There's three of us now. Four,' she added to Mr Mitchell, who shrugged.

'Just the hired gun.'

Pen jerked her head at Morgan. 'The kid's in on things?'

'He's our other consultant,' Alec said; 'our stepbrother.'

'Then you'll all have to promise to hush about what we find. I discovered something brilliant, you see—I don't want to wreck my bit of panax with chemicals so I didn't dare test anything on it. I don't know a thing about physics but I borrowed a load of old equipment to have a look. And one of them was an electrometer. For measuring tiny electrical outputs. It looks like a glass case, there's a rod attached to a sheet of gold leaf and the rod tips up when it's touched with anything charged. Well. I tested the panax.'

Morgan sat rigidly. 'What did you find?'

'The panax can't even be measured.' Pen folded her arms in satisfaction. 'A single grain has more voltage than a car battery. I should like to see if its electrical current is part of its curative properties.'

'Chasmeric emanations,' Morgan said. 'Really?'

'It makes perfect sense,' Rom said. 'That's what Mr Claker reads. It's what Kingsley smells. It's why they make a sort of crackle if you get too many of them in one place.'

'Can we build one of these machines?' Mr Mitchell asked.

'Not calibrated,' Pen said.

'We might be able to assemble something without a meter.' Morgan slid off the window seat. 'A simple indicator. Glass box, metal foil.'

'We can order things down from London if we must.' Alec was pacing. 'Proper materials. Is it necessary, though? Prideaux said we've got everything we need to solve it.'

'Prideaux's a wretch,' Rom said, 'I thought we all agreed.'

'What do we call our machine?' Pen asked. 'A magic-ometer. Demon-ometer?'

'It's called an electroscope.' Morgan reappeared at the door, unwrapping a chocolate bar.

Alec stopped. 'Is that my Toblerone?'

'It was.' Morgan tucked the chocolate between his teeth and smoothed the silver wrapper across his palm. 'Foil,' he said around the wedge of chocolate. 'Here.'

Alec took the scrap of metal. 'I'd rather have the chocolate. Not now,' he said irritably as Morgan took the bar out of his mouth again.

'Use a jam jar and some electrical wiring,' Morgan said. 'It might be an approximation, but it will work. We ought to be testing every chasmeric material we come across. Jasper said his work was dangerous. He seemed to take this seriously.'

'Jasper spent four pages talking about his rheumatic inflammation,' Rom said, 'his priorities are not our priorities.'

Mr Mitchell flexed his stiff fingers on the table. 'Give it a few years.' He nodded across at Morgan. 'Mock up a diagram and we'll make your box.'

He and Alec took the horse-cart into the village to buy copper wire and vanished into the parlour afterwards. After dinner he showed them: he'd taken the frame of an old glass lamp and set up the delicate foil hanging inside. Copper wire coiled out the top—the conductor, probably, a cunning little assembly.

'That is not a jam jar.' Morgan crouched to inspect. 'It should work perfectly.'

'It's working now,' Pen said, 'see the leaves of foil? They repel each other when there's an electrical field near the coil.'

Mr Mitchell nodded. 'It hasn't stopped since I put it together.'

'It's picking up on interference.' Pen touched her finger to the copper coil and the foil leaves inside fell flat. 'Now we can test it.'

'We should try it on Pixie first,' Rom said. She unbuckled the clasp from the neck of the dog, who watched with patient eyes.

They led Pixie up onto a chair beside the table and Rom held the heavy white paw beside the copper coil. Not touching, but close.

The frail metal leaves within the box lifted sharply apart.

Pen sighed. 'There,' she said, 'perfect. Something in the chasmeric magic has a particular frequency.'

Morgan discharged the wire again as Pen had. 'It's effective,' he said. 'Where's Pixie's collar?'

Rom held the gold links beside the copper coil, and within the glass box the foil reacted.

'Something's in there too,' Mr Mitchell said. He tapped the coil. 'If we had a machine with calibration could we isolate the stuff?'

'It's going again,' Pen said. 'Did you bump it?' She frowned at Mr Mitchell. 'You're wearing a wrist watch.'

'It's for diving.' He tugged up his shirt-sleeve and showed a silver-rimmed watch on a leather strap. 'Luminous dial,' he said.

'Must be interfering. You shouldn't be wearing that, anyhow; it's radium paint, strong stuff.'

'It's American,' Mr Mitchell said. 'It was a gift. The only kind you can see in dark water. I don't plan on replacing it.'

'Do as you like, but you need to take it off when you're here or we'll get mixed readings.'

'This,' Morgan said, 'this—' He pressed his wrist to his temple as though it ached. 'This is what I mean. The electroscope measures all sorts of emanations, not just electric. You said Jasper Teague left orders for his belongings to be destroyed?'

'Even the house,' Rom said. 'Nothing was supposed to be handled after his death. I thought he was just protecting his work.'

'He was protecting us. Everybody in his town. He knew it was contaminated.'

'You could be right.' Pen rubbed her chin. 'Before panax repairs a wound, it first consumes the damaged flesh. The only thing I've ever seen like it was in the War, we used to inject bad infections with a radioactive needle.'

'Ionising radiation.' Morgan sat heavily. 'Is that how how Jasper died?'

Rom rolled the cool gold chain between her finger. 'So this is dangerous to touch.'

'We don't know.' Pen bit her lip. 'We don't know nearly enough. May I borrow your horse? I must get to town and wire the X-ray labs.' She darted out, pulling on her jacket.

Rom replaced Pixie's collar, suddenly uneasy at the touch of gold.

Mr Mitchell was unbuckling his watch.

'Not in your pocket,' Morgan said, 'leave it down in the cottage. There's a lawsuit against that radium company. You're better off getting a new one.'

'It's military issue,' Mr Mitchell said with dangerous calm. 'They wouldn't use it if it wasn't alright.'

Morgan didn't look up from his writing. 'It needs to be encased in lead before you call it safe. Can you wire this when you're in town?' He handed his note to Alec as he stood. 'We can't take the collar apart by heat. No crucibles. Dissolving it is the only option.'

'That will take some nasty chemicals,' Mr Mitchell said.

'Father's suppliers will know.'

Morgan stayed behind, and Rom watched him shuffle his papers together. 'Is that true about the lawsuit?'

He raised his eyebrows as he gathered his thoughts. 'Yes,' he said. He looked down at his papers. 'Of course it's true. Father has shares in a radium mine in Uruguay.' Flatly. This wasn't a truce. 'What a perfectly stupid thing to wear on one's wrist. Does nobody pay attention to facts.' He put his notebook back into his satchel. 'The workers at the radium paint factory have cancer in their bones,' he said. He shouldered the bag on his way out, and glanced at Rom. 'If he doesn't listen to Dr Lloyd, you can try.'

He sulked through dinner. And all through the next day too; Alec was chatty enough that nobody seemed to notice, and Pen didn't know enough to see anything out of place. She'd been testing with the electroscope, propping Pixie behind an old refrigerator door and checking for radiation; lead didn't stop the emanations, and Jasper's notes suggested that sheet gold might be the only shield. Morgan paid no attention; Rom glimpsed his notes and suspected he'd started over again with the knotwork pattern.

The next day, though, when Alec whistled for Mr Mitchell to go swimming after lunch, Morgan put down his pencil and pushed back the chair. 'Wait up. I'll come.'

Alec mimed a heart attack behind him. But the muggy stillness in the sheltered garden was getting to all of them; even Rom was nearly tempted to the river.

'How are you all getting on with your holiday?' Aunt Minnie asked her that evening, as they dried the dishes in the fading kitchen.

'Brilliant,' Rom said, too enthusiastically. She sighed. 'Morgan's being monstrous but we've got some work done.' Aunt Minnie was too keen to have missed the hush of conspiracy that fogged her house. 'We're researching something. Following something Grandfather Teague was writing, partly a kind of archaeology. A buried treasure.'

'Here I was thinking both you children got your mother's temperament.'

'I never did,' Rom said.

'You two have always been mad for digging things up. But sometimes you're very like your father. He was a fanatic too, in his own way.' It probably didn't feel so long ago for Aunt Minnie, before the war and things. Her only brother. She put her tea towel over her shoulder. 'Let me show you something.'

Across the hallway stood the little under-room, as Alec called it, where Aunt Minnie did her ironing. It felt more like a sunny passageway, just a narrow place for a fireplace and a pair of sofas. Full of bookshelves, though, and Aunt Minnie gestured to a row of tiny notebooks stuffed beside a leather binocular case. 'I got a lot of Robert's things when he died,' Aunt Minnie said. 'Everything he left behind when he was called up for service.' She handed one of them to Rom, and flipped the tea towel wearily off her shoulder, and went upstairs.

It was a scuffed-up cardboard thing, pocket-small. The writing was loose and upright—recording days, days, glimpses of birds. One man and his binoculars, watching quietly.

Rom sat down, her lap full of little notebooks. She'd seen these in her father's hands, shoved in his pocket as they walked. Two years before the War; she'd been nine.

The birds were achingly common, finches and sleek jays. The notes when they moved to Egypt mentioned sandpipers, cranes. One memorable evening he'd heard a nightingale.

Green bee-eaters. Many mute swans. 1 lone flamingo (the children were ecstatic).

On the riverbank; she recalled it. Eating iced melon and waving at the stilted sugar-pink bird which existed, there, in that fresh land, like an extension of a dream. Her father's warm hand on her back.

And they had been ecstatic.

'Miss Godden?'

She rubbed her eyes. 'I didn't know anyone was still awake.'

'I'm heading down to bed,' Mr Mitchell said at the doorway, 'but I— well, I'm glad I caught you, actually. It's about Mckenzie.'

Not what she ever wanted to hear. Never quite a surprise. 'What's he done, Mr Mitchell?'

'Nothing, as far as I know.' The man raised his pale brows. 'He came swimming with us today. He's supposed to be resting his arm, isn't he?'

'He won't listen.' Rom put down the bird-books. 'It's nice he wanted to go at all.'

'He—ah, his shoulder. He injured himself playing cricket, I think?'

'Aunt Minnie thinks it will heal well enough.'

'School can be rough.'

'Yes,' Rom said, because he seemed to be waiting for an answer. She straightened on the sofa. 'Do you mean to say—'

Mr Mitchell was looking at the empty fireplace or something, not at her. 'There was something about him stabbing someone with a pen, Alec said.'

'Alec shouldn't have said. We don't know the full story and I—' She was going red, she knew it. 'What's the problem?'

Mr Mitchell cleared his throat. 'His arm, Miss Godden. It's broken, and his shoulder appears to be out of joint.'

Rom took a deep breath. 'He should have said something, we did ask. We'll get Pen to have a look tomorrow.'

'No. The thing is he has rather a lot of bruises. Across his shoulders, I mean. Almost faded now but I'd say somebody hit him over the arm until it broke. Probably a cricket bat.'

Rom held the back of the sofa. 'Who beat him?'

'D'you think he'd tell me?' Mr Mitchell glanced over. 'Somebody at school, most likely. It's no business of mine, but I mentioned it to Alec and he thought I should say something to you. I'm sorry if I'm intruding—' He faced her, probably relieved to be finished.

'Thanks for letting us know.' It was hard to talk. 'Morgan didn't tell us either.'

'Likely not,' Mr Mitchell said. 'Good night, then.'

The kitchen door closed and Rom was still standing in the sunroom with a notebook tight in her fingers. She realised she was crying.

21

June 26th

Dear Miss Rom,

    The big news of the week is my blister burst!! I know you were raving with concern but now you can sleep in peace. Last night was OPENING NIGHT and it was a perfect dream—partly wondrous but also feels like you gobbled too many sweets and can't recall your own name. I can't wait for you to see it.

After the show Hettie Gavreaux ran off with some rich nob and I thought it was the beastly Votaries again but all's well—just the ordinary sort of running away, elderly dick and a wad of cash.

Sorry Morgan is being a lump. At least he's learned to shut up a bit.

Ditto

Rom told Aunt Minnie early the next morning.

Aunt Minnie lit the stove in silence and made Rom some coffee. At last she sighed. 'I'll wire your mother. If she and Harry try to send him back to that school I'll be tempted to make trouble. And I'll talk to Morgan when he wakes. Don't tell him you heard; he wouldn't like anyone knowing.'

'I doubt he'd care much.'

'I'm sure he takes pains to make you think so. You could bridge the Atlantic with the pride of small boys.'

Rom listened to Alec's boots descending. 'We've been rather hard on him,' she said. 'I wish I'd known.'

'We all make a mess of things at some point. You can pretend you didn't, or you can apologise.' Aunt Minnie pointed at the chicken's bucket. 'Take that with you if you're fetching eggs.'

Morgan didn't come down to the parlour when the others did; Aunt Minnie took him in to town. Rom didn't see him until after lunch, on her way to hang out washing, when she got to the end of the towering rhododendrons and found him hunched on the garden steps with a book open. Bare knees above long socks. His left arm was tidily knotted in a clean white sling.

Rom stopped with the washing basket. 'May I talk?'

Morgan didn't look up from his page. 'I can't stop you.'

'I told your name in front of everyone,' she said. 'That was rotten of me.'

He stirred himself. 'It took you days to figure that out?'

'And I looked at your sketchbook.'

'I'm sure it was an accident.'

'When I said about your name, I didn't—' It was worse than talking to a stone wall. No wall ever had such terribly bored brown eyes. 'I knew I should have shut up but I didn't. I'm sorry.'

Silence.

'It's an interesting name.'

His fingers curled up like a spider on the open book. 'Alec told you about my arm.'

'That's why you wanted to move your seat in class? Someone was bothering you. And Mr Prideaux's puzzle—' She understood. 'Relix?'

'What is it you want?'

'I wanted,' she said carefully, 'to apologise.'

'Do you want me to say I forgive you?'

Rom paused.

'Because I don't.' He seemed to be reading again.

She moved on impulse and stopped. If she stormed away through the garden now they'd be just where they started, tomorrow and forever. 'I don't expect you to forgive any of us,' she said. 'But you ought to have told someone. I'm so sorry you couldn't. I don't suppose we've ever been that kind of family.'

She waded onwards to the clothesline.

Aunt Minnie had always called him Loveday when he was a small thing. He'd chattered even more than Alec back then, following them everywhere while Aunt Minnie let him ramble in that firm clear voice about the speckles on foxgloves and the petals on an apple blossom— they're related to roses. Did you know? Rosehips look like baby apples. But they taste very different. Yes, I know, Aunt Minnie in amusement, and she'd made him rosehip tea for breakfast and watched his mouth pucker.

Morgan didn't speak much to Rom all today, but he didn't do much of that anyhow.

'He looked at me when I passed him the salt,' Alec said when he caught her in the hallway. 'I think he might be warming up.'

28 Jun. '24

Ditto my dear,

I hope it's a little less stinkingly hot in London but I have serious doubts. Be sure to ice your feet if it gets too dreadful. All's well here: Alec and I compiling a Jolly Big Book of Demons (title pending) while Pen and Mr Mitchell yammer over science things.

Pen said half a dozen times we ought to test Pixie's blood in case she's made of panax, and at last we all agreed. Pen's very tidy with those things at least, and Pixie was very good about it—she knew it was serious and stood quite still. No luck with the blood though, it's pale as water and Pen said it's mildly antibacterial at most. Now she thinks it's only Coronets who have the panax—not so easy to nab one of those. She's returning to London soon, rather painful we haven't managed anything practical yet.

I do miss you. I wish you could have come down. But it's grand the show's done so well, I've seen all the reviews in the papers. I can't wait to see it and applaud till my silly hands fall off and one day—one day I shall see your name in the title billing, Lady Dido.

Yours ever so and warm enough to roast,

Rom

She was tempted to dip in the river once she got back clammy from the village post office. 'Parcel for you, Morgan. From Paris? Fancy.'

Morgan waved his hand from the window seat. 'It's for Mr Mitchell. My father sent a new watch.'

Alec looked up. 'That's decent of you. But he won't take it.'

'Probably not,' Morgan said. 'The dial isn't luminous. But it's waterproof; Father thought it might be appropriate.'

Alec grinned. 'It sounds like Father picked very well.'

The garden wavered in the heat. Pen was muttering to herself in the parlour and the others were busy with badminton; madness for mid-morning. Rom took her hat and a book and wound her way down through the garden.

She stopped to take an apple to Jubilee, Aunt Minnie's ancient cart-horse, and settled down at the river's edge where the willows shadowed the banks. River was too grand a word, it was just a noisy slash of clean water between heavy-headed grass, but it was deep enough to lose one's footing. A pleasant gushing while she read Wodehouse and ate apples.

'Swimming?' Mr Mitchell asked.

She jumped. 'Hell,' she said, 'no, just hiding from the sun.'

He'd come down to swim, no hat and a towel over his shoulder. He seemed uncertain whether to continue.

She turned a page. 'If you go around the bend I won't be able to see you. I promise.'

'You ought to go in yourself.'

'Not my style.'

He shuffled off his shoes beneath one of the willow trees. 'Not even to paddle?'

'I can swim,' she said. 'I learned at school. I'm quite alright in a pool. I just don't like rivers.'

'Why not?' His surprise was frank enough. She didn't know how to describe the uneasiness of sodden grass, gravel and wrong-textured mud.

At least a swimming pool sits still. A river wants to pull you somewhere.

'I can show you,' he said.

She wasn't sure if he meant it or just wanted to appear superior. 'I'm fine.' Her eyes moved to his wrist. 'You know they were both quite serious about your watch.'

He slung his towel over a willow bough. 'It's saved my life, on land and sea; they're fear-mongering.'

'Unfortunately I've never known Morgan to be wrong.'

Mr Mitchell kept his clothes on when slid down the bank. Even hampered by his trousers there was a sureness in the way he moved— none of Alec's exploratory manner, just a body slipping into clean water. Perhaps it's that easy for some.

He surfaced snorting like a horse. His hair was cropped too short to get in his eyes. But he flicked it back anyhow. 'Come in.'

She laughed aloud. 'You idiot.'

'It's shallower over here. I swear you'll like it.'

'Don't make promises, that's rather dangerous.' It did look blessedly fresh, though.

His eyes were a kind of challenge. 'You needn't,' he said. 'I just thought you might want to.'

Rom stood, toes curling in the grass. It would be easier to go in with just her underthings but she didn't plan to undress for anyone.

She sat on the bank, braced to slide in. He offered a hand in silence. 'You'll drop me.'

'I won't.'

She took it, his stiff fingers a quick grip, and slithered into the water. Grit and pebbles underfoot, a slink of hidden weeds. This is what she didn't like, the great pull against her legs. There was no logic to it. The same thing in the ocean rather excited her, though she never went in much deeper than her knees. She could swim entire laps of a swimming pool. But rivers are lean, winding, deceptive.

'Nice?'

'No,' she said, but it was far cooler. Better. Quite manageable, deep as her waist.

'See if you can cross to the other side. Then you return to your book and I stop bothering you.'

'Promises.' Her laugh chattered with the cold. He moved without warning and her foot slid on a stone. 'If you dare, you idiot—'

'Sorry,' he said. 'Better?' He held her properly, her arm and hip. No fumbling avoidance and he was, she realised, quite serious. He'd rather see her manage than fail. They splashed onwards, Rom kicking against her wet skirt and Mr Mitchell stepping backwards until it was shoulder deep. Then she had to bob on tiptoes and he let her push across the heady gush to the shallows.

She rested in silence, elbows propped on the bent reeds of the bank, and in silence hooked her hand over his shoulder to get back again. When she hauled herself dripping to the grass beneath her tree, the air draped warm.

His smile was golden. 'You faced one horror for the day. You've earned a biscuit.'

'I didn't say I was scared,' she said, but he emerged from his towel oblivious.

'You should do something terrifying every day. Only way to be sure you don't rot in your boots.' He handed her his damp towel, apologetic, and scooped up his shoes before he ducked away under the willows.

Aunt Minnie was over at Victoria's; for lunch they all ate in the kitchen. Selwyn chatted, slightly muted as he often was indoors, with the hampered courtesy of a man in a woman's house. Afterwards he disappeared directly to the garden for a cigarette; not avoiding Rom, but not available for conversation either.

A good thing, she thought as she and Alec washed the dishes. She didn't need complications in the way they spoke.

When they returned to the parlour, Morgan was seated cross-legged in the window seat, his dark eyes vivid. 'It's no use,' he said. 'I've had a lot of ideas.'

Pen looked tired. 'Isn't that a good thing?'

'I was drinking my tea,' Morgan said, ignoring her, 'and you were right.' He gestured to Alec. 'That pattern was in my tea-cup. If the spoon gets in the way of the current—'

This was too vague, grasping at similarities. Sharply un-Morganish. 'I've seen that too,' Rom said, 'but it's hardly magic.'

'No, it's liquid mechanics. I wired an associate of Father's, he deals in large earthworks. Which means researching local meteorology—'

'Weather,' Alec said flatly.

'Shut up,' Morgan said, 'listen. The pattern appears in clouds too. A stream of energy hits an upright object and the disturbance creates a wave. The windows at the Waldorf were vibrating, yes? Have you ever heard telegram wires singing?'

'On a ship,' Mr Mitchell said, 'if a mast catches the wrong sort of wind it sets the deck shaking.'

'Exactly.' Morgan's lips were tightly compressed. 'Jasper used chemistry as a tool, but it's not the source of magic. Chasmeric materials emit some kind of energy, like sound or light, that affects the physical world and the unseen field simultaneously. It could permeate anything.'

'What does that mean?' Mr Mitchell asked. 'We could use music?'

'If we had any clue of the notes. Or the pitch; I doubt a demon's going to respect a Continental middle C. Or it could be focused using some kind of mirror beam. Or something else; anything. Do you see? Maybe if I could understand every science, every application of it, I might have a chance.'

'The Coronets probably specialise,' Rom said. 'We know Desir does something with his voice.'

'Where are we supposed to start?' asked Pen.

Mr Mitchell snorted. 'How long is a piece of string?'

Morgan leaned back against the darkened window. 'Good question.'

'If magic is a force like gravity,' Rom said, 'it's going to work whether you understand it or not. Stop looking so far away.'

'I want to know,' Morgan said, his eyes fixed on the floor.

'Then you can start like everybody else, and be ignorant. Jasper's experiments worked. All we have to do is figure out his process.'

They spent the afternoon looking through the alchemical lexicons again.

3. It is also called Water of Life, for it causes the King, who is dead, to awake into a better mode of being and life. It is the best and most excellent medicine for the life of mankind.

4. Venom, Poison, Chamber, because it kills and destroys the King, and there is no stronger poison in the world.

'This is nonsense.' Morgan turned a page. 'Apparently there isn't even any point looking for a formula; *the philosopher's stone is made of one thing.*'

'That doesn't rule out our theories,' Rom said. 'If panax needs a combination of demon blood—the right birds—then it's the same material but not.'

Pen was flicking through her book. 'Jasper said the blood was sometimes toxic,' she said; 'when his demon cut itself the stuff burned like acid. Doesn't that remind you of something? *Alkahest, or atramentum, is nevertheless deemed to be mythical due to the inherent paradox: a universal solvent must also dissolve its container, and therefore can never be stored.* What if this is a type of demon blood? The chasma *are* the container.'

'That works,' Rom said slowly. 'But we haven't a clue which demon makes which kind.'

'What does alkahest look like?' Mr Mitchell asked. 'Is it the golden stuff?'

'It's probably dark,' Rom said, 'the Romans used the word atramentum for ink.' She stiffened. 'Oh, what if it's *nigredo*? The four stages of alchemy could be types of blood. Panax is just the one that heals.'

'Or,' Morgan said slowly, 'every demon has every kind of blood. The stages of purification are states of health.'

Pen's eyes narrowed. 'The healthy ones have panax?'

'They don't get ill,' Rom said. It struck her. 'They don't age, there's no change at all across time. But they do need to eat. We could assume a demon is strongest after consuming a soul. That would be golden. You said yourself that sometimes the blood seemed less effective; sometimes they only feed on human blood. Three stages of potency, and the mix is panax.'

Pen leaned forward. 'And the alkahest—'

'Is when they're hungry,' Alec said.

The room was silent.

Pen sat back in her seat. 'So that's how Jasper made it. He only needed to control how much his demon was fed.'

'Demons,' Morgan said, 'plural. They're efficient animals. A small amount of blood sustains them for weeks. It must take years to degrade. Creating alkahest at the same time as other ingredients—'

'Hell,' Rom said. 'You'd need a demon who drank blood, and one fed on mortal souls. And one who was starved. That's what Jasper meant.' She didn't dare look at Pixie. 'He said there's always a price to pay.'

Pen's eyes were bright. 'If somebody had the Phoenix, they wouldn't need to sacrifice any human lives at all. He's always golden. Nobody would ever have to die for panax.'

'No,' Rom said, 'they'd only need to keep a demon starving in a cage.'

'How do you think we discovered medicine? The entire basis of science is experimentation,' Pen said. 'If you want a surgeon you have to accept that somebody's been cut up. We could save every human life. Extend it like a miracle. Wars would—dear God—all the millions who died, you can't begin to think. These things would kill us if they had the chance, and you're worried about them being hungry?'

'If you'd met Kingsley—' Rom tried to keep her voice steady. 'You'd cage them for this?'

'We'll come to some agreement. There has to be some element of control over the process, even the demons would admit the need. It would be regulated properly. They must be clever enough to know what would happen to them if they start simply telling everyone.'

'There are hundreds of chasma,' Alec said. 'Maybe thousands. I don't think any of them will volunteer themselves for medical science.'

'It's a difficult question,' Morgan said. 'Medical ethics. This is a new situation.'

'And?' Mr Mitchell raised his brows.

'Demons show a high level of consciousness.' Morgan sighed. 'They would classify as human.'

'There's plenty of time to consider these things,' Pen said. 'You probably won't care to research panax much further than this, not now we know what we're trying to handle. This isn't amateur stuff, it's very probably deadly. It'll be up to the professionals. I do think we ought to be jolly proud of ourselves for solving it, though.'

'True,' Mr Mitchell said. 'True, then. I'm going back to badminton.' He pushed back his chair, and didn't seem surprised when Alec followed.

Pen waved at the microscope slides. 'I'll pack up this lot. Might nip into the village and stay at the hotel this evening—don't want to miss the early train.'

It was a relief to step out of the parlour to the dry blue dusk. They dragged the garden chairs onto the lawn. Rom didn't want to play just yet; her limbs felt numb.

She watched, though, with Pixie curled against her feet, glad for Alec's lightness. Somebody might as well be happy if they could.

He was playing Mr Mitchell, who did take his games seriously; maybe he'd have built a sandcastle with them after all. But Morgan was right. Selwyn was a man, despite his boyish restlessness, and Alec acted differently in front of him. She supposed she did too.

'Let,' Alec said.

Selwyn growled. 'You missed it, you donkey. Rom should umpire.'

'I didn't see. Morgan, was it a let?'

'Not even close.'

'Bastards,' Alec said, 'all of you—' He sprang around the grass, hot with energy, hitting as though it was tennis. Selwyn was stronger. Alec would tire himself if he didn't stop jumping about. At last he shook hands and Selwyn dropped into a chair. 'Good game, old man. Rom—'

'I'm on refreshment duty,' she said, and got away before Alec could drag her in. When she returned with lemonade Morgan was playing;

he'd come back down in one of Alec's white flannel shirts. She hadn't seen him without a tie since he was ten.

He'd taken off the sling and kept his bandaged arm close against his ribs.

'Don't let Aunt Minnie see you,' Rom said.

He moved slower than Alec, but he had a bullish stubbornness. Focused, a flush of colour high on his cheeks. Alec was saving his breath now. Trying to set the pace, swinging wildly to force something through. Rom wasn't even sure what she was looking at until he smacked the shuttlecock and Morgan didn't move for it. The shuttle flapped into the oleanders.

Morgan waited as Alec retrieved it. He'd known it wasn't worth trying for.

Alec served again, and Morgan's steadiness looked different now. Determination. Something else. Is this how he always was? Somewhere on the inside, click click react.

Alec shook his head when Selwyn called it and they pulled up. 'Well done, Mckenzie. That backhand of yours—'

'Lethal,' Selwyn said.

Morgan rubbed his hands on his shorts. 'Are you playing, Mr Mitchell?'

'Not today.' Selwyn paused. 'Next time.'

Morgan nodded and took his glass of lemonade inside, and later, when Rom brought the dinner plates out to the garden, she saw the upstairs window open and his dark head bent over his desk.

They ate on the lawn, sausages and Aunt Minnie's yellow tomatoes, but Pen didn't make an appearance. She was packing away her equipment. She had no need for any of them, after all, though she raised her head when Rom leaned in later.

'Oh? Fine. I've got plenty of work to go on with at home. Just have to get a good team of friendly fey together. It can't be too hard, they want our blood as much as we want theirs.'

She rumbled off to the station just as the late moon came over the hills, and the parlour was quiet when Alec got back with the cart.

'We'd better get this formula published,' he said. 'She's got all our research now.'

'Much good it will do her,' Rom said, 'she'll need to chain a demon if she wants alkahest. And she won't tell a soul. She's afraid the government will step in.'

'And if they do? We shouldn't have let her go.'

'It's better she's gone,' Morgan said on his way upstairs. 'Tomorrow we can start properly.'

Selwyn strolled after Rom when she went to close up the chickens for the night. 'Will you come for a swim?' He seemed wired with a need to do something, a mood she recognised.

'In the dark?'

'It's barely evening.'

After that she knew it hardly mattered. He wouldn't mind if she didn't want to swim. He didn't want to swim. 'Walk?' she said.

'Yes.' Quick with relief. They continued past the edge of the garden to the dim orchard. She ought to ease things, but talk felt silly. Words for the sake of it. And he seemed quite content to roam in silence, gazing up at the fruit. 'These aren't apples,' he said presently.

'Quince. Pears to the west, and plums by the river.'

'Nice place,' he said. 'Your aunt's a trooper for letting us all stay.'

'It seems wrong to have brought our mess with us, though. Her house is supposed to be peaceful.'

'If things go bad with these creatures there won't be any peaceful places.'

'You don't think it will come to that?' Possibilities felt far away. Her puzzles lay closer, her own tasks.

He didn't reply. Perhaps he felt the same.

'Do you ever think we might be delusional?''

'Often,' he said. 'Not much point worrying. The Front was useful for that much, you realise very quick your war isn't anyone else's. The officers are living something different. And the generals know things you never will, nobody ever has the whole map. You can only look at what you've got. Make it work.'

'And if we are delusional?'

They were near the river now; plums. He reached for one. 'Then I'd say we've all got quite an imagination.' He ate his plum and spat the seed thoughtfully.

'Is that the new watch?'

He held out his wrist. 'Double-cased stainless steel.'

'Cheapskate. Harry could have sent a gold one at least.'

'It's a solid thing. A Submarine, a little Swiss company makes them.' He glanced at her. 'I still don't plan to throw out the other one.'

'They were only concerned about you,' she said, 'Morgan and Dr Lloyd.'

'And you?' He brushed the back of her fingers. Heat seemed to roll from his skin.

She pushed up his sleeve, tucking her fingers under. It would be better to see him properly, spread in daylight. Maybe if he'd come to her earlier. But they wouldn't have. He'd been right to wait. This wouldn't have happened at any other moment, just here.

His touch along her wrist made her catch a drift of wanting as a sail might, caught and filled, and she reached on her toes and kissed him. He kissed back. The sandpaper warmth of his chin. But his mouth was too hasty and they pulled away again. She'd flushed hot.

His hand slipped beneath the strap of her dress. He rested it there on her shoulder. Did he want to know what she wanted?

She liked his hunger, instinctive and direct. She could find no shame in him. She reached down between their bodies and found the ridge of his cock.

'Ah, you—'

'Mhm,' she said, 'I didn't mention. I'm a bit of a rotter.'

His laughter was all breath. 'That makes a pair of us.'

The grass was cool against her legs when they settled under the willows. She touched herself first, dipping beneath her knickers to the humid lick of hair. When his fingers followed she guided the catch of his rougher fingertips. He moved her thigh, one hand braced in the grass by her shoulder, and she'd seen the way he handled glass. The way he hefted a tool. He'd hold her the way he did everything, with fierce consideration, and turn away simply as switching off a light.

She pushed her hands beneath his shirt. He eased himself into her. You'd think he'd eaten the sun, the way he burned. Under her touch, against her thighs. The living flinch of his cock, an ache of satisfaction. His solid shoulders bowed closer when she gripped them.

He wasn't entirely quiet, his breath coming in long shudders. He liked it when she moved with him against the grass. Restless tumult in her ears, no hurry at all but the natural way of things, the quickening urgency in their breath and that edge when she gritted her teeth—the seize of her whole being around him. A greed too intimate.

She eased her knees apart, flopping her legs around his own. The leaves stirred across the sky. He moved as though his head spun, leaning down to meet her lips, and it was hot. Sudden.

That's how you should kiss. Not because you've considered the options. Not because you've looked too long at a bitten lip and wondered how it tastes, but with a dizzy sort of helplessness. You kiss because you can't do anything else.

22

I have sent them away for the last time. Polly was worried by my worn appearance and no doubt will be relieved she need not bring her children near me—but my dear little Andromeda—a sturdy bright child. I know I have been weak.

Polly allowed me to photograph her and I dipped my plate in the stuff, the cursed alkahest, and when they left the house I rushed downstairs to develop the image with such a fear and a hope.

There I saw her, Andromeda on her chair, as solemn as you please—such a good girl to sit so still!—and next moment I saw the wings poised in the gloom at her back and thought my heart would stop.

I sent the picture to Polly today. Perhaps it was a confession of sorts. Perhaps they will not see what I see. Some days I cannot tell what I see; there is an ache behind my eyes.

JASPER TEAGUE, Journals, 6th July 1908

Morgan had been and gone when Rom descended for breakfast; his plate and tea-cup sat washed beside the sink. She was boiling the kettle a second time when Alec and Selwyn trooped in from their orchard huts, trying not to track damp grass into the kitchen.

'Tea, you lot?'

Selwyn met her gaze, a shy small shift in his eyes. Her face was probably reddening as she filled the cups. But the warmth over her neck was only pleasant.

A telegram had arrived for Morgan and he hooked Alec after breakfast. 'Can I get a lift to the train station? There's a parcel.'

'What for?' Rom asked, glad for something to work on.

She found out for herself when they unpacked Morgan's timber crate in the parlour.

'We'll need to do this outside.' He leafed through the invoice. 'This stuff will strip the wallpaper.'

'You're hoping to recreate the old man's work?' Selwyn asked.

'The chemicals are predictable,' Morgan said. 'The bittergold isn't.

Jasper might have used blood in the formula, or maybe panax. It should burn off with the rest of the impurities but it's hard to know whether to allow for it chemically. What do you think?' He unfolded the notepaper from his pocket. 'This part is from the pattern of the collar. This symbol means sublimation. It was in your notes.'

The cup-shaped sign with its curled rim. 'It's a process,' Rom said, 'a substance dissolving directly from solid to gas.'

'When you turn it up the other way it means precipitation,' Morgan said.

Selwyn leaned over. 'And linked together—'

'It's not Pixie's name at all. It's instructions. Basic chemistry. Just like every picture in that poetry book is a list of ingredients. All Jasper did was invent a recipe.'

'Kerckhoffs's Principle,' Rom said. 'All the pieces were in front of us.'

'Indeed,' Morgan said. 'Is the formula going to work?'

'God,' Alec said, 'you can't tell?'

'I only had an idea.'

Rom folded her arms in distaste. 'So you ordered a box of volatile chemicals?'

'I told my father we'd found some gold scrap and wanted to recover it. Basically it's true,' he said, affronted.

But Rom's glare wasn't for the lie. 'Were you even going to ask us whether you can chuck the collar in a vat of acid?'

'You're going to say yes. You want this too.'

'It could go badly,' Selwyn said. 'What's the worst case scenario?'

'Worst case,' Morgan said, 'the bittergold won't respond and we'll have a few quarts of fluids to dispose of. Alec, if you break that bottle the fumes will eat your eyeballs.' He folded up the invoice. 'Any other questions?'

They set up a trestle table on the edge of the orchard, beside the pickers' huts. Rom marked a circle first—a ring of salt scattered large enough to enclose them all, and the table, and Pixie lying solemnly in the cool grass.

Rom winced as they opened the crates. Heavy rubber gloves, glass beakers. 'I'm not touching any of this.'

Morgan was unpacking jars. 'I can do it.'

'Not a chance,' Alec said, 'you're still bandaged. If you blow yourself up we'll never hear the end of it.'

'Let me do it,' Selwyn said. 'One bomb's much like another. I've slapped together a grenade from a sardine tin and a handful of white phosphorus.'

'This isn't anything the same,' Morgan said. 'You won't know how to stop things if the reaction goes wrong.'

'If the reaction goes wrong,' Selwyn said carefully, 'there won't be much time to do anything at all.'

Alec fidgeted. 'Are you prepared to lose a hand?'

Selwyn didn't look up as he dragged on a glove. 'Usually.'

Rom brought over Pixie's collar. 'This is it, I suppose.' She and Alec stood within the rim of the salt ring as Selwyn lined up his materials. 'We begin with dissolution.'

Pixie sat close, her heavy haunches against Rom's ankle.

The shape of Morgan's mouth was uncompromisingly adult as he read out the instructions. 'Hydrochloric,' he said, his notes held open like a songbook. 'And then you add the nitric. With great care.' He glanced toward Rom. 'This is aqua regia, if you're a medievalist.'

Selwyn measured and poured, infinitely delicate. The liquids splashed into the beaker, clear as water, and he dropped in the collar. He looked over his shoulder. 'Stand back, you lot.'

Rom peered closer. 'Nothing's happening.'

'It's called a hangfire,' Selwyn said. 'Sometimes you fire a weapon and the thing takes a moment to catch.'

The beaker already swirled a dirty yellowish. 'Is that from the panax?' Alec asked.

Morgan made a long patient sound. 'It's a chemical reaction. You donkey. It's going to take hours,' he added, 'we'll leave it overnight.'

But the trestle table rattled. The solution seethed, amber red, the gold chain bobbing in the liquid. It fumed to a brownish fug.

'Smells like hell,' Alec said.

The bright orchard beyond was stirring but the wind no longer reached them. Their small sounds were amplified, the chime of glass and Morgan's focused breathing. Vaporous white breaths. Rom's cheeks felt stiff and cold. The temperature was plunging, bitter through her summer dress.

Alec's anxious laugh came bouncing from every direction. 'This isn't science, is it.'

Selwyn looked around. White shards stiffened around them in an arc of ice crackling up from the grass. It glistened overhead, ringed by the salt and contained, thickening as they watched.

Pixie dropped to her belly and whined. She rubbed her muzzle into the frosted grass.

'The off-gassing must have disturbed the atmosphere,' Morgan said, 'if we just get back—'

The beaker flared blue in a plume and Rom staggered. The air was swallowed, a terrible weightless lift. Her temples ached with pressure.

Alec said something but all sound was gone between them, lost in their cold breath and the turbulent shaking. He caught the edge of the table. Morgan's eyes were closed. Sel had dropped to a crouch, his face shielded. The beaker trembled against the table and it would have to shatter, nothing could hold forever. Not her breath, her ears.

Rom stepped back. Salt crunched underfoot and she fell.

Clean air hit her face as the fumes cleared, tugged by the wind, and the frost blew from their midst. The beaker steamed a clear honey colour.

'Shit,' said Morgan, breathless.

Pixie whined, her short fur prickling. Her shadow swung over the grass, abruptly stark, and reached for a moment over all the frosted lawn—hooked and curved, some bulk of restless flesh. The dog shook out her tail and slunk under the trestle table.

'Isn't she going to change?' Rom asked.

'The collar was probably only a lock,' Morgan said. 'They change form on their own. I'm betting, though, if you dipped your hand in a chasma's blood you'd see your Skein was gone.'

Selwyn flapped the heavy rubber glove from his hand. 'That was it.' He was breathing hard. 'The real thing.' He waved at the beaker. 'At least you've got yourself a jug of very costly necklace juice.'

'This isn't done yet.' Morgan hauled himself to his feet and pulled the gloves on. 'This should be stable, I'm only adding water and precipitant. No, don't touch it.' He leaned away from the vicious fumes as he tweaked the solutions. 'It will settle by morning.'

'What about Pixie?' Rom said. 'Must we ask her to change? We could try a summoning.' She leaned to look under the table. 'Hop out, you silly doggo.' Something struck her shoulder, small stones pinging her back and cheek.

Alec grabbed her arm. 'Get down.'

Rom scrabbled with him under the table, knees in the grass.

'It's raining black ice,' Selwyn said with immense calm as he pulled himself in beside her. 'Why?'

Morgan's eyes were bright as he tucked himself in at the end. 'Sublimation,' he said. 'Something in the bittergold turned straight into gas.'

'And now it's precipitating,' Rom said. 'What on earth?'

Morgan was laughing helplessly, a bump against Alec's shoulder. 'It's precipitation,' he said. 'Literal, chemical, metaphysical—' He dissolved again in a gasping laugh. '*Precipitation—*'

Alec looked rather dazed. 'It's not that funny.'

'It really doesn't matter if we're ignorant.' Morgan wiped his sleeve across his mouth and composed himself without embarrassment. 'We don't have a clue how it works, and it doesn't even matter.'

The scorching shower was slowing already, the grass left pitted with steaming puddles. Selwyn stuck his head out. 'All clear.'

'I say,' Alec began, but he didn't say. He only tipped up his chin to stare. Directly over them the sky was brilliant blue, a perfect hole punched through the clouds. The circular rim began to warp in the wind even as they watched.

'Chasma,' Rom said. The fumes had gotten to her head. Or maybe just the whole strange mess.

They sat limp in the shrivelled grass.

'We can tackle Pixie tomorrow.' Alec laughed shakily. 'It's what we wanted. Isn't it? We broke the ruddy thing and the dog didn't turn into a monster and nobody's been eaten. I should think that's a grand day's work.'

Aunt Minnie had left them a plate of lamb chops for dinner; they made a little campfire at the end of the garden. Alec cooked, brightly absorbed. And Rom sliced cucumbers and listened to their echoes.

From the kitchen window they were better observed. Morgan was describing something—she'd never noticed this. His hands moved when he was trying to find the right words, wide gestures from the shoulder. Selwyn's laugh—*ha, ha*, the dips of quiet marking Morgan's interjections; Alec's gusting voice. We're all just children playing with matches, she thought.

They ate like children, noisily. She filled a bowl with perfumed Gillyflower apples for dessert. 'I should have made a cake. Forgot, though.'

'You could always summon a demon,' Alec said. 'Tell him to wash the dishes while he's at it.'

Morgan rubbed an apple on his cuff. 'Would you ever?'

'Depends what they were offering,' Alec said. 'And what they wanted in return. You can see why people would be interested, everyone wants to wish on a star.'

'What if they only wanted blood?'

'I can think of plenty of things to ask for.' Alec shrugged. 'And I'm not all that convinced about souls. You mightn't even miss it. Non-existence can't be too painful, there's no self left to feel it. Wouldn't you say? Logically.'

Rom stopped chewing. 'You'd do it?'

'No.'

'Me neither.' She threw her apple core into the fire. 'We don't know nearly enough, what souls are worth or what the whole point even is. I imagine it makes more sense if there's an afterlife. The Egyptians made a world of it. Death hardly frightened them at all, they built a whole economy on that. I don't think that would be better, but there might be some kind of heaven—even just more lives, reincarnation. There'd be some relief, wouldn't there? It would make sense of things. We'd have a chance to fix our problems. It seems unfair to have only this.' She plucked the grass beside her ankle, rubbing the greenish juice between thumb and finger. 'Father always said we only have one life, nothing else. I used to think it was rather dull. Now I think that's brave. Braver than I am, maybe.'

The silence was a kind of exposure.

'I don't know what he'd have said if he met a demon.'

'If there are demons, there must be other things,' Morgan said, 'unlimited things we haven't seen yet.'

'Nothing you'd give a soul for?'

'No.' Morgan raised his dark brows across the fire. 'Mr Mitchell?'

Sel laughed. Uncomfortably, she thought. 'Not personally, no.'

'What about you?' Rom asked. 'I'm surprised you believe in souls at all. Something without a shred of proof.'

'I believe in demons,' Morgan said. 'Demons believe in souls. They find them valuable. I'd be stupid to ignore that.' He reached for another apple. 'There's plenty of things I'd want, though. If we're talking about wishes.'

Alec eyed him. 'Such as?'

'Rolls Royce.'

'Good lord, wouldn't we all.'

The twilight was silver. There was just a tease of wind; the cooling grass held the end of summer, snared like sand in the bottom of her pocket.

'The world's about to get strange,' Selwyn said. 'Are we ready, do you think?'

'We have to be.' Rom settled her chin on her knees. 'I was waiting for an adventure. Planning—like it was a place I could go to—but it came to us.'

'Coming for everything,' Alec said. 'I wonder if the Phoenix will get back to America. That'll be chaos.'

'I suppose we'll have the same here, once we make the panax.'

Selwyn hesitated. 'Panax sounds like bad news for demons. It weakens them, it's a weapon to us. Why is Mr Prideaux encouraging it?'

'Mr Prideaux would throw dynamite for fun,' Morgan said from across the fire. 'I don't think he concerns himself with outcomes.'

'His puzzle,' Rom said. 'Can you solve it now you know what to look for?'

'Too many things it could be. The thing we're always missing is context,' Morgan said. 'Mr Prideaux never told me there'd be an answer. I'm not sure I was supposed to find one.' He stood and stretched his shoulder. 'We'd better check on the necklace juice.'

They'd left the beakers on the trestle, sheltered by the empty garden shed, and the soupy fluid had already accumulated a glitter of sludge. Alec held a torch while Morgan decanted the acid. He looked pleased. 'We have gold dust.'

'There, Pixie.' Rom nudged her. 'We broke it for you. If you're just being stubborn, I'm going to be cross.'

Alec wanted music and set up the record player in the parlour—
quietly, for the sake of Aunt Minnie, who'd returned with a headache
from a day of picking. Selwyn went off through the garden to bed. He
seemed to wake before any of them and kept the irritating natural
hours of a small child. Morgan disappeared to his room upstairs, and
Rom paused over the kitchen mess; she wasn't in the mood for dishes.
She could drag herself down early to wash them, and maybe Alec too,
if she could bribe him with more picnics. Tonight she wanted a walk.

She hadn't had much of a plan, but it felt right to turn left at the
hydrangeas and wander down to the little wooden huts, propped on
timber struts like pigeon-houses in the clover. The hot eye of Selwyn's
cigarette showed in the dusk. He was sitting on the step.

'Nice night for it,' he said. That slow smile as he pulled himself to his
feet and lit the oil lamp inside.

Rom undressed by the neat low bed. Beside his cigarettes he set
another bright tin; 3 *Ramses*, said the label. But they weren't cigarettes.

'You're prepared.'

'Well.' He rubbed his chin. 'I thought it was better to, you know.'
Defensive. Did he think she could be upset by that?

She took his heavy head in both hands. His grey eyes were clear as
diamonds. 'Wise man.'

He drew her to the edge of his bed and opened the little tin, and he
let her take his sleepy cock in one hand and squeeze until they could
slick the rubber over it. 'Careful,' he whispered: oh, the tender burr of
his voice.

'Selwyn.'

'Hm?'

'Say *rubber prophylactic*.'

His laughter was an unresisting choke as he rolled into her.

They got through half the tin before they heard Alec clatter into the
hut next door, and Rom carried her shoes back barefoot to the
sleeping house.

Alec and Morgan went out to the garden early, checking the precious
gold mud. But when they came in for breakfast Morgan was
thoughtful. 'It's still precipitating; the filtrate was full of something
powdered. Perhaps it couldn't materialise until we'd removed the gold.'

Rom was trawling their books for summoning rituals, trying to assemble a ceremony for Pixie, and when she passed later Morgan and Alec had rinsed and dried the gold, packing it into the smallest jam jar they could find. Into another they'd decanted the strange dust.

'That's bone,' Alec said, 'from a demon, isn't it.'

'The acid would have taken anything that wasn't noble metal,' Morgan said.

'How much do you think it's worth?'

'Put it down, Alec.'

The wind was up, not too hot, and they dragged out the badminton racquets before lunch. 'Where's Sel? Is he playing?'

'I'll go.' Rom pushed herself from the garden chair and walked down to the buzzing orchard. The door of Selwyn's hut stood open. 'Are you in?' She didn't need an answer. His cough was rather dreadful.

'I'm here,' he said, 'coming,' and she stepped up to the doorway.

'Alec thought you might want to play.'

Selwyn stood by the creased bed. He'd been resting. 'Alec—' He cleared his throat. 'Alec just likes an audience.' He laughed. And interrupted himself to cough again, shoulders rounded, and carried on coughing into the crook of his arm while he felt for a handkerchief. Rom looked away until the rasp became a retch and he sat down. 'Damn.' He swallowed hard. His sleeve was stained pinkish with phlegm.

She stumbled up the step. 'Are you alright?'

He shrugged her away. 'Catching my breath.'

'I'll get you a clean shirt.' She had to find something to do. 'In the trunk?' His shirts were folded, thick pale-blue cotton. When she returned he'd taken off his tweed waistcoat and was scrubbing at the sleeve with his handkerchief.

She nudged his hand away. 'We'll wash it,' she said.

Selwyn shuffled his suspenders off, looking at the floor as he unbuttoned his collar. 'I should be dressing for lunch.'

'Nobody will fuss if you don't come up to eat. It's the country,' she said, so he'd know it wasn't a concession to an invalid. 'We're not very formal here. Anyway, you should be in bed. And there's a doctor in town.'

Displeasure shadowed him. 'I'll see one in London next week.'

Which meant *don't fuss*, clear as daylight. He moved stiffly, tugging the stained shirt over his head, and the rough gold hair under his arms was dark with sweat. So was his singlet, the cream wool dampened. It looked like he was shivering when she helped him pull the clean shirt on. But he couldn't be cold.

'You're feverish,' she said as she shuffled the shirt straight.

'Likely.' He breathed carefully in the pause. 'I say, I'm sorry.'

'Don't be.'

'You ought to be a nurse.'

'Never. I fret too much.' She was doing up the top button and he tipped his head away from her fingers.

'I wouldn't worry, it doesn't show.'

He was trying to amuse her, so she smiled as she lifted his wrist to button his cuff. But she wouldn't ignore the bloodstained shirt on the floor. He stood, bracing his calves against the bed as he tucked in the shirt-tail. He went very still as she got the steel buttons of his trousers open.

He'd been ill in the War. He was used to being tended, surely, but he didn't meet her eyes as she tucked in his shirt. The flush of hair at his groin showed briefly before she buttoned the flies again.

'All done?'

'You're as bad a patient as I am a nurse.'

'I'd rather you didn't mention this, it's nobody's problem.'

Quite true. And yet. 'Would you like some tea? It won't be lunch for a while.'

'I might sleep, if that's not horribly rude.'

She scooped his shirt from the floor and rolled it neatly. 'Alec will fetch you later.'

She left his door open to the bright air. Coming up through the garden she heard Alec's voice behind the rhododendrons, and Morgan with him. She cut past the clothesline to the kitchen door. On the staircase landing she stopped, and leaned at the open window for a long time.

The noonday glowed green with their distant noise. Rom's eyes followed a wasp as it crawled across the window-frame and butted the glass with fine uncertain legs. She bent and blew lightly. The wasp fell with a click, squirming with all the ugliness of a thing upturned.

There are many sorts of secrets. Just as many categories of betrayal.

She went upstairs to Aunt Minnie, and unrolled Selwyn's shirt. Aunt Minnie put down her iron and said it was pulmonary tuberculosis. They sent for the doctor.

Rom was feeding the chickens in the white noon when Alec found her. He looked ferocious. 'They're not letting me see him.'

'The doctor will tell us when he comes down.'

He kicked the nodding daisies. 'Utter rot. Sel's quite well. He was playing badminton yesterday.'

And had to rest most of the morning, Rom thought. But Alec wouldn't want to hear reason.

Rom returned to her bedroom. It was lunchtime but she couldn't go down. Maybe Aunt Minnie knew, because when she caught Rom skulking in the hallway she sighed. 'Make yourself a ham sandwich, I'm not calling anyone to the table.'

When the doctor left Rom didn't move from her desk. Barricaded with books, staring out the window. Ignoring the empty side of the room; the spare bed had been carried out and set up in the yellow-papered study for Mr Mitchell. Then Alec knocked on her door and together they waited in the hallway.

Morgan marched upstairs, hands in his pockets, and joined them in silence. She was surprised; nobody would blame him for keeping out of this, the awkwardness of a sickroom and someone else's troubles.

When Aunt Minnie let them into the yellow room, Selwyn was tucked under the starched bed sheets looking flushed and sullen.

'Hullo,' Alec said with desperate pleasantness.

'Dr Hillier agrees it's a case of advanced phthisis.' Aunt Minnie folded up her glasses. 'We'll track Mr Mitchell's temperature twice a day, and once he returns to his sister they can run some proper tests.'

Alec shuffled. 'Where do you think he'll—'

'The sanatorium at Birmingham has a good reputation.'

Selwyn's eyes were flat. Disbelieving, as though he'd been slapped. 'I'm not going to live in a hospital.'

'You can decide that for yourself,' Aunt Minnie said. 'But the x-ray isn't an option, Mr Mitchell. Each time you breathe you're endangering everyone in this house. We're all in good health; a little exposure won't do much harm. Not everyone with whom you come into contact will be so lucky.' She left the notebook and glass thermometer on the dresser. 'Alright,' she said to them, 'I shall give you a quarter of an hour to visit. Don't tire him out. And don't approach the bed, please.'

After she closed the door there was a ringing kind of silence.

'Rotten luck,' Alec said. Selwyn glared at the wall. And this wasn't how any day should go, in this house or anywhere, and Rom sat down on the end of his bed.

'I know,' she said to Alec, 'don't be silly. The windows are open, nobody's going to catch anything. I'm not afraid.' Then Alec sat too, on the other side. Morgan leaned against the wall with his hands behind him.

'Good lord,' Selwyn said, and she wished he'd swear instead. 'Cheer up, I don't intend to die.'

'You won't,' Alec said, 'you've gotten through worse than this.'

'Nobody's going to die,' Morgan said evenly. 'We have a recipe for panax.'

Rom's skin prickled. 'D'you have a soul handy that you plan to sacrifice?' But she already saw where his mind leapt.

'Dr Lloyd has a grain left in London,' Morgan said. 'And we know where the Phoenix is.'

Alec rubbed his hand across his eyes. 'Lucky. We'll see if we're right about this stuff.'

'No,' Selwyn said, 'I don't want it.'

'You can't be serious.' Alec's voice was quiet. 'You might get worse.'

'Death I can manage, but I'm not paying a demon anything.'

'You don't have to,' Rom said, 'not even relix, and you'll be fixed.'

Selwyn's forehead darkened. 'It's my own life. I can choose, can't I?'

'That's bloody stupid,' Alec said. 'It's medicine.'

'Medicine somebody died for.'

'Not if we get the Phoenix back,' Alec began, and Selwyn made a noise.

'I don't need anyone's help.'

'Fine,' Alec said, 'fine,' and it was beginning to sound like an argument. He tried to wrench things somewhere better. 'We're heading home in a few days too. You won't be missing anything here.'

'We haven't gotten through the last of Pixie's spells.'

'No,' Rom said, 'we must be very close, though. We couldn't have done it without you.'

Selwyn shuffled his head on the pillow. 'You shall have to write and tell me how it goes.' His eyes moved to the open window, his mouth pinched white, and she didn't want to leave him here alone. But the effort to face them was more than he should have to manage.

'Come along, you lot.' She squeezed Selwyn's wrist, his dry fierce pulse. 'Aunt Minnie will yell.'

They found themselves in the kitchen, a loose wordless assembly. Aunt Minnie joined them, sliding into her chair with a sigh. 'He's blazingly hot; his temp's permanently elevated. There's nothing we can do here.'

'What'll they do at the sanatorium?' Alec asked.

'Surgery to his lungs, if it's not too far gone. Bed rest; something for the pain.'

His eyes were wide. 'That's all?'

'Why do you think I've been asking him to go? I know the recovery rate. It's a bastard of a thing to have.'

It was quiet in the kitchen as Rom began to make tea. Morgan stood in the doorway with his arms folded, and Alec was drumming on the table-edge. Rom asked, eventually. 'How long, do you think...?'

'Five years, with luck,' Aunt Minnie said. 'And if he recovers he'll be at the san until he's clear. No more work.'

'Bugger that,' Alec said, 'he'll never agree.'

'It isn't a matter of what anybody wants. He needs to be quarantined.' Aunt Minnie patted at her pocket and frowned. 'My pencil's upstairs. Be a dear, Morgan—it's on the dresser in Mr Mitchell's room. He oughtn't be catching any trains,' she went on, as Morgan's boots echoed from the stairs. 'He'll have to, though, if his sister can't come down for him.' She took the tea-cup Rom handed her and began to spoon sugar.

'You're taking this very bloody calmly.' Alec's voice rose. 'He's our friend.'

Aunt Minnie didn't look up. 'I'm not a doctor. Not even a nurse, but I worked in hospitals. Your friend is lucky, if anything; he came home.'

'We must be able to do something or what's the *point* of—'

'Alec,' Aunt Minnie said. 'Go outside and come back when you're feeling better.'

Alec shoved back his chair and went. The kitchen door shook behind him.

Rom sat in the chair he'd left, perched on the edge. She poured herself tea. 'There's a medicine,' she said. 'Something Dr Lloyd was researching. It would probably fix whatever Selwyn's got, but he doesn't want it. And the medicine isn't—' Words. Words. 'It isn't good.'

Aunt Minnie nodded, very slowly. Maybe after a war nothing surprised her. 'Doctors have their own kind of courage,' she said. 'So do soldiers.'

Rom stirred another lump of sugar, just to watch it crumble on the wet spoon. 'He should live. If he can.'

'We had to call the doctor, that was right. Now it's up to Selwyn. He's young. It isn't over yet. And death's not quite the opposite of living.' Aunt Minnie sat with her boots apart and hands tired between her knees. 'Life is a difficult thing. It's grand, but surviving isn't always enough. Let the boy meet it on his own terms.'

Rom pressed the grit of sugar against the inside of her cup. 'I thought he just had a cough,' she said miserably, and they drank their tea in silence.

The front door opened a little while later and closed, and the sound stirred the wooden hallway. 'He forgot my pencil, of course,' Aunt Minnie said. Morgan's dark head passed by the far window, towards the back garden.

'I'll take him biscuits.'

'Leave him. He won't want anyone.'

'Did you really leave your pencil upstairs?'

Aunt Minnie smiled faintly. 'Yes. But I could have asked somebody else to fetch it.'

'That's good of you.'

'You know how Morgan looks at him. You must have noticed.'

Rom had noticed it. She hadn't expected anyone else to.

'Poor silly pup, I'd hoped it would do him good to have an idol.' Aunt Minnie gathered up the plates.

Rom looked down at the table, at her own folded hands on the chintz tablecloth. 'And Selwyn, does he—'

'Probably. But I think he's the honourable type.'

'Yes,' Rom said, because there wasn't anything else to say.

Dinner was a dismal thing; Alec took his plate outside and ate somewhere in the garden, and Aunt Minnie didn't stop him. Morgan didn't come down at all until she went up and knocked. Rom was already washing the dishes by then, but she saw his gaze fixed on the tablecloth, the utter steadiness with which he finished his soup.

Aunt Minnie's boots creaked on the back step. 'Morgan?'

He raised his head.

'Pack your things, love. I'll wire your aunt tomorrow.'

His mouth pressed tightly. But he went upstairs and they heard his trunk clattering, so perhaps he knew there was no point arguing.

Rom didn't see him again that evening. When she went to brush her teeth she found the sealed biscuit tin outside her bedroom door, weighty with the hidden jars of powder. Alec was taking him down early to the station, and the next morning she was in her bedroom when she heard the cart on the driveway.

She leaned out of the window, though, and saw Alec's hair as he led out the cart, a fox-bright flash beside the old horse, and Morgan huddled on the open bench beside him.

Alec was saying something. Morgan didn't look back.

23

I had a letter from Polly. She has had a second child—a boy. Little Andromeda is doing well, learning to speak. I wonder what her first word was.

Polly sounds foolish as ever; she and her husband plan to travel the Mediterranean—of all the stupidities—they're poor as churchmice. The husband is an artist, I believe.

I've had a luckless few weeks. My store of alkahest has been used, and there are difficulties obtaining more. Avery has mentioned how it must be created, and I cannot imagine imposing such cruelty on any creature—but there will be no panax without it.

Polly said she named her boy after me; Alexander Jasper. Perhaps if my success comes quickly I will be able to send them some money.

JASPER TEAGUE, Journals, 19th Oct. 1906

'So much for summer,' Alec said. 'Remind me not to bother next year.'

They'd wandered in late for breakfast and found Aunt Minnie out somewhere, her brusque note on the table, and Pixie dozing on the back step.

Selwyn's sister had picked him up, a small tense woman with burning eyes, and all their goodbyes had been pleasant and hollow. Rom and Alec spent a few strange days kicking around the garden, and once went down to the coast, but today the house echoed uncommonly empty.

'We've still got tomorrow,' Rom said. 'We ought to finish Pixie's ceremony.'

'Aunt Minnie won't appreciate us spattering ectoplasm over her kitchen.'

'They're demons, not ghosts. And she won't be back until dinner. Don't you think we should try?'

Alec sighed. 'We might as well get somewhere after all our work.'

They carried everything down, salt and candles and their notes, and led Pixie through the deep green garden to one of the pickers' huts. Their ritual pieced together lines from volumes of demonology and the oldest magic Rom could find, Sumerian things, and warding patterns copied from *The Nest of Amoury*.

'If there's no single perfect method then this can't be wrong,' Rom said. But the daylight felt distinctly un-occult, bright through the slatted walls.

'No robes,' Alec said. It might have been disappointment.

'Find a tablecloth if you want a cape.' Rom had the notebook open as she wrote on the wooden floor, slow strokes with a finger dipped in oil. 'Sit still, doggo.' She traced a ring enclosing Pixie, who sat high and tight and cattish on her heavy paws.

Alec followed, correcting the smudged shapes of the glistening oil. 'What do you think?'

'If it fails,' Rom said, 'it won't be due to faulty linework.'

'What if it rains hellfire again?'

'We're inside.' But Rom was ready to dive for the door if necessary. She knelt beside the circle. 'I know you can understand me, Pixie. Kingsley said you could.'

The dog turned her muzzle away, her tense flank rippling like a horse's.

'Pixie, I command you.' With a sewing needle Rom pierced the soft flesh beside her own thumb and squeezed up a speck of blood. She thought of Kingsley's oath before Corbin Quinn. 'By crux, string, and bone,' she said, 'speak and break what binds you.'

Pixie bent and licked over Rom's hand. She whined, a startled doggish sound. Rom's ears popped.

'Is that it?' Sunlight striped Alec's face and he looked sharp and puckish. But Pixie hadn't moved.

Rom groaned. 'You must let us, old girl. We're safe, you can change back.'

'I'd rather a hailstorm,' Alec said.

Pixie put her paws together and stretched. Her shoulders tightened in strange undulations, her skin crawling with colour. The flex of flesh uncurled too fast and her white body singed like paper, seized with a fierce blue light that couldn't be looked at. Clean fire tore silently across her.

The heat hit Rom's face. 'Speak,' she said. She heard the uncertainty.

Pixie raised her head. She wasn't a dog.

She crouched naked on the wooden floor, white hair tangled thick down her back, and she was beautiful. Strong-boned. Her lashes were pale as her eyes.

'That's her?' Alec's voice was high. 'That's what Pixie is?'

The girl wrapped her arms around her bare knees. She spoke. Her voice was deep and soft and the words tumbled out, lost sounds.

'Does she speak English?'

'Some's familiar but this—I haven't a clue.' Rom stepped forward and stopped against an impact. She stung like ice. 'Something's here. I can't get close.'

Alec stretched a hand. 'Electric?'

'She can't leave the circle. We can't go in.'

Pixie dropped her head to her knees with a low ragged sob.

'It wasn't supposed to hurt her,' Rom said. The grass outside chirruped with birds. The hut sweltered under the low roof, but Pixie shivered. 'We need help. You stay. I'll telephone.'

'In town?'

'We've got Jubilee,' Rom said, 'I can ride.'

She was halfway to the garden when Alec yelled after her. 'Who are you calling?'

She didn't stop. 'Who do you think?'

The old horse was sleepy but she jolted as Rom dragged down the saddle and led her from the stall. No time to put on boots. Her purse for the post office telephone, and then she was on the dusty road, swinging into the wide saddle and heading for the village.

The wind was up, flinging grit in her eyes, and she jammed her hat on harder. Her hands were certainly not shaking. The road was longer than she remembered, narrow between lush hedges, high under blinding sky. It snaked out of the valley to the whitewashed village— one mile, and she felt every second of it.

Mrs Polworth at the inn was staring when she pulled up in a scuffle outside the post office. She thrust her purse across the counter and dialled at the wall-mounted telephone.

'Yes?' It was Kingsley's voice.

'It's us. Godden. Is he in?'

'What for?'

'We need to talk to him, it's Pixie—'

'No.'
'It's urgent, she's hurt, we need—'
'He said no.'
Rom stopped. 'He's there? Can't you ask?'
'I'm sorry, Miss Godden.' And Kingsley sounded it, too. He hung up.
'Shit,' Rom said to the buzzing phone. 'Shit, shit—' and she ran back to the desk. This time she sent a telegram.
PIXIE IS DYING WE WILL PAY PLEASE HURRY
The post boy took it. Stamped it. Handed it to the man at the machine. 'Will you wait, miss?'
Rom waited. The fresh lawn beside the post office ran down to the river's edge, and she walked and waited.
All the mechanisms of speed weren't quick enough. Hum and wire transfer, a click at the other end as the message tapped out. A slip of card, prompt dispatch to the crowded street and the telegram boy in his badged hat trotting up the stationer's stairs. And if the Magician was up there—if he even opened the thing and thought it worth a reply, he'd give the kid an answer to carry through noon-day Holburn, swerving back to the post office. Tapping. Whirr. Two hundred miles as she paced the green beside the narrow river. Thirty-four minutes, and the post boy pushed the slip of paper across the counter.
MY DOCTORATES ARE NOT IN MEDICINE HARD LUCK CHILDREN
She dialled the Nest's number again. It rang for a long time.
And clicked. His quick voice. 'Kingsley?'
'No,' she said. 'It's us. Please, we're in terrible—'
'Crux.' Prideaux thumped something at the other end. 'It had better be a fen-sucked sodding catastrophe. I was very fucking specific in a way I rarely am. I was specific, wasn't I?'
'It's a catastrophe.'
'Good to hear.'
'Please.' Rom faltered. 'We did it. We changed her. And she's hurting.'
'You broke the collar.'
'Dissolved it,' she said. 'How can we help her?'
He was silent for a heartbeat. 'You can't. Where are you?'
'My aunt's house. It's in Cornwall, near—'

'Don't let anybody in. Don't leave. Put something gold at the front door, anything you've got, and I'll be there by dusk. Hold tight.' The dial tone stammered.

The road home was a long judder of dust. Jubilee's pace was anxious and Rom didn't want to rush her.

Alec met her at the edge of the orchard. 'Well? What can we do?'

'Nothing. He's coming.'

They turned out their pockets in the little hut. Alec's watch chain was gold-plated, and Rom's earrings; but that was it. 'Will it be enough?'

She didn't answer. She didn't know.

Alec was pacing. Rom's hands felt stiff in her pockets. Pixie's pale hair was stuck damp against her forehead and Rom watched her, unable to look away. It was strange and horrible and she knew the lines of that face so well, strong cheekbones and snowy lashes, but it was utterly unfamiliar.

Alec had brought down a blanket from the house but the unseen barrier stung him when he drew close to Pixie. 'Are you cold?'

The girl whined into her folded arms.

'I should wait on the road,' Alec said at one point. 'In case he knocks at the house.'

Rom shook her head. 'Stay where we are. That's what he said.' It was pitifully little, far too late, but she needed a rule to hold.

The sun was a low bloody sop across the sky when Alec jumped. She didn't know what he'd heard, the road was far distant, but the trembling whistle reached her. Pixie curled her lips. Close to a snarl. Her teeth were pointed.

'It's me,' said Kingsley's voice beyond the door. Bell-clear in the dark, unhappy. 'Will you open, please?'

He looked draggled and tired. Prideaux loomed behind him, sharp as if he was chipped from flint.

'Come in,' Rom said, so Kingsley wouldn't have to ask, and Prideaux pushed past them into the tiny lamp-lit hut. He was pulling off his coat. Kingsley took it, laying it over his arm, and Rom saw Prideaux had a gladstone bag hooked over his arm beside his cane, black leather like a doctor's kit.

'I'm sorry,' she said, 'we had no idea this could happen. If there's anything—'

'Sod off.' Prideaux tossed something to Alec. 'Light that up.'

Alec fumbled with it, some little box of pierced metal. Trays inside, a lump of wax rattling above a chunk of charcoal, and he took the silver lighter Prideaux handed him.

'Have you any salt?'

Rom jumped at the roughness of Prideaux's voice. She passed him the dish and he knelt beside Pixie.

'Has she said anything?'

'Nothing we could understand,' Alec said.

Pixie was growling. The sound wasn't from her lips.

'She has been caught between two bindings,' Prideaux said. 'You tried to cut it and you haven't a clue what it was holding together.' He scattered the salt with a shuffle of his hand and said something. He leaned forward, listening.

Pixie's tearing sound became a whimper. She fell silent.

Alec cupped the censor box. Resinous smoke twined from the lid. Prideaux took it and breathed lightly over it and the smoke dipped, coiled, ravelling across the dim cabin to the space above Pixie.

'Is the barrier hurting her?' asked Rom.

'Protecting her.' He brushed his gloved palms together. 'Stand up.'

Pixie slid her hands across her ears, huddling smaller.

'*Nūr sīn.*' *Moonlight.* 'What have you done, little dog?'

Pixie wrapped her arms around herself. 'Pixie,' she said huskily.

'No,' Prideaux said. 'That's not your name. Lower your wards.'

The snow-coloured girl looked up. Her mouth moved wildly. Morax. Rom read it. *MoraxMoraxMorax—*

'Stop it,' Rom said, 'leave her alone.'

'Miss Godden, you need to tell her to break her oath.' Prideaux was tugging off his gloves. 'Under Jasper's contract she can't be touched by bird, beast, or bookman.'

'But Morax—'

'She's already compromised. I can't help her if I can't touch her.'

Rom didn't know how to word this. She was useless at comforting anyone, that sort of ready helpfulness stuck in her chest.

But this wasn't comfort. She was Jasper's grandchild. It was business. 'You're worried,' she said. 'But we're trying to fix this. You can let go of the bindings now.'

Pixie's eyes squeezed shut.

Rom tried desperately. 'Please, the Magician said we have to—'

Pixie's hand clawed overhead. Something whip-like and numinous collapsed around them, sense more than sight, and Pixie's mouth widened in a bruising moan.

'There we go.' Alec shuffled the blanket around her bare shoulders. 'Well done.'

Prideaux didn't turn his head. 'Kingsley. Come here.'

Kingsley slunk back. 'You can't ask me to do that.'

'You were an Arbiter, weren't you?'

'No, sir. Only his tracker.'

Pixie began to whimper again.

It sliced beneath Rom's skin. 'If she's back in her other shape will it stop hurting?'

'It isn't pain,' Kingsley said. 'She's afraid. The Law is coming.'

'Coming here?' Alec stood and the stool tipped over.

'I can't stop it,' Prideaux said, 'I haven't the authority. Nobody does.' He set down his cane. It thumped oddly heavy and stayed upright, shivering as he took his hand from the gilded crook. 'Stop this, little dog. It will be hours until news gets to the Carnifex. Stop this, now.'

Pixie made a low sound. She inched her weight up the wall as she stood, her face dirty with tears.

Prideaux tucked his gloves away. He tapped Pixie's chin with two fingertips. 'You broke Lady Tyet's serpent?'

She raised her stained face. Nodded.

'But you attacked your master's kin. The boy.'

Her voice was a deep soft rush and Rom knew the tone of protest even if she couldn't grasp a word.

'The snake was on the stairs. You protected him.' Prideaux sighed. 'And your master, and all in her house. Well done, small thing.' He cradled Pixie's elbow and took hold of his cane. It came away lightly from the floor.

Pixie closed her eyes as Prideaux's hand slid flat-palmed to her back. 'Your master would have been proud.' His thumb rubbed at her soft nape. Smoothing, stroking. 'Nūr sīn.' He pressed the head of the cane to the back of her neck and something rushed through Rom's knees, a tug as though the room breathed in. Pixie slumped against the Magician's arm.

He lowered Pixie to the floor, her bare strong legs sliding limp. 'This will be simpler while she sleeps.' Behind his voice the silence surged. 'Kit,' he said, and Kingsley pushed the bag across.

Prideaux worked swiftly, an exacting economy of gesture as he lay the naked demon upon her back, set the bowl of salt at her head, and the smoking censer at her feet. He pointed to the bowl of water and Rom carried it over, and this he placed beside Pixie's right hand. It was an inversion. Salt should be earth and the feet that walk on it. Water is of the left, the secret hidden hand. He was laying out the properties in reverse. As a banishing should be, Rom finally understood.

Three of the four alchemical tools. Which left a blade; Rom opened her mouth to offer, she could fetch one from the kitchen. But Prideaux drew from his pocket a stumpy leather sheath. The knife had a bone handle, folded like a boy's pocket knife, or a farmer's—plain sturdy steel.

He was whispering. Rom couldn't catch the sound of it. It circled like an echo, spinning in the corners of the room and something flooded her mind, a vision collapsing over it like water, like a sheaf of paper. The earth had opened. Not here, but in some recess of sensation. She pressed against the wall. Alec did the same as though the floor had become some wide-mouthed pit.

Only Kingsley was still, his shoulders heavy.

Prideaux opened the blade and held it a moment, balanced on his palm. He said a single word, flat and clean and shimmering as a golden plate, and stabbed down. The blade struck Pixie's chest.

He slid the knife out and laid it over his knee. It was slick with transparent ichor. Pixie's skin gushed liquid, contorting like the edge of flame and it swelled, flickered. Blistered. Her limbs shook and gave way, a subsidence of red flesh, foaming black and splintering yellow bone. The bitter smell was cut with something noxiously rich. Pixie's body slumped inwards to the hissing floorboards, fusing into them. The bubbling stiffened as the mess became viscous, hardening. The floorboards smoked.

'They'll come looking for her.' Prideaux wiped the knife on his scarf and folded it. 'Before midnight they'll send a chit to finalise the ruling.'

Alec lunged but Kingsley caught his shoulder.

Rom couldn't look away from the steaming floor. Her voice was forced up from far away. 'You killed her.'

'No,' Prideaux said. 'You killed her.' He tugged his gloves on. 'You should never have called me.'

'Bring her back,' Rom said. 'You could, I know it.'

'One chasma cannot summon another.'

'Then tell me how.'

'You haven't the skill. Nor the relix. Your beast is gone.'

'Aren't you supposed to be powerful?'

'You misunderstand the difference between capability and responsibility. Why do you think she'd want to come back here?'

'Under the aegis of your house. All your *shite—*'

'Morax would have muzzled her,' Prideaux said. He flicked his fingers and Kingsley released Alec's arm. 'You don't know what happens when a chasma starves. Didn't you find that in your books? Their blood decays to atramentum; their veins leak poison; the flesh rots. Pain within a year but no death, not for centuries. I returned her to the underfires. It's more than the Law would have granted her.'

'We had to try,' Rom said faintly.

Prideaux pulled on his coat. 'Having fun yet?'

He'd travel a long way back tonight. He'd left his work. 'We said we'd pay you,' she said. 'And we will.'

'What do you think I am?' His face twitched. 'I wouldn't take all the salt on earth for this.'

Kingsley was waiting by the door.

'Don't call me again,' Prideaux said. 'Not for anything. I take it you comprehend that much.'

Nobody answered.

The door closed and the echo ran through her skin.

Rom sat on the sunken step of the hut. She didn't know how long it was. The acrid smell forced her out and for a while she prowled under the trees, a headlong wandering. But it felt wrong to move out of sight of the wooden roof and she returned to it. The sun dissolved behind the orchard.

'We should go back to the house,' Alec said.

'Prideaux said they'll send a letter. We have to wait.'

'What if he didn't—'

'He wasn't lying.'

Alec withdrew. Rom dropped her face into her hands. She knew nothing about the Magician. She couldn't know how much of him was empty, whether he even possessed some crucial spar of soundness, but tonight he'd been telling the truth.

She jumped. Alec had made a bleating noise from inside the hut. Now Rom heard a spitting sizzle and leaped back up the step in time to see a blue gash dripping in the air. It closed like a curtain as two people stepped out.

Identical. Wildly tall, their pointed caps brushing the rafters. Padded angles buttoned into strange tailored gowns of seamy yellow-white, swathes of faded skirt and high-collared jacket, head to toe, gloved to the elbow. They were masked like fencers, an oval of split wicker over their faces, and Rom had a crawling horror there was nothing underneath.

One of them jerked its arm. 'I am Mr Fyne,' it said, a woody whistling. 'And this is Mrs Gallow.'

The head of the other tipped like some central rope had snapped. 'Mrs Gallow,' it repeated. The same voice.

The first one bent over the pile of corruption. 'Oh,' it said. 'Oh. The dissident has been returned. Goodling.'

Rom's voice was thick. 'We didn't hurt her. It was a Coronet. He calls himself Naberius.'

Mrs Gallow looked at Mr Fyne. 'An Arbiter.'

'In exile,' said Mr Fyne, tinny with distance or mechanical playback. 'He has no authority to dispense Law.' The thing shrugged. 'But it is simpler than a trial.' It crooked an arm at Pixie. 'This was bounden to you?'

Rom swallowed. 'To my grandfather. I inherited the binding.'

Mr Fyne bent as though its hips were hinged and spread its gloved fingers above the body. It nodded at Mrs Gallow. 'The contract is cut. Morax accepts the debt as paid.'

The creatures stood stiff beside each other. One raised its arm and Rom realised they were about to depart.

'What about the relix?' she said. 'My soul was bound. If Pixie's dead does it mean—'

'Show.' The one called Mrs Gallow held out its leather palm. Rom touched it. Mrs Gallow took her wrist and pressed its thumb in hard and Rom felt a prickle up to the elbow, to the hollow of her armpit, and on her skin the familiar line surfaced like a thread. Mrs Gallow buzzed. 'The bind holds.'

Rom's head felt dull as cotton wool. 'But she's gone.'

'This is not the dogget's bind,' Mrs Gallow said. 'This belongs to a Named.'

'Who?' She breathed hard. 'Who—'

Mr Fyne trembled as though a new thought was ratcheting into place. 'We cannot comment on another's Skein.' It raised its hand. The air frothed and then they were alone: Alec, limp as death on the wooden stool, and her own shivering self, and the scorching rot of Pixie's body.

'An accident.'

'Yes,' Alec said, 'the entire hut caught fire.'

'We didn't mean to,' Rom said.

The kitchen leered in the electric lights. The smell of burning still drifted from the darkened orchard.

'And Pixie's dead?' Aunt Minnie's face was implacable. 'If I found out one of you hurt an animal—'

'I promise,' Rom said, 'I promise we'd change it if we could.' She couldn't go on. She'd make it all the way upstairs, maybe, and this sick weight would flood in. She could sink with it. But you're not allowed to wish yourself anywhere else when you deserve far worse.

'Was it something to do with this medicine?'

Her spine felt roped into stiffness. But she met Aunt Minnie's face. 'No.'

'I don't suppose I'll ever hear the truth,' Aunt Minnie said. 'I didn't want to treat you like children and I'd rather hoped you weren't. But you've done a terrible thing.'

Rom closed her eyes, stinging hot.

'We did what we could,' Alec said. 'And it's over.'

24

My own stupidity offends me. The solution lies in my hands yet I cannot see it. Avery assists me but he cannot do my thinking for me, as he quite rightly points out.

I want to weep and kick things but what would that mean? Townsend already fears for my mind. When he doesn't visit I go a month or more without so much as speaking to another soul.

Dear fellow, he's taken a liking to Pixie. He says she is a most uncommon dog. Whatever would he say if he saw the creatures as they truly are?

JASPER TEAGUE, Journals, 7th March 1905

'A translator spans two worlds at once.' Dr Carr looked over his glasses and the lecture room riffled with shaken papers. 'He must convey his meaning clearly while attempting to carry some essence of the original spirit. Too slavish a reproduction becomes obscure. Too loose an interpretation becomes meaningless.'

Rom's pen scratched mechanically but she already knew, she moved through her days knowing this. Everything you say is just translation. Mind to word; heart to head. A wonder anyone makes sense of things.

Ditto limped home from the theatre after midnight. 'How was it?' she asked, because she knew not to ask *How are you*. Rom understood.

She'd been back nearly a week. The familiarity was fractional comfort and great pain—the library, their apartment. Miss Gwen sleeping lonely by the sofa.

'I wish we could have told Aunt Minnie. Even something about it, something close. Everyone should know who Pixie was. It just seems cruel—' They divided up the last dregs of vodka. 'Dr Carr asked today about Mr Prideaux, if we had any luck with the book we got.' Rom swallowed the burn. 'I told him I'm writing my essay on something else.'

She needed to rest. It hurt to cry. Not the exhaustion, the numbness that thickened her, but the pointlessness. The void wasn't a rock to be dislodged. It hung vaporous and unreachable, a ring of smoke.

'How was the show?'

'Better than last week.' Ditto had her feet in a dish which clinked with ice from downstairs, pure luxury, because she'd given the landlady tickets to *Ducky Dear*. 'We should be perfect by the time you see things.'

Rom brought her another plate of eggs. 'I wouldn't miss it for anything, dear.'

It seemed impossible the world could stagger on, with or without her. She didn't want to go anywhere. Time passed like carousel music: but this was the world too.

Ditto waved at the sideboard. 'You got a letter this morning.'

'I saw.' She hadn't opened it yet. A cramped and busy little hand, sent from Birmingham. *S Mitchell*, the sender's name, but she didn't think it was his writing. Maybe the nurse, if he was too unwell. Or perhaps he didn't like to write things.

Later, though, after Ditto had told her everything about the day's rehearsals, when the room settled cooler, calmer, Rom felt strong enough to handle whatever the letter might say.

There was only one page inside.

Dear Andromeda, it said. *I hope you're well. Alec told me about Pixie. I'm sorry I couldn't help. I don't think anyone could, I'd have tried too if it was me. Hoping you haven't any more trouble with the fair folk.* He was being cautious in case his letters went astray.

I'm getting by, the usual sort of thing. The nurses are very nice. Nurse Miller in particular. I have to say that because she's writing this for me and she'll be cross if I don't.

Will you come to Birmingham some time? Although I shouldn't be having visitors they said, not for months. Letters are allowed.

If you like, anyway.

Yours sincerely,

Selwyn Mitchell

Ditto was watching her. 'Are you going to write back?'

'I might.' She would, but not tomorrow. She couldn't begin to know how she'd answer.

'Are you in love with him?'

'Don't be silly.'

'He's mad about you.'

'Not likely,' Rom said. But her palms felt prickly as she tucked the letter back within the envelope.

She hadn't told Ditto about her and Selwyn. His illness of course had been part of the story, and Ditto understood—she'd grown up in crowded London streets, she held the same horror for those clean-scrubbed sanatoriums and fouled air, failing lungs. Rom hadn't said about the rest, though.

She hadn't intended to conceal a thing but Pixie had been on her mind, the whole bitter collapse of summer, and now too many days had passed. No point bringing it up. Ditto had never been much bothered by her little flings anyhow and this wasn't any different; it was already finished.

Rom stood. 'Come along, you sleepy.'

Ditto's head was cushioned on the sofa's arm and slipping lower.

'Shall I carry you?'

Ditto splashed out of the iced water, hopping for her towel. 'Don't you dare.'

This nearly felt like home, Rom thought, when the lights were off and she was settled on the narrow sofa. The walls still held her. A century older, gardens burned and the well of memory boarded over. The most you can hope for, sometimes.

On Friday at Dr Brackburn's lecture she sat far up the back. She could hardly hear a word and didn't much care. She itched to go outside, to focus on the open air and something real—Aunt Minnie's garden. Or even the Park. A fly buzzed somewhere.

You know we couldn't have changed it, Alec had said before he boarded his train north. It made not a scrap of difference.

She hung around her usual phone box on her way back to the Tube but Alec didn't call. Out on assignment, likely; he'd have a stack of work to compensate for. It would have been good to hear him ramble.

Ditto stormed home with stage paint still bright on her lips. 'Good news,' she said. Her eyes were brilliant. 'The best of news.'

Rom put down her pen and rubbed her cheeks in hard little circles. 'I need good news, I really do.'

'Somebody offered me a job.' Ditto was on tiptoe. 'It's a film, Rom. A proper part and Mr Hayakawa is directing.'

'Film?' Rom caught her hands. 'That's gorgeous, oh, Dido—'

'No more stage, not ever. I don't care if I never have to sing again—I'll be in picture theatres. And the very best thing is I'm going to the Continent after all. I'll be in Paris. Actually really and truly.'

Rom hugged her to the hot tightness in her chest. 'How glorious. Not right away?'

'Gads, no.' Ditto stretched herself, knelt to unbuckle her shoes, and scruffed Miss Gwen from under the coffee table to snuggle her. 'I can't go anywhere until *Ducky's* finished up, and that's another two weeks if the reviews stay nice. And there's so much to plan, contracts and all that. Lists. I can't move a thing until October.'

'Three months.' Rom meant to say it brightly but her tongue dragged.

'You'll have to come to Paris for Christmas. Will you? I don't care how poor I am, it'll still be Paris. Don't mope, you silly, you must visit me always.'

'I'm not moping. Paris would be rather wonderful. You work dreadfully hard, dear, I'm glad they noticed. You'll be marvellous.'

'I know. I'll try.' Ditto stretched out on the carpet, bowed over Miss Gwen's head, and flexed her stockinged toes. 'I'll dance every morning. I do believe it will be the most wonderful year in the history of years.'

'I hope so. I'll be stuck here alone.'

'Not 'ardly,' Ditto said in flippant Cockney, 'you've got Alec.'

'At the other end of the country.'

'And Mr Mitchell. Did you answer his letter?'

'Not yet.' She hadn't found the right words to give him. 'I'm not the sort to lead anyone on. He must have known nothing would come of it.'

'Come of what?' Ditto's eyes were sharp as pins. 'Did you go to bed with him?'

Rom turned back to her papers on the table. 'It wasn't like that. It's not a romance, you don't have to worry.'

Ditto pushed Miss Gwen from her lap and stood, brushing off her dress. 'You never said.'

'We've had plenty else to worry about.'

'Were you planning to mention it?'

'I don't suppose it matters now. You weren't going to say you want to leave before Christmas.'

'You knew that.' Ditto stared. 'I've been planning all year. I always meant to go to Berlin if I could, and this is far better. A job. And *Paris*.' It sounded worse each time. 'My rehearsals, everything. You know it's what I wanted.'

Rom had known. She'd misled herself somewhere. She didn't even know what she wanted to say.

She found something. 'I knew this would happen eventually.'

'Rom.'

'It was always going to fall to pieces. I just thought we'd have a little more time.'

'Don't.' Ditto's eyes were glistening and Rom knew she should stop.

'It doesn't matter.' She shuffled her papers together. 'It was nothing very serious, was it?'

Ditto kept standing there. Rom didn't look at her.

And then Ditto was at the sideboard, opening the drawers. Closing them. Dragging her hatbox from the top of the wardrobe. She swept her clothes together in a heap and slammed the carpet-bag shut, and still Rom didn't turn around.

Ditto stopped at the door, wrapping Miss Gwen's leash around her wrist with a quick jerk. 'You're going to go and get married, aren't you.'

'Don't be stupid.' Rom shoved her papers away.

'You could have told me.' The door shut.

Rom filled a glass of water, cupped in careful hands. She sat down and drank it. It was nobody's concern. Only her own.

The wire arrived at breakfast time. Somebody called Asherford, postmarked Godalming.

HENRY LOVEDAY MORGAN NOTED ABSENT FROM SCHOOL GROUNDS YESTERDAY PLEASE ADVISE

Rom grabbed her hat.

The post office was noisy but the voice on the phone line cut nasal and direct. 'No idea, Miss Godden. Most sorry. We hoped you might know. We wired his parents this morning. And you were the other contact on file.'

'They're in Egypt,' Rom said. 'It's just me.' She hung up.

He could be anywhere.

She wanted Ditto, a quick impulsive need, and buttoned it away. She'd even take a cab straight to Great Queen Street, if there was any chance they'd let her in.

That left mortals and whatever good they could pull together. She dialled again.

Alec wasn't in his office, and when they put Tom Wells on the phone he was hesitant. 'I haven't seen him. He ought to be about today. Has he called you?'

'No,' she said. 'Thanks.'

Alec must be studying at home. Or hungover in bed. Nothing to be surprised about, that was the logical explanation, and she wished she still believed in logic.

The street glared with summer dust. She walked home, her dress sticking to her stomach. Her straw hat prickled. There's always a way. Kingsley would know someone who could help.

At home she dragged out her clothes-drawers and tipped them on the bed and found the biscuit tin. The collar had to be worth something, even in pieces. She hadn't opened the thing since she'd been back and the tape around the tin's lid was layered thick. She scraped with a chewed thumbnail. But something about the weight was wrong, the heavy balance on her knees, and her hand shook when she dug out a kitchen knife and cut the tape. She flicked off the clattering lid.

The little jar of gold nestled snug in newspaper. The jar of white powder was gone, replaced with a chunk of rock. There was a folded page.

Borrowed for research. You wouldn't have said yes so I didn't ask.

Rom put down the tin, her hands shaking.

She scribbled two notes and pushed them behind the marigolds down in the courtyard. *Morgan missing with bittergold, will pay.* One she addressed to Crowfolk. And the other was addressed to *Kingsley % Mr Prideaux, Great Queen Street*, because neither of them would like that and maybe if somebody was angry they'd answer quicker.

She went across to the Park telephones and rang Alec's office again. He hadn't been in. No message either, and he'd missed work. And Rom was afraid. The world shook like she'd tripped a wire and she couldn't begin to see how far it quivered.

'Oi,' said the high voice behind her. 'Godden?'

The little girl was barely ten, buttoned into a faded pink silk jacket. She held out a folded page. 'Quinn said propera posthaste.' She slipped back into the crowd, a wink of sequins, and Rom looked at the note. It was signed **q**.

kinchin ∧ *1st train Hollesley heri*

crown ∨ *go armed*

Heri meant yesterday. A Coronet coming south, and Morgan heading to Jasper's house. Had he taken the stuff with him?

Go armed.

Rom didn't even close her front door when she got home. She tumbled everything out of her college bag and packed some biscuits. A cardigan. Her purse and a kitchen knife. When she pulled on a jacket her hands felt numb on the buttons.

Morgan. You wretched fool.

She closed her door, and stepped into the feverish daylight.

There was only one bus through Hollesley and she'd missed it. She went by train.

The stationmaster told her the horse-cart at the pub might drop her on the edge of town. 'Shepherd's Race?' He wrinkled his nose.

'Did somebody else ask for it? A kid,' Rom prompted, but he didn't want to answer. Maybe he'd been paid well enough not to. Or maybe she was wrong, and it wasn't Morgan, hadn't ever been, and she wasn't looking in the right place.

The cart driver was every bit as silent as his horse, and didn't speak a word on the road. It was midday, relentless, dusty enough to cling to her sweaty arms. She'd worn dark travelling stuff and the grime showed yellow on her navy skirt. The rutted road hackled her bones, jolted her stomach, and she closed her mouth tightly and tried not to think about being sick. If he'd come this way yesterday he might be gone again, back into town and settled in rooms at the pub. Or already on the train home.

Or worse, he'd come to meet somebody. And met them.

The trees were lower here, sparse and sheltering quiet sheep, punctuated by low water. Canals slushed beside the road and the air had the tang of sea-rot. The coast was very near.

Where the fields broke into waterways, the road ended beside
Jasper's house. It was smaller than she'd expected, but she'd been
expecting that. Tucked behind scraggled bushes and sunk in the rank
grass, the faded pink walls gleamed with flints bedded like teeth. The
southern roof-line looked unsteady beneath the thatch. Western? She
had no sense of direction at the best of times.

She slid from the cart and paid the man and halted by the gate, still
waiting, she didn't know what for. The place looked deserted.

Not entirely. The grass around the gate was pressed down by recent
feet, permitting a half-shove, and she entered her grandfather's
garden.

A red-brick hobble to the front door. The wild but jolly garden and
the path she recalled, wading to the back terraces and the marsh itself.
The smell sank deep in her chest. Mud and salt water. Somewhere
back here was the old ice cellar, the bunker Jasper had made. She
thought she glimpsed it through the waving shrubbery, but she
needed to see the house, the kitchen, and if anyone had been here.

The back door was unlocked. She paused with her hand on the
door; Alec should have been the last visitor, with Mr Mitchell. What
had Selwyn made of all this? If he'd never come down to help a friend,
he'd be safe in Scotland yet. Except for the sickness was rooted in his
lungs; there'd be no escaping it. Maybe he'd rather have never found
out.

Rom closed the door behind her. Even if she had a right to be here it
wouldn't help much if a demon was hanging around the garden. She
wanted Pixie. And then it hurt all over again, wanting a quiet dog
beside her, when that was so much less than Pixie had been.

She went slowly upstairs. Everything smelled unwell. The plastered
walls were mapped with mould. The house was small, two bedrooms,
both empty; after she was certain nothing hid behind the doors, she
moved on. Back downstairs to the stiff little parlour and its curtains
shut tightly, the old man's stuffy office, and the brick-floored
bathroom. No sign of life, breath, anything.

Rom sat at the kitchen table and found her hands damp. Had she
been as scared as that? Relief and disappointment feel the same. Or
maybe she was frightened still, because she'd seen the house, but the
house wasn't what she'd come to see.

There was still the cellar.

The empty doorway loomed beside the pantry. Rom leaned through: narrow steps down to a chemical stench; no lights. 'Fuck that for barrel of dicks,' she said, and the sound of her own voice steadied her. She poked through the kitchen for a candle-stump. A flint lighter on the mantelpiece, and there: *'Fiat lux,'* she said. Let there be light. Hand on the clammy wall as she descended.

Fiat is an act of will. It is, because I command it to be. She paused on the stairs to listen but nothing rustled behind her.

Fiat also means *so be it.* It is; there's nothing I can do about it. There is light, and who am I to stop it?

There was no light here. No sign of a crucible, just the squint of glass when she reached the bottom of the steps and moved her arm, swinging shards of candleglare against the stacked bottles.

She checked the floor before she stepped, avoiding tangled wires. They led back to a steel vat, a hulking generator, and it did look like something from a horror film—if she hadn't known it was for gold-plating an old man's teaspoons, she might have believed it was dangerous. The place was a real laboratory, though. Her eyes stung with the caustic air, damp and acrid down her throat. She wanted to get out again but it was pointless to leave until she was sure the place was empty.

There was nowhere for anyone to hide; she'd see them. If they were visible. She couldn't even corral a comforting thought. Rom growled as she circled the dank work benches.

Sel had seen gunpowder somewhere, she'd have to be careful with the candle, which already dripped onto her fist and guttered in a draught from somewhere. From behind her. As though the kitchen door had been opened and shut again, and a puff of air were drifting lazily down to her.

Rom tried to hear past the beat in her head. Nothing she could make out, and now she didn't want to go back up. But she couldn't stay waiting for her nerves to fracture.

She swore as her hip struck the bench and the flame smoked out.

'Useless bloody thing.' At the flood of pain her stomach denounced her and she retched. She gripped the workbench, missed it.

The drone in her ears became a great heat.

25

...Clotho, Lachesis, and Atropos invented seven Greek letters—A B H T I U. Others say that Mercurius invented them from the flight of cranes, which, when they fly, form letters—W E Z F; Epicharmus of Sicily, two—P and Q. The Greek letters Mercurius is said to have brought to Egypt, and from Egypt Cadmus took them to Greece. Cadmus, in exile from Arcadia, took them to Italy, and his mother Carmenta changed them to Latin to the number of 15. Apollo on the lyre added the rest.

PSEUDO-HYGINUS

The glare sizzled through Rom's eyelids. 'Oi.'

She was lying on the stone floor. She must have fainted, damn and blast. An electric torch beside her pointed at the wall and the shadows bounced as someone stepped over her feet.

'Oi,' she said again. Croaking. The figure leaned over her. It loomed black, round-eyed and mouth cavernous. Her eyes burned and she hit out, both fists on its chest. Hard rubber. She choked. 'Stop—'

'Rom.' Muffled. 'Is Kingsley with you?'

The creature dragged its face off and Morgan crouched. His hair was rumpled. Gas mask, she thought stupidly, the black vent dangled in his hand.

She sat up and groaned. 'Why would he be?'

'Because you wouldn't be dim enough to come alone.' He tugged the mask on again and his voice was hollow. 'Upside. Before we combust.'

Rom hoisted herself vertical. Her shoulders hurt. Her stockings were damp from the puddles as she followed his leaping torchlight.

The kitchen was dankly warm. Morgan hung the gas mask behind the door as though it was an umbrella. His satchel lay on the table with a tin of apricots.

'You came here after all.'

'Mhm,' he said. He didn't look happy.

'You stole the collar.'

'No,' he said, 'I only took the bone-dust. Do you have a hotel room

266

in town? You should go before it gets dark.'

'I'm not going to leave you here, this isn't your house.'

'Not yours either.'

She was too furious to be upset by his pettiness. There were real things. Terrible things. 'It's the bones of the chasma?'

'It can't be the common sort or they'd all be making it; maybe it's not these bodies they have, it's something else. Would have been nice to study it properly.'

'You're going to give it to Tyet. The things she could do with bittergold—'

'Exchange.' He was fossicking in a cupboard. 'For Alec. She took him. You want him back, don't be idiotic.'

Rom leaned dizzy against the table. But it was the best plan they had. 'Has she arrived?'

'Should be here before nightfall. She'll release Alec when she has the dust.'

'How do you know she'll keep her word?'

'She has to,' Morgan said. 'They're ugly things but they follow through, if you make the terms specific enough.'

'You should have told us what you were doing.'

He didn't even answer. He was packing up his satchel again, pocket knife and tinned apricots and torch, and when he clumped back out to the garden Rom followed him; down the sunken path and under the dangling plums to the lawn, the shaken grass. In one corner, where the wild rabbits had cropped things shorter, a little canvas tent was strung between the trees.

'You slept here last night?'

'Didn't fancy the house.' Morgan threw his satchel through the open flap. 'Alec said the cellar smelled. Fumes can be toxic.'

She didn't trust him, not a bit of it, but his indifference was a relief. He was here for something that had nothing to do with her.

'You fainted down there,' he said. 'Cellar full of chemicals and you went down with an open flame. You're stupid.' His voice was almost awed. 'Really stupid.'

'You don't have to be so superior—'

'Have you seen the bunker yet?'

'I didn't have a light.'

'Do you want to see it?'

She was trying to decide.

'I haven't looked yet.' His face eased. 'I didn't want to go by myself.'

The garden glowed, sere yellow grass and shaking boughs. The reddish curve of the brick bunker looked like stained bone, a buried cranium. 'Dark as anything.' Morgan peered through the little window. 'Looks empty.'

'Help me get it open.'

'I wouldn't.' He bent over the unfettered daisies, brushing their ruffled heads with his thumb. 'We don't know what's inside.'

'You just said it's empty.' Rom unbolted the latch and hauled the steel door free, kicking the long grass away. 'Where's the torch?'

Three steps down. Morgan followed. A musty animal scent, sweet and metallic. The room was unoccupied and Rom breathed in relief. A bare stretcher bed; a pile of books, a wooden bowl on the brick floor. The arcing smooth curved walls were polished like mirrors. Her own reflection wavered, warped by the panelling. The torchlight gleamed strangely.

Rom touched it. 'Gold. The walls are covered in it.'

'Suppose we know where the old man's bullion went.'

The books were shabby but stacked neatly, worn engineering texts and some poetry. Arabic, Romanian. The pages were stained. Something dark had splashed the brick and left liquid gouges on the steel door.

'Corrosive.' Rom bent closer. 'Jasper was messing with acid.'

Morgan stood still. 'We shouldn't be in here.'

'I'm not going to touch it.'

'Rom. Get out.'

She looked at his tense eyes. She ran for the steps. Only when they'd stumbled out into the dry garden did Morgan stop.

'What did you see?'

'Nothing.' He slammed the door shut and ran his hands over his face. 'But the bolts are on the outside. Jasper wasn't hiding. He locked something away.'

'That was demon's blood.' Her stomach burned.

'The whole place will be contaminated, everything it touched. The books and dishes. Radiation.'

Rom had been picturing something like the plague, germs or something. 'Is that all?'

'Just because it's invisible you think it isn't there. You'd die horribly and never know why.' He plucked one of the daisies and held it out to her.

She cupped it in her palm. The yellow heart was split, the petals buckling into uneasy ruffles. The flowers, the whole swaying garden, malformed as it grew.

'A starving demon,' Morgan said. 'They poison everything around them. They have to eat, there's no way out. Somebody always has to die.'

She didn't have an answer. She hadn't even thought about it yet. Morgan had, of course. Morgan thought of everything. 'That's how nature works,' she said.

'I thought it might be bigger. But the laws are always the same.'

It's hard to pretend a creature is only a creature when it's got a stack of books beside its pillow. Jasper had pretended.

They crossed the garden silently. Plum trees hung across the hedge, boughs weighted with fruit, late season, and flecked with plushy blossoms. Time ran untimely here.

'Is that smoke?' The air beyond the house was white-hazed.

'Mist,' Morgan said, 'from the marshes.' Something hardened in his face. 'They've come by sea.'

At the gate they saw movements in the lank grass by their feet, glistening bodies of serpents passing silver through the garden. Rom shuddered. The mist thickened, closing off the world. She could scarcely see the waterbirds scuffling onto the road past the fence.

Where the lawn fell away into sodden flats, the air was parting. Up from the reeds, her high black boots sheathed in mud, came Lady Tyet.

She was dressed for sailing, in snug jodhpurs and a cream knit jacket, her wrists clattering with scarlet bangles. She called to them. 'You brought me the bittergold.' She stopped two paces away and addressed Morgan, one hand folded on her hip. 'Many thanks.'

Rom opened her mouth but Morgan was already asking. 'Where's Alec?'

Tyet pointed.

On the road past the gate stood Alec, hands bound, between two women in sturdy boots and jackets. His orange suit was a flame in the misty air.

Morgan breathed out sharply. He called across the shambling hedge. 'All well?'

'Perfectly,' Alec shouted back, and not a drop of his sarcasm was lost. 'Don't give the bloody stuff away, we should ask Mr Kingsley—' He broke off as one of the women pressed something to his ribs. A revolver, and Alec shrugged at them.

Rom felt faint again. 'If they dare—'

'They won't.' Morgan turned back to Tyet. 'We're taking him immediately. Yes? Unhindered and unfollowed.'

'Dear thing.' She smiled with curious indulgence. 'You don't interest me. Show me the collar.'

'Can't give you that,' Morgan said. 'It's Jasper Teague's. But this was extracted from the gold.' He unwrapped a jar from his satchel, the strange chasmeric powder.

Tyet made no motion to touch it. Maybe she couldn't. 'You cut the stinger from the bee? I chose a good time to bargain.'

'You already knew we were trying,' Morgan said. 'How?'

'I hear a lot of things,' Tyet said, one of those vague evasions that felt so much like Prideaux's.

'Who told you?'

Rom wished he'd hurry; Alec was waiting.

But Morgan held the jar in both hands. 'Kingsley wouldn't.'

'No.' Tyet shivered with surprise. 'The hound obeys his captain. I have many times offered Mr Kingsley a place among my People; long ago he served the Leopard, my sister, and he should afterwards have come to me. He could have run beside my chariot. But he chose the house of the Arbiters, and now he plays scout, guard, and nursemaid for a foolish scribe.'

'Lady Tyet.' Morgan didn't budge. 'Who told you about the collar?'

'You watch your folk well. But not well enough; I had a visit from a doctor. You did not tell her what the collar was.' Tyet shook her head. 'You were nearly wise enough.'

Rom broke in. 'Pen's working for you?'

'Not yet. She is looking for a patron.'

'She's already got the formula for panax,' Morgan said, 'she doesn't need—'

He turned. The air beside them leaked fire, a drip as the mist yawned open. Something staggered out and Morgan yelped. But Rom had seen this thing before, the nauseous whitish gown. The blank oval mask.

'I am Mrs Gall,' it said.

'Chits,' said Tyet. It sounded like a curse. 'Get back to the boats.' A thump of wet flame hit the ground and she hissed.

Sulphuric light behind them. Flaring by the gate. Voids opened for those pointed caps, the long white bodies. Rom whirled around but Alec was being pushed by the women towards the reeds as the mist broke with flashes.

'That isn't Tyet,' Morgan said uncertainly. 'That—'

Tyet was plunging back towards the reeds but something opened ahead of her, an eye onto darkness, bigger than the doors that poured Chits on every side—this was tunnel-wide, a blue rush as something lumbered into the evening garden. Thick-legged, horned and heavy-necked bullish creature, and Rom knew it. Shaped in bronze, bellowing in darkness. But this was alive, naked and pelted like a great beast, gripping a double axe.

Morgan looked sick. 'Minotaur?'

'Law is peace.' The creature's voice was trumpets braying underfoot. 'Glad tidings. Heralds sing. The Law will be kept.'

Tyet stumbled back. He was twice her height. His form seared lucid as he unfolded two slick arching wings, a vile mechanical clicking as their beetle-like transparency spread behind his shoulders.

'Shit,' Rom said.

They ran.

Chits leered around the shrubbery and Morgan darted, shying from the sticky fire that vented from the creatures' palms. A gob of the stuff caught Rom's shoulder and she flung off her cardigan as they reached the kitchen steps.

'Godden?' came a shrill voice.

Rom spun around. The boy was plump and earnest, bent double, waving at the back garden. 'Quinn comes,' he said, gasping. 'Hold thou and we'll harry the Bull-man's Chits.'

Rom felt a jump of hope. Colours wavered in the garden, red capes and gold and the flit of birds. They weren't alone.

'We'll try,' she said, and the crowchild ran back down the path. 'Hose,' she said to Morgan, 'and buckets. We need water.'

'Alec—'

'I know. We can't get to him. These things are Tyet's enemies too, she'll run for it. Once Crow gets her—'

She didn't know. But the thought was enough.

They worked in thunderous silence, dragging the garden hose to the rain-tank beside the steps. Morgan worked the pump and she aimed, swinging the hose, splashing the tinder-dry thatch of the roof and the spot-fires along the path. Wincing at the flash of firefight in the marsh and the growing shouts from the garden, the raw bright cries of crowfolk and the click of Chits.

'On your left,' Morgan said.

She got it, the figure tottering like sticks in a glove. It reeled backwards and she swung the other way to catch another Chit behind the hedge.

'Water won't hold them long.'

'We need fire.' She wanted whatever Morax's People had and this low deep anger made her choke. But a human could never hope to combat this, the slave-things or the Carnifex, creatures too old to fear a death that couldn't bind.

But it could still hurt.

'Shit.' She dropped the hose and ran for the house.

Morgan's voice cracked above the roar. 'Don't you dare—'

She didn't stop. Stairs and door and kitchen, a plosive thump as fire smacked the plaster wall beside her, and then the dim stairs beside the pantry. Morgan's torch was where he'd left it and this time she knew exactly what she was doing.

The glancing beam lit the mess of wires at the bottom of the cellar steps. She was looking for labels, poison and death's head stamped like a pirate.

'Don't.' It was muffled. A boy's voice through a rubber gas mask.

'I can make gunpowder. We're going to burn them.'

'Andromeda. Get out of here.'

'We learned about Greek fire with Dr Brackburn, it must have had saltpetre. You're the brain, aren't you? Do something. Do you want to die?' She threw open another box and leaned in, angling the torch. 'It'll look like salt, won't it? Sodium nitrate.'

'Everything looks like salt. Ammonium nitrate would be faster. You can't stay down here. Andromeda—'

'You don't have to stay. Go home.' The little box was heavy steel, labelled clearly. She dragged it out. 'Can we mix this with something?'

'Won't need to, we can drop a match. Can you just come *on*—'

She handed him the torch and hefted the box in both hands, and Morgan shone the light at their feet as they ascended.

'If the roof catches properly—'

'I know.' She was lightheaded, tense. 'It won't. It doesn't matter.'

'Careful with that.' As she scuffed the step. 'It'll go up if you drop it.'

In the kitchen she thrust the box at him and dug out her handkerchief. Her eyes streamed wet, stinging even in the clean air.

'Your respiration is slow?'

'I'm fine. Are they down on the boats?' She wanted to laugh with sudden hope. The nitrate was power, good as a bomb. They could burn the Chits and hold the house until Quinn arrived.

Morgan's face pinched. 'We need charcoal.'

'The roof's burning, we'll have plenty soon.'

'Proper charcoal, you donkey. You've been poisoned.'

It was only a sting in her throat. 'I'm fine,' she said, 'really.'

'You'll keep on being fine for about three minutes and then you'll be dead.'

She looked at him.

'Cyanide salts in the cellar.' His face was cold. 'What's charcoal made from?'

'Wood.' She breathed in. It made no difference. All the air burned. She aimed for the chair but the floor was closer, a bump as she sat, legs numb. 'Morgan—'

'Shut up. Please. What's charcoal made from?' He rummaged among his thrown-off coat and pulled out the gas mask. 'In the War they made charcoal from peach-stones. From cherry pits. Horse-chestnuts. They told all the Boy Scouts to gather horse-chestnuts.'

'Alec used to gather them from the garden.'

Morgan wasn't listening. He crouched with the mask over his knee and a knife glittered between his fingers as he slashed the seal around the goggle front. 'The government never said why they wanted horse-chestnuts. The government never tells anything. But what's the only thing they'd need them for?'

She could only watch, breathing raggedly. He wrenched off the rubber cap and pried out the scrunched-up filter.

'They made two things with the cellulose. Acetone for explosives and charcoal for gas mask filters. The weapon and the antidote. Here.' He took her wrist and shook the black grit into her hand. 'You have to eat it.'

Dust in her mouth, rough and choking. 'I can't just swallow it.'

He made a growling sound and was gone.

She tried again, licking her palm. But her arms were heavy. Her head squealed with falling fireworks and she was waiting for the burst. Morgan was gone for a long time.

When he came back he had a bucket. It sloshed at her feet. 'Hurry up.'

This time she managed to gulp some of the grit. But the water was salty and she sputtered. 'It's sea.'

'The tide's coming in from the estuary.' His hands curled at his sides. 'The tank's empty and there's no well, we're right on the marsh.' He was speaking too fast, small and clipped.

'It's alright,' she said, 'you did so well, kiddo. We just have to wait for Quinn.'

'It's too late.' His wet eyes were level with hers as he knelt. 'Lady Tyet has sailed. Morax is outside.'

If she could only find something to hold onto, this might not fall to pieces. She closed her eyes and felt the plaster wall shatter as something heavy thrust its shoulders through the doorway.

'You're the Carnifex.' Morgan's voice, low and clear. 'We know what you want.'

Light ached through Rom's closed eyelids. She blinked, ill with what she might see.

The doorway jostled with Chits. And a heavy man entered, solid, naked, his shaved head gleaming with golden glyphs like metal pressed into his skin. Bronze knotwork marked his belly, but it was the same bullish beast. The same silver axe and lightless eyes.

'Do you know the bittergold?' Morax's voice echoed in the flagstones. 'Then give.'

'Don't,' she whispered. 'They can bind anything if they get it.'

Morgan pointed. 'Down there.'

The Carnifex turned his polished head, a rotation to the open doorway.

'It's the alchemist's cellar. He had a vat and all the blood he could use. He made a whole set of chains. It was too heavy, I couldn't take it with me.' Morgan's voice was tight with regret. 'The dog-collar's gone but everything else he made is here.'

The demon's noise was an exhalation of fury. 'We go down,' he said. His People stepped ahead, and Morgan raised his voice.

'Don't use fire,' he said. 'There are burning powders down there. Use the electric lamps.'

The demon's mouth curved wet across thick teeth. 'I am stronger than human fires.' He made a motion to his Chits as he descended, though, and the creatures followed him cautiously.

Rom pressed the back of her hand to her eyes. 'Why must you ruin things.'

Morgan shoved his torch into her hands. 'Get out. In the garden, before the idiots blow the place.'

She stared, foggy. 'I can't.'

'Look for Quinn. Ask for medicine, he must have something—' His face was agitated.

'I'm fine,' she said, but she ached to sit down again and breathe past the stench of damp burning.

Morgan pushed her. 'Damn you—'

She stumbled down the stairs. It was bright gold, the whole garden, slanting light and smoke, the thud of Chit's fire. She couldn't see Quinn. She couldn't see anything, just a blear of tears and glittering boughs and sky, and a drift of birds above. She leaned her head back. Lazy, high. Gull, tern. Great wide circles, the grand awkwardness of a water-bird; egret, heron.

Maybe she should yell for crowfolk. But her voice was gone. And if she called, what monster would find her?

Sound broke like a wave as the sun rose from the earth behind her and swallowed her whole.

26

Polly has sent a telegram—she has returned from the Continent with her husband—when was she married? How could I imagine such a thing might happen—I could not. And Polly said they have a child—a daughter. I have a grandchild. I am undone. How could this happen?

My brain feels half frozen. It is monstrous.

The creature brought up the telegram. It had already read the words. It was smiling at me.

It sits at my desk now, sharpening a fresh box of pencils for me.

Sometimes I want to stab him with a pencil.

JASPER TEAGUE, Journals, 4th Oct. 1904

The wind lowered like wings.

She opened her eyes but they were covered with something soft, her head wrapped dark. The air stung her skin.

'Andromeda.'

Her parents, she thought, calling her in from the garden, from the heat of the noon-day sun.

'Should I check if she can open her eyes?' somebody asked.

'Better she doesn't.' That rasp of a voice.

'She might be awake.'

'Better she isn't.'

'I am,' Rom whispered. There was blood in her mouth.

'Of course,' Kingsley muttered somewhere.

Rom shifted her shoulders. She lay with a twig nobbling her back, and the air rang bitter.

'Her eyes aren't too bad, but I had to wash them.' Kingsley's voice wavered closer. 'The burns will heal.'

The cloth across her eyes was wet. Her dress was drenched. Grass tickled her hands. 'He's here?' Her whisper frayed. 'Mr Prideaux.'

'I am.' Somewhere on the right.

'You shouldn't be.'

'Is your objection moral or geographic?'

Rom put her hands to the cloth on her eyes.

'Not yet,' Kingsley said, 'can you sit up, Miss Godden?' He slid his arm beneath her shoulders.

Her dress clung to her legs. Chest full of fire and the stiffness of long sleep or no sleep.

'Alright, your eyes, now.'

He untied the cloth and Rom blinked. Late air gouged her lungs. A glow came through the branches. Kingsley's bright hair was rumpled and his bare chest gleamed pale as milk beneath his open blue coat. Not his coat at all. 'The place went up in flames,' he said, 'like a bomb. The house collapsed.'

She saw his lips move but her ears rang. 'Morax?'

'Gone,' Kingsley said, 'him and his People. He'll repair himself, but not in the next few hours. Quinn drove them out. And we broke a few Chits. Tyet called a ceasefire, her People were injured too. There's time to get away.'

'I'm soaking,' she said. 'Why?"

'We had to bucket you down.'

She shuddered for breath. 'Am I going to die?'

'Yes.' Prideaux's shadow moved on her right. 'Probably not today.'

'That isn't funny,' Kingsley said.

She wrapped her arms around herself. 'Where's Morgan?'

'He got out of the house before he brought it down,' Kingsley said. 'But he's gone. He went with Mrs Ash. She took Alec.'

Her eyes streamed but it wasn't tears. She wiped them on her wet sleeve, stupidly, and the smell of burning soured her mouth. 'Where's she taken them?'

'North. She can't let them die.'

Rom shook her brittle thoughts. No use wandering the dark looking for anyone. She needed Morgan's ideas. But he was far from here. 'He knew the cellar would burn.'

'Cyanide salts.' Prideaux knelt on the grass beside her. 'The place was leaking.'

Kingsley was scrubbing his hands in the bucket.

'You got the stuff on you,' Rom said. 'Won't you get sick?'

'Mortal blood is based upon an iron molecule,' Prideaux said, 'susceptible to cyanide binding, while chasma are chiefly sulphuric with—'

'Shut up,' she said.

He did; the only good thing that had happened all night. In the deepening shade his white shirt was barred by his suspenders, spattered with dirt or blood.

'When did you last feed?' Kingsley asked. For a moment she thought he was talking to her.

But Prideaux cleared his throat. 'Four weeks.'

'And he was fervent. Yours is the better chance.'

She looked from Kingsley's frown to Prideaux. 'I don't need blood. Morgan gave me charcoal.'

Prideaux said, 'I knew it must have been someone clever.'

'It saved you,' Kingsley said. 'But I wouldn't mind making sure.'

She wanted to go home. She wanted her mother. She wanted Alec. 'I don't want blood,' she said.

Kingsley wasn't smiling. Maybe he was offended, some etiquette she'd misunderstood. 'Sir—'

Prideaux sat back on his heels. 'Don't look at me like that, she'll probably live.'

'Likely, but I can't guarantee the child.'

'Gestating,' Prideaux said. 'Truly, Godden? Of all the stupidity.'

Rom's insides rolled over. 'Me?'

'How jolly,' Prideaux said. 'Congratulations all round. Well done, you silly mutt, she'll be useless all night.'

'Kingsley.' She was gasping. 'Are you sure?'

Kingsley's face twitched. 'Are you unsure?'

The storm behind her eyes threatened to break. She couldn't think of Selwyn.

The bucket dripped beside her, the one Morgan had dragged from the river, just before he dropped a house on the Carnifex. He'd met the day with only his great and terrible simplicity. How? First things first.

Rom pulled her knees against her chest. 'Is your blood safe?'

'It's not panax,' Kingsley said, 'but it's better than any medicine you'll get in the next few hours.' He turned back to Prideaux. 'Sir?'

'I can't spare it.'

'Can you not?' Something gurgled in Kingsley's throat. 'Three drops.

You useless fucking shite. Roll up your fucking sleeve.'

Prideaux's lips whitened. He unbuttoned his cuff and pushed it up. He dug out his pocket knife and nicked his inner arm and the bead of ichor swelled onto the blade, a dark rusty gleam. He held out the knife to her. In silence, with both hands.

She didn't look at either of them as she took it. 'Altruism?'

'You assisted the Phoenix when you didn't need to,' Kingsley said. 'The Coronets owe you.'

Prideaux sat back on his heels. 'And we need somebody alive to negotiate with Tyet.'

'Do I—'

'Just eat it.'

It looked as though it should be sweet, honey-like, but the bitter droplet scorched her tongue. Something loosened even as she winced and her lungs knocked open, deep breaths, and the rush made her vision spin. She closed her eyes over the tears. The Magician's fingers slipped the knife from her.

'Up, now,' Kingsley said, and began to unbuckle her shoe.

She pulled her foot away. 'I'll do it myself.' Her chest hurt when she leaned forward. 'Is there anything dry to wear?'

'Galoshes,' Kingsley said proudly. 'I left relix for them.'

They were rubber overshoes, too big, and she rubbed her stockinged feet together. 'No clothes, I suppose.'

'On their way,' Prideaux said. 'Crowfolk are close. We'll meet them on the road.'

'And in the meantime?'

'Coat, Kingsley.'

'I haven't got anything else,' he said.

'Don't tell me you've acquired some modesty in your old age.'

'Alright,' Kingsley said with some coldness. 'Look away, Miss Godden.'

'I *am*.'

The blue coat fell on the grass at her side. The light was a momentary shift behind her eyelids, and Kingsley sneezed. When Rom glanced up he was sitting on his haunches like any other dog in the world.

She began to work on the buttons behind her neck. Her hat was long gone and her pinned-up braid was unravelling wetly down her neck. She pulled on the coat, the silk lining sticking to her skin, and it smelled like a musty house, something sweet and salt and wrong. The heady rot of the ocean. Flesh, incense.

Prideaux got to his feet. 'I'll be at the gate when you're ready to go.'

'Go where?' Rom stopped with one stocking half rolled off.

'London. But first, a walk.' The burning house set an aureole behind Prideaux's head as he turned away. 'Make haste, Andromeda,' he said, and it drifted in the wind. 'I'm waiting.'

She pulled off her stocking. On a day of strange things, that might have been the strangest. Her name, in his voice, in her grandfather's garden.

When she came up the pathway they were waiting by the gate, man and dog. Not-man. Not-dog. Prideaux whistled, soft chirrups, and the fox-hound wriggled under the dark hedge and away into the night. She looked back at the blunt and crumbled walls of Jasper's house, the buried beams still blazing. Prideaux held the gate open.

And that was how it began, the night journey through the marshland under a burning sky.

Rom's feet slid around in the galoshes. She'd belted the coat tightly over her damp underthings and felt like a scarecrow. The ground was sodden; she tripped on tussocks before they were even out of sight of the flames. His stride was unforgiving. The sunglow had long faded and the moon was hours away.

'A walk.' Did she even want to know? 'How far?'

'Two hours should get us there.' He stopped. 'Possibly two and a half,' he added as she caught up, and she kept pace with him for a while after that. Perhaps he'd slowed. Difficult to tell in the squelch.

Her eyes stung from smoke and poison, welling with tears. Her nose streamed hotly. She wiped her face on her sleeve. It was hard enough to see without smothered vision.

Where was Alec now? Somewhere off the coast. Sel and Aunt Minnie wouldn't know about any of this. Somebody would have to tell them, if anyone was left alive. She pulled back from the thought, morbid circling would get her nowhere, but living held no comfort either— telling Selwyn. A baby.

Her body clenched afresh. The pink girl at Gordey's knew a doctor, the kind who can help, but those things already belonged to a different world. Her mind hung far distant, not daring to land.

Rivulets glistened in the darkness and she made small jumps. Her galoshes were already slopping inside. She waded, arms outstretched for balance in the peat. Was it peat? Morgan would know. She swept her thoughts onwards.

Prideaux walked through grass and water alike, unerring in the dark, steady in his limping pace. Her feet snared and she tugged against the suction. Fen-sucked. Fen-sucked sodding everything. The marsh air smelled of sulphur, like the cellar.

Or perhaps it was only him.

Worse than loneliness, their silence through the waterlands. She had to hold things at arm's length and begin again. But the future was in her blood and she wanted none of it. How can you make anything new when you're falling to pieces?

There must be an answer. One clean solution, her wish as sharp as a needle, all fate incised and banished. Maybe if she gave enough, a runnel of her blood in a silver tube—that was the source of all of this, Jasper's Skein and Pixie's death and the seed set to grow like a plant inside her. Kingsley could have every drop. It could slosh in a row of swollen jars, her organs neatly packed. They couldn't ask anything of her then.

Demons can step right out of the air, out of themselves, away from all flesh. Her heart caught with envy.

But even they have to feed.

The caustic taste of his blood still coated her tongue. It's a terrible thing, wanting to live.

The sounds of water ran louder. Prideaux had stopped walking. He was directly in front of her and her boots slowed. She stood, some tide of her pulse moving from head to foot; she still had feet. How curious.

'Cigarettes, please.'

Rom waited stupidly until she recalled. She was carrying them in the breast pocket of the blue coat.

Prideaux's bare fingers were icy in the dark. The scratch and flare of the match was followed by a glow between his hands and his face sharpened briefly in the red light. He returned the tin and walked on.

Firmer ground, damp meadow. Proper trees and a hedgerow. She fell over a tussock and found it was thistle. She caught a shinful of spines, wide awake now. 'You can see in the dark?'

'My direction's fairly reliable.'

His terseness frayed her. 'You're mad about something.'

'Not at all.' He didn't turn and it was difficult to hear.

'You're quiet.'

'You're not.'

'I didn't ask for blood. I never asked you to drag me through the countryside. Or turn up in fucking Suffolk.' She'd hit another thistle clump. 'How *did* you turn up in fucking Suffolk?'

The pale splash of his shirt was two paces from her. 'I flew.'

It was easier going now, moving through the scent of crushed grass and dozing sheep. She tripped in a rabbit hole, swearing. He hoisted her up by the collar.

They met a hedge, crossed by the stile, then a road; then more stiles, more hedges, field. But they were climbing a low rise among the endless dark flats, and there was light spilled ahead below: a village. Or an encampment. Wind stirred her legs and damp hair.

A stand of trees spiked the rise and Prideaux stopped in their shadow. Rom's whole body ached as she sank on the cold grass and nursed her blistered heels. She thought Prideaux was going to ask for the cigarette tin but he stood, his face turned upward to the trees.

Walking had lulled her into some rhythm of acceptance. It's easy to think you're making progress when you're on your feet. Now she sat, folded small against the ragged wind, and the streaming world caught up with her.

'When I was a child I fell into the Nile River,' she said. She didn't know how to begin, questions or accusations, but she knew this story. 'I don't remember much.' Only the stench of mud and wings. 'When they pulled me out of the water I was half-drowned. I told my mother and father I'd been rescued by a bird. Isn't that odd?'

He didn't reply and she plunged on, eyes shut, as though she'd grab her answers from the dark. 'It was a big white bird. Probably an ibis. Or a crane, maybe. Waterbirds all look the same to me. I don't suppose you know much about ornithology.'

'Is that a question, Godden?'

'Of course it's a bloody question. I'm asking you, Mr Prideaux.' She fixed her eyes on the camp below, and the sway of light detaching itself like a firefly.

'An ibis has a curved beak,' he said. 'A crane has a straight one.' The wind came over the rise and hissed through the branches overhead. 'When you were a child, you were pulled from the River Nile by an ibis.'

'Why would it do that?'

'The bird was bound to serve the family of Jasper Teague. As payment, Teague chose to pass the binding to the firstborn of his firstborn, a child he believed would never exist.'

'And Pixie?'

'There was a grandchild after all,' Prideaux said. 'So Teague changed his mind. He betrayed the chasma who taught him. He built a trap.'

Rom shuddered in the damp coat. 'I saw the bunker.'

'Then he bound a new chasma, the white dog, and believed she could protect his family from their creditor. He believed he could cut a knot with another knot.'

'He gave his soul as relix to Pixie,' she said. 'And it still didn't save things?'

'Naught's for naught,' said Prideaux in the dark. 'He shouldn't have tried to break an oath.'

'Who was the Ibis?' Quietly, but she knew he could hear it. Even the wind had stopped.

'Surely you've untangled that, Andromeda.'

Something rose within her like a muddy tide. 'Pixie knew,' she said. 'She never had the power to fight. You didn't have to kill her.'

'Indeed,' Prideaux said. 'I could have left her for the Carnifex.'

'Don't pretend you helped anyone.'

'I don't deceive myself.'

Lantern-light moved up the slope towards them and somebody was whistling. Rom watched it through the wet of her burning eyes. 'If we were to give you the bittergold as relix,' she said. 'Theoretically—'

'That wasn't the bargain.'

'I don't suppose anyone was going to tell me.' The light drew close and the grass moved as a dog bounded ahead. Her mind swayed with the swinging lantern. 'My grandfather kept a Coronet as his pet. I needed to know.'

Prideaux's voice was a powder of stone. 'I was not his pet.'

'That isn't how Jasper saw it.' Rom didn't know for certain. But everything was ash tonight, and this beast had let it burn, and she hoped there was something left in the world with power to hurt him.

'Eho,' a child called, 'Mr Quinn sends light.' He came into sight, a gangling boy in a yellow hood, with Kingsley in dog-form beside him. 'There's a cart for the kinchin, she may ride. But Crow says Mr Argent must walk his own road.'

'Crow can choke on my sword.' Prideaux unslung the suspenders from his shoulders. In the swooping lamplight his shirt flashed white and shadowed, bloodstained and shuffling off over his head in a pale crumple.

The boy pushed the lantern towards her. 'Cart, missus.'

Rom took it and walked, down through the whispering grass to the horse.

A rift of light behind her. The crowchild crooked his arm across his face, and Rom looked back at the rise of trees.

Something a book can't tell you about birds: their wings. The noise. Even a crow whips swiftly in passing, and this pale bird was vast against the shaken trees. The movement of wings deceives. It isn't up and down—it's rotation, hesitation, round and back and banking for wind shear. A lift and gone, beating against the sky.

There were clothes in the cart. Rom shrugged off the muddy blue coat and pulled on clean things by lamplight, shirt and rustling trousers and a jacket. Thick knitted socks. The cart was full of firm hessian wool-bales, and she laid her head down with shaky gratitude. Crow's People knew what roadlings need. Her streaming tears could have been real and she wouldn't know.

The crowchild tossed something into the cart beside her—stained shirt, glistening field boots. He took the lantern and murmured to the horse, and led the cart rumbling through the darkened fields, the scents of grass and mossy water. The child whistled sometimes, and was sometimes quiet. Or perhaps his whistling dipped into places Rom couldn't hear. Her ears rang seething.

The Magician's clothes lay on the bale beside her as though it was all the creature had ever been. Rom felt washed and empty, another bundle carried somewhere in the dark. Saved again; for what? Saved for later like some unnecessary luncheon. Unfair to have to think of her last days, any other days, when this one still had to be endured. Maybe she'd be drained to the final drip of blood—slung on a hook and flayed like the satyr Marsyas, who failed at the feet of Apollo.

No contest here. Not even Apollo, who'd slipped from these shores and taken his Sight with him.

Androméda. She whispered it aloud as though she could make sense of herself, holding the name as he'd held it.

Had Desir seen this future? Had her fate even stirred a ripple? Maybe not, if it always led to the orbit of the wounded bird.

The hedges fell away on either side and the wind keened across. Rom tugged the demon's coat towards her and pulled it on again, heavy wool around her shoulders. She curled in the corner of the swaying cart and slept. She dreamed of endless nights of water. Earth shaken with hooves, a bull's thundering. The clew of thread winding tight around her fist as she led herself in, and in, all things gathered to a knot.

She woke to an engine and the blink of headlights. Kingsley had a car waiting; not his own beautiful Packard but an ancient rusted thing. He was dressed like crowfolk in faded brown velvet, and he looked at her oddly as she clambered into the passenger seat.

'It'll be hours,' he said. 'You should sleep.'

She couldn't have resisted if she'd wanted to.

27

I have learned so much—my head spins and creaks like an astrolabe, a galaxy of the mad and wondrous. My notebooks are full but they are only the barest beginning—this alchemy is physical. I have seen the marvels with my own eyes. It makes me wonder what awaits me if I ever dare make the grander sacrifice of which he speaks.

But I must not allow myself to consider—down such a path lies only horror and I am not so weak.

It's human, though, to be curious.

JASPER TEAGUE, Journals, 26th Feb. 1903

'You're stuck full of thorns.'

'Thistles,' Rom said. She slumped in the window seat with one knee in Kingsley's charge as he sat cross-legged on the floor, hunched over the tweezers. A coldwater chill stiffened her bones.

At night, the Nest on Great Queen Street outshone the shop below. The place had been lantern-warm and bright when they ascended, and empty. Maybe not; distant water pipes shook the wall.

'Tymp and frisket, look at your shins.'

She sipped. 'I fell over.'

'I can see that. You didn't take very good care of her.'

'She fell over,' Prideaux said. When had he come in? Standing by the desk, buttoning links into his shirt-cuffs. His hair was wet. 'What's she drinking?'

Kingsley didn't look over. 'Tea.'

'I don't have any tea.'

'I got you some when the mortals last stayed here. These cuts will get infected. Have you got anything for it?'

'Probably.'

Kingsley looked up. 'Will you fetch it?'

Prideaux grasped his cane and went upstairs in silence.

'You spilled your tea,' Kingsley said.

'That bloody pinches. Are you always so obvious?'

286

'Crow told me to keep to obvious things when I talk. Otherwise—' he nipped intently— 'humans become anxious. I could always talk about the mice in the walls.'

'Sounds quite interesting.'

'It would take your mind off your headache.'

'Don't,' she said shortly.

'I wouldn't worry. You smell well enough. Both of you.'

Her ribs ached tightly.

'You're overtired, but apart from that—' He trailed off, absent. A door slammed overhead.

Rom drained her tea-cup.

She'd soaked in the strange green dim of the bathroom, flinching over blisters; the tops of all her toes were broken glossy pink. Burns woke in unexpected places; the back of her calves, her shoulder. Nothing to wear afterwards except the crowfolk's gifts, and Rom smoothed her sleeve, the riding coat fringed in metal braid, the loose silk trousers striped black and oyster-white. She hadn't known how to wear the corselet thing and just buttoned it over her shirt but at least everything was neat, dry. She'd lost her hairpins and the knotted braid hung heavy down her back. She felt childish.

Kingsley had scrounged a paper parcel of fish and chips and now Rom unwrapped it, looking over the midnight gleam of Queen Street.

'You like that. Yes?' He looked anxious. 'It's a people thing?'

She nodded. She felt only a remote nausea, but the hot paper let out fragrant steam and her throat tightened. She wanted to keep it for somebody who could appreciate it better, the piled salt chips and cheery lemon. For another self, this morning's self, dissolved.

Prideaux came back downstairs in his noxious yellow robe and set a green glass jar beside her. 'Antiseptic.'

'That's honey,' Kingsley said.

'It'll do well.'

'That's *my* honey.'

'We're all making sacrifices. Show us your war-wounds, Godden.'

Her folded legs were cosy under the warm lapful. The fish was sumptuous under a gilt crunch and she paused, bolstered by a stir of appetite. 'I can do it myself.'

'The cyanide's blurred her vision,' Kingsley said, 'she can hardly see.'

'You villain,' she muttered.

Prideaux settled himself on the window seat, angled opposite, and tucked one knee to his chest. 'May I?'

Rom narrowed her eyes. And unfolded, facing him.

'Kingsley, what have you done to her?' Prideaux steadied her bent knee beside his own. 'These thorns are absurdly small.' He took a pair of steel-wire spectacles from Kingsley's waiting hand and settled them on his long nose.

Rom squeezed lemon over her last few chips. 'What happened to your reliable vision?'

'Long distance.'

His fingernails were the same colour as his skin. Antique wax. His mouth tightened in concentration and for a flinching moment he looked too human. 'Don't hover, Kingsley,' he said, and Kingsley went. Out, apparently, because he took his cap from the hook behind the door when he left.

'Other one,' Prideaux said. Rom propped her knees together. Her feet were curled between his legs, her toes raw under the crowfolk's thick socks, stinging when she moved them.

'Don't wriggle.' He glanced up and his eyes blinked milky. Translucent second eyelids, there and gone. 'Are you crying?'

'My eyes have been watering all night.'

He passed over a pressed handkerchief in striped purple silk. 'They look like tears.'

'I'm not going to cry in front of anybody.'

'You're in the house of the only creatures who couldn't care less.'

'I think Kingsley cares, actually.'

'Tisn't Kingsley's house.'

Rom bit into the quarter of lemon and swallowed hard. She'd rather pluck each sting herself if only for the forced focus, drawing them out. One moment at a time.

'*Don't* bloody wriggle,' he said. 'Either kick me or touch it properly.'

She flushed and curled up her toes. 'Are you done?'

'I thought you admired truthfulness.'

She moved her shoulder against the window-frame. His thigh was hot along hers. Should it be, if he wasn't warm-blooded? His dark velvet slippers were embroidered like a Victorian bachelor's with pointed leaves and purplish pincushion-flowers. The spare line of his other leg flopped absently, the one he didn't lean on. Which war had done it? What quarrel, in which century?

She took the honey jar and began to anoint the reddened patches on her other shin. 'Occasionally I'm tempted,' she said, 'to ask you to lie to me.'

'You don't want that.' Prideaux took off his glasses and pressed the heel of his palm to his eye. 'You barely survived my honesty. How far do you think you'd get if I gave it up?'

'Lady Tyet said Kingsley used to work for her sister.'

'What else did she say?'

'Not much. We got interrupted by a Minotaur.'

'It's a hard-earned talent, chatting while you run.'

'Unless Morax is something else.' The honey was thickly resinous, melting into her skin. 'The constellation Taurus represents an ancient monster, the Bull of Heaven; the Sumerians named him keeper of the law. He was led by the goddess Ishtar, once, to attack her enemies. The Egyptians called her Isis—her symbol was the knotted belt she wore, a talisman called the tyet.'

'What a lot of thoughts you have.'

'I saw Phoenix at the Waldorf. I've read my history books. I know an Apollonian cult when I see one. But if that's true, if that's what they are —everything gets a little bit impossible, doesn't it.'

'You think they're gods?'

'I think they could be.'

'You'll live long enough to be disappointed by every deity.' Prideaux hooked his cane and crossed to the table. 'Tyet will bargain like she's already won,' he said over his shoulder. 'But I'll think of something.'

'I don't expect you to save me,' Rom said.

'Your survival is just a useful coincidence.' He returned to put one knee on the window-seat beside her. 'Think of it as saving ourselves in parallel. Are your eyes stinging? Chin up.'

'Piss off.'

'Not metaphorically, Godden.' He tipped her face with two cool fingertips and dabbed her closed eyes with the handkerchief. 'You're leaking again. I notice you wiped your nose all over Kingsley's coat.'

'It was Kingsley's coat, then.'

'Of course.' His dry voice resounded close by. 'I'd rather something in grey wool; subtle. Silver buttons. But he vertates without the least bit of planning and it's simpler to have his clothes ready.'

'Altruism?'

'It's my job.' Prideaux's voice shifted and she opened her eyes. 'You're not the only one who inherited a faery hound.' He hadn't moved as far away as she thought. Merely turned his head, and he swung back to her with a peculiar crease between his brows.

'I don't know what to do,' she said. 'About anything, I don't know what to do next.'

'At this particular moment it's out of your power.' His head tilted. 'That isn't what you wanted me to say.'

Rom didn't answer.

And he was close enough for her to catch the myriad tightenings around his eyes. 'You'll get used to it.'

The street door slammed. Voices bounded up the staircase. Kingsley with someone else, maybe news about Alec, and Rom wiped honey from her fingers as Prideaux stood. But the boy who filed in behind Kingsley wasn't crowfolk.

Morgan's chestnut-coloured boots were caked with dry mud. His hair straggled loose over his eyes and he'd never looked so tired.

Prideaux crossed to his desk and sank into the wooden chair. 'Was he followed?'

'No,' Kingsley said. 'Junius brought him. Morax's People had eyes on him to the edge of London, but they lost interest once they saw him under Crow's wing.' He pulled a chair up to the desk and Morgan sat, dropping his satchel. Boots together, hands on his knees like a school exam.

Rom looked at him as if he might evaporate in front of her. 'Where's Alec?'

Another voice slanted up the stairwell and she bolted to the portico as Alec reached the doorway. His trousers were singed over one blistered knee and his green-striped jumper gaped ragged over his ribs. 'Oz.' He didn't even mind when she hugged him. 'In one piece?'

'Mostly.' He looked crumpled, paler than he should have been, and tipsy with long exhaustion. 'Lady Tyet had a yacht off the coast. I caught a flashbolt on the way to the boat. I'll say that much for Tyet, she's got good medics.'

'You escaped?'

'She let us go.' He sat unsteadily, glancing at the Magician, who busily ignored them from his desk. 'We gave Tyet the bone powder. But she wants the skull.'

'Which?' Rom sought words. 'What?'

'The one Mr Harper found. She released us on the terms of its return.'

Rom felt cold. 'Dr Carr's got it.'

'He might let us have it if we explain. We're clear, anyhow, all we need to do is get the teraphim and it's over. Morgan's probably got a hundred plans already.'

Morgan hoisted his satchel to his lap, unpacking it onto the desk; torch and pencil box and notebook. 'Dr Carr won't help us.' He unwrapped a chocolate bar and began to eat. 'The museum knows about chasma.'

'You can't be sure,' Alec said, 'even if they heard the story they wouldn't believe.'

'Why does everyone say that?' Morgan's gaze was anchored on the fire. 'I don't know why you think they wouldn't be interested. I would be. You were.' He turned to Rom. 'We have to assume some prominent historians are aware. Dr Carr was involved with the War Office, so the government knows. Everyone knows. There are no secrets without somebody trying hard to keep it that way.'

'A plot.' Alec looked briefly excited. 'Makes it harder to get the skull back.'

'Mhm,' Morgan said through his chocolate.

Kingsley had aired out the attic rooms, and Alec went up with Rom and crawled obediently into one of the narrow beds. 'Quite glad to be on solid ground again,' he said, and Rom crouched beside the camp bed to hear his lowered voice. Morgan was dragging something around in the other room and he gestured to the sound. 'Don't be too rough on the kid, I think he was trying to help.'

'You got kidnapped.'

'Morgan didn't know that would happen. And Lady Tyet said he stopped the Carnifex.'

'He blew up Jasper's house.'

'He what?' Alec laughed weakly. 'Well. We're all safe, aren't we?'

There'd be time in the morning to tell him otherwise.

Morgan caught up with Rom on the stairway and she eyed his stiff-legged descent. The hollow of his ear held a crust of blood.

'Did Tyet give Alec any panax?'

'He wouldn't take anything,' Morgan said, 'but her People did a careful job. She was keen for you to know she didn't cause his injuries.' He dropped back into the chair by Prideaux's desk.

Rom sat slowly. 'She didn't keep her word about the exchange. I don't see why we should either. You're already safe. We don't have to give her anything.'

Morgan raised his hand, fingers spread.

Prideaux was writing and didn't look up. 'Tyet will have it off at the wrist if you break your word.'

'Only a finger,' Morgan said. 'She said I'm too young to bear a whole forfeit. We've got tomorrow to collect the payment.'

Rom understood. 'Alec doesn't know?'

'And you're not going to tell him. Tyet always planned to demand the skull.'

'Probably.' Prideaux leaned back in his seat. 'It belonged to a halfstar child. Give Tyet what she wants, she won't be merciful.'

'Kingsley told us there are no fey children,' Rom said.

'None alive.'

She moved on the hard wooden chair. 'Can't Crow help us?'

'Quinn's allegiance is to himself,' Prideaux said. 'If he's pushed he'll side with Bear. And Bear's now allied with Tyet.'

'But he was furious about Tyet and Phoenix taking all those souls.'

'The demons despise each other,' Morgan said, 'but they hate us more.'

Rom looked at Prideaux who listened with downcast eyes, his hands tucked behind his head. 'You work with us, though.'

'Mr Prideaux knows which side of his bread is buttered.'

The Magician lowered one hand to point at Morgan. 'Upstairs,' he said, 'or you'll be dead on your feet.'

Morgan stood, regarding Rom with a distant sort of pity. 'You ought to sleep, too.' He left his bag and headed for the stairs.

Prideaux raised his voice. 'How'd you manage with that puzzle in the end?'

Morgan stopped with his hand on the banister. 'There's only more questions,' he said. 'It should be easy as a piece of string. But how is it knotted? When wrapped up, what can it carry? If laid over stone, where do the knots lie? When plucked, what's the note? When stretched, how far does it reach? I don't know what to look for.'

'Is that your answer?'

'Probably,' Morgan said. 'I'm tired of it.' He went upstairs.

Rom watched his dragging boots. 'Is he hurt?'

'Not much,' Kingsley said from the doorway, 'Crow's People wanted relix to get him here. Took a bit of blood.'

'Monsters.' She couldn't speak.

'Morgan went north to betray them,' Prideaux said. 'Surely they were right to doubt him on the way home again.'

The day settled in Rom's mind like sand through water. A new reality. And this creature sat opposite, one cold fire in their constellation.

'Will you do it?' Prideaux asked. 'Quite a conclusion, stealing from your professor's office.'

At least it was something she could tackle properly, real action. 'Not many options,' she said.

'Indeed; Morgan can't manage everything.'

'How did he know Tyet had Alec?'

Kingsley was still leaning in the doorway. 'She sent a note, making her threat and demanding the collar.'

'I had care of Pixie. You'd think she'd have sent it to me.'

'She did,' Prideaux said. 'A message to your aunt's house.'

Rom paused. 'I never got it.'

'Morgan found it. He answered her. Crowfolk carried their notes. I think he fancied he could negotiate without giving up the bittergold, but Tyet doesn't appreciate games. She skipped directly to extortion.'

'So Alec got kidnapped.' Rom's throat was dry. 'He got burned by the slaves of a fucking Minotaur because Morgan stole my mail.'

Prideaux tapped the table. 'Answer the question.'

She gritted her teeth. 'Which?'

'Are you going to steal from the College offices?'

A sinuous silence. Not even the thump of Kingsley's heel; he'd disappeared.

'What are you suggesting?'

'I'm simply asking,' Prideaux said. 'Now Alec's safe, I wondered if you'd leave Mckenzie to his own mess. I thought that was your *modus negotii.*'

'Tyet would cut his finger off.' She was breathing hard. 'I'm not a demon. We aren't like that.'

'We? Crux, Godden.' Prideaux reached for Morgan's pencil box and dug out a pink eraser. 'Twenty years ago this rubber tree would have been from the Amazon. Have you heard of it? The Portuguese chained the locals into pillaging their own forests. It might even have been shipped from the Belgian Congo, the plantation gravesite of ten million people. But this one's probably direct from the Malaysian colonies where Britain grips the rubber supplies to pay off its war debts, so do not—*do not* talk to me about cruelty, Godden. Don't humiliate yourself with a boast of human morality while this penny rubber sits in my house.'

His eyes were scorching. She should go to bed and not even attempt to engage him.

'Alright,' she said, as though returning to a question. 'What were Jasper's terms?'

Prideaux didn't pretend to misunderstand. 'It's fairly standard. Your grandfather wanted to make the panax. He was unwilling to give his own soul for the privilege, but we negotiated an agreement.'

'And you got—what?'

'In the unlikely case his unmarried daughter should have a child, their soul would be forfeit. At the moment of their natural death. In which I cannot interfere.'

'What about the river? You saved me.'

'Clearly that was not the moment.'

'So you know when I'm going to die.'

'I know when you're not.'

'You told us to work on the panax, even now. It doesn't bother you if another demon gets caged to make alkahest.'

Prideaux rolled a pen between his fingers. 'They'd have to catch us first.'

'You don't much care for humans, do you?'

'They burned the sky. It rained poison.' His eyes were closed. 'I live here too.'

'So you'll continue to help me. As long as the contract lasts?'

'Until the terms are fulfilled, when the panax is released to the general population. With my assistance. Only in the field of alchemical science.' He half-opened one eye. 'We don't run errands.'

'Kingsley made me tea.'

'Kingsley's nice.'

'How can I break it? Is there another way?'

'Always, Miss Godden. You can pass the relix to one of your brothers. Or to your children. But I don't think you'll do it.' He settled his shoulder into the chair. 'I'm bound and somebody owes a soul. It's not ideal; you'd prefer not to lose it, and I'd prefer not to wait. The solution is, I kill you now or wait for somebody with half a business mind to come along and end it.'

'Morax would hunt you down. You can't kill me.'

'No, I can't.' She thought he sighed again. 'And the business mind obviously isn't yours. I'll wait if I must, but I really haven't more than a few years before I lose patience, and that one won't be ready.'

'Which one?'

He waved his pencil toward her. '*Relicus*.'

'You think I'd pay you with my child's soul.'

'Or grandchild, if you'd rather. Many do. It's easier; less personal attachment, I imagine. Some never pay at all, simply passing the debt through time. One of Forca's People has been with the same family for eight generations and they show no sign of paying out. It keeps him in fresh blood, and they have their problems taken care of. He isn't a hunter, of course, he's a Warrener.'

'I'm not about to drop my problems on to somebody else.' She'd never subject her children to this, nor their children, this fate like a thorn unhealed. 'What about the other way? What if you die?'

'I return, eventually, and the debt stands. And I'm much less pleasant than I was before.'

The silence lengthened and grew dangerous.

'A soul for a stack of books,' she said. 'Seems a little steep.'

'For a demon's assistance.' His eyes slitted open, unpleasantly bright. 'Is it? For the universal panacea. A decade of service. The four hundred sacred works of Trismegistus. The Holy Fucking Grail, Godden. You're very welcome, keep the change.'

Something faltered in her chest. 'It wasn't my idea.'

'It's simply commerce. You need us.'

'If you died tomorrow nobody would even notice.'

'Half the population of this piss-ant little planet would kill for a chance at—'

'But if we died,' she said, 'every single one of you would starve. I suppose that's why you make a fuss about contracts, so you can pretend there's some kind of equality. Nicer than begging to be fed.'

'Everything is a contract, every unspoken understanding. It's just buying and selling and owing and collecting. Nothing free, nothing without obligation and consequences.'

'Plenty of people do unselfish things.'

'Because it makes them feel nice,' Prideaux said. 'Your grandfather. Jasper.' A hard sort of voice. 'His intentions were of the utmost purity. He planned to make panacea for all the world. He spent every penny he had to shield his materials from contaminating the air and water. He was wonderfully righteous.'

Prideaux rolled the pencil over his knuckles. 'He gave his own soul to protect his family. His work will save the lives of millions.' The pencil flickered in a silver revolution around his fingers. 'And he starved a chasma in his garden for six years.'

'I'm sorry,' Rom said. 'But he didn't realise what it meant to make panax, or how many people would suffer. I've read his notes. He wasn't happy about what he was doing.'

'He came down to view his little project, with his checklist and his tests. He knew exactly what he was doing. I heard each of his confessions. He was looking for punishment, you understand.' Prideaux caught the pencil between thumb and finger, balanced. 'It became a little project of my own, speculating how far he'd fall before the end, trying to persuade him to change the contract while ensuring his mind didn't break too suddenly. I'm afraid I didn't succeed.' A mordant silence, not quite empty. 'His health failed. Nature had more mercy than I did.'

He stood, shaking himself out, and he was leaving. Rom didn't move. If she moved her head she'd be sick.

Prideaux paused at the bathroom door. 'A lot to do tomorrow.' He spoke as if they were planning a jaunt to the markets. 'You really ought to sleep.'

Rom whispered. 'In this place?'

'Are you afraid?' he said. 'I want you alive. You've never been safer.'

28

I can get no further on this path. I walked the mysteries, and they led me to the precipice.

But is this not the true beginning? The Fool upon the cliff-top stands in perfect unknowing. The journey cannot begin until he steps into the void.

The first step is the Magician. He has mastery of the elements, after all; the tools are his.

This is for all people. I have prepared the circle and the bones. I have painted the circle with blood and quicksilver, and I begin the great work.

I am going to summon a demon.

JASPER TEAGUE, Journals, 4th April 1900

Rom slept.

Kingsley had tea waiting when she emerged at dawn, feeling stiff and unready. He'd bought muffins from somewhere—an apology for Prideaux, for everything; or maybe they just wanted her in a good mood.

Morgan sat bathed and dressed beneath the window, with a map spread over his knee.

'Alec's fine,' he said, before she could ask. 'We're leaving him here until things are finished with Tyet, then crowfolk will take him home.' He gestured at the desk. 'One of them went by his hotel room; Polly sent a telegram.'

Rom paused on the stairs. 'About you?'

'She was pleased to hear I wasn't dead yet.' Morgan brushed crumbs from the map. 'And they'll be over here next Tuesday.'

She couldn't afford to think even a day ahead. 'I'll tell Alec the good news.'

He was half-dozing when she knocked at the little attic room, but he came smartly to attention when she sat on his bed. 'Problem?'

'Several.' She hadn't planned to bring it up until they were out of here, but safety seemed more distant than she'd reckoned on. She clasped her wrist. 'I know whose Skein this is.'

'I want to say I don't believe it.' Alec paled as he listened, his long face worn. 'Unfortunately I've met the Magician.'

'The term of a natural life, he said. It might not be so bad. Oblivion can't be all that painful.'

'Bosh.' Alec shuffled out of the stretcher bed, wincing. 'Total and utter. Come on, we're squaring this.'

Kingsley was busy with a kettle when they came down, and Morgan's voice murmured from the landing. Mr Prideaux was at his desk.

'Naberius, wasn't it?' Alec said, as though they'd never met. 'You're a rotten snake.'

Prideaux nodded with a kind of humility. 'How did you sleep?'

'What's a soul worth?'

'I know what you're planning,' Prideaux said; 'there isn't any point.'

Alec plunged on as though he hadn't heard. 'Does it have to be human?'

'The vital energies increase in proportion with an animal's consciousness; human pain is nearly unmatched.'

'Is there nothing you'll take instead?'

'No mortal treasure could compensate for your sister's relix. The scales might possibly balance over a lifetime of indentured servitude.' Prideaux rolled a pencil between two fingers. 'Or just over a billion litres of blood.'

'You said she could lump her relix onto someone else. Every soul's the same to you.'

Prideaux's eyes were liquid ink. 'Are you quite sure you want to do this?'

'Certain,' Alec said. 'No, shut up,' and Rom stopped, her throat burning. 'If we're all equally useful I don't see why he should bully us.' He turned back to Prideaux. 'How about we leave it to chance? Sounds like your sort of lark. Whichever of us dies first, Rom or me. Nobody's a victim and you don't get to choose.'

'Oz—'

'Rom. You know it makes sense,' he said. 'I'm not leaving it up to anyone else, least of all this doaty weasel.'

'Why should I?' Prideaux said.

'No loss to you,' Alec said, 'and better chance of an early pay-out. I'm a bad driver.'

'Fair,' Prideaux said. He was drawing off his glove. He pushed back his chair and stood, leaning across the desk. 'Shake, Mr Godden.' Alec held out his hand and Prideaux gripped it. 'I accept your terms. You'll bear the Skein of my house until relix is paid.'

'Superb.' Alec withdrew his fingers. 'I'm going back to bed.' He squeezed Rom's shoulder and turned away, stiff as he marched upstairs.

Through a ringing fog Rom heard his door close.

'Fascinating,' Prideaux said. 'How does it feel to be rescued two days running?'

She sat on the wooden chair. 'I'm going to need my clothes back.'

'I burned them,' Kingsley said.

Rom slumped. Her striped trousers winked back at her. 'Well then.' A pair of paper shears glittered on Prideaux's desk. 'Has anyone got a spare shirt?'

The scissors were for trimming the fringe on the circus coat; that's what she told herself. But once she had them in her hand she knew why she'd asked.

She did it in the bathroom, in front of the rusty mirror. Pulling her hair out of its braid, over her shoulders, and then she could grab it properly—hanks of wheaty-brown, singed and dank with smoke. One at a time, snipped unsteadily, all the way to her ears.

She put down the scissors and leaned against the sink. It felt light as nothing at all. She hardly looked like herself. No make-up, a strange scruff of hair. But when was the last time she'd been anything she recognised?

She pulled the striped trousers back on.

'Here,' Kingsley said through the door, 'I had a fresh one.' He passed through a pressed and cream-striped linen shirt.

She could wear the corsolet over it. She'd need to, without any underthings. The boots fitted well enough over the joyously mismatched knitted socks. And Kingsley had put in a tie, Alec's emerald green one, a dash of formality to offset the mad harlequin trousers.

She opened the bathroom door. 'Done.'

'What sort of slattern are you?' Prideaux held out a black scarf. 'Put a hat on.'

She knotted it around her cropped hair. 'You never wear one.'

'I left it somewhere and forgot to go back. I'm assuming you have a plan for breaking into the College?'

'If we knew when Dr Carr would be absent.'

'He has a meeting at half-past ten.' Morgan pulled the curtain closed as he stepped in from the landing. 'I telephoned, said I wanted to interview him for a school paper. The clerk told me his schedule.'

'Well,' Prideaux said. 'I think we make a rather brilliant team.'

They ignored him. 'I know his office,' Rom said. 'Even if somebody catches me I've got a reason.'

Prideaux looked interested. 'You plan to safeguard the whole floor while you break in and smuggle the teraphim out?'

'We should bring Kingsley,' Morgan said.

'You're staying with Alec,' she said. 'This isn't any kind of a lark, it's robbery.'

Morgan sighed. 'I'm risking a finger. This has to work. Which means I need to be there.'

'It's only theft,' said Prideaux, 'unless you're planning to threaten violence.'

'If your school finds out—you won't get out of this, Harry won't—'

'It's only school.'

'Really,' Prideaux said, 'you're planning a crime and nobody's asked me.'

'I'd rather take a dead cat,' Rom said. At least Morgan wanted this to succeed; no danger he'd betray them before Tyet had the teraphim.

'I'm protecting my investment,' Prideaux said. 'And I'm good at my job.'

'Which is what, stirring shit on every continent since the early Chalcolithic?'

'Talking,' Prideaux said. 'Watching. Wandering about.' He paused, wrapping his hand around his cane. 'Thieving.'

'We don't need a thief,' Morgan said. 'We need a sentry.'

'His hearing range is half a mile,' Kingsley said.

'Bloody—' Rom hissed. 'Alright, fine.' She nodded at Prideaux. 'No suggestions. No assistance. Don't order us about and don't touch anything.'

'I'll get my coat,' Prideaux said.

Morgan was frowning. 'We can't just walk in.'

'Carr knows Godden,' Prideaux said. 'She'll keep an eye on his meeting room. If he comes out early, she keeps him occupied while you're on lookout, and I get the teraphim.'

Morgan's eyebrows lifted. 'Lookout.'

'Not a chance,' Rom said, 'you'll switch the bloody thing. I'm getting the teraphim myself. You can watch Dr Carr.'

'*Lookout*,' Morgan said again.

'You've got a better plan?' she asked.

'Carr knows both of you,' Morgan said. 'That's going to end badly when he finds the teraphim gone. Of course there's a better plan.'

'So the metal-workers of Mesopotamia used moulds to create their bronze blades. Do you think this technique developed from their skill with clay?'

'Certainly,' Dr Carr said. 'They invented the potter's wheel. In a culture without a firm grounding in clay techniques, the craftsmen might have forged their bronze instead. What did you say your interest was in my article?'

Morgan smiled. 'Weapons, sir.'

Rom rounded the staircase landing and their voices in the corridor became a murmur. She made her way towards the professor's office, not lingering; just a student trudging with an armful of books.

Things had been smooth so far. She'd walked to the College with Morgan's bag over her shoulder, fast enough to stop her hands shaking. At a quarter past ten Morgan had marched to the front desk and passed her on his way up to the lecture rooms.

Kingsley had dropped Mr Prideaux half a block from the front steps, and he'd ambled up in his own time. She'd caught sight of his cloud-grey suit and watched him mount the stairs with painful slowness. Unconcerned, putting out his cigarette before he finally tucked his cane beneath his elbow and entered the College foyer. Coat over his arm, his signal all was well on the street outside. Her queue to join a gabbling crowd of students and sweep upstairs with them, past Morgan and Dr Carr and into the staff corridors.

She'd timed it well; the hallway was deserted and the few students

didn't seem to suspect. She paused, just a girl in striped trousers, knocking on her professor's door and entering as though she belonged.

When she closed the door it bumped on Prideaux's shoe.

'The little shit can talk when he wants to.'

'I thought you were staying on the stairs,' Rom said. Quietly. Not gently.

'Nobody's coming.' Prideaux hung his cane on his wrist and pushed past her. 'Go on, thieve away.'

'The bones don't belong to Dr Carr either.'

'*Hermes koinos*.'

'Something like that.' She peered into the cabinets. Then she dropped to a crouch. The bright faience pieces had been replaced with striped glass dishes, and the cushion where the teraphim had rested was occupied by a fragment of pot. 'It's not here.' Her insides curled up cold. 'It's gone, he must have moved it.' She dashed around to the other cases, the tidy desk. 'Is it in a cupboard?'

Prideaux was reading the titles on the bookshelves. 'It's not in the building; Carr transferred it a few days ago.'

'Where to?' She groaned. 'You didn't tell us.'

'I don't recall you asking. Would you like to ask for assistance?'

Her knees throbbed with the effort of locking them steady. 'Do you want us to fail? If Morgan—' She couldn't think that far ahead. 'Death's too good for you.' She swung the satchel over her back, her boots striking echoes on the stone steps as she charged back down and across the foyer.

Morgan caught up with her on the footpath. 'You don't have it.'

'No.' Furious. 'Did you know?'

'It wasn't there? That was a possibility.'

'Where the hell is it, then?'

They both turned. Prideaux leaned against the College wall, patting down his pockets for his tin. 'I don't know,' he said. He cupped the lighter in his palm, weighing it. 'If Kingsley hadn't ducked out, he could have found it quicker than anyone. But it's not far away. I can find a halfstar's bones in London, with a bit of time.'

'We don't have time,' Morgan began, and Rom shook her head.

'We already know where it is.' She turned back up the Strand, away from the river and towards the city. Prideaux muttered something and fell into step beside them.

'Dr Carr could have given it to the police,' Morgan said. 'Or locked it in a safe.'

'He'd put it in the most secure place he's got,' Rom said. 'With all the other bones. In the British Museum.'

'He wouldn't.' Morgan ducked to avoid a woman with a pram, his feet automatic. 'Shit. He would. This will work.' From his firm mouth Rom couldn't tell if it was certainty or hope.

'It might,' she said. 'But we can't just walk up—'

'Andromeda. You know we're going to, just find a way.'

He was right. If there was another way he'd be doing it.

She turned to Prideaux. 'Will it be there?'

His lope was longer than either of theirs, slightly uneven. 'Museum's the safest bet.' He scanned the streets as they shouldered through the midday crowds. 'I do think we could catch a cab.'

'No taxi,' Morgan said. 'If the police investigate, they'll advertise for information and the driver might remember us.'

'I appreciate your forethought,' Prideaux said, 'but I don't intend to walk.'

'Then go home,' Rom said. 'You've wrecked enough for one day.'

'That's a no to my assistance?'

Morgan stopped. His brown eyes were raw and wide, an awful kind of stare, and she was glad it wasn't aimed at her. 'What do you want?' he said, fixed on Prideaux but almost talking to himself. 'What is it you *want*?'

She'd never seen Prideaux stand entirely still. 'You're going to rob a museum,' he said. 'I want to see.'

Morgan sighed. 'Stay quiet, then.' And they walked on. 'How far is it?'

'A mile or so,' Rom said. 'We could take a taxi—'

'No.' Morgan's steadiness held no hostility. 'It's ideal. Enough time to make a plan.'

That was an optimistic word, thought Rom, a mile or so later, for the utter simplicity of what followed.

1. Enter the British Museum. Marble cold, antiseptic as a tomb, with Morgan tense on her left and Prideaux on her right. She whispered.

'You don't seem concerned by mortal thresholds.'

Prideaux shrugged. 'Public building.'

2. Turn left and head for the offices. No point applying for a study room ticket; if the teraphim was here, Dr Carr would ensure it wasn't available for viewing. It wouldn't even exist.

3. Descend to the archives. 'They're kept locked,' she explained on the stairs, 'but I can get a key.' If she was lucky, if the conservator was somebody she'd met one assorted Wednesday. 'And I can always say Dr Carr sent me.'

'The wondrous simplicity of the outright lie,' Prideaux said.

Backstage of anywhere has a utilitarian sameness. Everyone has the smug boredom of the insider; the corridors echo, and nothing's properly lit. The archives were storage for everything that couldn't fit upstairs, items under repair and artifacts in line to be processed.

It was far busier than Rom expected and the first store-room loomed with half-wrapped statues. Workmen with trolleys. The room she wanted was at the back, through a little passage between tidy ranks of boxes, close enough she could almost smell the old clay.

Worry rose like a flush. 'It might not even be here.'

'It's here,' Prideaux said. 'You get us in, I'll find it.'

She was aware of Morgan's expectant gaze as she entered the open door of the shabby staff room. 'Good afternoon. I'm over from King's College, I work in conservation on—'

'Where's your sign-off?' The harried little man looked over his clipboard. 'I'm not on conservation today, we're getting the Assyrian bits upstairs. Nobody said the workrooms would be open.'

'They're not,' she said, 'it's just one thing. It was brought in a few days ago, we need it back to show a specialist.'

'He can come down for a squiz like everyone else.' The man frowned. 'Artifacts can't be dragged in and out of humidity. I'll need that sign-off.' He saluted as he ducked back over to the canvas-wrapped Assyrian kings.

She walked back to the corridor, stiff and hot-faced.

'Amateur,' Prideaux said.

'If we could mock up a form ourselves—'

'It has to be now,' Morgan said. 'We're here.'

'You want to take the thing in full sight. And just walk out again?'

She wanted him to have a scheme, something clever enough to clear this mess. She wanted him to say no.

'Yes.' Prideaux was tugging off his left glove.

She turned on him. 'You need someone to hold your hand?'

'There's not much point, you don't have permission here either. We're all trespassing. I will not be invisible. You'll have to carry it out, you're less culpable if we're stopped. Get a taxi on Gower Street and go straight to the station. Kingsley will have the car at the other end, if crowfolk do their job. And I'll do mine.' He pushed his coat into Morgan's arms.

'We didn't ask you to,' Rom said. 'I'm not paying you for this.'

'You will.' Prideaux was counting the workmen around the statues. 'You have.' Eyeing the three clerks pointing to the stacked crates. Counting the head conservator and the doorways, left, right. He tapped his cane on the ground and hefted it.

The whole room slowed to silence. The light hardened. Unfolding shadows crossed the floor at Prideaux's feet as though a hand of cards had shuffled. He'd sucked something out of the air—noise, light—a hiss of sand, caught breath, and there was only the tap of his cane.

One of the workmen swore.

The Magician didn't even hurry himself. The man staggered as he caught the cane hard across the knees. Prideaux hooked an arm around him and pressed the gilt crook to the back of his neck, and the workman slumped. Prideaux lowered his silent dead-weight to the floor.

The other men spread out, blocking the doorway, and one swung a crowbar.

Prideaux slipped between the shelves. Another packer crumpled.

He didn't try to get within reach of the others. He stepped forward, too tall, his form billowing like a shadow, shaking and lengthening and stretching lightly in quick tapping steps. Looming like a dream between foolishness and horror like a vile stilt-jack. Somebody shouted.

Prideaux disappeared behind the shelves in the far corner, his shadow darting across the ceiling.

'We're going to have to run,' Rom said. 'Once we've got it.'

Morgan nodded.

One of the workmen bellowed, and charged between the aisles with a chair as though he faced a frenzied dog.

A rumour of movement whispered through the concrete floor and jarred her teeth.

'He's going to change.' Morgan's eyes were fixed wide. 'Kingsley said he's a bird sometimes. Do you think he can fly?'

The packer backed out of the aisle, stumbling, followed by the spilled shadow of the demon. The thing was silhouetted on the floor in a fuming light that showed massive slinking flesh, a jut of horn. The room seized up with the tortured grind of iron and the world pulled tight.

Rom's eyes spasmed with fireworks. Vision, breath. Then rumbling noise, a rush like a passing train, and time unrolled.

'Fuck me.' Prideaux was beside her, entirely naked, pulling his coat on. 'Fucking chronological classification, I can't find anything.' He cupped a box in both hands. 'Carry this.'

It was an archival box of ivory paper. She began to open it but he bared his teeth. 'It's the teraphim. Would I lie?'

Rom settled the box into the satchel at her hip. She didn't look at Prideaux's neck and chest as he knotted his belt.

'Go.' He was feeling in his pocket, tucking something into it or just looking for his tin. 'Go to the station. Don't stop. Kingsley will get you to Tyet.'

Rom caught Morgan's sleeve and walked briskly for the corridor, aware of slamming doors and shouts in the distance.

Morgan scuffled to keep up. 'We'll be stopped.'

'Won't,' she said. But they would be, they'd been noticed. A squarish suited man with a toolbox had rounded the end of the hallway.

Morgan's shout echoed. 'Help. Quick—'

'What's this?' A clerk flung open a door just ahead of them. His spectacles dangled. 'Who's messing around?'

Morgan pointed. 'Back there, someone's breaking things in the store-room.'

'Hurry.' Rom didn't have to act. Her voice was unsteady. 'You have to hurry—'

The clerk swore and bolted past them. They pushed onwards past the other man, and Rom didn't stop or speak as they marched through the echoing upper corridors—clattering down steps and heading for the crowds, stairs, the exhibits in their endless grand galleries that opened at last on the Museum foyer and released them into the buzzing street.

It was cool and gusting outside, a damp foul smell. Morgan whistled for a taxi.

She knew it was the stupidest thing she could do, pulling out a stolen item in public, but she needed to see. She opened the box and unfolded the cotton wool from the arc of smooth clay.

Morgan's eyes were hard. 'That's it?'

Rom closed the box. 'Yes.'

'You know he stole something else in there.'

'We did let him into the store rooms. It's not stealing, anyway—*hermes koinos*.' A taxi pulled up to the gutter and she glanced at Morgan. 'It means *something for all*. Finders keepers. Really it means *common to Hermes*; everything lost gets shared with the god of discoveries. Good luck is only theft from the fates. The ancient Greeks didn't always see much difference between stealing and finding. Neither does Dr Carr, apparently.'

Morgan settled beside her in the sour cab.

'Quick thinking. Back there in the hallway.' She held the satchel on her lap as they jolted into traffic. 'Were you always so clever with stories?'

Morgan rested his head back and closed his eyes. 'I had a good teacher,' he said.

29

'In the oldest times—so long as the gods themselves still dwelt in trees, springs, rude stones fallen (or reputed to have fallen) from heaven, and pointed columns... sacred groves furnished with a fence, served as the places of divine worship.' The night haunt of Artemis, with her ghostly troupe, was at the crossways.

ALFRED WATKINS, The Old Straight Track

Kingsley pulled up the car between open fields and cut the engine. The insect hum swelled. Boundless sky as they stepped out into some windblown corner of Berkshire, maybe; Rom had been lost since noon. After the sweltering car, the air was cool.

A girl in a Votary's mantle was perched on the stile. 'Welcome, mortals,' she said in her silly cooing voice. 'You weren't invited,' she said to Kingsley, and nodded towards the rise. 'Shall we?'

Rom and Morgan swished through the sallow grass. 'Do you think the Magician plans to show?'

'I don't suppose he's welcome,' Morgan said.

They came out on the hilltop. A huge stone leaned half-sunk in the grass, as though pressed under by the lowering sky. Rom knew everyone assembled here: Tyet, heavy-lidded and upright, her white dress flapping against her legs. Her shoes were stained with mud, all up the ankles of her leaf-green stockings. Four Votaries simpered alike in white robes. A Chit leaned like a stitched-up scarecrow beside the old stone.

And one more. Rom didn't notice her until she moved, a giant of a woman, tall as Prideaux and far stronger, wrapped in a brown tweed overcoat. She was barefoot in the grass. Her broad cheekbones were flecked like a fawn's hide and her straw-coloured hair was knotted at her nape.

Rom stopped with Morgan a few steps from the strange woman and Lady Tyet.

'Welcome, children,' Tyet said in her thrilling warm voice. Her eyes slid to the box in Rom's hands. 'Did you bring it?'

'Once you have it Morgan will be free?'

Tyet bowed her head. 'Of course.'

The rain was coming over in drifts. Rom's hands felt clammy around the paper box. 'Free him first,' she said. 'Please.'

Tyet raised her left hand. She twined her fingers, a slow writhe passing through her arm as though it shuddered boneless. 'You are unbound, little one.'

Morgan rubbed his knuckles. He nodded as if he didn't trust himself to speak.

Rom held out the box. 'Take it.'

'Witness,' the Chit said in its fluting voice. 'Witness, all.'

The tall woman stepped forward, the fair-headed stranger. Her broad and calloused hands received the box with infinite care. 'Despina,' she said. Her voice was husky and soft. 'That was her name.'

Tyet's great eyes gleamed sharp as stones. 'She was our sister's child. Where did you find her?'

'The Museum,' Rom said. 'Somebody gave them the teraphim—a professor.'

'It was not his to give.'

'He didn't know it was yours.' But Rom didn't think it would have made a difference.

'So we all have what we want. Yes? This is how a negotiation should end.' Tyet looked around. 'We have our halfstar safe.' She laid her hand on the woman's big soft shoulder. The woman growled in her chest, and Rom's hands prickled. *Bear.* 'I will go back to the Americas,' Tyet went on, 'and leave Phoenix to play his own games. We will see what dawn the fresh year brings us. What joy, what harmony.' Her fine fingers curled into the Votary's shoulder as she turned back to Rom. 'My brother has done well. You can tell him our bargain holds.'

'Tell him yourself,' Rom said. 'Mr Desir's got grand plans, I don't think I'll be seeing him soon.'

'No.' Tyet tilted her head. 'My younger brother. My canting, subtle, wondrous bird. Êkhos promised he would send us our halfstar, and the white dog's collar, and so he did. Give him my thanks. And tell him this also: if he crosses me again, I'll clip him like a barnyard goose.'

'That was me,' Rom said. Her head spun with ugly vertigo. 'I got the teraphim out of the Museum.' Because she'd heard Prideaux's story. Because Morgan needed help. She kindled with fury as she rounded on him. 'You knew?'

'No.' Morgan's voice was hoarse.

'Prideaux told you to steal the bittergold.'

'No,' Morgan said, 'he told me not to, I wasn't—'

'He played you,' Rom said, 'you utter fool.' She turned to Lady Tyet. 'Prideaux shouldn't have promised you. He couldn't have known—' The wind whipped her cropped hair and flung her voice into a distant gust. She hardened her face against the rain. 'He never said he was your brother.'

Tyet's golden earrings trembled. 'He is learning the wisdom of silence.'

Maybe the knowledge wouldn't have changed anything. Maybe this is how an ancient thing will always make you feel, like a single word in somebody else's story. How long had this story run? How does it end?

'He must have made a bargain,' Rom said desperately. 'What did he want for all this?'

Tyet turned away. 'Many thanks to you, small one.' She nodded to Morgan.

Rom was afraid she might cry. 'Little rat.'

'Mr Morgan is playing with a world that isn't ready for him,' Tyet said, pausing. 'He should have been a herald, standing in the battlefield to number the dead and decide the victory. To carry news to queens. But he is stuck in a pitiable time. What will you do, child?'

Morgan rubbed his sleeve over his nose. 'I'm going back to school.'

'We're finished here,' Tyet said.

Bear shuffled off her heavy coat and stood bare-armed. The wind caught her rust-coloured dress like a flag, sighing through the sere grass. The votaries whispered. Bear knelt on her strong knees and laid her hand flat against the ground. Her cry was long and rasping, and broke like thunder.

The earth rolled under Rom's feet.

The Chit clickered. 'Ben lightmans, all.' It lifted its hands and the air ignited briefly. Rain hissed where the thing had stood.

And the Bear was wailing, a deep guttural sound, her face turned up to the rain, rocking on her knees, her arm reached above her head as if she wanted to drag something from the sky.

Rom shivered. 'It's time to go.'

'I'm sorry,' Morgan said. 'About the collar. And everything. I didn't realise.'

'That doesn't help.'

'I'm sorry,' he said again.

Rom pulled her coat closer and turned back down the track. Long strides, brisk through the field.

She thought he tried to catch up, but she didn't wait.

Kingsley hovered at the car door. 'Done?'

A blue tartan coat was slung over the driver's seat.

'Not nearly,' Rom said. 'Where is he?'

Kingsley nodded towards the woodland. 'Scouting.'

She strode down the wet slope. She saw movement between the boughs and braced herself as she passed under the dripping trees.

Prideaux leaned against a gate-post, just down the narrow path, rolling himself a cigarette. His tweed trousers were stuffed into high field boots. The cane hung from his arm. A striped shirt showed under his old-fashioned waistcoat, and he had a knotted blue rag of a tie.

He flicked the lighter. 'Hullo.'

'Did you tell Morgan to steal the collar?'

He shifted his weight to the other foot. 'Morgan would have reached the same conclusion unassisted.'

'It was you,' she said, 'every dirty little idea. What was your bargain with Tyet?'

'Not your business, Godden.'

'It is. I'm paying.'

'I wanted Tyet to leave her alliance with Phoenix,' Prideaux said. 'That's all. She wants an amusement, and she can find one somewhere else.'

'You don't want them playing without you.'

His eyes were unreadable. 'Phoenix wants a war against the underfires. I did the clever thing. Perhaps even the right thing, as far as you'd see it. Should I have encouraged him?'

'The right thing? You've never been honest with us. We broke into the bloody Museum—'

'With my assistance.'

'Because you wanted something,' Rom said. 'You find every bit of leeway and worm your way in. What did you take?'

'I shouldn't worry. You'll be rid of me by the new year; you've got the key to panax. I keep my promises.'

It had been long enough for her. But even longer for him. 'You'll be free of us too.'

'One duty finished,' he said, 'another begun.'

Revulsion weighted her laughter. 'You despise us. And you're going to do it all again? So much for your restraint,' she said. 'Have you given up on asceticism?'

He pinched the cigarette to blow out a coil of smoke. His eyes were fixed on the muddy path, waiting for her to finish.

'No, that was Jasper's idea, wasn't it. He designed your martyrdom.' Rom inhaled the wet earth, the fetid smoke, and her thoughts gathered like a fist. 'He put it in the contract? He stopped you eating. You need to finish here so you can feed again.'

Prideaux took the cigarette from his mouth and twitched his nose.

'Is that the only reason you helped us?'

'Simple needs.'

But she could see now. 'You could have sat back and waited till we died of old age, but you were starving. You can't even get blood except from the others. All this time?' Her ears rang. 'All your scheming. You really are no better than a parasite.'

'I did my job. I'm good at what I do.'

'You lied.'

'Not once. I'm *good*,' he repeated, 'at what I do.' He was very tall when he straightened himself.

'You deceived us constantly.' She'd wanted for too long to say these things. 'You didn't have to bring Morgan into it, he's just a kid. Alec could have died.'

'They made their own choices.'

'Pixie didn't.' And that was a bad sick thing, cracking like a brick through her thoughts. Rom had spoken the words herself. She'd ordered Pixie to lower her wards. She'd undone the magic keeping Pixie from the Magician's knife, the only knot of puzzlement keeping her own soul out of his hands. 'Did you always guess I'd free her?'

'You were hardly honest either.' He waved his cigarette at her belly.

'That's none of your business.'

'And you can't extend me the same courtesy?' His anger was flat and horrible. 'Not even a scrap of privacy when I haven't the power to make my own.'

'You don't care about your own people either. You knew what the teraphim was as soon as you saw it. The way we choose to do things is important.'

'Which is why you intend to wake our barrow-children.' He exhaled vapour. 'You plan to commodify our blood with complete moral superiority. Is that the case? I'm going to enjoy watching it. I shall read about it in the papers.'

'You *told* us to, it's the only thing we have against Morax. No,' she corrected herself. 'You only said it would make us less afraid. Nobody has the power to stand against him. Once we make panax, how do you intend to keep us safe?'

'Crow might help, if he's feeling generous.'

Rom's skin prickled. 'Revealing the panax will get us killed.'

'The threat of mutual annihilation makes a stable bargain. You should have asked for the terms in writing.'

'Then tell me,' she said, 'the full terms. You can't lie.'

Prideaux sniffed. 'In return for one soul, of Jasper Teague's choosing, from amongst his possible descendants: full assistance in the production of a universal panacea. Duties include supplying materials; maintenance of the covenanter's house, paperwork, and physical health; and protection from interference or attack for the duration of the research period. Notice your grandfather failed to specify maintenance of his mental stability. Notice also that he forfeited his health when he decided he'd rather get a bulk discount on his alkahest instead of paying for it by the grain. Terms are considered complete upon the full publication of his chasmeric research, by the covenanter, without patent or restriction.'

'We can't do it,' she said. 'None of it.' The words loosened something exhausting, but she understood. 'The research, everything—we can't publish.'

'You plan to watch Dr Lloyd get there first?'

'She won't. They'll label it top secret, you know they will. Alec can go ahead and write his little articles but he won't get far, nobody believes in magic.'

'You'd turn your back on Jasper's work? I won't be forgiving in my interpretation of the terms. Any information about the chasma will be construed as relating to the panax—any discussion, any attempt at contact or investigation. You'll not be permitted to mention us again.'

'I can deal with that,' she said, though her mind pushed rebelliously back at her.

He laughed. Softly, and the toes of his boots nudged her own. 'You'd never. You've seen reality and you can't turn your back on it. What do you plan to do with your mortal life? You've only got a few decades to dig some meaning from the mess before you die. You've already promised your soul. And you're giving it up for nothing?'

Prideaux's contempt slid hot under her collar. 'I don't have an option.'

'Of course you do. Publish your research. Let me go about my business, and if you're worried about Morax you can come back on your knees to me and plead to be rescued. New deal, solid plan.'

'That isn't right,' Rom said. Something snagged beneath her ribs. 'If I bury everything, then your work's left undone. Jasper wanted to make panax. He wanted his name cleared, his findings published—that's the contract. If I don't finish it, you can't start another one. Correct?'

'Quite so.'

'How long have you got?' She spoke very low. 'Because you can hardly walk. I think it gets worse when you're hungry. How long before you rot in your own blood?'

'Five or six months before it's incapacitating,' Prideaux said. 'A year until you need to think about a gold-lined bunker.'

'Will you live?'

'*In spiritu*? Endlessly. Incarnate? The physical survival of an atramental chasma is round about a century. By that point their flesh decays to a liquid. The noise, apparently, affects a radius of several miles. Electrical disturbance. Gravitational anomalies. The structural integrity of their containment facility is usually the first to fail.'

'I see,' she said. The leaves above them scattered rain. 'But you will live.'

Prideaux flicked ash across the bracken. 'It is a pleasure, Godden, to see how perfectly you abandon your morality.'

'I can't endanger my family. I've made my choice.'

'Noble of you.' He seemed very busy with the tip of his cigarette. 'What do you propose?'

'Drop Alec from the relix.'

He let out a sharp drift of smoke and lowered himself, a slide down the trunk as he sat. He dropped his cane into the bracken. 'Alec, is it.' He tucked up one leg. 'Andromeda cannot bear to be rescued, not even from death.'

'Death happens without you.'

'Indeed. I'm only a facilitator.' He pressed out his cigarette in the moss beside him. 'All parties are supposed to be present for this. Are you content to allow alterations to the contract without a debtor's consent?'

'Nobody asked me if I wanted this. I don't need Alec's permission to save his soul.'

'Come here.'

Rom crouched in the scent of crushed violets. Prideaux pulled off his glove. 'Hand.' His own was cold when he spread her fingers. 'You wish to remove Alec Godden from the contract.'

'And make sure he can't come back and change it later.'

'Understood.' His hard thumb on her wrist sent a pang through her bones and she tried not to feel the hidden surge, her fate, the mark like ink that only blood could see. 'Alec will no longer be recognised within the terms. All other terms remain unchanged. You agree?'

Something pooled in her stomach. Magic. Or fear. Yes, I know what's involved. She wanted to say it. My soul, my life, it's not like you haven't talked about this.

He waited. And she couldn't shake the impression his face was a mask of clean stone, carved and gleaming—fragmentary head in alabaster, Twelfth Dynasty, suspended between the leaves and shade.

'Yes,' she said.

Prideaux shivered. 'Yes.' He released her hand. He sat back against the tree and rummaged for the tobacco tin. 'Yes, all's as it should be and no harm done, and it really could have been much worse.'

Raindrops fingered the bracken. Rom stood, brushing off her knees.

He didn't look up at her. He was tugging on his glove with the cigarette jammed in his mouth. This strange old thing and his machinations of deceit, shivering in the wind. 'You can have a few weeks to think about things,' he said. 'Time yet to decide how to flaunt your vengeance.'

'I already know,' she said. 'I'm not going to publish.'

'I see.' He flexed his fingers within the tight leather.

'This is so pointless. How much blood would it take?'

'It's already over,' he said. 'The only thing one can do is mitigate one's losses.'

'I'm *trying*,' Rom said. 'My soul's forfeit either way, that's done. How much blood to keep you alive?'

Prideaux felt in the bracken for the cane, his gaze steady. 'A contract's structure is algebraic. It must exhibit symmetry.' He hauled himself upright and Rom stepped back into the path. 'What are you asking for?'

'Nothing. You've done plenty. We'll be cleaning it up for years.'

'Your pity isn't needed, Godden.'

'Give us a Rolls Royce, if it makes you feel better.'

'It would take several pints a month. For the rest of your life. You couldn't manage it alone.'

'I'll ask Alec. He'll understand. I'll leave it my courtyard. Is that a yes?'

The silver lighter clicked like a beetle as he thumbed it. 'Perhaps.' He tucked the lighter away.

'In writing, please. If you've got an offer, send it by crowfolk.'

'I hope you know you're insufferable,' Prideaux said. 'Is it worth it, your little bit of condescension?'

Of course she wasn't sure. But she had to be sure; this is what beginnings feel like.

'It's worth everything to be done with you. And I'm done. Good afternoon, Mr Prideaux.' Rom turned away beneath the restless boughs.

'Not done,' he said, raising his voice, 'not quite, not until the moment you finally die. The day will come when we settle the account.'

She didn't reply. He'd be standing in the tree-shadow, watching her walk away.

'I'll be sure to make it perfectly fair.' He never could shut up. 'You'd like that, wouldn't you?'

Her throat ached with the effort of silence. But she could let him have the last word.

He had nothing else.

Morgan didn't speak on the road back, and Kingsley drove in silence with his cap low over his eyes.

Rom wasn't sure where he was taking them. She hadn't even thought about this part, now everything was finished. Each observation barely touched her. It was late summer, early afternoon; overcast. When they stopped for fuel she was sick again.

The car pulled up at last in a small town beside a weedy railway station, and Kingsley leaned across the seat. 'Will you be alright to catch the train back? Otherwise we'll be a few hours out of your way.'

Rom gathered her jacket automatically. 'Where's Morgan going?'

'Godalming,' Kingsley said. 'Lady Tyet said to get you both home. That's school for him.'

Morgan was staring out at the hedge.

'Will you be alright?' she asked.

He stirred himself and nodded. 'I won't be there for long, anyway.' He must have seen something in her expression because he gave a funny shrug. 'Father will be here next week.'

'They might not come.'

'They can't ignore this one. I burned down your grandfather's house.'

Rom had nearly forgotten. She reached over the car to shake his hand, but his fingers just squeezed hers.

'Take care,' he said. 'Tell me how Alec's doing.'

Then the car was moving again, and Rom mounted the steps to the station platform, and piled her coins together for a ticket.

She bought a faded apple from the sandwich cart as it passed her compartment. This day, this never-ending day, and the sobbing rattle of the tracks. Dusty carriage seats, farms beyond, restless and cloudswept. She took off the heavy riding coat. She didn't have money for coffee. Scattered railyards became backyard fences as the fields fell into London.

It was late afternoon, a blare of car-horns, and when she stepped down from the sooty station she walked for a while. Another train. She walked more. The city was pulled under the hood of night. Then Harrington Street, as the lamplighter clattered past with his ladder, his silhouette winding up and down each lamp post like a toy on a string, and all the street flared to life behind him.

Rom stood on her front step, feeling for her keys. There weren't any keys. She'd have to ring for Mrs Martin. All her things jingled loose in the coat pocket, ticket stub and two last pennies, and it wasn't even her coat. She looked down at her striped trousers. At Alec's tie, Kingsley's shirt, the black silk tail of the Magician's scarf—gathered scraps of all the lost and wandering. She'd marched across London looking like a clown. She might have laughed if she had any tears left.

30

Silver earrings. Her dress in sheer slate blue. Second-best hat—that old
glad twist of leopard print was long gone, and this yellow straw thing
didn't feel familiar. It fit neatly, though, over her fresh cropped hair.

She'd need a new gown this winter. It would be months until the
bumpling made an appearance; better to plan. Maybe better to wait.
Winter means the future; plans mean choices. Rom pulled her gaze
back to the mirror.

An envelope had arrived in the morning mail; from Selwyn, she
recognised the nurse's quick script. She'd pinned it carefully to the
wall as though it might be swept off by the wind while she wasn't
looking. Maybe she hoped it would.

The letter she'd written to him had been difficult. She'd tried to
differentiate, certainties and options; she could burrow in at St Veep
and have the baby herself if she wanted to. A family can be anything, if
you've got a good imagination. She wasn't going back to College, that
was a certainty; the world had cracked open, infinitely strange, and
not because of anything she'd learned in a book.

Nobody can have everything. That's only a devil's promise.

He seems the honourable sort, Aunt Minnie had said. Rom's throat
ached. She only wanted him to be honest.

*You needn't marry me. You needn't do anything. Does this sound
hateful? I hope not. I'll be quite fine. I won't be a mother unless I'm
certain. As certain as I was of you, when we chose each other in the
orchard. It ought to feel like that. Don't you think?*

*It's simply this—if I had to imagine a father for any baby, I'd rather
he was certain too.*

Rom swept up her purse and lipstick. She'd have to open Selwyn's reply eventually. But not this evening.

Soho flickered cunningly, throwing neon over the wet pavements. The theatre was hot with perfume. Rom sat three rows from the front and applauded until her hands were numb: one promise she could keep, at least.

And hell, the show was glorious—laughing, wicked, tender Ditto. A tug of joy caught all the audience. It was magic real as anything Desir had made, a perfect alchemy of place and audience, flint and powder, a temporary incandescence—the utter uselessness of trying to explain. Darling Ditto. Hers, everyone's, glitter on the stage.

Rom lingered afterwards in the crowded corridors where the dressing room doors slammed open and shut, pressed between yawning journalists and gin-flushed men.

'You came.' Ditto flung into her arms.

'I couldn't not.' Rom hugged her. 'An eight-week run? That's wondrous, dear. It was grand. Truly.'

Ditto withdrew, detaching her scarf from Rom's earring, and they both smiled. This is what you have to do when you understand you won't hold each other again.

The dancers' dressing room was jammed like Wall Street but there was a kind of quiet in their corner by the mirrors.

'How's your packing going? Tell me about your plans.'

When the trees faded to brown Ditto would be gone, sailing from Dover. 'I'm going to use my name again. My real one.'

'Dido?'

'No, my surname. Ditto Ito, isn't it dolly? My father's name. He's thrilled. They'll miss me shockingly. But I've got older sisters, Pa lets me do as I please.' A whole shining life bundled up in there; she'd always been good at keeping things to herself.

Rom had been too good at never asking. 'Ditto,' she said, 'I am so sorry.'

'Doesn't matter now. It's all panned out perfectly,' Ditto said, 'hasn't it,' and Rom looked away from the glisten in her lashes.

'I'll come to the station. See you off on the boat train.'

'No,' Ditto said. 'Don't.' She put down her make-up sponge and squeezed Rom's fingers. 'Will you write?'

Rom's heart snagged. 'Always,' she said.

She walked through the midnight West End glimmer until she couldn't stand the laughing crowds, and then she caught a cab home. She was tempted to direct it to Claridge's; Alec had been staying all month at Mother's hotel while Mother and Harry fussed over Morgan and threatened to hang about until Christmas. It would be easy to dissolve in the babble of their voices.

But that would be cowardice too.

And Alec had other things on his mind; two of the corpses in the Phoenix's hotel suite had been peers of the realm, and he'd started a new investigation involving a Brighton seance hoax and missing millions. He was off again, trailing stories, and Rom climbed the stairs to her empty apartment. She unlocked the smell of burnt toast and wet dog, the ghosts of company.

She took down Selwyn's envelope and looked at it for a long time before she opened it.

Dear Andromeda, it said.

That's rather a turn. I hope you're feeling well. I don't think your letter was rude and anyhow I think we always were straightforward with each other so I don't see any point in changing now.

~~*I hope you haven't made up your mind yet or if you have*~~

If you haven't made up your mind yet, let me know.

I ought to tell you I will ask you to marry me, whatever you end up deciding.

Rom had a cup of tea. She drank it, and felt a little less ill. Then she unpacked her letter paper.

Next week, she said, *I'll catch the train up.*

The sanatorium was outside Birmingham; a regimented place, low wards laid out like military barracks. Long before Rom got to the front office the scent of disinfectant clawed her throat.

'They're out in the garden,' said the nurse at the desk. 'I'll show you through.'

It was only a sort of wooden deck along the side of the ward, overlooking a space of grass between. A row of reclining chairs. Some men she didn't know. And there he was, flopped on his side in the pale sunlight.

His hair had been cropped to glistening stubble. 'Rom,' he said, and smiled.

They shook hands.

'I can't kiss you,' he said, raising himself on one elbow. 'They told me I'm not to.' He was too thin under his blue-striped shirt. His sleeves were rolled up and his shoulders looked raw-boned.

'It's cold.' She pulled her coat closer. 'Isn't it cold?'

'I don't feel it much,' Selwyn said, 'they keep the place fresh.' Behind them the windows stood open to the wind. Scrubbed floors and frosty air; no place for corruption.

'How has it been?'

He snorted. 'Should duck back to the Somme for some R & R.' He flexed his shoulder, a restless twitch. 'I can't complain, though, the little kids over in quarantine have it worse.'

It felt longer than six weeks. He had questions about everything he'd missed, though Alec had filled him in on most of it. Rom was in the middle of describing the Museum when he broke in. 'Are you well?'

'Same as always.' She wondered, though. And he wasn't the same either.

She didn't mention his letter. Her insides felt stitched together. He didn't say anything about it; he might have changed his mind, now he'd seen her away from the house and their nights together.

'Have you laid eyes on the fair folk?' he asked.

'No,' she said slowly. Not even a note among the marigolds since she'd left Prideaux on the woodland path. The hangfire silence wasn't a comfort. 'They did offer me some of their blood,' she went on, 'after Jasper's house went up.'

'You didn't take it?'

'Yes.' She'd always be entwined with the chasma, by debt or history. Her garden would always belong to crowfolk.

'I'm glad,' Selwyn said. 'I'd rather you lived.'

'And you. You don't regret it?'

He shook his head. 'I'll take my chances.'

Luck was with him, the nurses said, when they brought out a tray of tea—if he was cautious, if he didn't expect too much, which seemed the best way about it. He had one lung unaffected; the doctors would take a lancet to the bad one in a couple of months, and collapse it to let it heal.

'No drinking. No more diving. Meanwhile I'm supposed to lie on my right side. Continuously.' He sighed. 'And stay all next year.'

'That's—' Rom tried not to falter. Courage was the least she could offer him. 'That's a while.'

'Christ, yes. Can't afford it. Maybe till June. Doctor said I should live somewhere drier, as though I can just pack off to Italy.' He shifted on his chair. 'It'd be good to be free again.'

She looked sideways at him as he spoke, his sea-glass eyes.

His temper was terrible, of course. Brief, though, clouds over the sun. And she thought of cool grass and plum trees and unbuttoning his shirt in the orchard dark.

He smiled at her, waiting; maybe he was testing something too.

She settled into the sound of his voice. They spoke like old friends.

He asked after Ditto. He made no mention of Morgan. When he reached for his tea-cup she looked at the new steel watch-band, the face turned to his inner wrist as he preferred it.

'I got your letter,' she said.

'I know.'

Stupid, that's why she was here. 'I never much wanted to marry.'

He looked away towards the trees. 'Me either.'

'You changed your mind?'

'Not really.' He pulled himself higher in the sun-chair. 'Neither have you, though. Have you?' He glanced back. 'I don't mind if you haven't. But things happen. Kids would be fun.'

Marriage. A vote, a bank account, and the right sort of husband would even let her keep a job.

'If you like,' he added. 'I'm stuck in here—it won't be easy on your end once you have to start explaining things.' His glance fell to the front of her dress. 'You can say we eloped. And then—well. We could.'

'I'm poor as dirt.'

'So am I. Army pension—' He shrugged. 'It ends when I do. There'd be nothing for the little one.'

'One of these days I'll have to tell Mother about the baby.'

He considered. 'It could be a very quiet wedding. Nobody at all. Only the ones who matter. You and me and a witness.' He grinned. 'You know I'd be a dreadful husband.'

'That's a relief,' Rom said, 'I'd be a godawful wife.'

'A pair of rotters.' He rested his head back on his chair. 'Should we?'

It was a thrill, the thought of leaving London. 'Should we?' And they could run far. 'It wouldn't have to be mock-Tudor at all,' she said. 'You need a better climate. And I don't like white fences. What about Cairo?'

'With a baby?' He raised his brows. That quizzical arch. But he didn't say no.

'Mother did it. Hilda Petrie did it. She's an archaeologist; married on a Thursday, caught a steamer to Egypt on the Friday.'

He rubbed his cheek. 'Cairo.' And there was something in his eyes, a gleam of something when he walked with her to the gate.

In the sharp blue shadow of the trees they shook hands again.

'Rom.' Selwyn didn't release her fingers. 'Is this going to be alright?'

'It doesn't frighten me.' She wasn't certain. She never would be. But she cupped his dry warm hand. 'Do you know what Quinn said? *Good luck on the high road, and the low road, and the maze between where no roads be.* Maybe the third way looks like this.'

'Making it up as we go along?' Selwyn's eyes were very bright. 'Hold still—' He kissed her cheek.

'I suppose it's goodbye for now.'

'Not really,' he said. 'I'll see you soon. You might even get an invitation to my wedding.'

Mother bustled around the station platform, searching her purse. 'Mckenzie, pet, have you bought your sweets?'

'I'm fine,' Morgan said, 'thank you, Polly.'

He and Harry waited by the newspaper stand and Rom sent them a sympathetic glance. Mother was in a whirl of activity, very little of it useful; she and Harry were going back to Egypt for a few months until Christmas. Harry had family there and work to complete and then they were off to the States, apparently. Beyond the reach of telephones, the silent far side of the globe.

And Morgan was going with them.

'We're going to miss you, Captain.' Alec thumped Morgan's shoulder as hard as he dared.

'We will, you know,' Rom said, and he looked at her.

'I wouldn't go if I didn't have to.' Which seemed an odd way to put it.

'Rom, now—I'll wire from Calais.'

Mother's bright voice behind her, and she turned.

'I hope the crossing's calm for you.' She handed Mother a roll of peppermints.

Mother tucked them into her purse and stood irresolute, flapping her gloves against her hand. 'If you reconsider,' she said, 'even a small gathering—'

Rom had told Mother last week about Selwyn—clearly, incontestably, giving no mention of a baby and taking no questions afterwards. *He's nice. You'll like him.* Alec hadn't been surprised. Mother had been thrilled; but after the first shock, and the irritation of Selwyn being safely cloistered from visitors until February, she was left with the indignity of being forbidden to plan a wedding.

'No guests,' Rom said again, 'thank you. But you must come and see us when you can.'

Mother darted close and hugged her, thin as a reed, and Rom squeezed her with a sort of wonder. It was a dampish buffety day but she felt quite insulated from the bleak weather and Mother's fretting, steady on one point at least.

'Best wishes, dear. I love you ever so, you know.' Mother said it as she always did, a waiting pause, and Rom nodded.

'I know. Me too.' She tucked her hands in her pockets as Mother nestled back at the news stand, away from the smoky draught that came funnelling up the platform. Mother was still talking, her sharp freckled face turned away to look at the magazines, and Harry was still nodding. He took it cheerfully. Maybe he needed the tide of her talk to float him along the endless social crowds, a necessity, as he was to her. Independence is a privilege.

Rom turned back to Morgan. 'New school, kiddo?'

'Can't be worse than the old one,' Morgan said. 'Might even be able to make a research team.'

'I'm sorry you can't tell me anything,' Rom said, 'the fair folk wouldn't be happy.'

Alec was shuffling through a newspaper. 'Well,' he said brightly, 'I doubt Mr Prideaux will bother us again. We haven't heard from him, have we?'

'You will have to keep your head down, Mckenzie,' Rom said. 'You certain you want the mess?'

'There's entire worlds out there.' Morgan smiled warily. 'Don't worry, I'll start with this one.'

Alec grinned. 'You do like the impossible.'

'It's expensive and complex.' Morgan slung his satchel over his shoulder. 'And tiresome. But not impossible.'

'I suppose not,' Rom said.

'Not for me. So long, then.' It was awkward, his usual awkwardness. 'Do take care, won't you?' And then he was holding out his hand to shake. 'Come here,' Rom said, 'come here, you idiot.' She hugged him hard around the neck and he waited woodenly until she released him. But he was still smiling.

'Anyhow,' she said, 'I don't expect you to write. And we don't promise to. Then nobody's disappointed, are they?'

'I won't write,' Alec said. 'But you'll probably get a telegram on your birthday.'

'Good enough,' Morgan said.

Are people only themselves when they're leaving?

He stopped on the running board of the train, and up there he was taller than she was. 'Andromeda. I am sorry.'

'So are we. You needn't worry, it's fine.' She squeezed his elbow.

'Keep everyone safe,' he said.

The train hissed and shunted and shifted away. And Mother and Harry were waving, and Alec pulled off his cap and waved back. Morgan held his jacket close around him when he ducked back under his father's arm and disappeared into the carriage.

'It feels like the end of a year,' Alec said on the footpath outside. 'I refuse to believe it's not even September.'

Rom eyed the newspaper stand. The date winked back at her. 'Will you come for a walk?' she said. 'There's something we need to return.'

The afternoon scudded with clouds as they climbed the resounding stairwell on Great Queen Street.

The portiere curtain was pinned back; grey light swelled the landing. 'Miss Godden?' came Kingsley's voice. 'Hello, you lot.'

They stepped inside. Somebody had been organising the books in stacks; the shelves sat tidy. The air hung chill and stale, the hearth swept as clean as the corner beside it. A cleared gap held the centre of the room, just a foursquare indent on the rug where the desk had stood.

No desk, no papers, no bed.

'Kingsley. What happened?'

'He left. He does this, you know.'

'But where?' Alec said.

'I'm not his keeper.'

'Kingsley—'

'Baghdad, probably. He was tired of the cold.'

'He can't have,' Rom said. 'When?'

'Two weeks ago. Boat from Dover; his Lady sister was in a rage, you know, t'were better he go. He took everything, so I—don't think he'll be back.'

Kingsley's pause was troubling.

'What about you?' she asked.

'I have my orders. Bodyguard duties.'

'Guarding who?'

He was looking out the bare window. 'Monsieur Séraphin.'

'Oh,' she whispered. 'Kingsley.'

'It's a job. Same as any.' His boot-heel scuffed into the floor.

'He doesn't deserve you,' Rom said at last.

Kingsley unfolded his arms with a careless yawn. 'Don't I know it.' He turned to the mantelpiece above the empty hearth. 'Before you go, something here for you.'

She opened the lemon-coloured envelope.

Miss Andromeda May Godden,

You will no doubt be pleased to hear your uncomfortable Situation has been satisfactorily resolved. Due to a fortuitous change in circumstances your Relix will no longer be required.

She began again, eyes burning dry.

I don't fancy going hungry for the second time in a century and I certainly don't plan to do it for your amusement. As the proverb says, 'Better a dip between the teeth of Hades than slow necrosis overseen by a smuggery of Goddens' etc.

I leave you free, of course, from any hindrance or debt.

I wish you the best of luck and consider myself ever honoured to be working with such an extraordinary family as yours. Many thanks.

Yours sincerely—and a tense little monogram, *VA*. Possibly *AV*.

P.S. Thanks for returning The Nest *to the Nest. File it under P for Piss Off.*

She held the letter away as though distance could deliver her. 'What's this?'

Alec took the pages from her. He whistled. 'You're bloody lucky.'

'That's why I don't believe it,' Rom said. 'All luck's stolen from the gods.' She felt a toppling imbalance, her legs like water and head stony.

The room prickled with small absences, gaps on shelves and walls, the remainder of careful selection or great haste. The dust of his house tickled in her throat. She leaned against the window seat and looked over the street. The busy stationer's, the elegant facade of the Freemason's Hall. And maybe it truly had taken every moment, every single moment until now for her to understand where she stood.

'I'm a fool.' Her voice came from very far away. 'I'm a gibbering baboon. He called himself the Magician, Alec, he never even tried to hide. The French word, *argent*—'

'Silver?' he asked.

'Living silver,' Rom said. 'Quicksilver. It's mercury.'

Alec sank onto the window seat. 'We really are infants.'

Rom was swamped in comprehension. 'Hermes, Mercury. And Thoth—so many gods of words. Or the same god, different names. It's called syncretism in linguistics too, when a word's the same in every tense—it doesn't change with time.' Locating the words made sense of her blistering thoughts. Of course it would work like that.

'Did we ever have a chance?' Alec asked. 'Mercury's never been a god of truth.'

Stone shuddered behind them. Kingsley was dragging the herm from the portiere—Rom had never noticed the apartment door, faded green, pinned open behind it.

Kingsley took a heavy blue overcoat from the armchair. He pulled it on; a long coat, a good fit. 'Outside, please. I need to lock up.'

Rom looked around at the bookshelves. She slipped *The Nest of Amoury* back into her purse. 'Hermes Koinos,' she said, and wrapped her arms around herself as Kingsley closed the Nest.

They descended through the bustle of the stationer's shop.

Out onto the street, whipped by the gusting southerly. Traffic thundered. It was going to rain.

Kingsley held out his hand. 'I suppose it's farewell for now.'

Alec shook it.

Rom didn't. 'You knew he was a god,' she said. 'You never told us.'

Kingsley's brown eyes were puzzled. 'He has a lot of names.'

'If he breaks an oath, he's an outcast.'

'Is that what you think of him? I'm sorry, Miss Godden.' He nodded and turned away, his cap disappearing through the afternoon rush.

It was the season of departures.

Rom had to step aside; they were blocking the stationer's shop. She leaned against a terrace railing and read Prideaux's letter again. It was a conclusion, but nothing near an explanation. She wanted to believe. She always had. But hope seemed too breakable until she could be certain.

'Isn't it good news?' Alec seemed strangely buoyant. 'We dodged a nasty bullet there, even Jasper couldn't manage it. It's over, Rom. We don't have to worry any longer.'

She looked at him. 'Just say it. I've had enough of secrets.'

'Not a secret, I was going to tell you.' Alec pulled a rolled newspaper from his coat. 'Prideaux went missing in Greece last month.'

She didn't move. She was trying to hold her thoughts together. 'You had him followed?'

'My office has contacts at the Embassy.' Alec's narrow jaw was hard. 'I had news a few days ago but I wanted to be sure.'

She took the newspaper.

Missing British tourist feared drowned, says British Envoy to Athens. The personal effects of Mr Cranach Prideaux, a retired schoolteacher from York, were discovered yesterday—

'They found a touring car in a river gorge in Macedonia,' Alec said, 'all his travelling things. Official word says he met with an accident and washed downstream.'

Rom stared at the newsprint. 'What's the unofficial story?'

'The valley was burned out for half a mile around, every tree gone. I talked to the reporter myself. Could be a bomb, of course,' Alec said. 'But if Kingsley's right, if Tyet got him, or Morax—' Alec turned up his collar against the first splash of rain. 'It's done. He's gone. And he knew he was going.'

The notion was strangely final. *Sincerely,* said his letter. Maybe at the very end he was.

Rom's heartbeat shook her fingers and the newspaper whispered against itself. The hot unfolding of her pulse. Alive, alive. Jasper Teague had carried this fate for years, and she felt dazed to see a future without it—Egypt, the clean dry wind. A baby, and Selwyn, lugging their trunks with his easy smile—she needed to write and tell him. Immediately. And if by chance she and Alec stumbled over something about demons, and one thing connected to another thing, nobody could stop her from investigating.

Some people have a family ghost. They've never known the levity of losing one.

She rolled up the newspaper and rested her hand on her belly, warm and solid as a whole world.

Alec waved for a taxi. 'You know,' he said, 'next year might be rather better.'

'Worth a try,' Rom said.

EPILOGUE

December 30, 1923.
Majestic Hotel, Alexandria

Arrived last night. My hotel room is haunted by a century's mosquitoes.
Re: your letter of December 23rd, the Winter Palace would be an acceptable
rendezvous. The cost of flight from Paris was more than monetary but I don't
imagine I'll delay you much longer; the dahabiyeh is engag'd for today and the
weather is sweet for sailing.
I trust you are prepared. Be in the hotel garden, Friday evening at five.

Morgan laid down the letter and rested his fingertips on the paper.

'Isn't Luxor gorgeous in the afternoon,' Polly said, 'so atmospheric.'

Harry agreed. So did Mr and Mrs Pettle.

Morgan was silent; they rarely required a response.

'It's a pity we'll miss Rom after all.' Polly drained her martini. 'But she's not arriving until spring. After the baby.' Archly to the Pettles. 'Sly things, I do believe they didn't tell us till after we booked our passage.'

Sunlight glittered on the hotel terrace and Morgan had to squint to see over the roaring street to the river, warm and brown, and the string of Nile boats: dahabiyeh, from the Arabic. *Golden one.*

'We must duck back for a squiz next year,' Polly said. 'Meet this fiancé. Not that I don't trust her taste; engineers, you know. You said he's alright, Mckenzie?'

Morgan's eyes were fixed on the water. 'Yes.'

'I wish we could stay a few months more—even a week, until after Mckenzie's birthday. Must we go, darling?'

'We're not delaying,' Harry said. 'We'd be gone already if Loveday could haul himself out of bed for long enough.'

An attempt at eliciting guilt, but his father had no talent for it. 'I've packed,' Morgan said.

There was just enough breeze to stir the palms, to ripple the sequins on Polly's gown and flap the waiters' aprons as they jostled among the tables. Enough to angle the sails of every river boat; apart from one, coming from Cairo, furling as it approached the embankment and moored before the hotel.

It could have been any of a hundred boats. The disembarking passenger could have been any of a thousand tourists, inconspicuous among the crowd in his pale linen suit. Leaning on a cane; another foreigner escaping British fog and nursing his consumption.

Morgan refolded the letter. *Consumed*. Is that the word he was looking for?

'More drinks,' Polly said. 'And we can dine at eight when it cools down. It does seem rather a fizz for New Year's Eve, though, doesn't it?'

'Different calendar,' Mr Pettle said. 'Not Christians here.'

Morgan pushed back his chair. 'I'll be back before dinner.'

His father looked up from trimming a cigar. 'Studying?'

'Yes,' Morgan said, but he lied.

He descended the hotel's curved steps toward the river.

The northerly wind was pleasant and he didn't feel like waiting in the gardens. He crossed between idling motorcars, reaching the embankment as it spilled passengers from the Nile boat. The hotel arched white behind him, cradled by evening palms, and all these noises surged—the cars, chatter, calls from other boats and the green riverbank opposite—so festive and solemn it seemed like something else, an echo of the hollow temple sprawling just downriver, columns and white dust, the terrace that was garden when this place was Thebes.

Perhaps it still was, in some place outside time. This conviction pressed on his skin like the kick of heat: if he turned he'd see white-robed priests on the steps.

Morgan didn't turn.

It was an atmosphere, not an observation. Andromeda was correct; every demon has its power. Each Coronet has a particular talent and this one, lounging against the embankment to finish his smoke, had a talent for making things seem like other things.

'Not dead, then,' Morgan said.

Mr Prideaux slit him a sideways glance. 'How's your holiday going, Mckenzie?'

'Nearly over.'

'Family all well?'

Morgan could answer this with certainty. 'They're going to be fine.'

Prideaux fanned himself with his panama hat, though mood and shirt-collar alike seemed uncreased by the heat. 'Fine luck they had you lurking in the wings. Isn't it? If they call you a sibling, I can't see why any contract should quibble. What did Andromeda say?'

'I haven't told anyone,' Morgan said.

'It's chilling, actually, to think how she might have ended had nobody intervened.' Prideaux unhooked a pristine Malacca cane from his elbow and leaned on it heavily as he mounted the steps. 'Pressure compels most sediment to gold. Now your sister has a chance at living, and I avoid Tyet. And you get to practise your heroism. Pressure's only another name for fate, and I'm good at that.'

Morgan was silent. The equatorial dusk was dropping swiftly, but this was only a daybreak: he couldn't lose patience now.

'Very few people know this about me,' Prideaux said in a tone both detached and confidential, 'but I'm really fond of happy endings.'

'It's not my reason, you know.' Morgan's voice felt suddenly forced. But it seemed very important that he say this today, before whatever came next. 'This isn't heroism.'

'One hopes,' Prideaux said. He dropped the end of the cigarette and set his heel on it. 'Let's walk.'

Acknowledgements

Perseverance is not my strong point and if I'd really been as alone as writers are said to be—toiling in fits of glamorous solitude—this would be a stack of neatly labelled empty files instead of a book. I owe endless thanks to my early readers. To Dhara, for your enthusiasm, sharp-eyed patience, sprints, and wheedles: you endured multiple rough drafts and still encouraged the atrocities. To Miri, for vibing over Polari, thread magic, and the twink of all time: if you enjoyed this, I can rest contented.

And to Hom, my darlingest, who is always correct.

To everyone who ever read a thing I wrote, and told me that you liked it: this wouldn't exist without you. (If you enjoy somebody's art, music, or words, please tell them. It means so much.)

Lastly, to the chief forger and fancifier of words—thanks for showing how raucous life becomes when one takes a god of trickery as one's muse. *Hermes Koinos.*

About the author

L.B. Hazelthorn is an editor, artist, and author of fantastical fictions. Born in an Australian cane town and home-schooled by fanatical doomsdayers, they spent the first few chapters of their future memoir learning Latin and building an extensive network of escapist fantasies. After emerging into the twenty-first century they travelled for a decade, living in boats, tents, and various forms of artistic penury. They currently live in lutruwita/Tasmania with multiple offspring and a kitchen full of long-suffering ferns.

For news and updates you can find them at lbhazelthorn.com, or leave out a note for the faeries.

Printed in the USA
CPSIA information can be obtained
at www.ICGtesting.com
CBHW011920090824
12962CB00059B/664